PRAISE FOR
award-winning author

Joanne Rock

"Joanne Rock's heroes capture and conquer in just one
glance, one word, one touch. Irresistible!"
—*USA TODAY* bestselling author Julie Leto

"Sizzling chemistry with a splash of seductively
intense suspense—fabulous Joanne Rock
always delivers a page-turning read!"
—RITA® Award winner Catherine Mann

"The storyline is action-packed...and never slows down."
—*The Best Reviews* on *His Wicked Ways*

Dear Reader,

It's hard to believe that the Signature Select program is one year old—with seventy-two books already published by top Harlequin and Silhouette authors.

What an exciting and varied lineup we have in the year ahead! In the first quarter of the year, the Signature Spotlight program offers three very different reading experiences. Popular author Marie Ferrarella, well-known for her warm family-centered romances, has gone in quite a different direction to write a story that has been "haunting her" for years. Please check out *Sundays Are for Murder* in January. Hop aboard a Caribbean cruise with Joanne Rock in *The Pleasure Trip* for February, and don't miss a trademark romantic suspense from Debra Webb, *Vows of Silence* in March.

Our collections in the first quarter of the year explore a variety of contemporary themes. Our Valentine's collection—*Write It Up!*—homes in on the trend to online dating in three stories by Elizabeth Bevarly, Tracy Kelleher and Mary Leo. February is awards season, and Barbara Bretton, Isabel Sharpe and Emilie Rose join the fun and glamour in *And the Envelope, Please....* And in March, Leslie Kelly, Heather MacAllister and Cindi Myers have penned novellas about women desperate enough to go to *Bootcamp* to learn how not to scare men away!

Three original sagas also come your way in the first quarter of this year. Silhouette author Gina Wilkins spins off her popular FAMILY FOUND miniseries in *Wealth Beyond Riches*. Janice Kay Johnson has written a powerful story of a tortured shared past in *Dead Wrong*, which is connected to her PATTON'S DAUGHTERS Superromance miniseries, and Kathleen O'Brien gives a haunting story of mysterious murder in *Quiet as the Grave*.

And don't miss reissues of some of your favorite authors, including Georgette Heyer, Joan Hohl, Jayne Ann Krentz and Fayrene Preston. We are also featuring a number of two-in-one connected stories in volumes by Janice Kay Johnson and Kathleen O'Brien, as well as Roz Denny Fox and Janelle Denison. And don't forget there is original bonus material in every single Signature Select book to give you the inside scoop on the creative process of your favorite authors!

Enjoy!

Marsha Zinberg

Marsha Zinberg
Executive Editor
The Signature Select Program

SPOTLIGHT

The Pleasure Trip

Joanne Rock

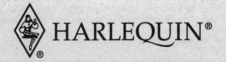

HARLEQUIN®

TORONTO • NEW YORK • LONDON
AMSTERDAM • PARIS • SYDNEY • HAMBURG
STOCKHOLM • ATHENS • TOKYO • MILAN • MADRID
PRAGUE • WARSAW • BUDAPEST • AUCKLAND

ISBN 0-373-83682-1

THE PLEASURE TRIP

This book is dedicated to my big sister, Linda, whose love and friendship mean the world to me. Her generous spirit is great inspiration for what sisterhood should be all about. And while our relationship bears little resemblance to Rita and Jayne's except in the best of ways, Linda's wizardry with needle and thread (and possibly a glue gun) did provide me with the idea for the sisterly gifts contained in this story. My glitter sneakers are on my list of top ten presents I've ever received.
Thank you, big sister!

ACKNOWLEDGMENTS

I'd like to thank the staff and crew members of the Carnival *Inspiration* for their enthusiasm about my book and their help to ensure my questions were answered. My fictional cruise line is not in any way modeled on the commitment to excellence that I saw around me every day on a Carnival ship, but I appreciated the insights about life on board so that I could create a believable world for *The Pleasure Trip*.
Thank you especially to Cruise Director Lenny Halliday and the Carnival promotion department.
Thanks also to our dining companions Al and Debbie Moy, who kindly shared their experiences from multiple cruises with a couple of first-timers. Not only did I learn a lot for my book, but I had a great time in the process and can't wait for another trip!

CHAPTER ONE

EVEN FOR A WOMAN with two left feet, pounding down eight flights of stairs in cheap flip-flops didn't present a challenge when fueled by anger and the desire to give a well-deserved butt kicking.

Silently fuming, Rita Frazer shoved open the stairwell door on the basement level of Roman Cruise Lines' flagship, the *Venus,* where she and her sister had worked for over a year. She glanced down at her insubstantial footwear with blue plastic flowers between the toes. No doubt about it, her flip-flops were a sorry excuse for butt-kicking shoes. But where there was a will, desperate women found a way.

"Jayne!" Rita shouted down the narrow corridor reserved for the ship's employees, steam hissing from her ears like the boiler beside her cabin. Everyone but her younger sister the showgirl was at work this afternoon, prepping for an influx of passengers after a day docked in St. Kitts, the second island stop on a ten-day Caribbean cruise.

Rita had done the same trip plenty of times as official seamstress for the *Venus.* But this wasn't just any cruise, and Jayne knew it. This particular excursion could be Rita's big financial break since she'd gone out on a limb to create new outfits for the show—outfits five times as good as what they'd bought from manufacturers in the past. She just hoped the cruise management company would agree and pony up an appropriate payout.

And of course, she hoped Jayne—one of the show's featured performers—didn't mess up Rita's big night.

When no answer was forthcoming, Rita stomped her way to the end of the hall, following the scent of the Chanel No. 5 Jayne preferred even though none of the dancers were supposed to wear perfume out of deference to the costumes. The familiar fragrance wafted from the same interior stateroom from which a warbling rendition of "Stand By Your Man" currently emanated.

Rita let herself into the compact room they shared in the bowels of the ship, a room Jayne never bothered to bolt no matter how many times they discussed the potential dangers with an ever-changing crew of nine hundred. The drone of shower water mingled with god-awful singing.

"You are so dead." Rita figured it would be okay to strangle her sister today since Jayne hadn't bothered to show for dress rehearsal this afternoon when she knew damn well this was Rita's one chance to shine in her peon job as a seamstress.

The singing stopped as Jayne popped her head out of the shower, all smiles amid a cloud of steam. "Rita? What time is it?"

"Past time for rehearsal and Danielle already wants your head on a platter for not checking in with her. Star status doesn't buy you exemption from attending show preliminaries." She torpedoed a towel against the shower curtain, nailing Jayne in the hip through the white waffle weave. "Besides that, do you know how many corporate managers I corralled into seeing the show tonight to see the new outfits? The boat pulls out in twenty minutes."

"Crap." The reference to the timeline at least got Jayne moving as she ducked back into the shower spray to rinse. "I've got to hurry."

Mildly disappointed no butt kicking had been needed, Rita gave her flip-flops the rest of the day off. She stalked out of the closet-size bathroom, noting the unholy mess scattered about their cramped cabin now that she wasn't focused solely on her beef with Jayne. Clothes were strewn everywhere, the twin beds both covered in discarded silk tops, scarves and skinny hot pants.

"I'm not even going to ask what happened in here." Rita flung her plastic thongs into the closet and reached for a more forgiving pair of sneakers to wear with her jean shorts. "I've got too much on my mind to wade through your wardrobe crisis."

"That's okay." The shower curtain rings scraped over the rod with a metallic *ting* as Jayne toweled off. "I solved my own crisis, thank you very much, although God forbid you give me any credit for it. I know we're all excited about your foray into costume design, but you forget your sister is the Queen of Vintage and a fashion force to reckon with in her own right."

Rita needed to be back at the rehearsal stage to help dress everyone before show time, but her sister's comment slowed her reach for the door. "What do you need a great outfit for anyway? You're going onstage as soon as the ship sails."

She peered across the wardrobe tornado at Jayne sliding into a floral sundress in record time.

"Can't a girl dress up for her man?" She winked over her shoulder, one long red curl plastered to her cheek. Presenting her back to Rita to zip her up, she smoothed the hem of her short skirt. "How do I look?"

"Flushed and overexcited." Rita fastened the hook and eye over the zipper and wondered for the umpteen-millionth time how Jayne could appear so movie-star gorgeous with her confident stride and graceful moves while Rita lumbered through life with as much finesse as a linebacker. They were sisters, for crying out loud. Same genes. Same ballet lessons. Same basic looks and size. Where was the justice? "You're practically bubbling over for that matter. What gives?"

Jayne shuffled around her makeup table that doubled as a desk and poked Rita in the arm with a lipstick case. "Can't I be excited for you? I'm still in shock you finally talked the management into new outfits for the opening number. They're normally so stingy about wardrobe." Uncapping bright fuchsia lipstick, Jayne smeared it on her sister's mouth in a futile effort to make Rita look pulled together. "Now all you need to do is drag me out of show business and you'll be happy, right?"

Rita rolled her eyes and tried to stand still for the makeup job even though she'd rather not have her face lacquered while she was working. Didn't Jayne realize they were going to be late? But some things weren't worth arguing with her over. Makeup for one. And the fact that Rita hadn't *truly* sold the costumes to Roman Cruise Lines quite yet. Jayne would have had a conniption to think her big sister—by all of eleven months—had accepted a work-for-hire job to force the higher-ups into appreciating her. But they'd worked the cruise ship for minimum pay long enough after back-to-back six-month stints. Time to move on to greener pastures.

"Oh please. As if I'll be able to haul you away from this business or Horatio the Latin lover any time soon." Although Rita could always hope. She'd tried before to get Jayne to consider moving to New York to make the most of her dance talent, but Rita had never succeeded in convincing her to leave boy-bimbo Horatio behind. "You're addicted to all that glitters, remember? I'm just happy my costumes came together in time for tonight."

Rita had been trying to coax her starry-eyed sibling into developing interests outside of dancing since high school, but Jayne had the same stage aspirations as their mother and no promise of any stable, long-term work had ever wooed her away. The job on the cruise ship had been reliable and working on a luxury liner gave the illusion of being on vacation all the time—a welcome fantasy after they'd done their share of waiting tables in dive bars while waiting for Jayne's big break.

Showbiz opportunities hadn't been hiding in any of the trucker hangouts on Interstate 95 north of Fort Lauderdale where they'd grown up. And Jayne couldn't be convinced to try Broadway since their mother had a gambling problem along with a mixed bag of other addictions that kept her daughters on their toes and perpetually bankrupt unless they hid their money very carefully. The cruise stint allowed Jayne to keep tabs on Mom while Rita kept an eye on her baby sister.

Somehow, it all worked. For now.

"I mean it, Ree." Jayne coated her sister's eyelashes with industrial-strength mascara. "I think I'm ready to blow this showgirl gig once and for all. Finally, we're both going to have everything we dreamed about."

"You really think my outfits are going to be a hit?" Rita had sewn until her fingers bled to pull together the new costumes to unveil at tonight's program. She'd paid off one of the other dancers to model the extra garments informally around the tables before and after the house lights went up at the main performance. When the dancers weren't onstage, they spent plenty of time walking around the ship in full showgirl regalia to pose for pictures with the guests, so it wasn't like Missy didn't have experience preening while she mingled.

"Absolutely." Jayne smeared gloss on her lips and finger combed her damp hair into waves around her face. "You're going to knock 'em dead tonight. It's high time you came out of hiding to show your talents to the world."

The words of sisterly support were as welcome as they were rare in a relationship marked by old rivalries and very different perspectives. But deep down, she knew Jayne wanted her to succeed. Didn't she?

"Thanks." Rita pulled open the door, feet itching to get back to the stage. She hated it that suspicion held her up once again. "You're not planning anything unusual for the show, are you? No special theatrics to highlight my outfits or impulsive gestures sure to get us fired?"

Flashbacks to their childhood and her sister charging money from their friends to see her inline skating on a train rail came to mind. Jayne lighting the neighbor's garage on fire when she practiced her flaming baton routine as a teenager. Jayne slipping a note to the star quarterback in high school, saying that Rita liked him.

And although that last stunt had worked out with rather exciting results for Rita, she'd officially started her first ulcer while waiting to find out if A.J. liked her, too. No way would she tread down Jayne's road of recklessness again. She'd weathered enough emotional storms from her sister's revolving-door romances to know she was better off focusing on work.

"Trust me." Sliding into her high heels, Jayne smiled that angelic grin that had won her Sweetest Sugar Plum in the school Christmas pageant three years running. "You're going to be very happy tonight."

Reassured she'd covered her bases with Jayne, Rita sidestepped the elevator that only came to the bottom deck once in a blue moon. With paying passengers finishing up boarding from their shore excursions, the elevator would be too jammed to make the trip to the employee-only level anytime soon.

Not until she hit the second flight of stairs did she remember she'd never pinned down her sister for an estimated arrival time in wardrobe. No doubt, Jayne figured she could slide into her spot late since she didn't go out until the second number. And for the first time, Rita realized she didn't care if her sister failed to play by the book.

For just this once, maybe Rita and her two left feet could enjoy a little of the spotlight for herself.

"TRY BENDING OVER and jiggling." Sweaty and frazzled two minutes before the curtain went up, Rita waited while the platinum-blond showgirl decked in buttery-soft blue leather leaned forward and shook her considerable assets.

Straightening, the jittery young dancer covered in self-tanning cream and a healthy dose of body glitter looked to Rita for approval.

No luck, damn it. Rita ran a skilled finger along the inside of the other woman's bodice and tugged the material upward. "The twins are still a little uneven, Missy. Do you want me to take in the costume before you go onstage?"

Sighing, the stressed-out blonde waved away the help as she dove for a pink duffel bag on the dressing room table. "My right is bigger than my left. I've got a silicone lift in my bag to fill out that side a little."

Ignoring the usual pandemonium in the cavernous backstage of the Aurora 2 Theater, Rita silently critiqued every costume that streaked by her as dancers and acrobats scrambled for last-minute makeup fixes and hair touch-ups. They were three days into the February cruise with two performances down, but tonight's show marked the first appearance of the new outfits.

And surprise of all surprises, the costumes looked fantastic for their debut number. As long as the dancers did their part tonight and Jayne showed up soon, Rita was well on her way to getting reimbursed for her hard work with—hopefully—a hefty bonus to show for it, too.

"Places, ladies!" Danielle Divine, a former showgirl and the current Aurora floor-show manager, gave the familiar nudge to her dancers over the backstage P.A. system. "I need everyone lined up now."

"Gotta go." Missy stuffed the lift into her outfit and tossed her bag on the nearest dressing table. "Your costumes are fantastic, Rita. And the showy feathered one I modeled earlier was a hit. You really ought to be in New York designing clothes instead of repairing frayed officer uniforms."

"Thanks." Uncomfortable with the praise and the thought that she wasted her talents, Rita figured she'd be happy enough once she received payment in full. She hurried past a rolling rack of outfits to follow Missy and the other dancers toward the stage for the first number. The excitement of an opening night still gave Rita shivers, probably a response inherited simply by being a Frazer. Jayne had cheered herself hoarse after she'd landed her slot in the show, launching her into the best gig she'd had since their mother's last run at the gambling tables had financially ruined the whole family.

"No talking, ladies!" Danielle Divine stepped between them, physically nudging Rita back three steps with her skinny, strong arms. Older than Rita by ten years, she still packed more strength in her toned body than most eighteen-years-olds. Miss Divine took her job as backstage manager damn seriously. "Out of the way, Ms. Frazer. Your costumes are lovely but your fretting mother hen routine is not wanted in this show. Understood?"

Rita might have told Danielle where she could get off, but the house lights were already dimming and the entertainers began to engage in their individual last-minute rituals—visualization techniques, breathing exercises, even a few scattered prayers. No time for talk now.

"Good luck, everyone!" Rita stage-whispered over Danielle's Miss Clairol number nine head. "And thanks for making the costumes look great."

Couldn't hurt to remind them her reputation was

riding on their high kicks tonight. Missy gave her two thumbs up as they all filed onto their designated places on top of a wheeled piece of staging that would bring them out onto the stage, the acrobats and singers hanging back as they waited for their turn in the spot-light later tonight.

Rita stood back to cheer them on, the boat rocking gently beneath her feet while she wished Jayne were there to help calm her nerves when the audience got their first glimpse of the outfits. Jayne never had stage fright and always danced like a pro. From preschool pageants to high school plays, she'd never been flus-tered onstage, never lost her supreme confidence in her ability to perform.

Rita was another story. She'd always done well in re-hearsals and could nail any routine in the privacy of her bedroom, but on opening night she froze like a deer in headlights. A supreme disappointment to her torch-singer mother who'd dreamed of seeing her girls onstage.

Thankfully Rita had found work that allowed her to stay backstage, and even tonight, she only sent a small piece of herself out into the bright lights.

"Ladies and gentlemen," the announcer's voice boomed over the house speakers as a drumroll hummed in the background. "Welcome to Roman Cruise Lines' world-famous *Venus* floor-show extravaganza."

Rita watched the wheeled conveyance full of dancers start to move. The synthesized, edgy rock music for the performance began. Danielle Divine whispered last-minute instructions to a very fidgety Missy, who Rita knew was in danger of losing her job just two months into her contract. Poor thing.

Dancing gigs were damn hard to come by and fiercely competitive. If the woman lost this job…

Damn it, the red-eyed dancer wasn't the only one whose job was on the line. Rita forced herself to stop thinking about everyone else in the show and concentrated on her own responsibilities—making sure her deceptively simple leather costumes looked good enough to eat on stage.

The whole idea for the biker babe number had been Rita's, from the outfits to the music to the core theme behind the choreography. It had been hell to convince the show managers that the unconventional material could work on stage given its tendency to stretch, but once they'd glimpsed the possibilities and made sure Rita would be on hand for free alterations, they'd been all over the concept.

Nervous energy charging through her, she grabbed Jayne's outfit for the next number and tiptoed to the edge of the backstage curtain to gauge the audience's reaction. Jayne played a bigger role in the previous night's production but in this show, she had a solo dance sequence in just one of the acts. The house was packed, but the only faces Rita could make out were the folks in the front row. Thank God Jayne's loser boyfriend—Horatio the ass-grabbing blackjack dealer—wasn't in attendance for once. He normally sat front and center and ogled Jayne along with every other dancer, but tonight that seat belonged to…

Come to mama.

Someone much more interesting.

Rita wasn't in the market for a man. Especially not a high-roller type who traveled alone and booked Caribbean cruises for the access to round-the-clock gambling. Traditionally, those were the kind of guys who reserved the front row tables at the nightly floor-show touted for a nearly nude revue capping off every performance. No, Rita didn't like that type of guy at all.

But if she *had,* her head would have been turned by the prime male specimen currently peeling the label off his bottle of beer while a battalion of leather-clad women sashayed past him. He was a big man. Big enough to make his chair look more like doll furniture than people seating.

His legs sprawled long and muscular beneath the cocktail table in front of him. His shoulders had the kind of width only a custom-made suit would accommodate. Which, of course, he wore. Navy-blue and pinstriped, the clothes gave him the appearance of a forties movie star, the kind of guy her mother would have fallen for in a heartbeat. But then, Margie Frazer had an unusual love of the forties and fifties screen icons, a fact advertised to the world by naming her daughters Rita Hayworth Frazer and Jayne Mansfield Frazer.

Licking her lips at the hot prospect seated in the first row, Rita momentarily forgot about the show and how much she had riding on it. Leaning one shoulder into an empty rolling rack tucked behind the backstage curtain, she indulged the urge to stare for just another moment. How many times in life did a woman feel that overwhelming sense of attraction at first sight?

She hadn't felt this way since A.J. the quarterback had given her heart palpitations in the eleventh grade. And as sweet as that first crush had been, Rita had to admit that with a woman's more mature and discriminating hormones at work, her attraction now was a hell of a lot stronger. Earthier. Yummier. Dancing biker babes flooded the stage in a swirl of color and feminine curves while Rita's gaze narrowed to just one man.

Close-trimmed dark hair framed the stranger's face, his brooding eyes glued to the bottle label he slowly mutilated. Although his sleek suit and narrow green-and-blue tie broadcast success, his forbidding expression and preoccupation reminded her of the desolate faces she'd seen at the ship's bar at 4:00 a.m. The shell-shocked folks who came onboard for a good time in the casino and somehow lost half their life savings to the roll of a die or hand of cards.

Foolish, clueless people who had no business indulging in the free drinks available at *Venus's* twenty-four-hour casino.

She hoped for this gorgeous man's sake he wasn't staring down the throat of a longneck for those kinds of reasons. Maybe his girlfriend had just dumped him and all he needed was a cynical, buxom redhead to put his life back into perspective for the night....

Rita debated taking a chance for once and sending him a drink. But as the music died away and the audience erupted into applause, she warned herself to get her head on straight and find Jayne to help with her costume change while a singing duo took the stage between dance numbers. The other dancers' next outfits weren't Rita Frazer Originals, but Jayne's was. Because Jayne played the central character in a very fluffy musical drama involving lots of feathers and coy smiles, her outfit could be different. Better. Hand sewn by Rita for a little extra spotlight.

Tearing her gaze away from the superstud with dark

disappointment in his eyes, Rita waited for Jayne at the edge of the stage, costume already in hand. Too bad Jayne was still nowhere in sight.

Damn it. What was her sister thinking?

Praying Danielle Divine—aka Danielle Domineering—wouldn't notice the absence, Rita waited to see her sister's Veronica Lake-style red waves bob around the corner.

And waited.

Until a bad feeling crept into her veins, chilling her skin and setting her every cynical, wise big-sister instinct on edge. Sprinting around the back of the staging area to another dressing room, Rita scanned the small expanse of lighted mirrors and makeup tables for a glimpse of Jayne.

To no avail.

Heart pounding, she mentally shuffled the image of Jayne's hopeful face with the fact that Horatio the loser blackjack dealer wasn't in his usual seat tonight. Hadn't Jayne said she was ready to get out of showbiz?

And hadn't Rita known damn well that couldn't be good?

Hightailing it to the other side of the stage where half the dancers were already naked and shimmying their way into their next outfit, Rita found Jayne's dressing table graced by a glittery star, her duffel bag beneath it. The bag was unusually light given all the stuff Jayne normally hauled around. There was no purse, no bulging makeup case. Just some tissues, hairbrush, masking tape and—a note?

The dread that had been knotting in her stomach traveled up her throat in a burning path.

Don't be mad at me, big sister! You know this routine inside and out and let's face it—no one deserves the spotlight as much as you tonight. I had an urgent appointment in St. Kitts because Horatio really wanted to—ready?—*elope!!!*

Love and kisses,
Jayne

Oh no. Oh no. Oh no freaking way.

Rita didn't need to run to the nearest porthole to know the big ship had already cleared St. Kitts harbor by a mile. Jayne must have slipped off the boat with seconds to spare considering Rita had seen her in the shower just twenty minutes before the boat set sail. Jayne had timed her defection flawlessly—no surprise there considering her perfect stage routines and the fact that she had every male security guard aboard the *Venus* wrapped around her finger.

Damn! Shoving aside the wealth of worries for her sister and more than a little resentment for herself, Rita's fingers tightened around the leopard-print notepaper in one hand, Jayne's dancing costume in the other.

With performers already lining up, Rita had zero time to make a decision. In fact, she didn't realize she'd actually made one at all until her clothes were sliding off and she found herself jamming one foot after another into the leg holes of the barely-there feathered concoction.

She could dance, right?

She'd sat in on all the same damn tap, jazz and ballet classes as Jayne until she'd emancipated herself from Margie's stage-mother stranglehold. Plus, for three months running Rita had rehearsed all of Jayne's dances so she could get a feel for how the costumes needed to be crafted to keep them fluid and feminine.

Shoving her bare feet into strappy rhinestone sandals that went with Jayne's ensemble, Rita nearly toppled over as Missy rushed by, headdress askew as Sammy the Somersaulting Albanian tried unsuccessfully to right the heavy tiara.

"Can you help her, Rita?" Sammy whispered, ever mindful of Danielle who wouldn't hesitate to axe any dancer who couldn't hold her own.

Or any dancer who did something really, really stupid like elope in the middle of the show.

"I'll take over, Sammy. Thanks." Rita let the wiry acrobat off the hook as she picked up speed fastening her rhinestone top, determined not to flub this. Why was she not surprised Sammy looked endlessly grateful as he hurried away with the fluid grace that came naturally to gymnasts?

"What are you doing?" Missy jammed fistfuls of hair into the headdress with no success. "Where's Jayne?"

What could she say? *Jayne's sucking face with the worst mistake of her life while our careers go up in flames?* Yanking her own headpiece off a hook over Jayne's star-spangled dressing table, Rita plunked the tiara on her head.

"She had an emergency, but that's just between us, okay?" Snitching a bobby pin from the jumble of accessories on the table, Rita thrust it into Missy's long blond curls and anchored the heavy headpiece to her scalp, the need to lend a hand still strong even when she had no time to help. "Don't worry about Danielle once you're onstage. Just dance."

As if she had time to dispense career advice while

undertaking the stupidest scheme of her life. Even Jayne had never been this impulsive.

Okay, taking into account eloping with Horatio, maybe she *had*.

"Places, ladies!" Danielle's throaty call for action multiplied the butterflies in Rita's stomach.

The last thing she needed was for Danielle to see her in Jayne's costume. With the headdress on, there was a chance she'd never notice. Thank God every Frazer woman had been given the same five feet ten inches to work with.

She had to at least *try* to get past Danielle for the sake of Jayne's job, which wouldn't be here for her when she came back—oh God, *if* she came back—without a little intervention.

The music changed as the performers lined up for the scene Jayne called the Wicked Angel. It looked like one big T-and-A fest to Rita's eyes, but Jayne insisted it was a fallen woman with a heart of gold act. Well, fallen woman with a heart of gold and sexual appetite the size of Texas since the dance involved substantial writhing around on the floor. Though the pastel feathers made the writhing look more innocent, according to Jayne.

Hence the Wicked Angel.

Rita had never explored her inner angel, preferring to barge through life being blunt and direct and simply asking for what she wanted. But tonight she'd play simpering and coy for all it was worth in order to save Jayne's paycheck.

She just hoped she didn't fall off her heels. Or turn

left when everyone else turned right and possibly high kick her neighbor right in the schnoz.

All of which had happened to her before in her long and colorful career as her sister's crappy sidekick.

"Hurry up, Jayne!" Danielle the Destroyer glared at her with a look that would have sent heavyweight boxers running for cover. Thank God the abysmal backstage lighting prevented her from discerning Rita's features under Jayne's headdress. "You're on in five. Four…"

Rita's bare legs quivered beneath her as she prayed for coordination and knew it wouldn't come. The only way she'd ever been able to get through a solid dance routine had been to isolate herself in a room all alone. Maybe she could close her eyes and pretend she was alone.

"Three. Two…"

The house lights swirled and changed from moody blues to brazen reds. The music kicked up volume. Her knees knocked so hard she wasn't sure she could haul herself out there. Closing her eyes would definitely result in her spiked heel planted in someone's instep.

She'd simply choose a focus point. Meditate the rest of the humongous amphitheater away.

"And you're on!" Danielle's threatening growl mingled with the beat in the music that cued the first step.

Where Rita's eyes promptly alighted on the only focus point in the room that interested her. The one man whose presence just might be the key to saving her feather-covered ass.

CHAPTER TWO

SPECIAL AGENT HARRISON Masters knew damn well he wouldn't find the answers to his problems by staring through the glass of his empty beer bottle like an amber-colored lens. Then again, he didn't think he'd find a fluffy white feather there, yet that didn't stop a downy quill from floating through his field of vision to land with a delicate sigh along the back of his hand.

Hauling his thoughts from his quickly-going-nowhere investigative work, Harrison scratched his nose and shook off the bit of fluff. He took in the extravagant floor show and searched for the source of the feather. Visions of snowy doves circling the all-you-can-eat buffet formed in his brain for all of two seconds before he locked gazes with a redheaded chorus girl in the front row.

And damned if he didn't get struck by a bolt of lightning.

Heat throbbed through him even as he realized the electric jolt had been a laser image broadcast across the dancers through the haze of fake red fog pumped through the amphitheater. When Harrison had left Naples, Florida, to embark on his first pleasure trip in years—even if he wasn't quite as interested in the recreation as he pretended—he'd briefly toyed with the idea of a vacation fling.

He hadn't seen a woman to pique his interest until now, however. The hot-as-hell redhead stared at him as if her life depended on maintaining eye contact—so much so that Harrison couldn't resist sneaking a look behind him to make sure he wasn't missing something. Like a seven-foot Martian at his six o'clock.

The bawdy, stripper-style music in the background played a mischievous accompaniment to the women garbed in angelic white feathers and strategically placed rhinestones. One dancer wore little more than a couple of quills over her breasts and a tiny G-string made entirely of red jewels.

Not that Harrison really cared what anyone else wore. He was merely curious to see how the rest of the women measured up to the auburn-haired bombshell with a pinup's body and mile-long naked legs.

They didn't.

Whoever this brazen dancer was, she seemed unique in her tendency to look right at an audience member. Him.

And yeah, he noticed. He was male and breathing, after all—and totally freaking free since his girlfriend of one year had dumped him eight weeks ago, leaving him high and dry but making him realize he'd never been all that fired-up about their relationship anyway. Too bad he'd been so busy figuring out his father's hotel business he'd temporarily inherited—a work world so different from the one he'd trained for—he hadn't even seen it coming.

Worse, he didn't really mourn the loss of her so much as the loss of her insights on the hospitality industry. No wonder she'd dumped his sorry ass and started dating the resort's golf pro, who also happened to be Harrison's best friend. Past tense.

These days, Harrison didn't think he would be ready for another serious relationship for a long time, at least until he'd untangled the mess he'd made of the last one. But now that he'd embarked on the cruise to follow his missing ex-girlfriend and a pile of absent cash from the resort that had disappeared along with the golf pro a few weeks later, Harrison wouldn't mind some nonserious adventure if it happened to sashay his way.

Something he'd bet the redhead could provide.

Settling into his chair at one of the handful of VIP tables up front in the theater, he shoved aside his empty beer bottle and concentrated on the woman onstage. Less made-up than her counterparts, she looked younger and older at the same time. Investigative instincts flared to life, cataloging clues to this woman's psyche for the best way to get into her head—and possibly under her feathers. There was less sophistication in the loose way she wore her hair and the lack of stage makeup around her eyes. Yet she was no nineteen-year-old college student, not with that intense stare of hers.

This woman had character. Some secrets, maybe.

She shimmied, she sashayed, she spun, her gaze always returning to him. To seduce him? Damn but he'd like to think so.

Loosening his tie by a fraction of an inch, he allowed himself to imagine taking this angel to bed. High, generous breasts supported a jeweled bodice that resembled a feminine version of chain mail. And suddenly he was thirteen years old again, studying the bra catalogs for a hint of nipple.

He hadn't made time for that kind of frivolous pleasure in the past year since he'd delved into the family business after his father collided with a mountain in a debilitating skiing accident. His dad had been forced into early retirement and his mother now dedicated all her time to his rehabilitation. Helping his family through a crisis had seemed more important than a career that once meant everything to him—even if he'd missed the intellectual thrill of cloak-and-dagger games, the adrenaline rush of tapping into big-league crime rings.

But no matter how much he itched to return to the FBI next week now that he finally had a temporary management team in place, he hadn't ever let himself screw up with the high-end Naples resort that provided much-needed income for his father's ongoing medical bills—far more than Harrison would ever see as a special agent. And he'd been doing a damn good job as the makeshift manager until Sonia had disappeared during a cruise on the *Venus* last month.

His instincts had twitched, but he'd wrestled them into submission. Until a considerable amount of cash vanished from the Masters Corporation accounts shortly thereafter. Then, he couldn't write off his concerns as sour grapes or even misplaced longing for some intrigue in a life grown tedious. He'd hired the temporary management team to ease his transition back to his work as an agent, then he'd driven all the way across Florida to jump on a boat and find out what sort of Bermuda Triangle effect was taking place in the Caribbean these days.

He wasn't onboard just to play spy. The *Venus* would

dock in Antigua for a day, where he could visit Masters Corporation's newest hotel property. It was all practical with just enough time for some pleasure in the mix.

The redhead's sudden high kick right over his table gave him a view of her French-cut bikini bottoms. Long ropes of clear rhinestones seemed to tie the panties around her hips while allowing the trailing stones to caress her pale thighs. There was no way this woman could have been onstage in the first number. She had a knack for commanding his attention, something he didn't give to many people in a life grown too fractured. He would have noticed her.

Lowering her body to the floor, she rocked her hips in provocative fashion. Writhed on the ground as if she couldn't wait for fulfillment. For sex. For him.

Damn but she was hot.

Renewed interest in his trip had him clapping and on his feet when her number ended. A wolf whistle fell from his lips without thought.

He didn't know if she had more dances or if she was done for the night, but either way he made up his mind to go backstage and find out. He might have squelched his aptitude for spontaneity over the last year of putting family first, but he'd always had a flair for closing a deal.

And the brazen bombshell hurrying offstage in glittering silver sandals was one opportunity he wouldn't let slip away.

HAULING BUTT OFFSTAGE, Rita wanted to slip out of sight and slink away before Danielle the Demoness could get a hold of her. She'd missed two cues by a fraction of a second. Not enough that the audience would notice, but enough to soften the performance and take off the edge of crisp perfection Danielle drilled into their brains at Jayne's rehearsals.

It was the man in the front row who'd thrown Rita off. When he'd turned to look at her head-on… She closed her eyes to recapture the hot sensation of desire that had showered over her.

Deep. Dark. Delicious.

If she didn't need to search for Jayne, she might be tempted to track him down and see what happened. Resigned to giving Danielle the slip and helping her sister keep her job instead, Rita hurried out of her costume before the show manager realized what happened. Luckily, Jayne's stage perfection usually bought her a wide berth from Danielle who—while she liked to nitpick every detail of her productions— possessed a healthy respect for star talent.

Sliding into her shorts and knit halter top she'd been wearing earlier, Rita rushed out of the backstage through a lesser-used side door out onto the Mercury deck while still securing the knot around the back of her neck.

"Can I help you with that?"

Through the veil of her hair with her neck kinked down, Rita spied the object of her stage fantasies framed by the dark night of the open deck. The man in the navy pinstriped suit looked even better close up. He reached for the tie on her halter top.

Sex-starved lunatic that she was, she actually moved her hand away to let him take over the task. For a nanosecond.

"Wait." She slapped her hand back on the half-formed knot, dismayed to find his fingers already there.

And she was already turned on. Her legs that had been shaking from the performance quivered a little more. Just from this man's proximity. Amazing.

"What?" His voice was too close. *He* was too close.

Rita reminded herself she was not the impulsive sister. She was the rock. The stabilizer in her family since she'd pulled her first babysitting gig when she'd been eight and Jayne seven. Rita prided herself on being the only Frazer female not driven by her hormones.

Although in this man's case that seemed hard to remember.

"I can get it. And I don't even know you, so I have no intention of letting you dress me."

He slid his hand out from under hers, although he didn't remove it altogether. Instead, the warmth of his fingers drifted fleetingly along her shoulder underneath her hair for a moment as she finished tying her shirt into place. The touch was so light she could almost think she'd imagined it.

"I'm Harrison Masters and I run a resort called Masters Inn on the outskirts of Naples."

"Rita Frazer." She found herself extending her hand to shake his, even though she didn't normally fraternize with passengers. But maybe just this once she deserved a little reward for her efforts since she'd gone above and beyond duty by dancing Jayne's number. She hadn't even been able to stick around to meet with the Roman Cruise Lines executives to ensure they were pleased with her costumes.

"Nice to meet you, Rita." His smile created crinkles around his endlessly blue eyes. His hand engulfed hers, the warmth of his fingers stroking the heel of her palm, the sensitive inside of her wrist where her pulse throbbed with awareness. "I hope you don't mind me following up on our connection during your show."

"Umm." She backed up against the rail as an older couple shuffled past them. "I'm not sure I know what you mean."

"I think you know exactly what I mean." He leaned against the rail while the ship cruised easily through open water, crossing his legs at the ankle as if he had all night. "I'm pretty sure I wasn't the only one engaged in the long, hot looks out there."

She hesitated, knowing she could hardly deny her unusual behavior. "Sorry about all the long, hot looks."

"Don't be sorry on my account. I'm a gentleman and all, and I'll leave now if I misinterpreted the staring. But I'd be lying if I said I wouldn't be disappointed."

"I *was* staring at you. But not for the reason you probably thought."

"Meaning you didn't hope I'd come backstage to proposition you?" He shook his head, his broad shoulders slumping just a bit. "Damned if my dating skills aren't getting rusty."

She remembered him peeling the label off his beer bottle before she came out onstage and felt a twinge of empathy. If he'd given her a hard-sell pitch to have a drink with him, she could have blown him off in a heartbeat. But she hated to think she'd led him on.

"I didn't mean to give you the wrong impression." And God knows, she'd thought about jumping him the moment she laid eyes on him. "I just got into a bit of a pickle with the whole dancing thing and I needed a focus—"

"No need to explain." He held up his hand to halt her,

a flash of regret in those gorgeous blue eyes of his. "It's not your fault and I'm just going to get out of your way so you can—"

"Wait." Rita's heart pounded with the need to explain. Or maybe she just didn't want to let him go. After the day she'd had, Harrison Masters seemed like a lifeline, a rare opportunity to enjoy herself for a few stolen hours since she probably wouldn't have any luck tracking down the partying newlyweds until dawn at the earliest. Maybe she could forget about being practical just this once. "On second thought, a man with rusty dating skills might be just my speed. You want to get a drink?"

TWO HOURS LATER, Harrison guided Rita toward the uppermost deck of the ship under a fat full moon and had to admit maybe his dating savvy wasn't as bad as he'd feared. At the very least, he was right to follow the attraction to see where it led because he'd had more fun getting to know her over drinks tonight than he'd ever had in a crowded bar.

"I never date," Rita blurted as they strolled side by side around the running track on the small, nearly vacant deck.

"Never?" Harrison had discovered speaking her mind was part of her unusual charm, a part he appreciated greatly since he'd never been much for decoding the complicated thought processes employed by women. "I'm positive that's not because of a lack of offers. Your line of work must bring you a lot of attention."

"Not exactly." She slowed down as they reached the forward curve of the rail where they could see six other larger decks sprawled out below them.

From their perch they could see conga dancing around

the pool, a teen disco party on another deck and an Irish pub night around one of the other outdoor bars where revelers all wore shiny green plastic leprechaun hats.

Her hedging answer made him wary to press further. "I totally get it if you don't want to talk about your love life. I'm just glad to be here with you, Rita, because I don't take much time off to hang out and relax. I've had a great time tonight."

Rita looked too good to contemplate with only a couple of inches separating them. She tossed her thick red curls over her shoulder, releasing the apple scent of her shampoo. She flicked her fingernail gently against her wineglass, creating a soft ringing sound.

"It's not that. We just got to talking about so many other things downstairs, I forgot to explain to you—" She stopped herself. "I never even told you about the staring thing onstage, either, did I? I got a little nervous before I went out and I thought it would help calm me down if I had a focus point."

"I was your focus point?" He settled at the rail next to her, enjoying the way their hideaway isolated them while giving them a view of so much of the ship. "And just what is a focus point, if you don't mind me asking?"

"I think it's a meditation aid or something. My mom told me she used one to help get her through childbirth after the doctor told her Valium wasn't an option, so I guess I adopted it for other painful experiences. I'm not even really a showgirl. But I was covering for someone." She shrugged, a flirtatious grin playing about her fuchsia painted lips. "Worked like a charm for me."

Her brown eyes glided over him, the bold stare at odds with her light words. Only an idiot wouldn't make a move after a night that couldn't get much more romantic. Then again, why rush something great when he was enjoying every second in her company? He wasn't twenty years old.

"It worked damn well for me, too. That costume you wore—" he'd be seeing rhinestones in his dreams for the rest of his life "—I've never seen anything like it. You'd never know you weren't supposed to be onstage. From where I was sitting, you looked like you were born to do high kicks."

"You liked the outfit?" For some reason, the notion seemed to really please her.

"I'm pretty sure I'll never forget it."

"I made it." She finished off the last of her wine and set the glass at her feet. "I'm the ship seamstress but that kind of sewing doesn't really scratch the creative itch, so I created a lot of the costumes for the show tonight."

Intrigued by this newly exposed facet of Rita, Harrison figured there would be no time like the present to reveal he wasn't a resort manager. But was it so much to ask to have one perfect night in his life? One date that wasn't overshadowed by his work the way so many other dates had been?

"I'm no sewing expert, but I don't think I need to be to guess you must be talented." Reaching to skim her bare arm with his fingers he settled his hand on her shoulder and simply savored the feel of her.

"Thank you." She shrugged, but somehow the movement seemed to bring her closer. Had he stepped nearer or had she? "For the compliment and for—" she waved her hand vaguely "—this. Tonight. It's been fun."

Even though he only touched a few square inches of

her smooth flesh, Harrison could feel her heart pounding, could sense the hot rush of blood through her veins. He would have never guessed he could deduce a woman's attraction so keenly, but he felt hers in every pore of his flesh.

Almost simultaneously he realized he hadn't been this tuned in to his ex-girlfriend—Sonia. God, he had deserved to be given the boot. But he wouldn't let past regrets rob him now.

In fact, he welcomed the chance to think about something other than the past few months. Not that any red-blooded man could do much thinking at the moment. Cupping Rita's bare shoulder in his palm, he made up his mind to seize the moment.

"Trust me, the pleasure has been all mine." Leaning close, he watched the way her tongue ran round the rim of her lips and his throat went dry.

Without a single thought to practicality, he slanted his mouth over hers and gave her the kiss he'd been thinking about all night.

CHAPTER THREE

JAYNE MANSFIELD FRAZER HAD never believed in luck, preferring to think life handed out plenty of opportunities for those smart enough to make something of them.

So she could hardly blame a run of bad luck now, when her fiancé for all of twelve hours failed to show for their appointed rendezvous outside St. Kitts' "Island Dreams" gift shop, which just so happened to double as a wedding chapel for eager—or stupidly impulsive—couples.

No, Jayne couldn't blame anything or anyone but herself for the farce of her plan to elope with Horatio. Even when it started to rain—big, fat earnest drops that meant a serious tropical downpour was on the way—she refused to whine and curse her fate. She tucked deeper under the overhang of the store's sheltered front porch, her shoulder scraping a blinking neon swordfish mounted on one wall, thinking there wasn't anyone around to whine to anyway. The whole tiny tourist town shut down once the *Venus* pulled out of the harbor, taking all of its spendthrift passengers with it and leaving Jayne no place to go tonight.

Nope. She was certain she'd figure out something. Find some hint of opportunity to turn this watery night from hell around and help her get back to the boat before it hit Barbados. Or before her sister hunted her down and kicked Jayne's tail from one end of the island to the other.

But as she stepped off the protected wooden porch of Island Dreams to get a better look at the small assortment of St. Kitts storefronts for any sign of life, two things happened which convinced Jayne to rethink her stance on bad luck.

Turning on her heel to size up her situation, she snapped off her four-inch stiletto on a brand-new pair of shoes Rita had simultaneously declared divinely gorgeous and a colossal waste of cash. Rain streamed down Jayne's skin, plastering her silk sundress to a body which—she now recalled—was completely commando since she'd thought she'd be engaging in nonstop monkey sex right after the ceremony. And she slowly realized the only place of business still open and within walking distance housed the one man she never wanted to see again.

Unfortunately, she wasn't thinking of Horatio. Because while some women might never want to lay eyes on the creep who ditched her in front of a gift shop that doubled as a wedding chapel, Jayne would be all too glad to find Horatio Aldo Garcia and wring his worthless neck with her own—wet—hands.

The man Jayne Frazer didn't ever want to see again was the proprietor of a dive bar at the far end of this stretch of tourist traps, and he also happened to be the only living man Jayne had ever wasted tears over. A man who had provided her with the hottest sex ever to melt a woman's knees before proposing three months after they first met on the *Venus,* planning out their lives together before she'd even caught her breath.

She'd tried to stall him, but the man in question—a big-deal New York corporate type before purchasing the bar and retiring at thirty-five—drove a hard bargain with an all-or-nothing price tag. So, because Jayne had no plans to settle down, the sex god of her dreams had sailed back into the sunset nine months ago.

Now, limping through the warm February downpour into Emmett MacNeil's bar after all this time seemed to be her only hope of finding shelter before she either caught pneumonia, or washed out to sea. Instead of Emmett hearing rumors through the St. Kitts grapevine that his former lover had gotten married on a romantic whim— and she couldn't deny the appealing scenario had occurred to her when she agreed to marry Horatio here—*now* Emmett would see his former lover looking like a drowned rat, complete with the stage makeup she'd nervously applied under Rita's watchful eye ten minutes before escaping the cruise ship dripping down her cheeks. So much for her grand plan to flaunt her happy bliss under Emmett's nose to prove his high-handed ultimatums and heart-stomping exit from her life hadn't fazed her one damn bit.

If ever there had been an argument for the existence of bad luck, *this* would be it.

Cursing the lack of cabs or buses—hell, she'd settle for a rickshaw—Jayne hobbled through the haze of sheeting rain and steam rising off the ground toward the Last Chance Bar, her existing heel sinking into the muck of the washed-out street with every step. Although even if there *had* been cabs to take her to a hotel on the island, Jayne would bet her last ten dollars that Horatio hadn't bothered to make reservations any more than he'd bothered to follow through on the wedding date.

In fact, thinking back, he'd probably only proposed yesterday in a last-ditch effort to get in her pants, and when she hadn't fallen into his arms then and there, he'd promptly forgotten about all their plans. Horatio hadn't taken her pledge of celibacy seriously when they first met six months ago, but Jayne meant it when she told him she wanted to be a born-again virgin. She'd given herself away too cheaply the first time when she'd lost it at sixteen in a semimutual romp with one of her mother's boyfriends.

Definitely not the best way for a girl to lose her innocence, especially since the experience had been all tangled up with guilt at going behind her mother's back because she'd been mad at Margie that day for— But she wasn't going to think about that anymore, was she?

Anyway, after ten years of taking sex way too lightly, Jayne had decided to make a change. Hence, her vow of celibacy six months ago.

Number one probable cause for Horatio's bogus proposal.

She'd worked herself into a full-blown hissy fit by the time she arrived at the little establishment Emmett was rumored to have bought from the island family who had built it. Jayne hadn't even gone out of her way to find out gossip about Emmett after their breakup, but the crew members who took shore leave here came back from island layovers full of news and word traveled fast when a bar changed hands at one of the boat's primary stops.

Jayne never told anyone—not even Rita—about the incredible night she and Emmett had shared on the beach in St. Kitts during his cruise. She'd told herself she wasn't the marrying kind and hadn't looked back.

Which, of course, called to mind her thwarted attempt to elope with Horatio. What made her say yes to a man with as much live-for-the-moment attitude as her, when she'd turned down a heartfelt offer from a sex god who took his responsibilities as seriously as a woman's pleasure? Funny how the answer bitch-slapped her in the face now that she'd been stood up. Maybe deep down she'd known all along that "forever" with Horatio wouldn't be a super-binding agreement.

And wasn't this a fine time for an epiphany? Apparently a tropical downpour could wash away even the most persistent of self-delusions.

Swallowing old wounds, Jayne refused to let them stand in the way of getting off this godforsaken island and back to the *Venus*. If Rita had taught her anything in the past twenty-six years, it was that you made your own luck.

She straightened her sodden dress, noticing with a wince her outfit had turned completely transparent, and teetered up the stairs to the aptly named Last Chance Bar. Facing her old lover today would take industrial-strength chutzpah. But never let it be said that Jayne Frazer couldn't pull off a hell of a good show.

Yanking off her shoes, she tossed them both in a trash can outside the front entrance before tugging open the door.

The scent of cigars and polished wood wafted over her as she stepped into an establishment gone utterly quiet now that the rush of cruise ship patrons had vacated the island for the day. Huge brass ceiling fans whirred quietly overhead in the dim interior, stirring the breeze drifting in from a wall of windows left slightly open on the far side of the bar. A bit of water dripped on the hardwood floor, but no one seemed to notice since the place was completely empty.

Maybe her luck was turning?

Jayne scanned the bar for signs of a pay phone so she could call for a car to take her to the nearest hotel, wondering if she could be in and out of the Last Chance without anyone being the wiser. She peered down a darkened corridor off of one wall but found only a couple of restrooms.

"Can I help you?" A brusque feminine voice from behind caused her to jump.

Turning, she came face-to-face with a lean brunette dressed in a tank top and shorts, a yellow bandanna wrapped around the back half of her head, a burning cigar still perched in her fingers.

Definitely not Emmett MacNeil. Thank God for small favors. Maybe this gorgeous woman with the great legs and golden skin was his bartender, treating herself to a smoke after fending off advances from drunken revelers half the day.

"I missed the cruise ship earlier. Do you have a phone I could use to make some arrangements?" In the silence that followed, the woman eyed Jayne with a wary gaze while her dress dripped audibly on the floor. "Sorry about the outfit. I'll mop up behind myself, I promise."

"You're a passenger on the *Venus?*" The woman took a drag on her cigar and tipped her head to the side to exhale. Clearly she didn't believe for a minute that Jayne had booked passage on one of the Caribbean's pricy luxury liners.

"Actually, I work on the boat." No need for subterfuge. Jayne took a page from Rita's book and decided to be as direct as possible so she could get out of here before Emmett put in an appearance. "I'm Rita, a seamstress with the ship's costume department."

Okay, so maybe she still needed a *little* subterfuge. She didn't want Emmett to get wind of who'd really been in his place today.

The brunette balanced her cigar in a dish on the shiny surface of the wooden bar before thrusting out her hand. "Claudia MacNeil, proprietor of the Last Chance. Pleased to meet you."

Shock froze Jayne's hands to her side.

Who knows how much time passed while she stared dumbly at this gorgeous creature who was…probably *not* Emmett's sister since he'd once told her he didn't have any siblings.

"Claudia *MacNeil?*" If she was going to have a brain malfunction over the idea of Emmett possibly being married, she might as well be sure she'd heard properly.

Belatedly, she remembered to shake the woman's hand, surprised by how warm and alive Claudia's skin seemed, while Jayne suddenly felt very cold.

"That's right, sugar." The woman retrieved her cigar and took another puff as she pulled out a bar stool. "You just have a seat while I get you a phone. Do you think maybe you spent too much time outside today? You seem like you might have a touch of sunstroke."

"I've got it, Claudia." A masculine voice rolled through the bar, low and authoritative.

A voice Jayne hadn't forgotten.

She cast a sideways glance toward an open arch in

the back that seemed to lead to an outdoor patio. Emmett MacNeil, the only man ever to come within spitting distance of breaking her heart, stood framed in the door. His gaze remained fixed on the woman who shared his name.

"Thanks. You'll close up for me, won't you, love?" The brunette swept past Jayne to meet Emmett in the breezeway, her long fingers patting his face with definite familiarity, her body invading his personal space so far there could only be intimacy between them. "I've got to go help my dad move some boxes."

The impact of seeing Emmett now—with a woman who couldn't possibly be a blood relation—threatened to level her. She hadn't wanted him or his ring, hadn't wanted this life he'd offered that sounded ordinary and boring compared to the glamorous dreams she'd had for herself just a year ago. So why did she feel like a very big bubble had burst?

Leaving her very soggy and more than a little sad.

She took in Emmett's rough-hewn features, thick dark eyebrows and coal-black hair as he nodded at Claudia and received her kiss on the cheek.

"Bye, Rita." Claudia gave a jaunty little wave over her shoulder, her yellow bandanna fluttering in the breeze stirred by the ceiling fans. "Nice meeting you, doll, and good luck getting back to your ship!"

Jayne forced a smile that probably only amounted to a fractional lift of one corner of her lips. This was *sooo* much worse than bad. She'd mark this day on her calendar as the one performance she'd ever flopped.

"Rita?" Emmett's eyebrows lifted in curious amusement as Claudia disappeared outside, and any semblance of feeling sorry for herself vanished like money on payday.

Summoning her best showgirl posture, Jayne lifted her chin and flounced her way to the bar.

"It's an alias in my new undercover work, *doll*. And as long as you're here, I'll take a gin and tonic on the rocks with lime. And could you make it quick?" She glanced at her watch gone cloudy from moisture under the glass. Peering back at him, she narrowed her eyes to convey precisely the right amount of hauteur. "I'm in a hurry."

HARRISON'S KISS MADE Rita dizzy in the best possible way. She wanted to lose herself in that kiss, to cling to this sexy, gorgeous man for dear life and simply revel in the pure pleasure of the moment. Arching up on her toes, she allowed herself a more firm hold—just for a little longer.

She'd never been an impulsive person before, but then she'd never had to literally step into her sister's shoes. What if she was turning into Jayne in some sort of *Freaky Friday* switcheroo? On the plus side, if that were the case, she wouldn't have to sweat this whole moonlight encounter. She'd simply do whatever felt good, the way Jayne had her whole life.

And Rita had to admit, Harrison's fingers drifting up her shoulder to the crook of her neck was feeling incredibly good right now.

A bark of drunken laughter drifting up the stairwell from the deck below forced her to pull back. To think. Not easy to do anymore when every breath she took contained a hint of his woodsy scent. His minty breath. His male heat.

"I might not be able to kiss you again without getting carried away." His whispered words loomed close to her ear and something about a male voice cutting through the utter darkness made her crave a man— him—all the more.

"Maybe that's not such a bad thing." She shivered as his thumb smoothed over the small of her back. Hadn't she always prided herself on speaking her mind? Being blunt and direct was her forte and she'd be a hypocrite to deny she wanted to take this further so badly her whole body hummed in anticipation.

The group of late night revelers didn't stay on the top deck for long since there were no lights to illuminate the Jupiter level and the only features were the running track, some shuffleboards and a great view. Rita knew the area was most popular with early risers, part of the reason she'd steered Harrison this way after drinks.

"I don't want to spoil a night that's been—" He looked out to sea for a long moment, as if his answer might be in the dark waves below. "Damn, Rita, it's been perfect."

"Trust me, I'm very practical, and getting carried away is the right thing to do." Taking a deep breath, she reached out to him through the darkness. Sliding her arms around his neck she plastered herself against him. Lips, breasts, hips—every part of her sought him out to cop a feel.

She threaded her fingers through his close-cropped hair, savoring the spiky strands as she drew him close.

Her breasts molded to his hard male chest, tongue tangling with his as easily as if they were long-lost lovers.

Only she didn't have lovers. Long-lost or any other kind. She only had relationships with nice men. Nice, foolish men who didn't realize she was content to be committed to her career and her sister since it was easier than being tied to a guy with normal dating expectations. Marriage. Picket fences. Family that didn't include Jayne and Margie and all their combined problems.

But Harrison wasn't a regular guy. He was fantasy material. A vacation fling. Maybe tonight she could let loose and simply enjoy the moment. And it's not like she had to worry about setting a bad example for Jayne since Jayne wasn't around.

Not that Jayne had ever paid attention to what kind of example Rita set, damn it all.

"What if we take this back to your place?" Rita walked her fingers down his scalp to the back of his neck, slipping just under his shirt collar. "Would that be okay?"

A low groan rumbled in his throat. "You don't know how happy that makes me."

She smiled against his mouth, her thigh grazing the proof of his happiness. "I have a fair idea."

She didn't know how long it had been since her previous sexual encounter. Her last relationship had ended…almost two years ago? No wonder she was unraveling in this man's arms faster than a spool of thread in a sewing machine.

Although that didn't explain why *him*. Or why now. Questions she didn't want to answer while her blood simmered through her veins, her skin tingling with a combination of hot flashes and sensual shivers everywhere he touched. Good God, how had she ignored her own needs for so long?

"If we do this, there are no regrets, right?" Harrison halted his kiss to cup her face between strong hands. "I'm not going to mess things up with you just because I want you. Badly."

Her pulse fluttered at his words, the notion soothing some insecure part of her that had always lived in Jayne's sultry, uninhibited shadow.

Despite her lifelong attempt to be the logical sister, tonight she had every intention of being a bad girl.

CHAPTER FOUR

DECISION MADE, RITA tugged Harrison toward the stairs, hormones kicking up a conga line more enthusiastic than the one they'd watch snake through the pool area two decks down. His kisses had aroused all her senses, tuning her into his every movement, his every breath.

They took the stairs together, striding more quickly now than their leisurely stroll around the running track earlier. But then, they had a very definite, a very delectable goal in mind.

Turning the corner at the end of one flight of stairs, they needed to enter one of the restaurant areas to find the next flight down. But before they re-entered the closed part of the ship, Rita's heightened senses heard a noise along the rail. A muffled cry?

"Did you hear something?" Harrison stopped short as Rita bumped into him, his suit jacket framing a set of abs any woman would drool over.

"Yes." She strained her ears to listen while she forced her eyes to look away from rippling male muscles.

"It sounded like a whimper or a sniffle."

At the mention of a whimper, Rita was immediately plagued with a vision of her sister returning to the boat, crying in the hallway, forsaken and forgotten by her no-account boyfriend. Even as she dismissed the idea as impossible in the middle of the ocean, Rita heard a distinctively feminine sob from underneath the stairwell.

The crying female on the other side of the wall wasn't Jayne. Even in the vacated dimness of the stairwell, Rita could see the tall blonde perched at the rail, her head buried against a pink duffel bag.

Missy.

Hurrying over, she could hear Harrison's steps following more slowly behind her.

"You okay, Missy?" She reached to touch her friend's shoulder, instantly on alert even though a part of her still longed to be heading back to Harrison's room. "What's wrong?"

Lifting her head to reveal red-rimmed eyes and traces of tearstained stage makeup, Missy shook her head in sniffly despair. She swiped a hand across her face when she noticed Rita wasn't alone.

"I got fired." Voice breaking on the last word, Missy fell into Rita's arms to cry harder.

"Danielle did this? Damn her for a heartless—" Anger burned away the feel-good endorphins Rita had been savoring from Harrison's kisses. She had the sinking feeling her night to be self-indulgent was rapidly going down the tubes, but how could she walk away from her friend?

"It's okay." Missy hiccupped as she swiped more tears away with the sleeve of her shirt. "I'll find something when we get back home. Sammy—the somersaulter—said he knows some club owners around Fort Lauderdale, so maybe he can help. I just wish Danielle had let me earn out the rest of the week's paycheck. I could have been at home playing with Annabelle if I wasn't going to be making any money this week."

Missy had an eight-month-old daughter back home who stayed with Missy's mother while she worked. Rita knew they barely made ends meet since the baby's father—an international crew member Missy had met on a Fort Lauderdale beach—had returned to his Eastern European home rather than help support his family. Missy had hoped the dancing gig on the ship would lead to something more stable. Gazing blankly around the darkened stretch of deck under the stairwell, Rita willed words of encouragement into her head. Too bad her eyes couldn't move past the abandon-ship evacuation route placard on the wall over Missy's head, which pointed passengers in the direction of the nearest lifeboat station. The whole ship seemed to be coming apart today.

"Could you go after them for wrongful termination?" Harrison straightened his tie while he seemed to size up the situation faster than Rita. "Some companies are willing to work with you if they're afraid you're going to cost them a lot of time and aggravation."

Missy smiled through her tears as she acknowledged his presence. "I'm Missy, and I'm sorry to ruin your night." She looked back and forth between Rita and Harrison. "But I wouldn't ever try to cause anyone aggravation."

Rita's gaze met Harrison's and she felt the heat crackle between them as they both remembered what they'd been about to share. Still, he seemed to understand her growing sense that things weren't going to progress any further tonight.

"You didn't ruin anything." Rita slung her arm around her friend's shoulders, knowing Jayne could be in the same situation tomorrow if Danielle had realized she'd skipped out on her performance tonight. Gesturing toward Harrison, she introduced him. "And this is Harrison Masters. A really nice guy, but he probably has no idea how little entertainers make for this cruise line or how much power the cruise industry wields."

"I'm in the resort business, too, remember?" He pulled a handkerchief from his pocket and passed it to Missy, his mussed dark hair brushing his eyebrows in a way that would make any woman's fingers itch to brush the strands aside. "And no matter how powerful the employer, the rules remain the same for their personnel practices. They can't fire you without just cause."

Rita wasn't sure how sound his advice was about pursuing wrongful termination, but she appreciated his calm insights on the situation. In her family, getting fired would be a major drama involving days of histrionics. The whole family would have to weigh in with an opinion—always a vehement, fiery stance—and then they'd argue the merits of that person's ideas until they were all hoarse. And if ever there was a cool voice of reason in the mix, it would invariably be Rita's. So to have Harrison preempt her with such rational logic seemed sort of…deflating.

Which was utterly stupid. She should be grateful Jayne wasn't around to start a public brawl with Danielle.

"What reason did Danielle give for letting you go?" Rita had never heard of a dancer getting the axe in the middle of a cruise week before. They still had two more shows and a handful of smaller responsibilities like helping the Karaoke King on Open Mike Night or posing for photos with passengers around the pool.

"She said I was late on my cue again tonight." Missy speared her hand through her long hair, sweeping aside the mass of curls from her face. "I thought I'd done a pretty good job this time but Danielle hauled me aside as the show ended. She asked me a million questions about you and Jayne, then she dropped the bomb that I wouldn't be returning to the show."

Her face crumpled as a new round of sobs began.

"She asked about me?" Rita drummed her fingertips on the rail.

"This Danielle is in charge of the performers?" Harrison seemed to be following the conversation better than most outsiders would. For that matter, didn't most guys bolt at the first sign of tears?

He seemed like a nice guy. A nice, *smart* guy, which was doubly rare in her experience.

"Yes. She runs the floor show with an iron fist and considers it her job to inspire fear in the hearts of all her dancers. I think she suffers from the delusion this makes them dance better." Turning back to Missy, Rita needed to get back to an important point. "You said she was asking questions about me?"

"You and Jayne. I don't think she realized that you covered for Jayne tonight but apparently your stage time ran over by a couple of seconds and that might have tipped her off. You know how she prides herself on running the whole thing by the clock."

Damn it. Damn it. Damn it.

Rita had purposely exited the stage on the wrong side to avoid Danielle in case she hadn't realized she'd taken Jayne's place. But that opposite stage exit probably took a little longer after the music died, causing the smallest ripple in Danielle's rigid time scheme.

"By the time she tracked down the problem, I was probably already—" Rita's gaze went automatically to Harrison "—busy somewhere else. And her frustration with the show was my fault, not yours."

"You don't know that." Missy shook her head in emphatic denial, sending curls flying. "Rita, I've messed up a ton of times, and she knows it."

"But you didn't mess up tonight." Rita could just picture Danielle in one of her snits. The obsessive manager had looked for a target for her anger and found someone totally undeserving, someone who'd been working hard at her job while Rita was drooling over a total stranger. "I'll make sure we straighten this mess out and if there's a way to get your job back you'll have it back or we'll sic Jayne on her."

Assuming Jayne came back onboard.

Her sister was going to have hell to pay for putting them all in this position. But until Jayne came back to fulfill the position of token Frazer woman gone off the deep end, Rita wouldn't hesitate to engage in a few histrionics of her own.

Squeezing Missy's shoulder, she hoped she could find a way to fix this.

"Missy, would you excuse Harrison and me for a few minutes and then I'll meet you at my room so we can come up with a game plan?" She needed to talk to him. Owed him an explanation, or a makeup date…or a quickie in the elevator to tide over her hunger for him.

"Sure." Missy scooped up her duffel bag. "And you

don't need to meet with me. I've taken up enough of your time already."

"Don't be silly." She nudged Missy forward with big-sister muscle she couldn't help but flex whenever someone needed help. "I'll catch up with you in a little bit."

As they waited for the sound of Missy's footsteps to disappear, Rita could already feel the heat of the man beside her. But as much as she still wanted him, she wasn't sure how to maintain her Jayne-impulsiveness once they left the dark cocoon of intimacy the Jupiter deck offered.

"I understand you need to help your friend." Harrison's blue eyes saw right through her despite the shadows of the stairwell. "I just hope you're not having second thoughts about us."

"No second thoughts." Although now that they'd been interrupted, Rita wondered if it wasn't for the best anyhow since they barely knew one another. She was normally a certified chicken when it came to men, even though she liked to tell herself she was just extremely practical. "And I'm sorry tonight didn't work out."

"That's okay." He squeezed her hand and planted a kiss on the back of her fingers, an old-world gesture that stole her heart.

"Maybe another time." She couldn't believe she was angling for another date with him when she'd just convinced herself she didn't know him well enough to sleep with him. But sometimes, there was no accounting for chemistry and, oh baby, did she have it for him.

"I'd like that. I want you bad, Rita Frazer, but only when you're one hundred percent into the moment. And for what it's worth, I'm sorry about this, too." He watched her with lazy eyes, reminding her how hot things could be between them. "You have no idea how sorry."

Her body still humming with good vibrations he'd brought her, she shot him a smile and hoped she could find a way to be bold and brazen with this man again soon.

"I have a pretty good idea."

TAKING DEEP BREATHS, Jayne steeled herself for confrontation as her long, lost lover poured her a drink. Heavy on the gin, easy on the tonic.

Thank God his bartending abilities were better than his dating skills.

"So you're traveling incognito these days?" He passed her the drink and the question she didn't want to answer, all the while staring at her with a lazy look that married men should be forbidden to bestow on unsuspecting females.

The rain still pounded the thatched roof over the bar, the fans whirring gently over the lounge to stir the sultry air.

"It protects my privacy to use my sister's name now that my fame has spread throughout the Caribbean." She toasted him with her glass before indulging in a sip, knowing damn well he'd see right through the lie and not caring a bit. "I've never been one to cause a stir, you know."

"And you find the general public immune to transparent clothing?" He leaned forward to peer over the bar, his chocolate-brown eyes raking in every inch of her dripping sundress. "I'll admit I'm surprised."

Her heart stuttered for an instant as a shark-tooth pendant clanked against the bar when he'd leaned near, bringing his features into too-enticing focus. He'd grown a patch of hair beneath his lower lip, a close-shorn triangle that she wondered what would feel like against her chin if she…

Snap out of it. Jayne forced herself back to reality by inhaling the scent of damp bamboo. If Rita were here, she would have nudged Jayne in the calf with a sisterly kick.

"I had an unexpected run-in with bad weather." The gin burned her throat before hitting her veins in a sizzling jolt. No, damn it. That was Emmett's eyes on her body giving her the sizzling jolt. The gin couldn't begin to dull senses so sharply attuned to this man's presence. "Perhaps you could just hand over the telephone and I'll remove myself and my transparent clothing from your fine establishment?"

She heard the bristly tone in her voice and refused to care that he'd gotten under her skin. He was married, after all. Completely out of her jurisdiction. What did it matter if he thought she was a washed-up has-been in her soggy clothes? He had another woman—a gorgeous, dry woman—waiting for him as soon as Jayne placed her call.

"Technically, it's no longer my establishment." He reached under the bar and came up with a telephone. "But feel free to call long distance. I hear the new owner has deep pockets."

"You sold the bar?" Jayne ignored the phone, her problems of ten minutes ago suddenly less significant. "I thought you were going to stay in St. Kitts forever?"

He'd told her as much when he'd been trying to convince her to give marriage a shot. She'd panicked at the idea of settling down in one place—a fate almost as scary as settling down with just one man—and promptly accused him of loving St. Kitts more than her.

In retrospect, she'd realized it hadn't exactly been a rational argument. But then, she'd never tried to be the world's most rational woman. That was Rita's niche. Up until Emmett, Jayne simply hadn't been used to men taking her too seriously.

"I guess forever didn't turn out to be as long as I'd hoped." He picked up the bottle of tonic and poured himself a glass. "Mind if I join you?"

Without waiting for her answer, he walked around the bar to join her on the other side. Her side.

"I don't think that's such a good idea considering you're married and I'm in a transparent dress, remember?" She tossed out the most obvious obstacles, knowing she didn't dare let Emmett within five feet of her when she was feeling more than a little vulnerable. "In fact, I promised your wife I'd just make my call and be on my way."

She meant to reach for the phone. Really, she did. But the visual of Emmett swinging his thigh around one side of a bar stool kept her gaze fastened to him with superglue sticking power.

"Ex-wife." Emmett's eyes remained fixed on a manila envelope at the end of the bar for a long moment, as if totally oblivious to Jayne's presence. "She's officially no longer mine as of today."

The hollow hurt of his words was unmistakable.

If Jayne had been a more sensitive woman, maybe she could have murmured something sympathetic and comforting. Hell, even a total stranger would offer up condolences on his failed marriage. But as his ex-lover, Jayne couldn't help but ask the question burning through her brain with all the insistence of a migraine.

"How long were you married?" The question would

shatter any illusion she might have created of aloofness, but the answer seemed too important to overlook. He'd asked Jayne to marry him nine short months ago.

"Seven months." Tearing his gaze away from the envelope she could only assume carried his divorce papers, Emmett grinned over the rim of his glass. "A hell of a track record in married life, isn't it?"

"You *bastard*." Hurt reeled through her as her brain computed the proximity of his proposal to her with his proposal to another woman. "What did you do, ask the first woman you saw after I got back onboard the *Venus* last spring to marry you?"

"You said no." He shrugged a shoulder the same way he must have shrugged off his so-called love for her. "And I respect that when a woman says no, she means it."

"I said I wasn't ready." As he no doubt damn well remembered since she'd explained to him in detail all the reasons she needed more time. "Last I checked, 'I'm not ready' doesn't mean *no*."

"It didn't mean yes, either, did it?" He swiveled on his bar stool to face her, his long legs almost touching her hip. "And you can take all the haughty feminine satisfaction you want from knowing I made a dumb-ass mistake by getting married in a hurry since I'm now divorced and I lost my bar in the bargain. So why not just make your phone call and you can high-kick your way back to the *S.S. Good Times* or wherever it is you make your home these days and we'll forget this little encounter ever happened?"

Jayne felt her mouth drooping open at his unexpectedly heated words and promptly snapped it shut. Reaching for the phone she realized she didn't have a phone number handy to call for a ride and she didn't personally know a soul on St. Kitts. Present company excluded.

Settling the handset back in the cradle in the rather awkward silence, she was about to request a phone book when Emmett slammed his glass on the bar.

"And for crying out loud, would you put some damn clothes on?" He reached over the counter and dug blindly around until he came up with a bright orange T-shirt. Even at six foot two he didn't exactly tower over her, but his strong arms and lean, surfer's physique gave him a solid power that…communicated itself to her so clearly that it was all she could do not to lick her lips. "Wear this. Or drape yourself in cocktail napkins. But Jesus, woman, put on something."

"Fine." Recognizing an old-fashioned snit when she saw one, even if the fit-thrower in question would surely wring her neck if she called it as such, Jayne dutifully dropped the promo T-shirt touting orange-flavored rum over her wet dress.

"While you're mighty quick to point fingers at me, I'd be willing to bet you haven't been celibate since we broke up, but you don't hear me asking you about the whys and whens of your personal encounters."

She wasn't touching that one with a ten-foot pole. Even if she'd tried her very best to be a born-again virgin for the last six months, she couldn't forget that she'd been pretty quick to drown her sorrows after Emmett.

What a screwed-up, self-destructive pair they made.

"Sorry to hear about the divorce." She'd never been skilled with an olive branch, but considered this a fair attempt at making peace. "Just because I take offense at the idea of you offering up a marriage proposal to another woman mere *days* after you made the same offer to me, that doesn't mean I would wish you ill-will."

Who said she couldn't be magnanimous?

"You need a ride somewhere?" Rising off the bar stool he replaced the phone under the bar and fished a set of keys off a hook on the wall. "I thought I heard you say you missed your boat, right?"

"I do need to find a hotel." She took another half-hearted sip of her gin and tonic, wondering what Emmett had in mind. Desperate women couldn't afford to be super-choosy about their rescuers and at least he'd had the decency to admit he'd messed up by marrying someone else.

"As luck would have it, so do I. What do you say we blow this clambake and call a truce?"

Let her guard down around Emmett? She'd have to be crazy to make peace with a newly divorced stud in a dangerous mood. But then again, no one had ever accused her of playing it safe.

Besides, she needed a ride.

"Truce." She reached for her tiny purse, telling herself this was a practical solution to her problem. Even Rita would have to admit Jayne was making the best of a bad situation. "Just as long as we go separate ways once we get there."

"Fine by me." He walked over to the manila envelope and jammed the whole packet under his arm in defiance of the Do Not Bend dictate scrawled across the front. "But I've got dibs on the bar since I plan on getting rip-roaring drunk tonight. You think you can stay away?"

"I'm sure I'll hold myself back somehow." Sailing through the front door he held open for her, Jayne welcomed the raindrops that still poured in earnest from the sky. It was the next best thing to a bucket of cold water being splashed on her face—an age-old cure for a woman thinking completely inappropriate thoughts about a man she had no business daydreaming over.

And no matter that she was furious with him—not to mention hurt—over his rapid defection, Jayne couldn't deny frequent mind wanderings picturing the man buck-naked. She had to admit he looked damn good. Both in her fantasies and in real life.

He jogged through the rain to a garage beside the bar and hauled open the door. Hurrying behind him, she saw the waves foaming with the storm on the other side of the road, the ocean empty of any ships for as far as the eye could see. She followed him into the dark and dilapidated clapboard structure that looked more suited to a backwoods farm than a tourist street. Squinting, she could see him unlocking the passenger door of a mud-encrusted Jeep.

Holding the door wide for her, he held his hand out to help her inside. She hadn't touched him yet but couldn't see how to avoid it now without making too big of a deal about it. No sense letting him know he got to her, right?

She reached for his hand, but his gaze had already fallen to her feet.

"Damn it, why didn't you tell me you needed shoes?" He lifted her by the waist as if he couldn't get her bare feet off the garage floor fast enough.

The imprint of his hands on her remained after he set her inside the vehicle, her skin warming all along her side.

"I guess I thought it was obvious I didn't have shoes."

She wiggled her toes and had a flashback to a day in third grade when she'd outgrown her shoes and Rita had insisted she take hers since money was nonexistent in the years their mother had big gambling losses. Rita had worn an old pair of boys' tennis shoes a neighbor had donated so Jayne could have their only pair of size five Mary Janes.

"Hell no, it wasn't obvious since my eyes never made it past the dress." He pulled a blanket out from behind the seat and tossed it in her lap. "Do me a favor and dry off."

It had been on the tip of her tongue to tell him to do *her* a favor and go screw himself, but she would cut him some slack since she'd obviously walked into his life on a bad day. She didn't know squat about marriage or how to make a go of a relationship but she knew divorce sucked—plain and simple.

Her childhood might have been fairly impoverished from a financial perspective, but at least her family had always been tight-knit and her mother had protected them from the upheaval of divorce by never remarrying. And Jayne had no doubt in her mind that no one besides their sainted father—God rest his soul—could have put up with Margie for long. Wrapping herself in the blanket Emmett had tossed her way, Jayne settled in for the ride while he started the Jeep and pulled out of the garage into the rain. She caught a glimpse of the Last Chance Bar through the downpour and wondered idly if Emmett would ever go back to the business now owned by his ex-wife.

The same business Jayne had made a beeline for in her darkest hour.

God, she'd been so caught up in seeing Emmett again she'd forgotten all about her fury with Horatio and the disappointment of her thwarted elopement. What a sorry excuse for a wife she would have made. She smiled as she tipped her head back against the seat and stared at the pattern of rain blowing across the passenger window.

"You'll never guess what I was doing in St. Kitts today."

CHAPTER FIVE

HARRISON BYPASSED the wealth of restaurant options onboard the *Venus* the next morning, ordering his breakfast through room service while he struggled to put Rita out of his mind long enough to brainstorm a game plan for digging up information on Sonia's disappearance.

No easy feat considering the attraction of a sexy redhead and their thwarted night that would have probably blown his mind. But this cruise couldn't be all fun. He'd known even when Sonia left on this very same ship that she'd been seeing Trevor, but Harrison still hadn't been prepared for the blow when Trevor took off for Grand Cayman a week later. And even though the *Venus* passenger records had shown Sonia went ashore at St. Maarten and never returned, he couldn't help but think she'd made connections with Trevor afterward.

Blow to the ego, sure. But when 10k had turned up missing in Trevor's golf store accounts, followed by almost 20k in weeks prior, Harrison had been pissed off on more than a personal level.

He needed to find her, to find the money and figure out what happened, but despite his best efforts over breakfast, he found himself thinking about Rita again and figuring out what happened with her sister. With

Missy's help last night, he'd eventually pieced together enough information to realize his high-kicking date had been filling in for her absentee sibling.

Now, as he carried his tray from room service out onto the ocean-view balcony, he wondered how he could wrangle time with a woman whose list of priorities put his own to shame. She filled in for her sister, gave her friend a shoulder to cry on…plus she had her own job and she'd sewed costumes for a whole production on top of that.

Something about Rita's unique blend of fiery demeanor and cool practicality appealed to him on a gut level he couldn't explain, powerful enough to have distracted him from his primary mission on the cruise. He needed to 'fess up to his quest for information about Sonia's trip before much more time elapsed since he wouldn't want Rita to think he'd been using her. Not in six years with the Bureau had he ever found cause to kiss a woman for the sake of his job and he wouldn't let Rita think as much for even an instant.

He debated calling her room and offering his services for the day while she searched for her sister when a knock sounded on his door. Could she have come looking for him instead?

Logically, he knew it was probably housekeeping, but that didn't stop him from vaulting over an armchair in his haste to get the door. Telling himself it was just the sex—or promise of sex—that had him so keyed up, he forced himself to wait another two-count before opening the door as a penalty for being too eager.

But it wasn't Rita on his threshold. Missy waited there instead, her blue eyes huge and punctuated with dark circles underneath them. Technically, he recognized her as an attractive female, but she didn't come close to Rita in his book.

"Sorry. It's just me." She apparently read the disappointment on his face in all of a second. "I hate to bother you again, but you were so smart about offering advice last night, I wondered if you could be persuaded to talk to Rita?"

"I was just having my breakfast." And plotting his way into spending time with the ship's seamstress. "But I can make time. Everything okay?"

"I think she's content with giving Danielle a little cool down period first, like you suggested." She teetered on the threshold of his stateroom as if scared to put so much as a pinkie toe in his suite. "But she's getting frantic about her sister and—"

Harrison didn't hesitate. Turning his back on his work, he slid into his shoes and scooped up his cell phone while he listened to Missy pour out the Tale of Two Sisters. It was a lot to absorb, even if they had thirteen floors to descend in order to reach Rita's cabin on the lowest level of the ship. But Harrison took in everything he could, gleaning that Rita was as much a workaholic as he'd ever been and that her sister played a crucial role in her life. And as Missy related what she knew of the events of the past few days, Harrison wondered if it was such a bad thing that Jayne was missing.

He began to revise the opinion when Rita opened the door for them, however.

Ear glued to a telephone, she had red-rimmed eyes and wild curls flying in every direction as if she hadn't slept all night but stayed up to pull her hair out. She gave him a halfhearted wave as she admitted him, but when he turned to let Missy enter first he realized the dancer had apparently tucked her tail and run, leaving him to deal with the crisis. From somewhere down the hall he heard the bing of an elevator car and silently cursed Missy for a coward.

In the meantime, Rita paced with the corded phone tucked between her shoulder and ear as she carried the base around the room with two fingers. Her room was strewn with half-finished sewing projects, uniforms of all kinds on hangers dangling from a makeshift stretch of rope at the foot of one bed, pins jabbed in hems and sleeves at every angle.

"…can't you just double-check? Her name is Jayne Frazer. Or else Jayne Garcia. And sometimes for fun she books herself under a code name like Cinderella. Or Ariel. Do you have an Ariel?" Rita covered the handset with her palm while mouthing words to Harrison. "She's big-time into Disney."

He knew then and there he had zero chances of getting to know Rita—let alone ever quizzing her about Sonia—until she found her sister. Now, he focused solely on how to find yet another missing person. All his leads on Sonia had dead-ended because he'd allowed the trail to grow cold. He wouldn't make the same mistake with Jayne.

"They hung up on me." Rita slammed the receiver back onto the base and stared at him with cold fury in her eyes. "Do you believe that?"

"We'll find her." He was a patient man and he didn't mind working for the things he wanted. His wild fantasies about Rita would keep.

"We need a boat." He started working up a plan to help. They should have a real boat. Not some fifteen-story mega-cruise liner that put as much room between their guests and the water as possible. "You could get around the island in a hurry and check with all the harbormasters."

Too bad Rita didn't look hyped about the idea. Her face was pretty pale for a woman who'd just inherited the dedicated help of a special agent as an answer to all her problems.

"My God. You don't think they ever would have tried boating over to Barbados from St. Kitts to meet up with the ship?" In an instant, the phone was tucked back under her ear. "It never occurred to me to check in with the harbormasters."

Panic welled in Rita's throat at the idea of brainless Horatio possibly talking her sister into sailing into the port at Bridgetown. But it made perfect sense in a screwed-up way. He wouldn't want to lose his job aboard the *Venus* any more than Jayne would want to lose hers.

And Rita had to find Jayne as soon as possible—not only to make sure she kept her job, but also to corral her into helping manage the latest Margie scare. Their mother had telephoned well after midnight in a rare and very expensive phone call to inform Rita that the bar where she'd been singing a couple of nights each week had just installed video poker.

Just exactly what Margie didn't need. The machines were probably illegal but Rita knew those kinds of laws were poorly enforced. And the Frazer women couldn't withstand another bankruptcy. Margie could be homeless by the time the ship docked in Fort Lauderdale.

"I think you'd be able to wrangle your answers faster if we rented a boat. Any harbormaster worth his stripes spends more time out on the docks than taking calls anyway. You can bring your phone to keep making calls, but we'll look around all the docking areas for ourselves once we find a boat." Harrison explained the strategy patiently enough but he looked ready to bolt from her tiny, cramped cabin. He couldn't walk two feet in any direction without stepping on Jayne's strewn clothes, Rita's sewing jobs or bumping into furniture. "How about we check with some of this guy's—Horatio's—friends to see if they knew where he planned to take his bride?"

"Of course." Nodding at the practical wisdom of his plan she slammed the phone down again. "I don't know why I didn't think to do that right away."

"You want me to go ask some questions while you get ready to disembark?" He backed toward the door, careful to sidestep a shimmering gold satin bra.

He would do that for her?

"That'd be great." She'd never had smart, sensible help before while facing a crisis, so having Harrison around seemed really…nice. Most guys who were interested in a cruise fling would have zero desire to play private detective for the sake of a missing sibling, but Harrison Masters was obviously not most guys. "Horatio is friends with a few other casino workers. Mostly a lady pit boss—Fiona, I think—and a nerdy security guard named James who makes sure nobody pockets chips that don't belong to them."

"Got it. Meet you by the atrium on the Bacchus deck in an hour? We should be docked within thirty minutes."

He checked his watch before his eyes went to the clock radio beside her bed. Just that brief flex of his muscles and the sight of big, male hands brought back memories of those hands on her. Amazing how being with him had made all her worries retreat into the far recesses of her mind last night.

"Let's meet in twenty minutes." She could pull it together in ten if need be, but she figured Harrison would need at least that much time to track down some of loser-boy Horatio's friends. "And I can't tell you how much I appreciate the help."

"Not a problem." He shrugged as he stepped out into the corridor of the ship's lowest deck. "It was high time I had a little excitement in my life anyway."

She had to smile at the thought, even if she wouldn't exactly classify Jayne's disappearance as "excitement." What woman wouldn't be attracted to this smart guy who led a sensible, low-key lifestyle without a lot of drama?

"Stick with me, handsome. There's plenty more where that came from in my family."

I CAME TO St. Kitts to elope.

Emmett replayed Jayne's confession in an endless audio loop in his brain the next morning, his attempts at drowning out her admission with a particularly fine Kentucky bourbon having failed miserably. As he rolled onto his back and smacked a pillow over his eyes, he had to own up to the fact that all he'd succeeded in doing was adding a headache to the news that Jayne had wanted to get married, she just hadn't wanted to marry *him*.

Well, welcome to the freaking club.

Claudia hadn't really wanted to be married to him either, although she seemed damned happy now that he'd signed over the lucrative Last Chance as part of their divorce settlement. Son of a bitch, but he couldn't get used to seeing all his dreams incinerate before his eyes. He might have the Midas touch when it came to business, but he'd acquired some sort of cursed ability to decimate anything he tried to grasp in his private life. His marriage? *Boom.* Explosive failure.

Jayne? *Pow.* He'd sent her running so fast he'd gotten whiplash as she peeled out of his life.

He'd promised to drive her to the local landing strip to catch a charter plane to Barbados today so she could meet up with the *Venus,* but for all he knew she'd left already. She'd gone real quiet in the Jeep last night after he'd spluttered in disbelief—and possibly yelled a tad about the foolishness of rash plans—at the news of her elopement.

But what had she expected him to say? *Good job ditching work to marry a blackjack dealer with zero plans to make a real future with you?* For that matter, what kind of loser stood up his bride-to-be?

It'd been on the tip of his tongue to tell her she sure had shit taste in men, but caught himself just in time. Pretty damn humbling to realize he'd fallen into the same category as a guy who couldn't say "I do" and then didn't have the balls to say "I don't" to a woman's face.

Nice.

An efficient knock at his door echoed through his hungover skull with all the subtlety of a sledgehammer. He moved the pillow off his head to shout back at the knocker.

"I'm still in bed." And he wasn't moving until he had proof positive that Jayne was still in the hotel and needed a ride. If not, he was making the Seawinds Suites his new home now that his divorce was official, his house had become the sole property of his ex-wife, and Claudia had neatly boxed up his every freaking possession and shipped everything to a local storage facility.

His ex might not love him, but she sure as hell had efficiency down to an art form.

"If that's an invitation, your technique has really fallen apart over the last year." The voice on the other side of the door sounded both sexy and bitchy and totally turned him on.

What kind of defective libido did he have that a haughty, high-maintenance woman like Jayne could inspire a hard-on even in the midst of a hangover from hell?

"If you get an invitation, woman, I guarantee you'll know it when you hear it." Shouting and wincing at the same time, he swung his legs off the bed and pulled on a pair of pants while he went to brush his teeth.

She could damn well wait.

"Emmett?" The conciliatory note in her voice was a surefire clue she needed a favor. He hadn't dated Jayne for long, but for those few months he'd known her more intimately than any other woman. And he damn well recognized now just from the way she said his name that she needed help.

Did her moronic blackjack dealer understand her needs half so well?

Rinsing and spitting, he stalked to the door and opened it.

"What?"

He'd caught her by surprise. He could tell by the way she quickly pulled her softened features into a mask of cool collectedness. Still, he'd seen the hint of vulnerability on her face, felt her uncertainty for one disconcerting instant.

"There seems to be a problem with my bill because it's ridiculously high." She had folded and unfolded the piece of paper in question ten times over as she stepped around a matching sheet on the floor of his suite. "I think I got charged for your room, too."

Her gaze dipped to his bare chest for a fleeting moment before she breezed past to pull open the curtains on the window overlooking the water.

"This looks right." He scooped up his bill and compared it to hers, noting his ungodly bar tab and her dry cleaning bill for her dress along with the purchase of a pair of cheap rhinestone-studded flip-flops from the gift shop. "I've got it."

"I don't expect you to pay for my room. Or my shoes." She flashed him a better view of her glittery pink thongs as she reached to take back the paper. "I just hadn't realized these resorts were allowed to rob their guests blind for the chance to sleep in a dry bed."

"I'm paying the damn bill and I'm not arguing about it since every word I utter reverberates in my head like a steel drum, you understand?" He hadn't given a thought to the cost when he brought her here last night, but he knew most cruise companies didn't pay their employees much for their efforts.

Jayne had never shared much about her past, but he'd gotten the impression she came from fairly humble roots

not all that different from his own. Life had been kind
enough to him since he'd figured out how to translate a
gift for stock market prediction into cold, hard cash, but
he'd seen the inside of the welfare office enough times
in his youth to appreciate not everyone was lucky
enough to find an honest means of living well.

"You play, you pay." She stared out over the endlessly
blue water. "Sometimes I have a hard time remembering that one myself."

Emmett wasn't touching that one. For all he knew
he'd misunderstood what sounded to his clueless ears
like an admission of normal human weakness, something completely uncharacteristic of the most proud
female he'd ever encountered.

He remained silent so long she finally twirled on her
heel to face him, her sundress swirling gently around her
thighs with the movement.

"Are you ready to take me over to the landing strip
yet, or did you change your mind about the ride?" She
nodded toward the vast expanse of ocean out the
window, her glossy red curls·slithering seductively
around her shoulders. "I've got to get back to the *Venus*
to kick a certain man's ass and apologize to my sister
before a seven-o'clock rehearsal tonight."

"You don't think this loser ex-fiancé of yours is still
on the ship?" Emmett reached for his shirt, his head
clearing at the thought of losing Jayne for the second
time in twelve months.

"He really likes his job. We weren't planning to quit
when we eloped, we just figured we'd take the night off
to be wild and crazy." Shrugging, she fished around in
her purse and retrieved a pair of sunglasses. Shoved

them on her nose. "Or so I thought. Guess I'm the last of a dying wild and crazy breed."

Something about seeing proud Jayne Mansfield Frazer duck behind designer knockoff lenses clenched strangely at his gut. She'd changed since their first meeting a year ago and some sucker-for-punishment facet of his ego wanted to know how. Why.

Ignoring the pounding in his head to follow the stupid thrum of his clueless heart, he made up his mind to find out more about The One Who Got Away. For that matter, it'd been months since he'd taken a cruise and now that his divorce was official he found himself homeless and in need of some high seas revelry.

"Hell no, you're not part of a dying breed. Give me five minutes to shower and I might just be wild and crazy enough to fly you back to Barbados myself."

RITA WAS CALLING IN favors at an alarming rate as she sweet-talked the most junior member of the ship security team into telling her everything he knew about Jayne's illicit escape from the ship the day before. But she'd sewn a prom dress for the guy's little sister last spring and he 'fessed up without a wince since Jayne had promised to be back onboard the next day.

While the news was reassuring, Rita knew better than most people that Jayne didn't always stick to a plan.

Now, as she stood on a pier on the opposite end of the marina and watched Harrison shake hands with a local charter boat captain, she wondered how she could ever repay him for all the help he'd given her last night and today. Jayne had never had a problem with accepting kindness from strangers, graciously smiling when-

ever passengers—men, women and little old ladies—
brought her flowers after a performance. But Rita was
uneasy with anyone who offered to do too much for her.
Somehow, she'd find a way to make it up to Harrison.
Maybe he had a sister young enough to need a prom
dress?

"We've got the boat for four hours." Harrison stopped
in front of the small craft he'd picked out with a practiced eye the moment they'd arrived. "We'll cruise
around to a few of the marinas on the western side of
the island and see what happens. The guy in charge of
the charter vessels said he's been here since dawn and
hasn't seen anyone fitting your sister's description get
off a boat."

"How do you know what my sister even looks like?"
She took his hand as he helped her onboard and
reminded herself to pop a few ginger tablets as soon as
they got settled. It had taken her weeks to get used to
the rocking motion of the *Venus,* never mind that most
people on cruise ships never felt the swaying at all. A
boat like this would have her seasick in no time if she
didn't take precautions.

"I figured she must look a lot like you since you
escaped the show manager's radar last night." He moved
around the deck like an old sea hand, untying ropes,
hauling in buoys or bumpers or whatever they called
those fat pads used to make sure a boat didn't get
scratched up by the dock. "By all accounts this Danielle
the Dastardly runs a pretty tight show, so if you danced
your way out there under her nose without her noticing… I put two and two together."

"I don't look anything like Jayne." Okay, small inevitable family resemblance aside. "She's the cover of *Vogue*. I'm the 'before' photo on the makeover page when they strong-arm the average woman on the street into a makeup chair."

"All I know is you look mighty good to me." He slid behind the steering wheel and fired up the engine. "You like boats?"

"I like them fine once I pop some ginger pills." Shaking her purse to free up all the infrequently used items in the deepest recesses of the striped satin lining, she followed the sound of rolling tablets in a bottle until she came up with her medicine case chock-full of everything from sleeping pills for the nights when Jayne blasted her radio full-power to aloe caplets for sunburns.

"Is this outing going to bother you?" Harrison moved away from the steering wheel to push off the dock, giving the boat a gentle shove by planting his foot on the pier and propelling them deeper into the water.

Chewing the pills quickly, Rita shook her head. Determined. Ready to make headway.

"Not nearly as much as it will bother me if I don't find Jayne."

"You two are pretty close, I take it?" He jogged the few steps back to the wheel and steered them slowly around the docked boats, being careful not to create too much of a wake.

He looked perfectly at home there, the strong Caribbean sun bearing down on his dark hair to give it a burnished glow, his feet spread on the deck like a man who'd navigated plenty of rough waters in his day.

"It's a relationship forged in fire." Sinking onto the seat beside him, Rita shoved her heavy purse off her shoulder and tried to relax. Concentrate on the pleasing vision of Harrison's legs in khaki shorts. "We've been through a lot together and that makes us good friends as well as…women who know far too much about each other's weaknesses."

"Sort of codependent?"

She bristled at the very idea.

"Hardly. We watch each other's backs." Often whether they really wanted to or not.

"So how was she watching your back last night when she ditched you on what Missy seemed to think was the turning point of your career?"

Surprise—and anger—reminded her she couldn't relax too much around a man she didn't know all that well despite the romantic night they'd shared. No matter how charming and helpful Harrison seemed, he wasn't family. He might not understand the world according to a Frazer.

"It wasn't a turning point. I sewed some outfits for extra cash. And while it would have been helpful if Jayne had been there to do her job— Everybody makes mistakes." Wrenching her gaze off his fine butt, she retrieved her sunscreen out of her bag to slather over skin with a high tendency to burn.

"Some more than others." He cranked the boat into a higher gear as they cleared the marina and hit the open water. "I'm close to my family, too, and I can't remember a time I would have left them holding the bag to chase dreams that could have easily waited a day or two."

"And your point is that I must be some kind of messed-up enabler to allow my sister to take advantage of me?" She'd heard that one before, although usually snippy fans of gossip liked to cluck about enabling her mother as opposed to Jayne. Still, the same principle applied. She was cast as the sucker. "Or are you suggesting my sister must be a complete waste-case to flee her job?"

She scrubbed the sunscreen into her skin with extra force.

"Rita—"

"Or worse." Another scenario smacked her upside the head with more force than a high kick to the temple as she tossed the SPF 45 aside. "You think *both* those things."

"Hardly." He slowed the boat as they neared another marina beside a stretch of ocean-view resort hotels. "I know all about the desire to help out your family and I've been down that route too many times myself to blame you for doing that same thing. I just hope your sister realizes what lengths you went to in order to cover for her because from the handful of people I talked to on the *Venus* about Jayne, I got the impression she takes the spotlight most of the time while you do twice as much behind the scenes."

"I'd love to know who told you that, especially since you've been on the ship for all of three days." How could her coworkers confide such intimate details to a perfect stranger? Curse the man's sexy dark stare.

"Nobody said it straight out." He slowed the motor as they closed in on a small dock. "I gathered as much from other things I heard from your friends and Horatio's."

"I forgot you talked to them." She'd been slowly losing her brain cells to anxiety and fear since last night. Add to that the fear that her skin was burning from want of Harrison and not because of the Caribbean sun, and she was forced to admit she wasn't thinking clearly at all.

"Did you find out anything helpful? Anything besides the fact that Jayne and I are codependent enablers?"

She squinted toward a throng of tourists on the dock, a man and three bikini-clad women stepping aside for a young couple on inline skates.

"Only that Horatio was scheduled to work last night and they hadn't heard anything about him ditching." He eased the boat around a mammoth-size yacht to give them a better view of the pier. "But I couldn't locate the casino workers you mentioned, just a couple of bartenders on a different deck from the casino and they were just barely crawling out of bed when I talked to them."

"Bastard." Rita's gaze fixed on the man on the pier as the guy's hand strayed over one of the women's tanga swimsuit bottom. Squinting, she couldn't believe her eyes as the man's familiar features came into focus. "Maybe they didn't know about Horatio skipping work because he never left the ship last night."

"What do you mean?" Harrison cut the motor, presumably so they could ask the group on the dock a few questions.

Indignation pumping through her, she didn't even bother lowering her voice as she pointed out the ass-grabber a few yards away.

"That's Jayne's so-called fiancé right there."

CHAPTER SIX

ON AN INTELLECTUAL LEVEL, Harrison processed the news that the jet-setter type on the dock was the same tool who'd stood up Rita's sister. But the information seemed less important than the primary data Harrison currently received from his personal observations of the scene on the pier.

Horatio and three fawning females had all just stepped off the big-ass yacht beside the dock from which obnoxious techno-pop music still blared. A party seemed to be in progress onboard the hundred-and-twenty-foot monster where a couple of guys and three other women sipped a rainbow range of bright cocktails, their swimsuits as expensive-looking as the designer sunglasses perched on almost every nose. Money oozed from the yacht along with the mindlessly repetitive club music, and Horatio the runaway groom looked fairly at home with it all for a guy whose paycheck couldn't be any fatter than what Harrison had pulled down during his time with the Bureau. And Harrison sure as hell could never afford the Breitling timepiece this bozo sported.

"Hey, scumbag, say cheese." The shout came from Harrison's elbow as Rita lined up her disposable camera for a shot of Horatio's hand on the bikini babe's butt.

She clicked the camera before calling over the lens. "My sister's going to annul this marriage so fast you'll be a single man by nightfall, dip-wad."

Harrison secured the boat in record time, recognizing quickly the shit was going to hit the fan. He would have liked to look around the dock more discreetly now that all of his agent instincts were up and running about Horatio's big money connections, but discretion seemed out of the question since Rita fairly launched out of their rented boat to confront the dealer.

"Sorry to disappoint you, babe, but I'm definitely still a single man." He squeezed his lady friend's butt cheek for emphasis. "Good thing, eh?"

Harrison could practically feel the fury rising off Rita as she bared her teeth at him.

"Too busy to elope?" She edged the words past her lips despite the clamped jaw.

Harrison looped an arm around her shoulders and hoped she wouldn't shove it off or start a big confrontation.

"Come on, Rita." Horatio shifted his weight in a subtle show of discomfort Harrison wouldn't have caught without years of experience at reading liars. "You know Jayne's not the settling-down type. If we tied the knot she would have thrown me over in two months max."

"With great reason, obviously." Rita moved toward the back of the boat as if to exit, but Harrison held her back.

Hoping to defuse the tension before Rita knocked this guy's teeth clear down his throat, Harrison kept his tone casual. "You know where we can find Jayne today?"

"We were supposed to meet at Island Dreams last night on St. Kitts and then catch a hop to Barbados this morning." He checked his watch in slow motion as if to be sure he kept his name brand visible. "If she caught the flight we talked about, she would have touched down a few minutes ago."

While Rita assured Playboy Joe that no dancer would ever look twice at him again once she spread the word of an unfortunate condition he'd contracted, Harrison noted the name of the yacht emblazoned on the bow. The *Over-Under*.

"Nice boat." Harrison interjected while Horatio's miniharem stepped back, their high heels a chorus of taps on the dock. "You have friends who like the over-under?"

"I've got a lot of friends." Shrugging, he started to follow the females heading up the pier toward a water-front restaurant and marketplace. "Who knows what they all like?"

Rita's hand slipped around Harrison's elbow, reminding him he couldn't follow up on his instincts about the blackjack dealer now, even if those instincts were blaring loudly in his ear that something wasn't right.

"Let's head over to the landing strip and see if she's there." Rita's simple red flip-flops smacked the back of her heels in rhythmic time as she walked the length of the boat with smooth, efficient strides bearing little re-semblance to her stage strut of the night before.

Funny how the practical woman appealed to him as much as the fantasy siren. More, even. He appreciated people who valued hard work and family the way he did.

"Done." Harrison untied their rented vessel and cranked up the engine, figuring the trip over to the landing strip was as good a time as any to let Rita in on his real motives behind taking the cruise. "But once we're underway, I need you to tell me everything you can about Horatio."

"Besides that he's a two-timing snake with no moral system in place?"

Rita seethed inwardly as Harrison guided the craft away from the creep who'd thought nothing of leaving her sister at the altar. Forget that the altar doubled as a gift shop checkout counter. That didn't diminish the magnitude of Horatio's desertion in the least.

"Doesn't it seem strange to you," Harrison pressed on, "that a lowlife like him could attract not one but three women to keep him company today? He's running with some big-money friends for a guy who makes pretty average wages."

"You're suggesting anyone who works on the *Venus* must be low-class?" She hadn't expected economic prejudice from Harrison. He seemed so down-to-earth. So normal.

"Of course not." He checked the map of Barbados the charter boat captain had given them, the sun casting a glare on the paper no matter where he positioned it. "I couldn't afford a boat like the one he was on either, but if he doesn't have any personal charisma and he's got the morals of a snake as you pointed out, what basis does he have to form a connection with some multimillionaire yacht owner?"

"I'm sure there are plenty of multimillionaires whose morals suck, too." Rita kept an eye on the coastline, trying to remember where an airport might be, but she'd never made much use of shore time like most of the crew, preferring to sew onboard the ship rather than party in Caribbean clubs.

"My point exactly. And if Horatio is hanging out with those kinds of wealthy, unethical people and sporting a Breitling watch that would be tough to afford on a dealer's salary, doesn't that make you suspicious?"

"So you think he's doing something illegal? When would he have time between working and juggling five different women? The bastard." Resenting Horatio's treatment of her sister, she couldn't get past that anger to think about whatever else he might be doing. "Don't you hate people who have hidden agendas and stupid little secrets?"

"Uh, in theory, yes."

"Why can't people just be honest with each other and say, 'I have three other women I'm screwing on the side. Would you care to be added to the list, or not?' That might be skeevy, but at least it's honest." Rita knew Jayne had at least made an effort to get her life together over the past six months since she'd really streamlined the number of men she dated. This blow from Horatio had to hurt.

"There's something we need to talk about."

The quiet seriousness in Harrison's tone called her from her sisterly outrage. Then, the stern set to his features as he steered the boat across open water gave her the distinct sense of impending doom.

She *so* could not handle more bad news today.

"Don't tell me you're sleeping with three other women?"

"It's not as bad as that, but I don't want you to think I have a secret agenda."

Although she would have rather simply enjoyed the view as the wind plastered Harrison's shirt to his muscular chest, Rita didn't mind playing a few rounds of Worst Case Scenario to keep whatever he had to say in perspective. She couldn't afford to let him hurt her when she could barely stagger through all that she had on her plate.

"Okay, I've got it. You introduced yourself to me last night because you have a thing for showgirls and now that you know me for the seamstress I really am, you want out?" She'd known plenty of guys who could only appreciate glitz and glitter and didn't have a clue about what lay beneath.

"Hell no. You don't need rhinestones to look hot." The look he slanted her confirmed the words, his gaze dark and intimate and providing an instant thrill. "But things escalated so fast last night I didn't have a chance to talk to you about why I took this trip in the first place."

"Maybe you're a bigwig fashion designer traveling incognito for a little R-and-R and you can't wait to produce my exotic costumes under your label for some naughty lingerie catalog."

"I'm with the FBI and I took this cruise because my ex-girlfriend disappeared during the *Venus's* eastern Caribbean run last month."

Rita considered revising her stance on the absence of luck in the universe since she seemed to inherit plenty of the negative kind.

"You're law enforcement and you're using your skills to stalk an old flame who's trying to put some space between you." She peered around at the expanse of water and felt very alone with this man of secrets. In the distance, closer to shore there were at least a few sailboats.

Would they give her safe harbor if she survived a swim through shark-infested waters? "Should I be scared?"

"You don't think like anyone I've ever met before." Shaking his head, he checked his navigation system and veered closer to the coastline, and thankfully, closer to those sails she'd spotted. "I'm not a stalker, Rita, just a sorry excuse for a significant other because I tend to get lost in my work."

"As an FBI agent?" She wondered if he was just trying to impress her with the worldly credentials. "You know how you said you can see beyond the rhinestones? Well so can I, and I have to say I'm very content with a man who simply runs a hotel."

"I did." He scrubbed a hand through his dark hair and she was struck with a vivid memory of what those short, spiky strands felt like beneath her fingers. "I took a leave from the Bureau a year ago to help out my family with their resort business and it's required all my time and energy to stay on top of it. So I wasn't surprised when my girlfriend dumped me two months ago, but then she hooked up with my best friend."

"Which pissed you off."

"Yes, but I was still okay with that until she disappeared from her cruise ship when they docked in St. Maarten, and then he took off to Grand Cayman a week later."

"So they're living in sin together in the Caribbean and you want to track them down to tell them how much you don't need either of them, and you want to flaunt your new showgirl babe under both their noses." She could probably be persuaded back into Jayne's rhinestones one last time to help Harrison after all he'd done for her today. God knows she'd dabbled in petty revenge a few times in her life, so she could hardly claim some great moral superiority now.

"Rita, they both worked with the resort—him as a golf pro and her as an independent retailer with a jewelry storefront in the hotel. And their accounts were short a lot of money after the fact, so I think they took me for a ride in more ways than one."

"They robbed you?" She squinted through the early-afternoon sunlight toward the hum of an aircraft overhead. Jayne's plane?

"All signs suggest yes, but I came onboard the *Venus* to duplicate Sonia's trip and see if I could find out what happened. It's bad enough if they just took the cash, but they might have ended up in some kind of trouble."

"You don't think Horatio had anything to do with that, do you?" She knew he was a vile creature, but she'd never pictured him doing anything worse than being a player.

"I'm not sure yet." As they neared land, the sound of the plane engine grew louder in its descent. "But what can you tell me about Horatio's work as a blackjack dealer? Do you know much about gambling?"

Visions of Margie sneaking her and ten-year-old Jayne into every casino in Vegas flitted through her mind. Nights at the homeless shelter when Margie's addiction had cost them their house.

And, oh God, Rita needed to find Jayne and come up with a plan to get Margie away from video poker before they all wound up right back in the soup kitchen again.

"More than I want to know, but it's not a topic I care to visit, especially with a man that it seems I don't know so well after all." She'd worked too hard to rebalance their lives to get caught up in whatever mayhem Harrison was involved in. "And if you're really FBI and that's not just a pickup line you use to impress naive women, I have to tell you here and now, we're through."

Keeping her eyes on the shore, she searched for glimpses of hot pink or leopard print that announced her sister's presence from miles away. Rita might not appreciate Jayne's antics that were giving her a premature case of ulcers, but bottom line, her family came first.

Even if it meant turning her back on the first man to tempt her in a very long time.

JAYNE'S HEART HAD inched up her throat when she'd sat beside Emmett in the cockpit as he landed his tiny private plane on what looked like an even tinier island from her bird's-eye view above the Atlantic.

But even that fear didn't compare to her marginal terror at facing Rita when she got back to the ship. Stepping out of the plane and into the relentless mid-afternoon sun, she counted her blessings that at least she had the ride over to the pier to collect herself.

And maybe she could sneak Emmett onboard long enough to get her through the worst of the confrontation. Big, strong Emmett who wasn't scared of anything could surely smooth things over for her and provide enough conversational distraction to keep Rita from blistering her ears with an hour-long tirade on the dangers of impulsiveness. She could smuggle him past security by saying Emmett was a new entertainer. Ships picked up new acts in different ports all the time.

Well, sometimes.

"Jayne Mansfield Frazer."

The cool fury of Rita's voice on the salty ocean breeze froze Jayne in her tracks as her rhinestone-dotted flip-flops met the landing strip.

"Rita?" Jayne could send Danielle the Diabolical running with a strong show of hauteur and a perfectly delivered routine, but in all her twenty-six years she hadn't figured out how to stand down her big sister.

Spotting her sibling stomping through a hibiscus hedge with her hair in a haphazard bun that did nothing for her, Jayne reached for Emmett strictly as a diversionary tactic and not because she wanted to cop a feel of the muscles she'd been drooling over in their close quarters on the plane.

"You'd better not ever tie the knot without inviting me to your wedding, or I'll kick your scrawny butt from here to Broward County." Meeting her near the tiny building that served as a terminal, Rita pinched her on the forearm in an age-old gesture Jayne tried to tell herself was love.

Damn it, she'd really wanted to give marriage a shot. Something about life without the Frazer name attached held definite appeal.

"You got it, sis." Smiling with open insincerity, she placated her sister even as she realized Emmett was taking total advantage of the situation to wrap his arm securely around her waist. Knees weakening just a little at the contact, she remembered why she'd said no to him back when she had been more sure of herself, more certain she could take on showbiz on her own terms.

Ha. She'd never make it big as a dancer and her time to be even marginally memorable was running out. But back then she'd had other ideas, bigger dreams, and she knew Emmett's strong personality would always call the shots. Jayne could B.S. her way around a lot of people but the straight shooters like Rita and Emmett poked holes in her every plan, saw right through her every artifice.

"We need to talk." Rita slanted a warning glance at Emmett, apparently unconcerned with any man Jayne had roped into flying her around the day after her failed elopement. "Will you excuse us?"

For a scant moment she felt herself being pulled in two directions and then Emmett let go.

"Sure. I'll call us a cab while I file some paperwork inside." He gestured toward the terminal building where a handful of tourists milled, comparing multicolored toy drums and cheap sarongs from the gift shop.

Idly, Jayne wondered if they had any sarongs in leopard print while she nodded to Emmett. She was about to ask her sister about the cute guy who seemed to be shadowing her, even though he lingered on the outskirts of the landing area to talk to a guy tinkering with a small plane, but then Rita pulled her even closer to whisper.

"Missy's been sacked and our parental unit called to say the top-notch lounge where she's singing has just installed video poker machines."

"Oh shit." Jayne accidentally swallowed her cinnamon gum as she raked in a deep breath.

"You're not kidding. We've got to get to the *Venus* and start putting out fires before the latest phase in Frazer Family Purgatory goes up in flames, agreed?"

"I'm there." Not even Danielle could be so cruel as to axe the mother of a fatherless eight-month-old, could she? And Jayne didn't even want to think about how much damage Margie could do at a video poker machine. "I mean it, Ree. I won't let you down this time."

Rita's raised auburn eyebrow seemed more damning than a twelve-hour tirade.

"You obviously have no idea how determined I am not to sing for my supper ever again." She didn't want to ask why Missy got canned because somehow she knew it had to be her fault. "We'll fix it."

"*You'll* fix it. I've got enough problems of my own since I didn't talk to the cruise line execs about the costumes because I didn't want to stick around with a suspicious Danielle breathing down my neck."

The argument would end faster if she just buttoned her lip. Zip it. Close it. Don't say a freaking word.

Damn it. That lasted all of two seconds.

"You didn't have to worry. I needed to be back onboard for rehearsals tonight since there's no show. And you sure as heck didn't have to search for me, Ree, I was gone less than twenty-four hours."

"But you were with an ass-grabbing blackjack dealer who's throwing around money like there's no tomorrow and according to Special Agent Masters who I've been hanging out with, it sounds like Horatio is well on his way to being wanted by the FBI. So I damn well *did* have to find you."

"A wanted man? For what?" Jayne could think of ten different times she'd seen Horatio throw wads of cash around that struck her as awfully fat for a cruise-ship casino worker, but she'd always figured he just managed his money better than she did. And Jayne had known her sister to stretch the truth a bit when it suited her purpose—usually to bring Jayne in line.

Her gaze skated over her sister's head as the door to the terminal opened and Emmett stalked toward them. He was so different from Horatio. So much more sure of himself. Horatio had seemed like a co-conspirator in fun, a fellow daredevil who liked to sneak into the ship's pools at night with her after the nets covered the water or drink shots at out-of-the-way island hangouts until they were silly.

But Emmett—she couldn't picture him ever getting drunk just for the fun of it. He'd indulged in a few too many the night before, but when she'd peeked into the bar on her way to the hotel gift shop she'd seen the way he drank—like a man on a mission. As if scotch were a means to an end and not a joyride in and of itself.

"I don't know for what." Rita hissed out a sigh between her teeth as she caught sight of Emmett. "Isn't it enough to know he's up to no good? And who the hell is this guy you're hanging out with now? The last thing you need is a transitional man. They're invariably worse than the guys they're playing cleanup for in the first place."

Rita didn't remember Emmett? Jayne couldn't help a small wince at the thought her sister paid so little attention to the men in Jayne's life. But by the end of Rita's speech, Emmett loomed two steps away, forcing her to whisper even more quietly.

"You ready?" He looked to Jayne for confirmation before giving Rita a smile that would charm the socks off any woman. Any *normal* woman who didn't pride herself on cold practicality, that is. "I'm Emmett."

If it had been even remotely socially acceptable to growl, Jayne had the feeling that would have been her sister's response. She shot Jayne a look that proved she already thought the worst about her hooking up with another guy on the heels of her failed elopement, but Jayne was too pissed—and yeah, damn it, too hurt—to correct her.

"I'm Rita." Her big sister offered up a terse nod. "But we really need to get back to our ship."

"Great. I got us a cab." He pointed toward the taxi stand out front where two guys smoked cigarettes as they lounged against the hoods of their respective vehicles.

"We rented a boat, actually." Rita shot down the taxi idea while the mystery man who'd been with her continued to talk to people around the airfield. "We'll be fine."

"We?" Jayne had to ask since curiosity about the silent hunk in the background was all but devouring her.

Too bad Emmett talked right over top of her.

"Then Jayne and I will meet you back at the ship." Unswayed by Rita's demands, Emmett turned his attention back to Jayne. "I just talked to the ship's bursar's office from a phone inside and it turns out they have enough vacancies to let me come aboard."

"You're going to be sailing with us?" Jayne couldn't imagine keeping a wise distance from Emmett when she was facing crises on every front of her life.

And if she got close to him, she knew somehow that would explode in her face, too.

"They just e-mailed me confirmation for purchasing a ticket." He flashed a piece of paper from his back pocket. "Lucky for you, I didn't have any plans for this week."

Emmett and Rita both nearby to give her hell? Jayne had visions of herself being steamrolled in no time.

Rita shook her head and backed up a step toward her mystery man who Jayne supposed was the FBI agent.

"Believe me, luck didn't have a damn thing to do with this cruise," Rita assured him.

Amen, sister. And for once, Jayne couldn't find a reason in the world to argue.

CHAPTER SEVEN

"SO HOW MUCH did your ex take you for?"

Harrison knew Rita meant no offense by the question she asked as they stood at the rail of the *Venus* and watched for the prodigal sister to return shortly before sunset. She just had a straightforward way of speaking unlike any woman he'd ever dated. Add to that the fact that she seemed wound tight with nervous energy and he wasn't the least bit surprised at her prod for details.

At least she hadn't told him to take a hike after her suggestion on Barbados that she wouldn't want to be with a Fed. Maybe she'd just been tense.

"I don't know if it was Sonia or Trevor, but in all, there's a little over thirty thousand missing." A drop in the bucket compared to what his family had paid out for his father's medical bills and rehab over the past two years since he'd needed extensive back surgeries and nerve repair after his accident. But that was all the more reason Harrison couldn't afford to simply write off the loss.

"You said she took this same cruise?" Rita fidgeted from foot to foot, neck craning to see the passengers who wandered toward the ship on the crowded board-walk below them where guests reboarded after their day ashore.

He had the distinct feeling she'd bolt the moment she spotted Jayne in the crowd with the new man on her arm. Not that Harrison had any right to judge, but he'd been a little surprised to see the body language between Jayne and the new guy. Emmett MacNeil, who hadn't offered up anything besides a name when they'd shook hands briefly back at the landing strip. Rita's sister sure didn't waste any time filling the Significant Other vacancy.

Somehow, he couldn't picture Rita ever being so fickle with her affections.

"Yeah. One month ago Sonia took this same trip and never came back to port."

"Don't you have a picture?" Her dark eyes slid up and down him, as if questioning his investigative abilities that he hadn't already thought of this. "Maybe I saw her."

Had she not been so wired after a day of panicking about Jayne, he might have reminded her it wasn't wise to look him over like that if she didn't want him to cart her off to his room so they could finish what they started the night before. Gritting his teeth, he swallowed the comment but not the thought.

"I have a photo from her resort ID." Withdrawing his PDA, he clicked through a few files until he found pictures of both Sonia and Trevor. "I haven't shown these around the ship yet since I was waiting to get a feel for who to trust. Nothing shouts 'cop' quite like a guy flashing photos and asking questions."

"But you trust me?" Rita studied the images on the screen, clicking between the two pictures at her leisure.

"I thought I owed you the truth after what happened between us." He slid the PDA from her hands and jammed it back in the pocket of his khaki shorts. "I've been trying to give you some space to handle your family crisis, but now that we've found Jayne, I have to tell you I can't stop thinking about you."

She blinked up at him as if reseeing him as the man she'd kissed and not just some average Joe who could drive a boat to help her find her sister.

"I…um…have thought about you a few times today, too, but I don't know if now is such a good time to—"

"We don't need to sort it out today." He remembered all too well her dictate that his FBI status meant he might be out of the realm of possibility as far as she was concerned, and he didn't want to argue the point with her now. He could bide his time. Even though it would be damn hard. Literally. "I just wanted you to know that being around you makes me want to touch you. Taste you."

The handful of other passengers lounging around the deck faded away, the pool area half-deserted since most people were getting ready for dinner after a day exploring Barbados. The band playing calypso music rattled the speakers loudly enough to make their conversation private.

Intimate.

Rita swayed closer, bringing her coconut sunscreen scent and soft, full lips into tempting range. He skimmed his hand up her neck and under the silky length of her auburn ponytail cascading down one shoulder, the unruly waves having slid out of the lopsided topknot she'd been sporting earlier.

What he wouldn't give to watch the rest of her come undone.

Abruptly, she pulled back.

"I haven't seen her." She shook her head fast, as if she could shake off the heat between them. "Your girlfriend, that is. I didn't recognize her face or your friend's, either."

"Ex," he clarified, wondering how to regain lost ground with this woman who he guessed didn't trust easily. "On both counts. Ex-girlfriend. Ex-friend."

"Look." Her gaze swept down to the pier and then back to him again. "I tried to tell you before. Things are complicated for me right now, and—"

"Things are always complicated." He'd never gone out on a limb for a woman before, probably because he'd never really been intrigued enough to give a relationship a hundred percent. But something about Rita made him want more. "We're smart. We'll figure it out. A few complications aren't enough to send me running."

"Because you're a big, bad, FBI guy, right?" She arched an auburn eyebrow, clearly skeptical of his credentials.

The jab might have held more punch if he didn't know she wanted him, too. He rested one foot on the lowest of the four rails ringing the deck and tilted back to study her.

"I'm going to cut you some slack because I know you're worried about your sister and doing your damnedest to scare me off."

"Is it working?"

"Put it this way—if I wasn't cutting you slack," he leaned closer to make his point, "I'd be touching you right now to remind you how meaningless complications become when you want someone so much you can't keep your hands off that person."

His thigh brushed hers and he heard her breath hitch in soft response. Definite green light.

"And if I wasn't trying like hell to give you some space today," he twined his finger around one red strand and watched it slide over his skin, "I'd be finding out right this second if you taste as good as I remember or if I dreamed that sweet flavor on my tongue last night."

Her gaze went a little sleepy-lidded and it was all he could do not to kiss her. Since when had he gone all noble holding back?

Her hand fluttered through the air in a sort of helpless gesture before it landed on his chest. A light caress that lured him more powerfully than if she'd dragged him to her with a grappling hook.

"What's one more complication in the big scheme of things?" Her lips hitched up into a lopsided grin.

Her coconut scent filled his nostrils, the late-afternoon Caribbean sun burnishing Rita's hair with a fiery glow. He hovered a scant breath away from her lips when a silky feminine drawl floated over the calypso music.

"Rita Hayworth Frazer, you come away from that man before he devours you."

Rita straightened, her dazed stare focusing on a point over his shoulder.

"Jesus, Jayne, you sounded just like Margie."

Harrison eased away enough to drag in a breath. Turning from the rail, he spotted Rita's troublemaking sibling and the tall, quiet guy whose clothes—the creases, the cut—suggested a certain amount of affluence. No obvious status symbols like Horatio's watch, but the signs were there, offset by sun-streaked, overgrown hair and what looked to be a shark tooth hanging around his neck.

"Rita *Hayworth?*" He glanced over at Rita as she flipped her long mane over one shoulder.

"Don't ask."

"Our mother is obsessed with movie idols," Jayne supplied as she sidled closer. Her hips swayed in a way designed to draw attention, the woman's every movement a subtle flirtation. "And she loved to forestall any of Rita's teenage suitors by flicking on the porch light and warning them not to devour her precious baby girl."

Rita rolled her eyes. "Harrison, would you excuse us?"

"If you promise me you'll come ashore with me tomorrow when we dock in Antigua." He hadn't pressed for the kiss, but he wasn't budging on the day ashore. Whether she recognized it or not, Rita needed to get away. "I've got to check up on a new property there."

And I want you with me.

He hoped she heard the words he didn't say because he couldn't go another day without touching her. Getting to know her.

"I'll see what I can do." She nodded absently as Jayne drew her away, leaving Harrison staring after them.

But he wasn't alone.

"Frazer females do that a hell of a lot."

The tall, quiet guy finally had something to say apparently. Emmett followed Jayne's swaying hips with his eyes, even as he leaned back on the rail a few feet down from Harrison.

"They do what?" Harrison didn't know who this guy was or how he figured into whatever was going on with Jayne, but since Harrison didn't have any clues about what happened to Sonia or his money, he was willing to simply keep his ears and eyes open for a few more days.

Besides, anyone connected to Horatio and Jayne was beginning to pique his professional curiosity.

"Walk away." Emmett waved over a bartender as the deck began to grow more crowded with sunburned passengers returning from shore excursions, arms loaded with souvenirs. "Trying to hold onto a Frazer woman is sort of like nailing down the wind. Can't do it. Stupid to try."

HEY, NOBODY COULD SAY he didn't warn the guy.

Emmett ordered a beer in an effort to ward off the last of his hangover from the scotch. Since he had no intention of chasing Jayne while she was busy playing apologetic little sister to the unsmiling redhead with all of Jayne's gorgeous looks and none of her over-the-top sexy style, he figured he might as well make the most of his vacation. God knows he'd been too busy trying to mold himself into an upstanding husband the last seven months to have much fun.

"So why do you bother?"

The guy next to him waited to pose the question until the bartender departed to take other orders. Soon the masses would thin out again when the dining rooms opened for the first seating. Emmett recalled the ebb and flow of the days on a ship well since he'd taken enough cruises in his late twenties while still working as a day trader, making money hand over fist and looking for ways to spend it. Enjoy it.

He hadn't even come close to succeeding until he'd met Jayne.

"It's MacNeil, right?" The guy next to him pulled out a PDA and started clicking through files. At Emmett's nod, Rita's boyfriend continued. "Why bother chasing a woman who has no intention of being caught?"

Emmett's gaze went to Jayne and Rita where they sat at a secluded table with no view of the pool or the calypso band. The two of them leaned close, redheads bent in sisterly conspiracy—one glittering from head to toe with her rhinestone shoes and gloss-slicked lips, the other frowning darkly, her bare mouth and utilitarian shorts as different from Jayne as possible.

"Besides blind stupidity and lust?" Emmett dragged his gaze away for two seconds before he followed that lust right back to where Jayne's ever-twitching curves resided. "Hell, I don't know. Sucker for mouthy redheads, I guess."

Even though Jayne was the only woman in that category he'd ever dated. His old girlfriends—even his ex-wife—had all been connected to the overprivileged world he'd worked hard to infiltrate ever since he left home at eighteen.

"You didn't just meet her on St. Kitts last night?" For a guy who appeared totally taken up with whatever he was looking at on his PDA, this Harrison Masters sure had a lot of questions. "Because Rita was under the impression you and Jayne only just hooked up."

Thank God his beer arrived at that moment since the dodging and weaving waiter with a tray full of drinks helped hide Emmett's flinch. How the hell could Jayne's sister not remember him? Sure Jayne had kept their relationship on the QT when they'd dated that first week on the *Venus,* but what about all those weeks afterward when he'd flown to one island after another to be with her on her days off?

For that matter, what about his freaking proposal? Hadn't Jayne bothered to mention it to her family?

"We've known each other a long time." Slapping his passenger ID card on the waiter's tray along with some extra bills, Emmett took a sip of his drink. "I used to own a bar on St. Kitts."

"Yeah?" Masters quit clicking the PDA keys. "I've spent some time in the hotel management business lately. I can't quite get used to the customer-is-always-right thinking. Sometimes don't you want to just tell people who are too demanding or too brainless to keep track of their bills to go screw themselves?"

"It's not so bad at a bar. You serve the rowdy ones another drink, or call the drunken ones a cab." Emmett would miss the Last Chance and the insulation from his old life it provided. Hell, how could a smart guy blow his last chance anyhow? "It's different in the Caribbean. Laid-back."

"Ever meet the numb-nut Jayne was about to marry?"

"Fortunately, no." He'd wasted too much time at the bar last night thinking about why she'd chosen such a loser over him. "I'm hoping it'll stay that way."

"I think he's mixed up in something shady. You might want to keep an eye out for him if he comes around again."

The beer soured in his throat as he swallowed. "What do you mean, *shady?*"

"Too much money. Questionable connections." Masters shrugged like that statement should somehow explain everything. "You ever see a boat around St. Kitts called the *Over-Under?*"

"Big-ass yacht that probably cost in the eight-million-dollar range, right?" Emmett had seen it. Might know something about it from his days on the jet-set circuit, but warning bells were telling him this Harrison guy was asking too many questions to be a hotel manager on vacation. "Why?"

"Horatio was partying on that boat this morning." Harrison twisted the PDA screen so that Emmett could see a photo of the *Over-Under.* "I e-mailed a friend about the boat and he found out who owns it—some guy named Seva Yurek. But apparently he's got about twenty other aliases even though my friend couldn't find a photo under any one of the names he uses."

"Holy crap. You're a cop?" He lowered his voice, not sure what the hell this guy was up to, but knowing enough to be discreet. Nobody accessed information that fast except law enforcement with the best connections. Emmett had worked with enough Securities and Exchange Commission investigations in his past to know you couldn't be too careful about who to trust and he didn't like the idea that someone in Jayne's past had flagged this kind of attention. "You think Jayne is in any danger? And what the hell makes you think you can trust me?"

"I looked you up, too." Harrison clicked back to another PDA file and pulled up a stock photo shot of Emmett from his days as a trader. "You check out."

Emmett whistled low under his breath and decided to play his cards close to his chest until he had a better handle on things. What if Jayne had gotten herself into some kind of trouble, too?

"Then I'm guessing you're not just a cop."

"FBI, actually, although I've been on leave lately."

Nodding, Harrison pocketed the PDA and turned his attention to the table where Rita and Jayne seemed to be having a more heated discussion. Arms were flailing. Cheeks were flushed. "And Horatio isn't just a blackjack dealer, either. All I'm saying is keep your eyes open."

"Done." Emmett would love an excuse to put Horatio through a wall. His vacation just started looking up. "I'll make it my personal mission to keep Jayne out of trouble."

"Uh, judging by the murderous look on her sister's face right now, that might be a full-time job."

"YOU CAN'T *QUIT.*" Rita could feel every last freckle on her face heat up with the very idea her sister would consider resigning after Rita had danced her ass off to keep the position and probably cost Missy a job in the process. "What the hell is that going to solve?"

"Obviously one of us needs to be in Lauderdale to oversee Margie." Jayne might wear her anger more demurely than Rita, but her jaw clenched from the same temper. "I'm not going to worry every time we leave port that we won't have a house to come home to. This job isn't worth it."

"So you say today." Rita made an effort to lower her voice when she noticed the karaoke director turn to look their way. "But when we were waitressing at the truck stop, you said you couldn't stand another day of microwaving frozen burritos for a bunch of caffeine addicts who couldn't keep their hands to themselves."

"And I meant it." Jayne waved at the Karaoke King and blew him a little kiss, effectively sending the married man scurrying away, albeit with a guilty grin on his face.

"Well that's what's waiting for you back home, hon. Sorry to be the bearer of bad news but remember how many jobs you can tear through in a month if you're not given a star on a dressing room door—or a dressing room table, in your case—and all the hoopla that goes along with it?"

Out of the corner of her eye she caught Harrison and Emmett MacNeil watching their conversation intently from the spot along the rail. The last thing she needed was Jayne's new man whisking her away so the Dancing Queen wouldn't have to suffer the annoyance of making a rational decision.

"What about New York?" Chewing the inside of her lip, Jayne cast a wary glance over her shoulder toward her latest boy toy. "Maybe we can sell the house and we can all check out Broadway, far away from her old gambling haunts."

"You'd really consider going?" Rita tried not to hyperventilate. Where was the catch? Jayne had never shown any interest in leaving before. "Why the sudden need to leave?"

Call her cynical, but Rita found it hard to believe Jayne would be all that broken up over her failed elopement.

"Let's just say it's time for me to be moving on." As she peered backward again, Jayne's long earrings dangled against her bare shoulder, a purple sunset coloring the whole deck with a lavender glow. "Margie needs to get away from her old bad habits, and maybe I do, too."

Well, knock her over with a feather.

That actually sounded sensible.

"Okay. We can start looking into the possibilities. Just promise me you won't quit this job before we have something else lined up."

They had pulled out of port a few minutes ago as the sun began to set, but the pool deck suddenly hummed with activity.

"Absolutely." Jayne pressed a hand to her chest, fake tennis bracelet winking in the overhead party lights strung from the ship's wide-open rafters. "I wouldn't dream of doing otherwise."

"Okay, save the heartfelt declarations for your new man." Rita couldn't shake the sense that Emmett MacNeil was going to swoop in and drag Jayne off for another ill-fated eloping scheme. "Where did you find this one?"

"At the altar, of course. Also known as the Island Dreams checkout counter. He was buying a shell necklace while I was purchasing a Little Mermaid negligee for my wedding night." Smiling, she didn't bother sewing up the details of a story that could easily be fact or fiction. "You know I don't believe in wasting time between men."

"I just hope he's better than Horatio." Spotting Missy curled up in a window seat next to Sammy the Somer-saulter, Rita waved her over. "We saw Horatio this morning in Barbados, by the way. I got a nice picture of his hand on another woman's ass, just in case you ever get a case of amnesia where he's concerned."

Rita didn't blame Jayne for giving her an evil look at the implication, but she didn't have time to cater to her little sister's ego. If Jayne was serious about taking her dancing to Broadway, she needed to be focused for once.

"Missy." Standing, Rita dragged their friend closer

so she could hear over the music that seemed to get louder by the minute. "Why don't you tell Jayne what happened last night with Danielle? Maybe she can give you some hints for getting back into her good graces."

"Jayne." Missy's smile was genuine for the traitorous Frazer whose absence had caused total chaos the previous night. "I'm so glad you're back."

"Duty calls then." Jayne rose from her seat, her innate grace making even the most basic of movements a visual treat to turn male heads all around them. "Tell me all about your run-in with the Evil One before I set her straight about your employment. I've got rehearsal in ten minutes and I'll talk to her after we finish up."

While Missy looked slavishly grateful, Jayne turned back to Rita with a hair flip Farrah Fawcett would have envied. "And while I'm negotiating with the Demoness, you're going to call Margie and make sure she's behaving."

Nodding, Rita could think of five million better ways to spend the rest of her free evening. She immediately sought out Harrison with a glance around deck. "Sure. I'll call her Gamblers Anonymous sponsor, too."

"Good. Because if she loses the condo somehow, we've got nothing left but our credit union savings."

Disguising her gulp, Rita shoved away thoughts of tackling Harrison as she realized their savings account was actually empty since she had gone out on a financial limb to pay for the fabric for the costumes she'd created for the ship's new floor show. A fact she never had shared with Jayne since she'd known damn well she'd get the money back as soon as the production was a big success.

"At least the condo is in our names now," she re-minded Jayne in an effort to reassure herself. They'd known better than to give their mother anything tangible to gamble away. "We're totally safe."

But just in case, she needed to speak to Danielle about getting reimbursed for her work-for-hire job with the costumes now that the show had debuted. She'd for-gotten all about the fate of her costumes after Jayne had disappeared. And wasn't that a slap in the face to realize she was as quick as her sister to shove aside work re-sponsibilities to indulge her personal life?

Except for Rita, her personal life meant taking care of her family. While Jayne's personal life continually seemed to mean taking care of Jayne.

But as Rita watched her sister saunter slowly toward the dining room with Missy in tow, she couldn't help but think maybe that was going to change.

CHAPTER EIGHT

SOME CHANGE WOULD do her good.

Jayne spun alone on the deserted stage in her dance shoes, her perfect high kicks wasted on an audience of empty chairs just past midnight. Spotlight warming her face with its relentless shine, she savored the stage even when no one watched her. The custodial crew had finished cleaning ten minutes ago, leaving the room locked at her request. She hadn't wanted any stray passengers to wander in and see her dance her way through the routines she'd missed the night before when she'd been waiting for one man and finding another who seemed far more dangerous to her mental health.

Missing a beat in a jump sequence that should be second nature to her, she cursed her weakness for a guy with the power to get under her skin. She'd done well enough in her rehearsal earlier, but now that she danced alone she found her thoughts straying. Before Emmett she'd always controlled men with the same fluid ease she'd exercised over her dance numbers. Now it seemed she was losing her touch between the bungled jump sequence and Horatio's absence last night. He hadn't even bothered to show up for a marriage that would have given him the green light for sex. Totally unheard of, in her experience.

And Emmett…well, she never had figured out how to push his buttons.

Correction. She remembered pushing certain buttons with electrifying results when they'd first met. They'd christened every square inch of his stateroom onboard the *Venus* with a different sex position, unable to pull away long enough to do anything but eat, drink and shower. But she'd never really understood him or what he wanted from her, and that scared her. Sex hadn't been nearly enough for him and giving more than that… Well, hell. She'd never been quite sure what to give.

Ending her routine in a partial split onstage, she sagged into the move, her thighs aching pleasantly with the stretch. Her body craved workouts all the more since she'd given up sex six months ago. Born-again virgin thighs needed the discipline of regular cardio sessions since they lacked the acrobatic challenge of wrapping around a man's waist. Sometimes his shoulders.

She shivered at the memory of a night spent on the beach in St. Kitts with Emmett a year ago. They'd cavorted around, shamelessly naked in front of the birds and fishes, their private stretch of beach protected from prying eyes by verdant green foliage.

Pressing her thighs together against an ache that had nothing to do with stretching, Jayne stood slowly. She had no idea why Emmett had decided to join the cruise, but she knew she needed to tread carefully if she didn't want to end up right back where she'd started with him—unable to move forward and commit herself to a man she didn't understand. Unable to go back, his kisses more addictive than a good workout.

"Hey, gorgeous." The masculine voice emanating from the back of the theater wasn't the one she'd been daydreaming about.

"Horatio?" Tensing with residual anger from her long walk in the rain the night before, she squinted into the rear of the small theater. "How did you get in here?"

"The janitor just opened it. He said to tell you they're not allowed to keep it locked except for during rehearsals." He stalked closer, his slick, Latin-American good looks so different from Emmett's lanky height, sun-tipped dark hair and soul patch. "I missed you last night before you left the ship, but I couldn't get away. The pit boss spotted me on the way out and threatened to turn me in."

It was not a bad excuse since they'd both agreed they couldn't risk their jobs to elope. Too bad Jayne didn't buy it for a second.

"Never lie to a liar, sweetie." She allowed Margie's perpetually overdone southern sweetness to infiltrate her speech, her fallback dialect when she wanted to turn up the bitch-factor. "We make for the toughest audience."

Still, Horatio didn't take the hint, swaggering closer with his cocksure stare and an expensive suit—damn, was that a Ralph Lauren?—she'd never seen before. Rita would have been able to pinpoint the threads.

"Come on, Jayne." Lowering his voice now that he had climbed the two stairs at the foot of the stage near the grand piano, he turned up the charm another notch. "You know I would have been there if there'd been any way in hell I could have arranged it. Nobody knows better than you how much I want you."

His hands stretched to touch her waist, but she forced herself to remain still. Calm. Margie-sweet.

"Touch me and you can kiss your balls goodbye."

"Jayne." He looked ready to argue, but the hands sure as hell stopped moving.

"Jayne?" A deeper voice rolled through the auditorium with a projection level a performer could appreciate.

And didn't she just love perfect timing?

"Up here, Emmett baby." She gestured her long-ago lover closer with a lazy wave of her fingers even though she hadn't actually spotted him in the shadows of the darkened theater yet.

No sense getting mad at Horatio who wouldn't know a nice girl if she sat on him and wiggled. Not that a nice girl would, she supposed. Jayne would simply get even.

"I've been looking for you." Emmett's voice went right through her with words that seemed half threat and half delicious promise. If she dared to let herself remember things they'd done together, she could kiss all her noble virgin intentions goodbye.

"And just my luck you found me." She tilted her head at an inviting angle, filling her eyes with plenty of come-hither steam. If Horatio hadn't been there, she would have never flirted so openly, but she'd be damned if she'd miss an opportunity to let him know his no-show stunt hadn't hurt her.

"You can't be serious." Horatio's lowered voice was meant for her, but it was all too obvious he wasn't prepared to mouth off in front of the six-foot-four tower of male muscle coming up the stairs.

She spared her ex-fiancé a sideways glance and

spoke in a stage whisper. "You should know I take sex *very* seriously."

"Any trouble here?" Emmett closed in on them, not coming to a halt until he stood a scant inch from her. He held out his hand to Horatio and introduced himself. "I'm Emmett."

Excess testosterone fogged the stage as the two men faced off. It did her heart good to see Horatio pale ever so slightly beneath his perpetual tan as Emmett gripped his hand with what looked to be excessive force.

"No trouble." Horatio took a step back toward the stairs leading off the stage, but he paused before leaving. "I was just telling Jayne she should be careful about taking unauthorized time away from the ship. You never know who might hear about things like that."

A string of appropriate curses bubbled up her throat, but Emmett palmed her back, his hand grounding her. Keeping her level.

"Making threats?" The spotlight cast shadows under Emmett's prominent cheekbones, his angular nose. He looked scary as hell, as far as Jayne could see. "Because the ship's entertainers have some strict clauses in their contracts about what sorts of harassment they don't have to take, and I'll be damned if that didn't sound like a threat to me."

Horatio's hands went up waist-high in the universal surrender sign. "I'm not looking for trouble, bud. Just making an observation to help her out."

Jayne suppressed a shiver at the smarmy insinuation in his voice and she had to wonder what was wrong with her to have dated someone like him for months. Was she that blind? Or had she simply ignored her in-

stincts about the guy so that she wouldn't have to be—
heaven help her—alone?

Damn, but self-realization bit the big one.

"That's right." Emmett nodded with smug victory at
the sight of Horatio walking away. "You wouldn't want
to lose your good gig as a dealer. Can't blame you for
not wanting to piss off a guy like Yurek."

Jayne had no clue what Emmett was talking about,
but whatever he was saying caused her slick ex-
boyfriend to stop in his tracks on the purple-carpeted
aisle leading toward the back of the theater.

Turning, he glared up at the stage with a level of
ugliness she'd never seen from a man who'd worked
hard to charm the pants off her.

"I don't know what you're saying, but I'd stay out of
the casino this trip if I was you." He allowed himself a
superior smile now that he was out of fist-range of
Emmett. "I've gotta warn you that I have a good contract
protecting me, too. A real good one."

Pivoting on his heel, he stalked out of the theater,
plowing through the metal double doors with a bang.

"What was that all about?" Wrapping her arms
around her waist, she stepped away from the warmth of
Emmett's hand on her back. "You know him?"

Somehow she couldn't help but feel a bit one-upped
by Emmett's exchange with Horatio, which seemed to
focus on a tension between them that didn't have a
single thing to do with her. Selfish, yes. Immature, no
question. Wouldn't be the first time she'd been guilty on
both counts.

Striding over to her water bottle at the edge of the
stage she heard the door at the back of the theater open

again. Spotted a small throng of old-timers settling into the back rows, probably looking for a quiet place to sit until seating for the midnight buffet eased up.

"I know his type," Emmett clarified, his eyes on the back of the theater and the newcomers still dressed in evening formal wear. "But I don't know him personally. You done rehearsing?"

Nodding, she moved to exit stage left but paused once they were behind the curtain, out of view. She flicked off the spotlight she'd been dancing under, leaving her and Emmett with only a few floor lights to illuminate the backstage full of stage props and speakers.

"What are you doing here?" She couldn't wait to ask the question that had been gnawing at her since this afternoon.

"Protecting you from the wolves of the world. What does it look like?"

"No. I mean, why did you come onboard the ship today when you could have just flown back to St. Kitts or New York, or wherever you wanted to go?" He'd been a jet-setter when they first met. An admittedly restless man with no experience sitting still for long.

Yet here he was, revisiting a place he'd already been with a woman who'd already told him no. And he looked suspiciously at ease with the situation that made her as jumpy as the acrobat act that came on after the floor show.

"Are you sure you want the truth, Jayne?" He took her water bottle from her hands and polished off the rest of the drink before setting aside the container on a speaker. "Or would you rather I whip up an answer you might actually like?"

"You don't need to lie to me." Her hands felt twitchy without the bottle to hold on to. And even though Emmett's insinuation that she needed a fairy tale pissed her off, she still wondered what it would be like to settle her hands on his chest and the taupe-colored dress shirt he wore rolled at the sleeves.

"Then I'm here for two reasons. One, because Horatio Hotshot is attracting the wrong kind of attention if Rita's boyfriend has taken an interest in him and I'll be damned if I let that dip-wad anywhere near you."

"I don't need a watchdog." Her feminine pride really bristled that he would come aboard the ship on some mission to protect her from loser-boy Horatio. "And I think Rita's new man is a Fed. Or former Fed." She flipped away the matter with a wave of her hand since she hadn't really been paying much attention to Rita's explanation of her cop suitor. "You said there was another reason?"

She hoped it was a hell of a lot better than the first.

He braced his hands on the speaker behind her that came up to the middle of her back, effectively trapping her. Breath catching at his proximity, she took in the scent of bay rum and sea wind. *His* scent.

Mind flooding with vivid memories of his touch, his taste, Jayne suddenly felt the weight of every hour she'd spent as a born-again virgin.

"You walked into my bar on the very day my divorce was finalized." His voice triggered chill bumps on her arms, her whole body tingling with remembered passion. "And I don't believe in coincidences."

Blinking, she tried her best to follow that thinking. "I didn't know anything about your marriage, let alone a divorce."

Come to think about it, she hadn't forgiven him for marrying the first bar bimbo he spotted after they broke up.

"Doesn't matter." His shirt brushed the front of her leotard, the gentle swish of fabric against her body causing every nerve ending to tighten. Tense. Anticipate.

"I've never chased a man in my life, MacNeil." She refused to chase anything in fact. Being raised by a woman who shamelessly schemed, scammed or begged for her every need, Jayne made it a point never to appear desperate.

Although if she was completely honest with herself, she might admit to being a bit desperate for a taste of Emmett again. Just for old times' sake.

"Fate put you there yesterday." He skimmed his thumb down her bare arm, right where he had to feel her skin reacting to his nearness. "So I thought I'd come along on the cruise to find out why."

She'd give her best dance shoes for a flirty comeback and the ability to sidle past him. Hell, she'd trade the damn star on her door to scrounge up even a hair flip. But she only seemed capable of a deer-in-the-headlights stare, hypnotized by the sight of Emmett's mouth so close to hers.

"I never asked Fate to intervene." Under better circumstances, she could have made that sound like a blow-off. But Marilyn Monroe in her heyday couldn't have huffed out the sentiment with more breathy promise than Jayne had.

Damn it all.

"I'll keep that in mind while I'm watching over you this week." Emmett's smile was slow and knowing and practically screamed out his intention to kiss her right there backstage.

Heaven help her, she puckered.

His lips met hers with slow reverence, as if he didn't remember she could combust at just the stroke of his palm over her breast. Or the feel of his thigh between hers.

No, he kissed her softly, gently, until her head buzzed with warm satisfaction and the need for more. Much more.

Too bad he pulled away when she opened her lips.

"I'm not going to push you this time, Jayne." He stared down with sleepy-lidded eyes, his mouth still damp from her kiss. "But I'll be here if you ever feel like tempting Fate with me."

Heart throbbing in her chest from too much… excitement, Jayne wasn't completely sure she understood what he was saying. But she figured it out when he turned on his heel and walked away.

Two men standing her up in as many days?

Thank God for the speaker behind her to hold her up since she thought she might honestly be going into shock. And yes, damn it, that's what it had to be because there was no other acceptable explanation for the sudden ache in her chest.

SIX DAYS INTO THE cruise and Harrison hadn't accomplished jack shit on his private mission to figure out what happened to his money or his former friends, but considering Rita sat by his side in the cab they'd caught to his family's newest hotel acquisition, he could hardly consider the trip a total bust.

"So your family owns two hotel properties?" She fidgeted by him now, her fingers smoothing a straight yellow skirt with a line of peach-colored ribbon ringing the hem.

He'd all but dragged her off the ship this morning after they'd docked in their next port of call, but he'd finally convinced her to leave her pile of sewing since she was entitled to two days off each week. He'd discovered she stayed up late most nights to finish her sewing because she liked to attend Jayne's dance rehearsals during the day and sew garments on a freelance basis for friends of her mother. All of which meant she worked way too much.

Now, a Bob Marley tune drifted through the cab from the radio. Sea breezes floated through the open windows as the driver stopped for pedestrian traffic. And all Harrison wanted to do was find a stretch of secluded beach where he could feed her oysters and tip cups of fruity sangria to her lips. Memories of her sizzling kisses wouldn't let him be for more than five straight minutes.

But before he could indulge his fantasies where she was concerned, he needed to make his visit to the new Masters Inn.

"We've got two hotels for now, but we're in negotiations for a third." He'd squelched some of his restlessness by acquiring the Caribbean property during his year of running the business and he'd started the paperwork to acquire a third before he'd turned the whole company over to the temporary management group.

"Sounds like a fun way to make a living." She gave him a tight smile, furthering his impression that she was uncomfortable or maybe miffed at him for twisting her arm into spending the day with him. "Did you find out anything more about your ex-girlfriend?"

Salt in the wound of his investigative skills gone to the dogs. Nice.

"Zilch." He spotted the hotel up ahead and reached for a file full of paperwork for the new manager. "But I think Emmett might know more about her lowlife former boyfriend than he's saying."

"What makes you say that?" Straightening, she seemed less interested in the spectacular coastline or the rambling, Victorian-style Masters Inn that had been a historic site since the 1970s, having been built in the late 1800s.

And she sure didn't look ready to seduce him in the privacy of the hotel room of her choice.

"Instinct, mostly. We talked for a little while on deck." Struggling to pull his thoughts away from peeling Rita's clothes off, he forked over the fare before they stopped. "He says he's known Jayne a long time."

He reached for the handle, but the valet guys were too quick, pulling open doors for him and Rita simultaneously.

"You're kidding." Frowning, she seemed to forget all about the hotel until he reached her side and escorted her up the steps to the resort.

Hand skimming the small of her back, he caught a whisper of subtle scent. Jasmine, maybe. Some sort of heat-loving flower a Floridian ought to recognize.

"No. I'm not." He tilted her chin upward so she had no choice but to take in her surroundings. "What do you think of the hotel?"

A smile broke over her lips as she dutifully shifted focus.

"I think you have too much money if you own this." Her gaze swept the grounds, lingered on the white walls and red roof of the sprawling building and the long, railed porch to one side where wicker chairs sat comfortably in the shaded overhang. Closer to the water, wooden loungers surrounded a pool overlooking the beach. "Seriously, it's gorgeous even if you are filthy rich by my standards."

"You'd be surprised how narrow the profit margin can be in the hotel industry." He hadn't known squat about hotels until a year ago since his family had never pressured him to take over the business. "It helps if the properties are more upscale like ours so you can pad the markup, but if you want to offer competitively priced lodging—forget it. You need to be a huge chain to make money."

He was proud of what he'd accomplished with the family assets, but that hadn't been enough to take away the hunger to do what he did best—busting up criminal rings by asking questions until he had answers.

"You're trying to tell me you own multiple properties and you still think you've got it tough?" Her eyebrows shot up in unison. "My heart bleeds for you."

He ran out of time to dispute the point when half the hotel staff piled in the lobby to greet him—no doubt the work of Brad the overeager manager who'd been running an Antigua hotel a quarter of the size of Masters Inn just two months ago. But Harrison hadn't cared about how many beds Bradley had overseen. He just wanted someone familiar with the fluctuations in business at Caribbean resorts.

"Welcome, Mr. Masters." He heard the greeting twenty times over and shook hands with a slew of middle managers while introducing Rita around the palm-filled room with massive ceiling fans humming softly overhead.

She slipped away soon enough though, excusing herself to walk on the beach while he tied up business. Made sense, but watching her walk away reminded him how much he'd prefer to see her moving toward him instead. MacNeil's comment about Frazer women echoed hollowly in his ears.

Mind wandering, he went through meetings on autopilot, already sliding Rita's bathing suit strap off her shoulder in his daydreams. He'd caught a tantalizing glimpse of that strap underneath her blouse this morning on their cab ride. He'd since decided his day would be a failure if he went home without seeing that swimsuit up close.

"And this is Ivan, the casino manager," Brad continued, apparently determined Harrison wouldn't overlook a single staff member on his visit.

But for the first time in an hour, Harrison couldn't deny his genuine interest.

"You run the casino?"

"We've been very profitable recently if you'd like to see our books—"

"I'm more interested in if you've seen some friends of mine." Brandishing his PDA, he put Sonia and Trevor on a split screen just for the hell of it. "Have you seen either of them recently?"

Brad frowned as he peered over Ivan's shoulder. No doubt the manager recognized one or both of them from his interview trips to Naples at the original Masters Inn.

Ivan nodded as he straightened the knot on a thin, brown tie. "They're employees of yours, right? They flashed Masters Corporation ID cards out on the floor last week to try and buy chips at a discount but I told them that didn't apply in the casino."

"You're sure it was them?" What the hell had they been doing over here at a Masters property when they had to know Harrison would be pissed off and looking for them?

Glancing toward the conference room windows that looked out over the beach, Harrison hoped Rita would wait a few more minutes for him. He'd spotted her a minute ago, but she seemed to have vanished amid the sun seekers and tourists having their hair braided by locals on the white sand. Tension threading through his shoulders at losing visual contact, he couldn't afford to go look for her now and ignore his first real lead on Sonia and Trevor. They hadn't touched their credit cards in the last two weeks and there hadn't been any activity on either of their cell phones so Harrison had had no way of tracking them.

"The woman is a bit of a high roller, yes?" Not waiting for an answer, Ivan pressed on in his languid island accent, tapping the PDA screen. "She didn't stay for long because my floor manager thought she was disturbing some of the other guests. She seemed to be intoxicated and wavering on her feet. Security asked her to leave an hour or so after they arrived."

"They?" He wanted to get the details right, and he had the impression Ivan was a man who didn't miss much. "The man was with her?"

"They didn't come in together, but I noticed they left at the same time."

"Can we find the valets who would have been working that night and find out if anyone remembers what they were driving?" He'd check out the hotels himself later, but his gut told him the pair wouldn't be on the island any longer.

"Anything else we can do for you, Harrison?" The hotel manager clapped him on the shoulder, blocking his view of the beach outside the windows. "Anything else you'd like to look over while you're here?"

Aside from tracking down the money that rightfully belonged to his family, he could only think of one more thing he wanted today. Searching for any signs of a willowy redhead in a yellow skirt, Harrison wanted Rita Frazer as close to him as humanly possible.

But damn it all, she was nowhere to be found.

"Actually, there is one other thing." He just hoped like hell he hadn't lost Rita, too. "I'm going to need a room for the afternoon to shower before dinner. Do you have a suite free?"

CHAPTER NINE

SHE WAS A FAKE and a fraud and she had no business being here.

Ducking into an empty cabana on the beach, Rita retreated in the shade of the bright white canvas roof and gently billowing bleached cotton walls, frantic for an escape from a beach full of overprivileged travelers sipping mai-tais and flashing gold AmEx cards. She so didn't belong here. Jayne could fake her way through anything, and high-class shindigs were her specialty, but Rita had never believed in pretending, preferring to shoot straight.

Only now she'd met a great guy who seemed sort of upstanding and honorable in that old-school, chivalrous male way, and for the first time, she found herself wishing she could slide into a different lifestyle to fit in for a few hours. One where she could close her eyes in the hot sun and sip her own umbrella drink without the gut-clenching fear in her belly that something would go dreadfully wrong on the *Venus* during these few stolen hours.

Her mother would call to say she'd gambled away her car. Their condo. Her soul.

Or Jayne would lose her job. Or piss off the one fashion-house executive who might have actually shown interest in Rita's new costumes. Or attract attention from the FBI because Jayne had been dating a criminal…

Oh God, this had been a mistake.

With the gentle lap of ocean waves on the sand ten yards outside the cabana to soothe her, she removed her wide-brimmed hat that protected her freckles and tried to tell herself she deserved a day to play. Sure the timing sucked since she should be hunting down Danielle the Demon Witch who'd been out of her office every time Rita went to talk to her about payment for the costumes.

But when Harrison had showed up at her room this morning, ready to take her ashore, she couldn't imagine wanting anything more. Partly because she'd love to jump him again, but also because she suspected he needed the break even more than she did. As a lifetime Overdoer, Rita recognized the quality in other people, and Harrison had it bad. He took care of everyone around him—from his FBI connection that still made her a little nervous, to his changing careers to help his parents, to his automatic response to help her when Jayne was missing.

Knowing how much that kind of generosity could suck right out of you, Rita admired the quality in other people. Modeled her own life on the principle that she didn't come first.

Now, breathing in the salty scent of the ocean, she fought to shake off the sense that she shouldn't be here even while she hoped Harrison would finish up his meeting soon so they could…

Nervous anticipation skittered through her as she acknowledged the attraction factor that had been gnawing at her ever since that first night she'd set eyes on him. Sex proved to be a damn strong selling point.

"Rita!"

His raised voice echoed across the beach, penetrating the gauzy walls of her hideaway along with the lulling gush of gentle waves.

"Here." She called out to him before she was even all the way out of the cabana, her eyes momentarily blinded by the strong afternoon sun. And what did it say about her long-neglected sex life that just the sound of this man's voice made her want to purr? "Harrison?"

Scanning the terrain with whitewashed vision from the abrupt transition from shade to sun, she spotted a tall man stalking toward her. She'd chosen a spot on the quieter end of the shore, the sand deserted except for a couple of beach towels with sleeping sunbathers and a roving waiter taking a drink order from a man with a Russian accent.

"I've been looking all over for you." Harrison finally came into full-color view as he closed the distance between them, his khakis and blue dress shirt a little formal for the beach, although she had to admit he looked damn good.

"Sorry. I slid into one of the cabana tents for some shade. I didn't think you'd be done with your meeting so fast." Even Frazer family powwows took longer than he'd spent inside the swanky resort property that—holy crap—he *owned*.

"I was afraid you'd disappear if I left you alone for too long." His hands caught her waist, fingers spanning down to her hips and inciting a swirl of heat that didn't have anything to do with the Caribbean sun.

"I'm trying to relax today. I ditched my watch on the ship so I could just have fun." So she wouldn't think about all the extra hours she was going without getting paid for those costumes she'd busted her butt to sew.

"Rita Frazer? Relax and have fun?" He slid one arm around her waist to lead her back toward the cabana where she'd left her hat. "I don't know. You think you're going to be able to do it?"

"I'm working on it." She ducked into the tent.

"Wow." He stepped back to get a better look at the cabana before joining her in the shade inside. His gaze roved over the jute mat and the taut canvas loungers positioned on either side of a lightweight table. "Looks like something out of Arabian Nights."

"They were giving massages in one of the other tents when I first came down to the beach." She'd hardly been able to watch the man's hand on a woman's bare back without getting…twitchy.

Awareness of Harrison's presence now brought that jumpiness back with a vengeance. Even though she was a fraud and a fake masquerading through his upscale world as if she'd never passed her days in a homeless shelter.

"A massage sounds just right for your day of enforced relaxation." He eyed her from no more than two feet away, his presence making the spacious cabana feel suddenly smaller. "Did you let them work your kinks out?"

"Me?" The thought of indulging in a rubdown hadn't crossed her mind for a second. Even the cheapo back rubs from locals trying to make an extra buck would set her back twenty dollars, minimum. She'd never get ahead if she blew cash on frivolous stuff. "No."

She wouldn't lie to him if he asked her why not because she'd be damned if she'd keep on being a fake, but the heat in his blue eyes suggested his thoughts had taken another turn.

"So you've still got all your kinks intact?" He reached for her, his hand skimming along the shoulder strap of a sleeveless linen blouse she'd made out of left-overs from one of Jayne's skirts.

"I work out often enough to keep myself from getting too tense, I think." Practicing Jayne's routines was rigorous exercise and Rita appreciated the benefits of long, lean dancer muscles. Those muscles shivered in response to Harrison's hand on her shoulder, sliding down to bare skin on her arm.

"Oh you're tense, all right." His fingers traced her bathing suit strap down her back with two warm fingers. "I can feel it."

A smile built inside her as she let him touch her with that slow, knowing way of his. They were shielded from anyone else on the beach unless someone crossed in front of the opening facing the water where the cotton was tied back to provide an ocean view. Harrison reached for the tie now and tugged at the string, allowing the fabric to sweep down to the sand and curtain them in total privacy.

"Maybe there are a few kinks." A massage didn't sound so bad if this guy's hands were doing the work on her. His touch was addictive and she'd been craving it like a junkie.

Unable to keep her hands to herself any longer, she found her fingertips smoothing along his shirt, pausing meaningfully over each button. Something about the heat of masculine skin through the starchy cotton of a well-ironed shirt struck her as endlessly delicious, a tactile sensation that came in second to only one other she could think of....

Spearing right through her with his dark blue gaze, he moved closer. Leaned. Hovered. Kissed her hard on the mouth with the same kind of feverish urgency she'd been feeling ever since that night on the Jupiter deck.

A hiss of breath sighed through her as she fell into him, soft curves pressing against taut male muscle. And taut male...ooohh.

Her hips rolled deeper against his at the feel of him pressing her belly. An unfulfilled ache tightened. Heightened.

"That's it." She angled back enough to run her finger over his jaw, to trace his lower lip. "I think you've pin-pointed the tension."

Nipping her finger gently with his teeth, he molded her hips with his hands, sliding over her rump to draw her even closer. "And *I* think I'm starting to get a little tense myself. Do you want to continue this back at the hotel?"

He flashed a keycard from his pocket, making his intention clear.

Visions of a presidential suite and more luxuries to make her feel out of place cemented the decision for her.

"How about we just stay here instead?" They were staked out at the far end of the beach where only a few Frisbee players and antisocial newlyweds ventured. "You can just tie the doors shut."

"Here?" He pocketed the card and pushed a hand lightly on the white cotton wall closest to where they stood. "I guess you can't see through."

"We can be quiet." She liked the idea more the longer she thought about it. "And that's important because even if no one can see in, they can still hear us." As much as she wanted Harrison right here, right now, she didn't want to be a total exhibitionist about it. A small jolt of nervousness kept her babbling when she should be kissing Harrison. "I could hear a Russian guy ordering a vodka twist outside the tent just before you got here and he sounded close enough to be—"

"A Russian?" Harrison gripped her shoulders, gaze intense, all traces of her lazy-eyed, would-be lover gone.

"Either that or it was some kind of Slavic accent. I hear so many kinds of accents on the islands and on a ship with fifty different nationalities represented that I probably don't have a great ear for the differences anymore." She sensed her answer was important from Harrison's alert stillness. "What does it matter? The point was just that sound really carries."

Releasing her, he plowed through the curtains covering the entrance, leaving the cabana. He'd set a new record for how fast a man could walk away from her.

"Harrison?" Not sure if she should be miffed or worried or both, she followed him out into the sun where he made a visual scan of the whole beach.

"It's nothing." Wrapping an arm around her waist he guided her back toward the tent, but Rita had no intention of moving until she got some answers.

Planting her feet in the sand she faced him. "It's not nothing or we'd already be halfway to naked right now."

"I'm not thinking straight." He lowered his voice even though no one lingered near them and the Frisbee players had packed up and gone home. "I made a stupid connection in my head when you mentioned the accent even though there could be a hundred tourists with that same inflection on Antigua any given day."

"Doubtful." She might not have a degree in intelligence gathering but that didn't sound right to her. "That's a small demographic on this side of the world and Antigua is an even smaller island."

"But you said you couldn't even be sure what kind of accent it was. Besides, I've got no business dragging you into my investigation when you've made it clear you're running at the first sign of my life as a special agent."

"Forget about that. I was spooked about Jayne when I tossed those words out there." And Jayne had broken up with the criminal, thank God. Rita could deal with dating a Fed, at least for a fling. "Besides, you helped me when I needed it. I'm not going to repay the kindness by distracting you with sex when you've got to take care of business."

He curved his hand under her hair to cup the back of her neck. "But I've been dying to be distracted with sex."

His words lulled her even more than the rhythmic swish of waves at their feet, calling her to hide away in the cabana and lose herself in his strength.

"Me too," she admitted, allowing herself to imagine what that might be like just for a moment. "But you can't ignore a lead when this Sonia chick might be around the corner with all the cash she stole from you."

The money-grubbing wench obviously lacked a big sister to keep her in line and Rita wouldn't mind donating an ass kicking to the cause.

Harrison hesitated; she could see it in his eyes even though his grip on her remained firm.

Pressing her advantage, she probed with the only bit of information she had.

"So, we're looking for a Russian?"

EMMETT HAD BEEN LOOKING for Jayne since breakfast.

He stared out over the Antigua coastline from his position on the Jupiter deck and hoped she hadn't taken it into her head to go ashore without him. Soft breeze blowing across his face, he scanned the pier full of duty-free gift shops in the hope of a glimpse of red hair.

She wasn't in the ship's theater. Not in her room. Not by the pool.

Of course, with thirteen decks, that left a lot of ground he hadn't covered. It also meant she could be in trouble somewhere, chased down by her shady former boyfriend who had possible criminal connections.

Cursing himself for not sticking closer to her, he was about to search the shipboard gym when he heard a wolf whistle from a lower deck.

Surely that was a good sign?

Peering down over the rail, he could see most of the other decks from his high position. The closest held a view of an empty kiddie pool. Two decks down he spied a couple of teenage guys drooling and grinning.

Bingo.

Pounding down two flights of stairs, past the ship's library where a bridge group dealt a hand of cards, past a couple of crew members testing out the rock wall while no one was around, Emmett finally spied Jayne. Perched on a red mat in a *Karate Kid* type stance, she seemed to be finishing up some yoga-looking moves on an unused shuffleboard. No one else was around except for the teens ogling Jayne's breasts peaking against her spandex exercise halter.

"There's at least a thousand girls in bikinis on the beaches around here." He gestured broadly toward the shore. What the hell was the matter with kids today? "Why don't you go gawk at someone your own age?"

The guys left, although not without a few muttered obscenities that Emmett chose to ignore.

"You make me sound like an old lady." Jayne didn't look overly appreciative. Her black tights and purple, two-piece dance outfit molded to her fine curves and bared her midriff. She stretched up and twirled on her toe in a move that looked more ballerina than showgirl. Her long braid spun out away from her as she turned.

He'd caught her show the night before and she'd been even more fantastic onstage than he'd remembered from his long-ago cruise. She rehearsed every day there wasn't a show, and she seemed to snag extra workout time on her own whenever she wasn't busy making the rounds posing for photos with guests.

"You can't tell me you wanted them here." He didn't want to argue with her today but how could he ever make headway with the woman when he didn't come close to understanding her? Why did a woman with so much talent and intelligence date losers and wink at salivating boys?

"No." Halting her spin abruptly she faced him with flushed cheeks. "But I don't know that I appreciate you suggesting they'd have more fun staring at girls in bathing suits than me. Since when do I rate second to any bikini?"

She sounded petulant and self-centered and maybe

even a little insecure, which he hadn't expected. And damned if he didn't want her anyway. Emmett stifled the urge to smile as he wondered if he was any smarter than those drooling kids.

"They're idiots if they'd rather look at anyone else." The words came easily because they weren't flattery to his way of thinking. That was the honest truth. "But I had to get rid of them somehow because I wasn't about to let them steal my view."

The smile she gave him bowled him over, dazzling him far more than any Caribbean sunset and reminding him why he'd fallen for her so fast. No other woman had ever knocked him flat on his ass the way she could with one simple smile that wasn't her stock flirtatious grin she shared with any man who walked by her. This was the real deal, the genuine article.

"Don't you dare flirt with me, Emmett MacNeil." She tugged the elastic band off the tail of her red braid, freeing loose red curls to tumble over her shoulders. "I could hardly sleep last night after that kiss two nights ago and I'm *not* treading down that path with you again."

She could hardly sleep? Hell, he'd gritted his teeth through the longest cold shower of his life in an effort to catch a few Zs. Even now, just a whiff of her sun-warmed skin and Chanel No. 5 could turn him inside out. In the weeks after she'd turned down his proposal, he'd caught himself lingering by a department-store fragrance counter in the hope of breathing in that scent that made him crazy.

"What path? What do you mean?" Was she trying to keep him from proposing? Because considering his newly divorced status, he was in no hurry to be that hasty again. "I told you, I'm willing to listen to your timetable on this."

"I mean I'm not going down the sex path—especially with a guy who's been divorced for like, ten minutes." She glared at him as if he'd been the one to bring it up. "So you can keep all kisses to yourself because I'm not that kind of girl anymore."

This time, he couldn't swallow the bark of hoarse laughter that escaped his throat.

"You think it's funny?" Huffing with obvious feminine outrage she folded up her mat as if she planned to leave. "Fine. You can laugh yourself all the way over to the Antigua beaches to find some bikini-wearing bimbo to share your kisses because you and me—it's not happening."

"Wait a minute." Struggling to process what she was telling him before she marched out of his life again, Emmett snaked an arm out to hold her back. "You're serious?"

"I think Horatio only proposed because he thought I'd change my mind if we were engaged." Tightening her grip on the mat, she stood rigid in his arms. "Apparently, he thought six months was long enough to hold out, but I'm not messing around with anyone who's not worth my time ever again."

"You never slept with him?" For six *months?* He'd known she'd changed somehow since last year. Maybe that was it. Or maybe that was only part of a bigger change he had yet to uncover.

"Not that it's any of your business—no, I didn't." Breaking out of his arms, she moved toward the stairs. "I only told you so you'd know I'm not the same woman you met last year and I have no intention of making dating decisions based on where I can get great sex."

Sneakers slapping down the steps while he wiped his jaw off the deck, Emmett stared after her. "Does that mean you thought the sex was great?"

She stopped at the bottom of the stairs to peer up at him, her hip curving seductively to one side because no matter how hard she tried, she didn't stand a chance of reining in the natural sensuality that emanated from her more strongly than any perfume.

"If you have to ask, you're not nearly as smart as I pegged you for, MacNeil." Sashaying away with the sweetest walk he'd ever seen, she slowly disappeared from view.

But hot damn, she'd given the sex two thumbs up.

Unfortunately, he had no idea how he would keep her out of trouble for the rest of the cruise if she refused to let him woo her back into his bed. Since a former federal agent had given him specific instructions about keeping an eye on her, Emmett considered it his civic duty to at least make an effort. And thankfully, Jayne had clued him in to the most surefire method to make her change her mind.

Hustling down the stairs behind her, Emmett would savor the task of figuring out exactly how—and where—he would kiss her next time.

CHAPTER TEN

"PASSENGERS MASTERS AND Frazer, please report to the *Venus* for embarkation. Passengers Masters and Frazer."

Harrison heard the words booming through the loud-speakers around the marketplace at Heritage Quay in Antigua's main port, but he wasn't quite done talking to a local silver merchant who had dealings with one of Seva Yurek's many aliases—Simeon Valenka. The sun slipped lower on the horizon, bringing them close to departure time.

"I'd better go back," Rita whispered at his elbow while the weathered old woman behind a wheeled jewelry cart hunted through her ratty three-ring binder for a shipping address he'd requested. "I can't afford to lose my seamstress gig."

"Go ahead. I'll meet you onboard." Guilt pinched him for spending their whole day searching for traces of Sonia or Seva—a man who probably sounded like a Russian even though his FBI file said he was technically Ukrainian.

"They'll pull out in ten minutes whether you're back or not," Rita fretted, her responsible nature spilling over onto him. Peering down the long dock covered with duty-free shops that separated the quay from the *Venus,* she drummed her fingers on her folded arms. "It takes almost that long just to walk that far."

"I'll run. You go." He didn't want to be responsible for her missing the boat, let alone losing her job, but he had to grin at the thought of her worrying about him. God, he was an idiot for not taking her up on her offer back in the cabana tent. Skimming his hand along her shoulder, he cupped her face for a moment before letting go. "Hurry."

She took off faster than he would have expected, her long, lean legs covering ground in rapid strides. As his gaze snapped back to the silver merchant's book, he spotted something that caught his eye.

"Wait a minute." He reached for the binder, halting her slow progress through the pages. A Naples, Florida, address jumped out at him. "Have you done business with Shine On Jewelers in Naples?"

He moved to lean over her records, but the old woman clutched the book like it required top security clearance.

"What if I had?" Dark eyes narrowing, she peered at him with undisguised suspicion.

"Just curious." He removed his hand from her files, knowing damn well he'd seen a Naples zip code in there. Hadn't Sonia mentioned doing business with a few Caribbean merchants? He should have paid more attention. "I'm looking for a connection between Shine On and the guy I told you about."

"I have sent some pieces to Shine On." Loosening her hold on her book, she allowed Harrison a short glimpse before she flipped more pages while the *Venus* blew its ear-splitting horn. "But not nearly as much as I do with Simeon Valenka."

He had to go. Now.

Damn.

Gesturing to a long list of entries on another page, she read off an address on the top of the paper. "The man, he picked up his most recent delivery at the Masters Inn on the other side of the island a week ago. That's all I know. We do not ship to him."

Memorizing at least a few of the dates and pickup spots at what looked to be hotels around the Caribbean, Harrison flipped a twenty onto the woman's ledger before he sprinted down the dock toward the *Venus.*

Toward Rita.

Legs propelling him as fast as they could, he grabbed an empty skateboard on the pier and used the wheels to whiz past the duty-free shops at lightning speed. Normally, ship security hung out there to check passenger IDs, but since the boat would be pulling out in another minute—maybe less—he didn't have to worry about flashing a card.

He had a good idea where Simeon—aka Seva— might show up next and lucky for him, the *Venus* just happened to be going in the right direction. Then again, luck didn't have much to do with it, since Harrison was beginning to realize Seva had targeted the cruise industry for wealthy travelers.

Leaving the skateboard on the pier where a Roman Cruise Lines seaman was currently unlooping the first of three massive ropes used to anchor the ship, Harrison whistled to the security guard closing up the gangplank area.

"Harrison!" Rita shouted from behind the security woman and gestured to let him onboard. "You made it."

"Don't tell me you doubted it." He resisted the urge to wipe the sweat from his brow. Damn, but that was close.

After not one, but two security guards briefed him on the need to be onboard half an hour before sailing, he led Rita to the creamy-colored elevators framed with gilded moldings incorporated in a huge mural of the goddess Venus arising out of a shell. A bit tacky and overdone, perhaps, but the depiction of a half-naked woman sure made the old men onboard linger around this elevator bank.

"We need to talk." As the elevator door swished open, Harrison held it for Rita, thinking he'd far rather stare at her even with all her clothes on. And Rita *naked?* The thought made him too edgy to contemplate unless they were alone. "Can you come to my room?"

A loudspeaker announcement overhead listed the highlights of the evening events as they stepped into the elevator.

"Your room sounds better than line dancing on the Aurora deck." She fanned herself with the wide straw hat she'd worn ashore as she stood a couple of feet in front of him. "Even if all you want to do is…talk."

She didn't even turn back to look at him, opting instead to watch the numbers light up as they changed floors. He stood very still as he watched her back, her straw hat swinging like a slow pendulum from one side of her body to another.

"Are you suggesting I have ulterior motives for taking you back to my cabin?" He reached to run a knuckle down her spine through the linen fabric of her blouse.

"You mentioned something about getting a room earlier today." Turning her head, she peered back at him with knowing eyes. "And I don't think you were much interested in talking then."

"Maybe because I've been hanging by a thread ever since the first time I kissed you." The heat between them swelled, filling the small space with sultry awareness until the elevator beeped for his floor.

Guiding her past a small throng of passengers dressed to the nines for dinner, Harrison wasn't letting her go this time. Screw Emmett MacNeil's insistence a Frazer woman couldn't be held. Harrison had been studying Rita, learning about her, figuring her out. He could at least make sure she stuck around long enough to drive them both to the brink and back again so many times neither one of them would walk straight tomorrow.

Besides, Rita wasn't the flighty sexpot that her sister seemed to be. She had serious substance. An admirable-as-hell work ethic. And killer legs, too.

If Sonia hadn't just recently proven to him in no uncertain terms that he sucked at relationships—or at the very least, that he was in no position to deserve one while his head was screwed on sideways—he might have fallen for Rita Hayworth Frazer on the spot.

"Here." He slid an arm around her waist to stop her as they arrived outside his stateroom, keeping his hold loose so as not to tempt himself to take her the moment they crossed the threshold. "This is it."

Swiping his keycard, he did a visual scan of the room, the bathroom and the balcony before letting her inside. Old habits and all that. The bed had been turned down, chocolates placed on his pillow, a towel animal—looked like an elephant tonight—crafted neatly by the cabin steward on the vanity. A single lamp burned over the bed, highlighting the sprawling mattress like a featured performer. Otherwise, everything was just as he'd left it.

Only then, when he'd confirmed the place was all clear and he'd locked the door behind them, did he allow himself to look at Rita and her long, luscious legs in the yellow skirt. The skinny red bathing suit strap still peeked out of the neckline of her blouse, the spandex fabric tantalizing him with what might have been in the cabana if he hadn't been too busy chasing a damn lead.

A good lead. But, still. A new clue didn't satisfy a man's needs quite the way this woman would. Just the sight of her and her wild red hair springing out from its half-hearted braid was making him crazy for her. The coconut-jasmine scent of her mingled with perspiration in a way that smelled like slow, sweaty sex.

"So?" She flung her hat on the vanity with a flick of her wrist. "What was it you wanted to talk to me about?"

EVERY NOW AND THEN, Rita was graced with a smidgen of her family's theatrical style. And right now, as she watched Harrison's sky-blue eyes darken to sea-swept gray, she thanked the saints for her well-played sense of timing.

She didn't have long to revel, though, because he charged her like a bull at the first hint of red, his head lowering on his way over to her. Then his hands were on her, his mouth meeting hers, tongue demanding entrance as if he'd picked up exactly where he left off two nights ago.

His lips slid over hers in hungry rhythm, fingers stroking up her waist and under her blouse to the skin bared by the modest two-piece bathing suit she'd never once gotten to show off for him today.

She'd been so determined to leave the mess with Jayne and the costumes behind her today, so sure she'd have time to indulge her much-ignored sense of adventure with Harrison. Not once had she imagined his trouble might use up all their time together.

"What about Jayne?" Harrison's head lifted from the curve of her neck, eyes at half-mast. "Do you need to check in with her before we take this any further? Because once I start peeling clothes off you this time—"

"There'll be no stopping." She wondered how he'd read her fleeting thoughts about her sister. But this time, Jayne's latest crisis—and there was always something—could wait. "I know. And I'm *very* okay with that."

"Thank you, God." He brushed aside the collar of her blouse to trace the strap of her swimsuit down to her breast and lingered there, igniting a shiver of pleasure.

"No offense, but I don't know that God had much to do with it." Head tilting sideways, she gladly gave him unobstructed access to her neck as he leaned in to kiss the curve of her shoulder. "Maybe it's me you ought to be thanking."

"Yeah?" He twined his finger in the strap and tugged gently, easing her breast upward, closer to his waiting mouth. "Are you expecting some big show of gratitude?"

Her skin tightened as his jaw scraped against the soft curve of her cleavage. His warm breath teased her senses, urging her to peel the suit down and away.

"I've got several ideas for how you can show your appreciation, actually." She hadn't forgotten the way he'd made her practically crawl right out of her skin two nights ago.

"I've got plenty of my own damn ideas, thanks." His other hand speared up into her hair to cup the back of her neck, anchoring her against him while he rolled the fabric of her suit to the very edge of her nipple. "And I'll thank you thoroughly in a minute, but I still think it was an act of God that kept me from missing the boat just now."

Her blood burned with a slow fire as he scraped her hair away from her shoulders to clear his view of her breasts. Deft fingers unfastened the buttons on her blouse. Desire hummed through her, heightening every sensation while demanding more.

"I would have been very disappointed if you hadn't made it back." Maybe she ought to wing up a few of her own prayers of thanks for delivering this incredible man safely to the ship. She'd never had much cause to love her job as seamstress aboard the *Venus,* but despite all the stress and worry, she'd still rank this cruise as the best pleasure trip of her life.

He blew a stream of cool air over her hot skin until it was all she could do not to wriggle her way into his mouth for the more thorough kiss she needed.

"I nearly broke my neck on a skateboard to get here." Parting the rest of her blouse with his hands, he shoved the fabric off her shoulders to float down to the floor at the foot of the couch in the small sitting area of his suite.

She wound her arms around his neck, purposely pressing herself against him, her hips rolling closer to the hard heat of him beneath his fly.

"You've been driving me crazy all day." He muttered the words into her skin while sliding his hands down her back. He unhooked the suit, unleashing the full weight of her breasts against his chest. "Ever since I caught a glimpse of red beneath your blouse."

Feminine pride preened at his words. "I may not wear feathers and rhinestones every day, but I know a little something about snagging a man's eye when the need arises."

His touch grew rougher, more insistent as he molded her hips with his hands then slid upward to cup her breasts. Her throat went dry. Words became too much of an effort.

"Need is definitely rising right now and standing at rock-hard attention." Bending at the knees he scooped her off her feet and settled her on the bed. Beside them, a sliding glass door led out to his balcony overlooking the ocean.

The sights and scents swirled together in one vague impression as Harrison moved her. Blue waves behind him turned to white ceiling above him as he bent down over her to plant a slick, deep kiss on her lips before moving lower to lave a taut nipple.

She threaded her fingers through his hair as he tugged her into his mouth. Pressing him close, she savored the sensations fanning out from that kiss, the ache in her womb becoming sharper with each passing second.

"That's *sooo* good." She hadn't been touched, tasted, held like this in forever. And never by a man who touched her with such consummate skill.

Her restless hands skimmed down his arms where he propped himself off her. Hot skin stretched over sinewy strength, the feel of his powerful body inspiring a shiver of anticipation. Sensual delight. He was a large man. Tall. Well-muscled.

The thought sent her hands on a quest down his chest, fingers unfastening buttons along the way. Too many clothes. Too much interference. She'd had all day to get worked up over him, and now that she found him within her grasp, she refused to waste even a second when she could be enjoying him.

The final shirt button popped free and rolled to the floor in a testament of her urgency. Or maybe it was the proximity of his fly that made her fingers a little unsteady on that last fastener.

"I can't get enough of the taste of you." He relinquished her breast to growl over her skin.

"I can't get enough of you, period." She tried edging up on her elbow to grab his belt, but he pinned her to the bed.

"I'm a little low on willpower this time, babe." The flex of his jaw muscle fascinated her as he held her easily in place. "Adrenaline overload and all that."

"Skateboarding gives you that much of a rush?" She arched her back just enough to draw his attention south over her body again.

My, my, but she loved to watch his eyes grow dark and intent.

"Nearly falling ass-backwards into the ocean to finally get you all to myself gives me a rush." Drawing her arms up over her head, he secured both her hands in one of his and used his free hand to tug down the zipper of her skirt. "So be a good girl and lie still while I have my way with you as a well-deserved reward."

She might have argued the point about who would have their way with whom, but then his fingers tunneled under her skirt and she forgot all about setting him straight. He explored the stretchy Lycra hugging her hips, fingers snagging now and again on the silky finish of her swimsuit as he followed the dip along her hipbone. Palmed her belly. Cupped her mound.

Pleasure warmed her thighs, tightened her insides in a coil of longing for more. Before she could plead her case, he bent to capture her lips again, his tongue swiping hers, stabbing into the recesses of her mouth with an unmistakable message.

A whimper escaped her throat, the need for him too urgent to hold back any longer.

Clothes began peeling away, melting off their bodies with gratifying speed until he was stretching himself over her, positioning himself between her legs where she wanted him most.

He'd let go of her at some point and she used her hands now to anchor herself against the tide of sensation rising inside her. Fingers clutching the bedspread, she steadied her body trembling with heady anticipation.

She didn't know when or how he'd rolled on a condom, but her quick glance down told her he'd taken care of everything. Taken care of *her*.

An unusual event, and not entirely unwelcome.

And as for the visual he made in all his naked glory—well, that was one mental picture she would commit to memory permanently.

He feathered a touch up her calf, behind her knee, before his knuckle smoothed along the inside of her thigh.

"Would you believe me if I told you I used up every shred of my patience the last time I kissed you?"

"Is that the truth?" Her words caught on a gasp as the tip of his shaft nudged her sex.

"I'll be damned if it isn't." Sweat beaded along his brow as he brushed a negligent finger along her cleft.

She lifted her hips in blatant invitation. "Then I believe you."

He thrust inside of her in one smooth motion, the slick heat of her easing his way. Her body stretched to accommodate him, her muscles clamping around him so tightly he had to know it had been a long time since there'd been anyone else.

And *oh God,* how could it have been so long? Pleasure poured through her veins as he slowly withdrew and then nudged his way inside her again. And again.

But then, as he reached between their bodies to find the taut bundle of nerves there, she realized exactly why it had been so long for her. She didn't believe in sex just to scratch an itch, even if the itch was being scratched supremely well.

Yet here she was, writhing beneath a man she'd known for less than a week and fighting off an orgasm in a battle she was quickly losing, probably because— heaven help her—he meant something to her.

Crying out her release, she allowed wave after wave of sensation to drown her in seductive bliss, unwilling to let fear of feeling too much ruin this moment. Her hips ground into his for the pure joy of feeling him buried deep as he filled all the empty places inside her.

His hoarse shout followed hers all too soon as he found his own pleasure and she gladly ducked her head against his warm chest, his heart hammering in her ear.

Words eluded her even though she felt some need to break the magical spell that seemed to linger over the bed and all around them. People didn't just have earth-moving, profound sex like that and then bounce back to casual repartee. Yet how could she acknowledge the degree of toe-curling perfection he'd just given her without sounding like a lovesick nitwit?

Better to stay silent and be thought a nitwit than to speak up and remove all doubt.

She inwardly amended the saying to suit her own needs and prayed she wasn't falling hard and fast for a fantasy, vacation fling lover who would only run his own way once they docked in Fort Lauderdale.

"You're incredible." Harrison's rough voice penetrated her hair to tickle her ear and stroke her feminine ego.

"Umm?" She shifted contentedly underneath him and tried not to think what it would be like to sleep near his big, beautiful body. She'd get up soon. Call her mom. Check on Jayne. Put some distance between herself and Harrison—physically and emotionally—so their return to Lauderdale in a few days' time would be simpler. "You haven't seen anything yet."

Way to go, Rita. Instead of putting distance between them she was implying there would be a next time. More sweaty sex.

More opportunities to lose her heart.

CHAPTER ELEVEN

"I CAN'T FIND my mother."

Panic pinched Jayne's muscles tight as she hit the redial button for a tenth time on the phone in her room. She stared up at Emmett in the hallway outside her quarters. She'd been dodging him all day that they'd been docked, using rehearsals and her brief stint as a photo prop with passengers as an excuse, but he caught up with her in the gym an hour ago and somehow she'd agreed to have a drink with him tonight even though she'd promised herself she was going to stay away from him. She may not have the *Mrs.* sign of respectability in front of her name the way she'd hoped she would earlier this week, but she'd been stocking up on self-respect lately, and that counted, too, right?

Now, she didn't have the option of sitting on her duff and mooning over this man's charismatic allure while sipping a crisp pinot noir. She needed to find out where the hell Margie had gone.

"She's not gambling again, is she?" Emmett ducked inside the narrow cabin's hallway jammed between the closet and the bathroom.

On the other end of the phone, Margie's answering machine picked up with her crooning a line from a Patsy

Cline tune before the beep sounded. Frustrated, Jayne slammed down the receiver and tried not to be turned on by the sight of Emmett's shoulder brushing up against a slinky, diaphanous pink gown sticking out of her closet.

Even her damn clothes wanted to get next to the man.

"I'm not sure if Margie's gone astray or she's just not home." Jayne had forgotten she had told Emmett about some of her history with her mother. Nothing too scary, but she'd felt close enough to him at one time to at least outline the basics of her mother's addiction. "She's also the genetic force responsible for my inability to be on time for anything, so for all I know, she could simply be out shopping with no desire to turn on her cell phone."

Irritated, she picked up the handset again.

"Wait." Emmett's hand snaked out for the phone and replaced it on the cradle. "Don't you have neighbors you can call?"

Jayne thought about the residents of their condo building and wondered if the gap between her and Emmett could yawn much wider.

"It's not like our neighbors are a bunch of ladies who lunch and hang out around home all day to know what's going on. Who am I going to call? The crack-ho in the condo upstairs or the sixteen-year-old mama who hangs out in a shoebox watching twin toddlers all day ever since she dropped out of school?"

"The sixteen-year-old sounds like the safer bet." Emmett guided her backward to her bed and sat her down on the unmade tornado of sheets and covers. "You want me to find a number for her or do you know it?"

Shaking her head helplessly, Jayne didn't necessarily

appreciate his kindness since too much niceness always had an uncanny—unreasonable—knack for making her cry. She could handle a smart-ass like her sister. She could deal with her mother who could say the most cutting things with a sweet smile on her Botoxed face. But kindness?

Crap. She could already feel the backs of her eyeballs burning.

"I don't know it." She snapped the words in an effort to deceive herself that she needed to take the defensive. Which was so wrong. Sighing, she settled for the truth. "The whole place depresses me. When we go home for a day or two, I pretend that we don't really live there and that we're just staying at a really crappy hotel."

Damn it. The place wasn't really that bad and she wouldn't be sharing anything half so revealing if she wasn't scared brainless that Margie had fallen off her recovery plan for the love of video poker. Jayne would be spouting off about how much his defection hurt her last year if she didn't stuff a sock in it soon.

Either that, or she needed to distract herself.

Her dinky twin bed suddenly loomed large in the cabin.

"What's the girl's name?" Emmett settled himself in a chair covered with stray stockings and bras that she'd hand washed the night before. "I'll call information."

Sharing what she knew along with the name of her building complex, she allowed nervous energy to propel her around the room, sweeping undergarments into a drawer and hurling shoes under the bed while dodging Rita's ever-present clothesline of mending projects.

"Doesn't your sister usually look after your mom?"

Emmett asked after he'd dialed information for the number.

"I haven't seen Rita since she went ashore with Harrison." A fact which bugged her. Hadn't they agreed they were going to put a tighter watch on Margie?

"We've been at sea for over three hours." Emmett glanced at his watch. "Where do you think they— Oh."

"Yeah—oh." For the first time in a dog's age, Rita was surely the one burning up the sheets while Jayne was clinging to a false sense of purity she'd probably never really feel. "Looks like I've got the room all to myself tonight."

Before Emmett could take the bait on her loaded comment, someone must have picked up the other end of the phone since he launched into a diatribe about needing to speak to Margie Frazer in the condo next door—pronto.

Jayne tensed, hoping with every last breath her mother was just coming into the building from a hard day of drooling over shoes she couldn't afford at Neiman's. *Please God, let her have been doing anything but gambling.*

"No luck?" Emmett spoke the words into the phone but shook his head to pass on the news to Jayne. He chatted amiably with the woman on the other end for a few more minutes, charming her into posting a note on Margie's door to call her daughter, then commiserating about the demands of twin toddlers. Finally, he wound up the call. "Let me at least send you over a pizza for your trouble."

Jayne's damn eyeballs were scorching again by the time he was done finding out what the adolescent mama wanted on her pie and insisting it was courtesy of Margie's daughter and no trouble at all.

Too damn nice of him. Even if he *had* gone and married someone else.

"I can call her Gamblers Anonymous sponsor." Blinking hard, Jayne seized the idea with both hands, springing off the bed to find her sister's address book. "Rita was supposed to do it the other night, but I haven't seen her much lately so I don't know if it ever got done."

Chances were slim to none that Ms. Organized had failed in her duty, but since Rita was surprising Jayne in a lot of ways this cruise, there was no sense taking chances. Jayne figured *she'd* been the one accomplishing everything this trip between breaking her engagement with Horatio—well, sort of—and twisting Danielle's arm into giving Missy another chance. A coup she'd couldn't believe she'd managed to achieve.

Now, Jayne flipped through Rita's red, satin-covered phone book while Emmett called information for a Fort Lauderdale pizzeria and sent a huge order of food to the harried teenage mom.

"So your mom's in G.A.?" Emmett asked after he hung up the phone. "I hadn't realized her habit was serious enough to need a program."

"It's been a good thing." She reached for the receiver, trying her best to avoid the lazy, masculine sprawl of Emmett at her built-in vanity table. "The hardest part is getting addicts to see the problem and she's past all that."

It had taken half a lifetime and the loss of their home, but Margie had finally owned up to an obsession with gambling. Proving slow learners could still see the light, a lesson Jayne was taking to heart these days.

Aside from the eloping mistake, of course.

"Must be hard to worry about her from so far away." He repositioned the phone to face her, his forearm brushing against hers as he did so. Only Emmett could turn her on with something so unassuming as a damn forearm. But it was exposed by a rolled-up shirt cuff, the tanned skin sprinkled with dark hair and prompting her to think about unveiling more bare flesh for her viewing pleasure.

"I'm a—" What had she been saying? Her fingers hovered, unsure, over the telephone buttons. The close proximity of this man affected her at a cell-deep level, her very molecules seeming to remember his touch and revving up in anticipation of more. "I'm not usually this worried about her, but—" she licked her lips, struggling to focus "—the club where she works recently introduced the wonders of video poker and it's not really fair to dangle so much temptation in front of a woman who wants something so damn badly."

Her words slowed down until they ground to a halt and she realized she was talking about her own need for self-denial more than her mom's. Hell yeah, it was hard to resist temptation.

Really, really…*hard*.

Dear Lord, save her from herself.

"Do you want me to make the call?" Emmett's deep voice seemed to roll right through her, the rich timbre as seductive as the rest of him. "You look a little…distracted."

He reached for her, his hand stroking down her arm when she wanted him to stroke far more intimate places. Still, the shiver that tripped through her was undeniable.

Subtle, unexpected pleasure warmed her insides—until she realized he was only reaching for Rita's phone book, which she still held.

Crap, crap, crap. Where was her head?

"I can do it." Yanking back her hand and the book, she called herself every kind of bad name that other girls had called her in high school. Maybe she really was a sex-crazed serial dater if she couldn't keep her panties in place for more than two days now that Emmett had showed up in her life again. Somehow, it had been easier to say no to Horatio for six months than to ward off Emmett's appeal for a few days.

Punching the buttons with extra force, Jayne collected her self-control and told herself what she needed was another night onstage under the spotlight to get back her attitude and a little backbone where he was concerned. Dancing always made her feel unbeatable, unbreakable. Ready to call her own shots.

The phone rang and rang until an answering machine picked up at Margie's sponsor's house. Leaving a detailed message, Jayne explained the video poker threat and her concern for her mother before disconnecting.

"Maybe the sponsor is already with your mother somewhere," Emmett suggested, clearing aside the phone and the phonebook. "It's possible Margie called for help if she felt tempted."

"I need a sponsor," Jayne blurted without thinking. Maybe she should join Sex Addicts Anonymous and solicit help for staying away from Emmett. "That is, it's good to have a friend to keep you from making big mistakes."

"You've got a sister." Leaning back in the chair,

Emmett slid out of his leather moccasins and put his feet up on the bed beside her, crossing at the ankles. "She seems pretty committed to watching your back."

Not tonight.

The words blared in her mind so loudly she wasn't entirely sure she didn't actually give voice to the notion. But Emmett just lounged there, staring at her until she thought her bloodstream would combust.

"Should we go on deck to grab that drink now?" Bolting off the bed, Jayne thought a straight shot of whiskey might be just the thing to clear her head. Possibly a double. Too bad she hated whiskey.

"You didn't leave your cell phone number, did you?" He tipped back his head to peer up at her, his tall, rangy body blocking the path to her door. "I'm still game for a drink, but I don't want you to miss a call."

Curses. Foiled again.

Her womb did little backflips to be so close to mouth-level with him. God, she could remember times when he'd…when they'd…

Her lips were too dry, her brain too fired-up with memories to make any kind of response. She tried to ignore the need to moisten her mouth with her tongue. Lord, did she try.

And failed.

Emmett's low growl clued her in to the error along with his lightning-fast rise out of his chair.

She half expected him to pull her down to the mattress. To pin her to the bed and not let go until she admitted how much she wanted him.

Instead, he skimmed his thumbs lightly over the

insides of her elbows, making her acutely aware of an erogenous zone she'd never known existed.

"I'm not going to try to talk you out of the no-sex rule if that's really want you want." The heat of his touch drifted higher along her arms, up to the short sleeves on her sequined organza blouse that she'd slipped into earlier. "But I'll be damned if I'm going to let you get away with all that hip-twitching, lip-smacking, hair-flipping flirting you like to do without letting you know what it does to me."

She was still processing the rapid-fire accusation of his words when his mouth fell on hers like a ravenous man who hadn't tasted a woman in a long time. Not that it had been a long time for him, damn the man.

Bless the man.

It was difficult to stay mad at a guy who kissed like Emmett. He still had a way of taking possession of her whole body with just a flick of his agile tongue, the velvety stroke sending heat waves to every nerve ending.

The good news was he possessed every bit of sexual firepower he'd ever had and more.

The bad news was the kisses were making her very, very distracted.

EMMETT GUESSED—hoped—he had two more minutes of self-control in him before he tossed Jayne on the bed and yanked off every piece of clingy, insubstantial fluff that she called clothes.

She'd had him on the verge of insanity ever since she waltzed barefoot into his bar in her dripping wet, see-through dress. The vision of her in that clinging flower print…

Ah hell.

He had one more minute left at the most. She burned in his arms, her trim dancer's body so finely tuned that she responded to every shift of his hands, every movement of his mouth. Her breasts flattened against his chest, the two peaked points obvious through her blouse's silky fabric.

He'd learned a fair amount of self-discipline since his wife had booted him out of her bed two months into their doomed marriage declaring him to be too rough, too uncouth and too frigging demanding for her taste. He'd worked his ass off to bring a little more gentility to the bedroom but he'd be damned if he could scavenge up any more right now.

Breaking off the kiss, he smothered a string of curses unsuccessfully, while he stared into Jayne's dazed, dark eyes.

"That's not the kind of response I usually get when I lock lips with a man, MacNeil." Her fingers smoothed her hair where he'd tangled it.

"Lucky for you, I'm not a grabby bastard like the guys you usually date." Though his fingers sure as hell wished he was.

"Really?" Her eyes sparked with an inner fire. "I seem to recall a time when you were a lot more in touch with your Inner Grabber."

She wrapped her arms around herself in a defensive posture, scraping his conscience raw. The room seemed to shrink two sizes from its already closet-like dimensions, leaving no room for anything but him, Jayne and a bed with sheets that smelled like her perfume.

"I've changed." Not enough to suit Claudia, but

maybe enough to be a better man to another woman in the far off future after he got his head on straight. After he figured out how to reconcile his hell-bent determination to kick back and have some fun in his life and his Type A personality that insisted he do it right now. "A guy can't go through his whole life being pushy and demanding. Didn't you tell me that once?"

"I meant you shouldn't give people ultimatums to marry you then and there *or else*." She pushed a gold bangle around and around her wrist. "Not that I'm suggesting *I* would have married you in a million years, but it strikes me as a little insincere to make such a serious offer and than swipe it back off the table ten seconds later."

"You had days to think about it." He wouldn't let her twist the truth since it had eaten away at him while she thought it over. "How much blasted time did you need?"

Releasing the bangle, she glanced up at him, her lips still close enough to taste.

"All I'm saying is that I would have never asked you to hold back while kissing me out of some need to be…undemanding. Kissing isn't a problem for you, if you ask me. And frankly, if that's how marriage changed you, I'm not sure it was such a good thing."

Emmett closed his eyes to keep himself from reacting automatically to her words. Too bad the image that flashed across the backs of his eyelids was Jayne gleefully tossing gasoline and a lit match on his already simmering sex drive.

"What in the hell are you thinking?" Eyes flying open, he closed the space between them so he was practically on top of her, his nose grazing her forehead until he angled her chin up toward him. "I haven't slept with a woman for almost as long as you haven't slept with a man since there was something off about my marriage from day one. And considering you and I once had sex six times in a day, I'd say that's too freaking long for a guy who wants you as bad as I do."

It was exactly the kind of confrontation Claudia would have booted him out on his ass for, claiming he needed anger management. But Jayne smiled her slow siren's smile that Mae West would have envied.

"Ah. Now *this* man, I know." She pressed her hips to his in acknowledgement of the wooden salute he'd been giving her for a hell of a lot longer than she probably realized. "Welcome back, Emmett."

Anger at her—at himself—for being so incredibly screwed-up rained down on him, soaking him in enough regret to force him a step back but not nearly enough to make him take his hands off her.

The phone ringing beside them slowly penetrated his brain. She blinked with surprise before picking it up.

"Hello?"

While Emmett thanked God for the intervention before he did something Jayne would regret—like sleep with her despite the no-sex rule—Jayne listened to whoever was on the other end.

A small, selfish part of him wished it was Margie so that her crisis would be solved and he could get Jayne out of her tiny cabin that reminded him of too many other times they'd been alone in this same room. He'd wanted to keep tabs on her today, knew he needed to make sure Garcia stayed the hell away from her, but he'd ended up following the prick dealer around the last two days instead of sticking close to Jayne since he wasn't totally sure he could trust himself not to touch her when she was around.

"Then we need to talk. Now." Frowning, Jayne nodded at something the other person was saying. "I'll meet you outside the piano bar in five minutes."

Obviously, it hadn't been Margie. As Jayne hung up the phone, Emmett reached for his jacket.

"Your sister?"

She nodded, slipping into her shoes. "Apparently Rita finally decided to check in with her family. It's probably just as well you and I go our separate ways tonight anyway since I'm obviously pissing you off at every turn."

Chin held high, she brushed past him, all haughty and snooty in her pink frilly blouse and tan skinny skirt.

Hauling her close to him for one last kiss, he figured there was no point in restraining himself if she didn't mind a little grabbiness.

"Don't mistake sexual frustration for me being pissed off." Hell, why not go for broke? He copped a feel of her oh-so-fine butt and hauled her even closer. "I'm mad at myself for not knowing how to talk to you anymore, but that doesn't mean for a second that I don't want you."

To prove the point, he kissed her hard, thoroughly and as long as he possibly could before she needed to meet her sister.

Then, with a mingled sense of regret and satisfaction, he pulled himself away and opened the door to the hallway.

"Push me away all you want, lady, but I'm still going to be here tomorrow."

HARRISON STALKED THE ship's corridor outside the piano bar where late-night revelers sang show tunes and a few old ladies cackled and tap-danced their way through "New York, New York."

He hadn't wanted to leave the bed where he'd finally had his first full, uninterrupted taste of Rita Frazer, but they'd both realized they couldn't indulge their own wants when they each had leads to follow. He'd needed to pull up some reports from Sonia's jewelry business to see if he could find any links to Seva Yurek or other underworld types in the Caribbean while Rita worried about her mother who she hadn't been able to reach all day.

She sat quietly at a round booth along the ship's outer wall now, overlooking the dark waves while he walked off his bad feeling that something had gone wrong today. Had he overlooked something on shore because he'd been so eager to get back on the *Venus* to be with Rita? A new worry for a guy who'd ignored his last girlfriend in favor of overseeing business.

He spied Jayne and Emmett stepping off the elevator when his phone rang.

A "blocked call" according to the ID pane.

Answering it anyway, he strode farther away from the noise wafting out of the piano bar, pushing through a nearby door leading out to a deck open to the night air.

"Hello?"

"Harrison, it's me. Trevor."

The voice was slightly distorted and sounded a million miles away but it sure sounded like him. Traitorous bastard.

A stiff wind gusted off the sea, whipping past his ears with surprising force.

"Where the hell are you, Judas?" Anger he'd been suppressing roiled up in him now, glad for an outlet even though he'd regret the moment of self-indulgence if it scared off Trevor. "I'm not going to stop searching until I find you and Sonia and the generous withdrawal you helped yourself to on your way out of town."

"We need help." At least, that's what it sounded like he was saying. The connection crackled and the gusting wind didn't help. "—can explain."

"How about you help *me* out for a change instead and tell me where you are so you can do all the explaining you want in person?" He hated to shout his frustration for the whole ship to hear but he wasn't losing this connection.

"—tomorrow in St. Maarten." The miles of dark Caribbean Sea ate up most of Trevor's words. "Don't go…" Words faded. Words came back. "—lot of trouble."

"What?" He shouted the word as loudly as he could but by then the connection had broken off completely, leaving him in sudden silence except for the snap of wind through his clothes.

Puzzling over what any of it meant, he tapped out a couple of digits to try a callback before patching into an old friend at the Bureau for help tracing the call.

When he'd taken care of what he could from a public place in the middle of the sea, he shoved through the doors to go inside. He paced back toward the table where Jayne and Rita talked in low tones when they weren't wolf-whistling encouragement at the old ladies now dancing in earnest to "Copa Cabana."

Emmett, the perpetual man-in-the-shadows, intercepted him before he could reach the table.

"You realize Rita and Jayne are going to be just like that when they're eighty years old, don't you?" Emmett stared at the feisty elderly ladies lifting their skirts enough to accommodate a modified high kick.

Harrison started to grin at the image until he remembered Emmett's other, less enjoyable prediction—that no man could hold onto a Frazer female. What did this guy know anyway?

"You been watching out for Jayne?" He changed the subject, not ready to think about what sleeping with Rita meant. "Keeping her away from the numb-nut?"

"He tried to move in on her the other night like nothing happened." Emmett paused as a pack of teenagers on the prowl walked by. "And I'm pretty damn sure he's got some kind of unholy alliance going with this Seva guy you're looking for."

"You've got every reason to hate Garcia's guts." Reserving judgment, Harrison waited for more information. He'd occasionally run into people who liked to play cops and robbers and dug the idea of feeding information to agents. "Are you sure you're not just being hopeful that he's up to no good?"

"I was trying to give Jayne some breathing room today so I figured I'd keep tabs on Garcia instead of sticking right next to her for twelve hours straight." Shrugging, the poor sucker could barely take his eyes off of Jayne. The day must have been hell for him. "Serves the same purpose right?"

"Not a bad strategy." Harrison's admiration for the guy ratcheted up a notch. "Good not to wear out your welcome when you're protecting someone."

"Turns out creepy dealer boy is giving a sign to one of the cruise guests when he's got a high roller."

"A sign?" Deflated, Harrison knew that any sign he

gave could be intended for security to flag their attention toward someone dropping a lot of dough.

"Very subtle. A turn of the head to the left or right. A clearing of the throat. But if you watch the guy for a whole shift you can see the pattern in how he moves, because he's incredibly still otherwise."

"How do you know he's signaling a guest and not security?" Casino security was notoriously high, even on cruise ships. Dealers didn't get away with squat. They had to flash their hands at cameras before and after their shifts and they had roving pit bosses looking over their shoulders all night. "High rollers can either be big casino moneymakers or potential threats to the house's odds. I'm pretty sure they watch them closely either way."

"Which is exactly what I thought until I saw the same guy dressed in a goofy-ass Hawaiian shirt approach all three of the high rollers Horatio pegged."

"Could be security in plain clothes." Although Harrison was definitely paying attention now.

"Not unless security is running illegal poker games outside the casinos." Emmett finally dragged his eyes off Jayne long enough to give Harrison a level look. "Because that's where all the high rollers and the Hawaiian shirt dude ended up. Smoking stogies in room E-5 and clinking a hell of a lot of chips around."

CHAPTER TWELVE

"I'M NOT LEAVING until Emmett comes back."

Jayne's disgruntled declaration alerted Rita to tread warily as they sat in their booth outside the piano bar alone, their drinks long since drained—Jayne's virgin Bloody Mary and Rita's whiskey sour that she'd nursed right down to ice cubes and orange rind.

Rita knew her sister didn't make idle threats. Even if she dressed like a sex goddess and occasionally appeared a bit featherheaded, Jayne had stubborn determination and grit down to a science when she chose to apply it. If she took it in her head to sit in their vinyl booth and wait for Emmett to reappear, they could be here until the wait staff changed over to the breakfast shift.

"It's Harrison's fault they've been gone so long." She didn't know exactly how or why, but she'd seen the way they'd been talking earlier and knew their conversation hadn't been small talk about the merits of the piano player.

"They barely know each other," Jayne retorted with a tone that suggested Rita examine her head. "What earthly reason would they have for disappearing into thin air for over an hour?"

Jayne checked her watch, frowning.

"Remember I told you Harrison is a former FBI

guy?" *Former* being a word he seemed to use rather loosely since he'd be returning to duty next week. "He's working on some kind of investigation and I think he's got Emmett pegged to help him. Maybe because your new boyfriend knows a lot of people in the Caribbean."

Rita waited patiently for Jayne to offer up more information, hoping if they put their heads together for a change, they could figure out what was going on this trip. Her patience wore thin in about five seconds, however, so she tried another tack while waving away an overeager waiter.

"Harrison said you and Emmett knew each other before this voyage to St. Kitts, but I don't remember you mentioning him."

A man walking past their table opened the door to the deck and a cool gust of air whistled past them.

"I met him on the *Venus* a year ago when he was a passenger. I'm sure you must have seen us together." Jayne chased her ice around and around with her straw while Rita tried to process the information.

"So what you said about meeting him in the St. Kitts gift shop was…not true?"

"Sometimes it's easier to tell you what you expect to hear from me." Shrugging, Jayne didn't bother with any further explanation.

Warding off the hurt inherent in her sister's suggestion, Rita concentrated on remembering Emmett's facial features and sifting through her memories of past cruises.

"He did look sort of familiar to me, but I thought that was just because he has that tall, dark and sexy thing going you seem to like." Rita had to admit she felt a little ashamed not to have remembered him straight off.

Maybe she had been unfair to jump to the conclusion that Jayne picked up a new man while waiting for her fiancé to show up in St. Kitts. "Plus I was nervous when we first started here, convinced I'd sew a costume to my own pant leg."

"And don't forget all that time you spent being seasick." A smile eased the furrow on Jayne's brow. "As I recall, green wasn't all that becoming on you."

Seeing Jayne's returning good humor as a chance to get her back to their room without an argument, Rita stood and tugged Jayne up with her.

"How kind of you to recall. Can we please go back to our room and forget about the guys?" Easier said than done, she knew, since she couldn't shove Harrison out of her mind to save her life. Just thinking about the time they'd spent together made her weak in the knees. "They don't deserve hot chicks like us anyway if they can't stick around for ten minutes straight."

"Fine." Reaching for her purse, Jayne followed her toward the elevator. By now, it was so late there weren't many passengers using them anyway. "It's just as well since you should call Margie's work to see if they know anything."

They both knew it had been their mother's night off. But since the advent of video poker, maybe someone had seen her playing a few hands. Or a few hundred hands.

Silence reigned in the elevator on the way down, neither really anxious to consider the prospect. When they reached the lowest level of the ship they could hear parties still going on in the crew cabins, the music almost as loud as the laughter and the shouted, drunken conversations that went on in a dozen different languages.

"There's Missy." Jayne pointed out their friend with the big blond cheerleader hair farther down the corridor near their rooms. "Did I tell you I got her job back for her? I also thought of a new routine today. I was very busy while you were off gallivanting in Antigua."

"You got Missy her job back?" Rita couldn't believe her ears. She waved at Missy down the endless hallway that ran over half the length of the ship. "You talked to Danielle?"

"I had to promise to spend as many hours rehearsing with Missy as Danielle says." Jayne slicked on another coat of lip gloss, soliciting a chorus of whistles from a handful of cabin boys hanging out in the hallway. "Oh, and I had to swear to Danielle that neither of us would badger her for anything else. No more favors for the Frazers, she says."

What? Rita's toe caught on a small step leading to the last stretch of hallway just as they met Missy.

"Whoa!" Missy caught her with one arm before Rita fell face-first. Missy's free hand still balanced a plate of something wafting a chocolate-y scent. "You okay? Did Jayne tell you I'm rehired? I snuck into the kitchen to pilfer a few of the hot caramel brownies that were left over from tonight's menu so we could celebrate."

While Missy practically bubbled over with excitement, Rita tried to discern if Demonic Danielle could actually be trying to weasel out of paying Rita for the costumes with her dictate of no more favors. Danielle could never consider payment for services rendered "a favor," could she? A sick feeling in Rita's belly told her not to expect normal consideration from a woman who prided herself on her reputation of pure evil.

Still, that kind of financial slap in the face would be devastating. Rita couldn't afford to get screwed out of her money on this. *Their* money. Half of her initial outlay belonged to Jayne.

"Ree?" Jayne looked expectantly at her as they stood outside their cabin door. "Do you have your room key? I think Emmett must have mine since it's locked and you know I never do that."

Rita couldn't take even a smidgen of pleasure out of her ever-prepared possession of a room key. She'd be hard-pressed to ever feel remotely more responsible than Jayne again since at least her younger sibling hadn't gambled away their savings on costumes she might never get reimbursed for.

Opening the door to their room, Rita wished she could have spent the night with Harrison so she wouldn't have had to face this news yet. But one thing was certain, she couldn't afford to spend another day ashore with him tomorrow even if she sewed all night long to get ahead.

She needed to set things straight with Danielle as soon as possible and she had a feeling that conversation would turn into a first-class showdown. Fully expecting a catfight, she predicted a hell of a lot of fur would be flying before the matter was settled.

THE NEXT MORNING, Rita swiped an apple off a buffet table in one of the ship's more casual dining rooms and munched it outside on a deck. The bow overlooked the pier along the Dutch portion of the island called St. Maarten while the French half was St. Martin. Lots of flash and Vegas-style glitz on the Dutch side and European charm on the French made it one of Rita's favorite stops in the Caribbean.

Pity she couldn't be down there today. She wanted to postpone her conversation with Danielle until Jayne was off the ship, and she watched the sea of departing passengers to make sure her sister left before confronting their longtime nemesis on her own. No need to worry Jayne about Danielle's weasely tactics yet.

Harrison would be departing soon, too. She still didn't know what was going on with Harrison and his search for the bimbo who didn't deserve him. He'd called last night to say all the right things—that he'd been thinking about her, that he couldn't get her out of his head—words that touched her cynical soul and made her smile. But he'd clammed up about new developments on his investigation even though she'd known damn well something must have happened or he would have wanted to spend last night with her.

Right?

It scared her to think how much she hoped that was true. He seemed so different from anyone else she'd ever dated. So much more thoughtful and yet—why couldn't he confide in her about what he was doing?

On the pier below she finally spotted him exiting the boat, his dark hair and his big, gorgeous body dressed in jeans and a T-shirt easy to pick out among the Hawaiian-shirt-sporting tourists and the older crowd wearing tailored seersucker jackets like her grandfather used to wear.

Rita was contemplating how she could create her own vintage evening wear from a stroll through Margie's closet when something went wrong on the pier below.

Bodies separated from the crowd in a semicircle around Harrison. Five men all seemed to move at once, surrounding him. Bad guys?

Fear for Harrison made Rita shriek out a warning, but even from her high vantage point she could somehow sense the tension in his posture. He'd already seen them. She thought she saw a flash of a gold badge and the cord of an earphone trailing down someone else's neck, but she wasn't sticking around to watch the action from far away.

Her confrontation with Danielle would have to wait since Rita planned to offer Harrison whatever backup a seamstress with a mean left hook could offer.

EVEN WHEN THEY didn't have a gun jammed between your ribs, foreign cops could be scary.

Harrison could hold his head up in any FBI outpost around the globe and state as much without feeling like a wuss since foreign law enforcement didn't give a rat's ass about what U.S. agency you were with or what mission you were trying to accomplish. If these guys wanted you badly enough, they could make you disappear or, if they were feeling particularly generous, they could send your broken body back to the States with their greatest sympathy for your windsurfing accident.

The local cops trying to haul him away spoke Dutch, which Harrison could understand about as well as Swahili. But he knew damn well most of the islanders could speak English, too. No doubt the language barrier was intentional. Now, they flashed a few photos under his nose of the silver merchant he'd talked to yesterday on the quay in Antigua, photos which showed the old lady badly beaten and bruised.

Oh shit.

"This woman was fine when I left her." He debated making a ruckus on the pier, but figured he'd be better off trying to get these guys to call the States to confirm his identity. "There have to be twenty witnesses around that quay who saw me leave her cart peacefully."

"Wait just a freaking minute." A pissed-off female with a slight—and possibly purposeful—southern drawl stopped the five cops in their tracks, proving they damn well knew English.

Rita.

God almighty, what was she thinking?

"Get back on the *Venus,* Rita." He spoke using as few facial muscles as possible, not wanting to provoke Trigger Finger, a tense-as-hell kid of no more than twenty who looked to be the youngest of the local cops.

Blithely ignoring him, Rita stepped forward while she had their attention. And damn but did she ever have their attention. Whether it was the flaming red hair draping her body down past her shoulders or her screaming red blazer and skirt that looked like she'd purposely armed for battle. She looked like some sort of Olympian goddess ready to start throwing bolts of fire at the next man to piss her off.

"I'm the cruise director for the ship you see behind me, gentlemen," she lied smoothly. "And this man you've accosted is one of our VIP guests whose comfort I'm personally overseeing this trip because of his business connections that Roman Cruise Lines values."

A small crowd started building around them now, from tourists to natives, shopkeepers and even a couple of ship security guards who—interestingly—hadn't spoken up to contradict Rita's story.

"This man assaulted an innocent woman yesterday in Antigua!" Trigger Finger shouted back at her in flawless English, gun kissing Harrison's kidney now.

One of the older guys with him, the more reasonable-looking black man with a stoic expression and grizzled streaks of gray through his hair, shushed the kid with a lazy lift of his hand.

"This man was with *me* all day on Antigua because it is my duty to ensure his trip is pleasant. Perhaps I should contact our ship's captain to help you sort this out?" Rita turned to a security guard as if to send the surprised woman off to do her bidding, but Grizzled Gray spoke up.

"We just want to speak with him," the older cop assured Rita. "No need to get anyone else involved."

"Then I think one person talking to him should be plenty as opposed to five men and a gun in his gut." She stared pointedly at Trigger.

"We can talk," Harrison jumped in, relaxing along with the easing of the weapon behind him. He pointed to the older guy who seemed to be in charge. "But I'm only having this discussion with you."

As the older man nodded, the other four guys backed off.

"You have five minutes before I call down our captain," the phony cruise director shouted while Harrison followed the other man to the far side of the pier.

Not even 10:00 a.m. and he'd already had a gun pressed to his flesh, a run-in with foreign police and the woman he'd slept with playing rescuer. A hell of a start to the day. On the plus side, he'd gotten to stare a little longer at the best set of legs he'd ever seen in his life and he was that much closer to finding out what had happened to Sonia.

All in all, not a bad trade.

"I'M NOT LEAVING." Rita tapped her toe in a rapid, nervous rhythm on the street outside of a casino called Golddiggers in the city of Phillipsburg two hours later. She would not allow Harrison to shove her away today. Not when this much trouble brewed.

Harrison had provided identification and information to the St. Maarten officials, along with an explanation of what he'd been doing in Antigua the day before. They'd finally released him after talking to the FBI headquarters in Tampa who'd vouched for his stellar arrest record and spotless work history even though Harrison had been on leave the last year. After much discussion, the cops finally cleared him but had taken years off Rita's life in the process.

She'd ridden off in a cab with him after explaining she didn't want to look like a liar to the foreign police and needed to follow through on her alibi as his personal tour guide during this trip. But mainly, she wanted to come along with him to find out what in the hell was going on.

Now, as the repeated beeps and dings of the slot machines inside Golddiggers drifted out onto the street from the casino, she discovered a confrontation with Harrison could be more difficult than standing down five foreign law enforcement officials.

"It's too dangerous for you to be here, damn it." He spared her a fierce glance before staring back into the casino where he was obviously dying to go.

How could she be attracted to him even when he

thoroughly ticked her off? But she'd been scared out of her mind when the St. Maarten police had been swarming around him.

"If what you're investigating is so flipping dangerous, how could you wrangle my sister's boyfriend into helping you?" She pointed a warning finger straight into his scowl. Okay, a little south of his scowl since he didn't look like a man who'd appreciate finger pointing. "And don't pretend you didn't get Emmett involved in this, because I have sixth-sense radar when it comes to trouble near Jayne, and believe me, she attracts it like a magnet."

"Emmett went ashore with her?" His scowl deepened. "That must mean Horatio Garcia got off the *Venus* today, too."

"He's following around the ass-grabbing bastard who stood up my sister? For what purpose?"

"We have reason to believe Horatio is part of an illegal gambling ring operating in the Caribbean. He's pulling in marks onboard the *Venus* and at nearly every port of call he can for the guy who owns that behemoth yacht we saw docked in Barbados two days ago."

"Much as I'd love to see Horatio rotting in prison for what he did to Jayne, I can't imagine it's a good idea for you to recruit innocent bystanders to do FBI work." What would Emmett do if he caught up with Jayne's old boyfriend? And what was Emmett thinking to bring her ashore with him when she had a show tonight?

Frustration combined with the growing heat of the high noon sun was slowly setting Rita's neck on fire. She hated feeling helpless, hated not knowing what was going on and damn it, but it sucked to have someone else calling all the shots while she sat in the dark.

"For all purposes, I'm an innocent bystander, too, since I'm not with the Bureau for this investigation. I didn't recruit Emmett for squat other than to warn him about Horatio's connections." His expression softened, the dark intensity fading long enough for her to see glimpses of the man she'd first spied peeling the label off his beer in the Aurora Theater. The guy she'd mistaken for a bored businessman. "Wouldn't you rather have Emmett know what's going on so he can look out for your sister?"

"I don't see how he's looking out for her very well by dragging her around to keep tabs on a man with deep, dark connections." To illegal gambling? Warning bells started buzzing in her overheated head, making her remember her mother and the new video poker machines back in Fort Lauderdale. "You said he spots targets for some kind of gambling kingpin?"

She must have raised her voice too much since he grabbed her by the arm and yanked her none too gently into an alley between the casino and a seafood restaurant with a juggler out front to catch the eye of cruise ship passengers that filled the area.

"It's all conjecture. I don't know anything for sure, and I'm not— *Holy hell.*" He broke off, his sharp blue gaze glued to the street as he dragged Rita closer to the edge of the casino building.

"What?" Her skirt snagged on the rough stucco of the building.

"Sonia's here." His sharp whisper cut her unexpectedly.

All this investigative work on his part had been prompted by the ex-girlfriend who'd hurt him. Stupid of Rita to be jealous. And yet…the thought of him leveling that keen glance at another woman made Rita's personal green monster roar inside her head.

"Let me see." She had to get a look at her, scooching forward to glimpse a slender woman leaning into a van window to pay the driver. She'd seen a photo of her on Harrison's PDA, but a static image never told a story the way the real-life person could.

A platinum blonde with well-tamed curls tucked neatly behind her ears, the woman turned on one aqua-colored mule to enter the casino, her striped pastel skirt and crisp linen blouse belted loosely at her waist. She looked cool and elegant, a woman at ease with privilege and wealth, and she strode toward the doorman with a confident air.

Rita felt like a sweaty, unruly mess by comparison. And damn it, what had possessed her to take a peek at his last girlfriend anyway? The picture he'd showed her of Sonia didn't come close to doing her justice.

"Should we follow her?" Rita wasn't sure she'd care for investigative work if it involved following around the skinny twig Harrison used to sleep with, but if solving his case meant keeping Jayne out of danger, Rita would find a way to keep her green monster at bay. She hoped.

"Wait." He held her back when she would have moved forward.

"What if we lose her?" Rita wondered how good a special agent this guy had been. "We spent all damn day yesterday trying to find her and now you're just going to let her walk on by?"

"Wait. Where's Trevor?" He eased forward a step and then back again when another van and a sleek silver Mercedes pulled up in front of the casino. "I think she's being followed."

Biting her lip hard not to tell him he was being far too cloak-and-daggerish about all this, Rita forced herself to simply watch a guy hop out of the passenger seat of the Mercedes, his bodybuilder-style physique giving the poor man no neck to speak of.

"That's not Trevor." She remembered seeing a photo of Harrison's former friend and he'd definitely had a neck.

"No." He stepped out of the alley as soon as No Neck entered the building. "And I'm not arguing with you anymore, Rita. You've got to get back to the ship."

Skimming a cooling hand underneath the blanket of her hot hair, she gently fanned the base of her skull. Somehow, some way, she was going to stick with Harrison today because she could smell trouble as clearly as the scent of smoked salmon wafting from the seafood place next door.

"I'm not arguing either." She was so glad to hear they were done with that since she had no desire to squabble in eighty-five-degree heat. "Your old girlfriend won't even recognize me if I keep an eye on her. Besides, remember how well I handled the cops for you earlier?" Darting past Harrison, she made a beeline for the door. "I think I'm gonna make you a hell of a partner."

CHAPTER THIRTEEN

"AND JUST HOW LONG did you want to hang out here?" Jayne resisted the urge to drum her fingernails on the dashboard of the Jeep Emmett had rented for the day.

Newer and a whole lot cleaner than his Jeep that they'd left parked at an airfield three islands back, this vehicle was shiny black and they'd rolled the top off to explore St. Maarten. At least that's what she'd *thought* they were doing until Emmett pulled over on the opposite side of the street from the Golddiggers casino shortly past noon and stared at the entrance.

For at least three minutes straight.

"Just a little longer," he answered finally, eyes barely flickering in her direction. "Have I told you how damn incredible you look in that dress?"

"So incredible you can't peel your eyes away from the casino doors for five seconds?" She knew her dress could slay most men at ten paces. Pale green, sheer organza covered a creamy white silk slip dress, the two layers swishing delicately as she walked. It felt sexy, looked sexy and even *sounded* erotic.

The fact that Emmett had turned blind and deaf in the course of the past few hours ashore definitely wasn't the dress's fault.

"God, Jayne, if it was up to me you'd be on my lap right now instead of sitting way the hell over there." He slanted her a glance that flash-fried her skin and nearly sizzled the ends of her hair. "Have you got no use at all for a gentleman in your life?"

Tapping her lips, she considered the question carefully. She'd never had a gentleman before, so she couldn't be sure.

"A gentleman would have offered to take me into that seafood restaurant over there, I think." The scent of grilled salmon permeated the air, but it didn't make her as hungry as Emmett's suggestion. "But if I remember correctly, your lap isn't such a bad place to be."

Now she had his complete, undivided attention. It didn't matter that they sat out in the open with the top rolled down or that tourists crowded both sides of the street in front of the casino. The whole world faded away to just Emmett and his dark eyes.

"If I pull you over here, my hands are going to be up your skirt a whole lot faster than you can say 'I'm saving myself.' Understand?"

Her thoughts flared into meltdown mode as her gaze drifted down to Emmett's hands. One rested on the gearshift, the other on the door where the window was rolled down. She could practically feel them on her thighs already. Even though she would never allow such a thing.

Or would she?

Even as she considered the possibility, her heart slugged slow and hard in her chest as she lifted her eyes to meet his again. But something odd diverted her attention midway.

Horatio Garcia stood in front of Golddiggers casino, escorting a couple of older men toward a waiting limo. Why was it stupid Horatio had to ruin things just when she was starting to have fun?

Emmett turned to follow her gaze.

"Shit." His expletive didn't surprise her as much as the fact that he suddenly pulled out the rental car brochure and started writing down the limo's license plate number along with the exact time.

"What are you doing?" Mood effectively broken even if her hormones were still spinning around her insides like a lucky slot machine ready to hit the jackpot, Jayne couldn't fathom why Emmett would write down a license plate. Unless Rita was right and he really was playing amateur spy. "Oh sweet Eliza Jane, Emmett. Don't tell me you've had me following around my ex-freaking-boyfriend all day today."

On the other side of the street, the limo sped off with the old-timers while Horatio walked back inside with an arrogant little bop in his step. Why had she never noticed how obnoxious he could be before? Thank God she hadn't married such a conceited twit.

"We're not really following him." Emmett tore off a corner of the brochure and shoved the slip of paper in his wallet before tossing the pen back in an open slot on the dashboard.

"Then what the hell are we doing here when we could be sipping margaritas and getting schnockered on the nearest beach?" She couldn't even let herself consider that Emmett might be more interested in spy games than spending time with her. Kissing her. Following through on that threat to touch her….

"We're keeping tabs." He shrugged it off as if shadowing her ex-fiancé around town wasn't a totally twisted thing to do. "Just to be sure you're not working on the *Venus* with a big-time criminal. I want to be certain you're safe."

"I dated that guy for six months, Emmett. I could walk past him and tweak his nose and I'd be safe. If he's a criminal, it's not like he's killing people or anything."

"Even if what you're saying is true—and I'm not so sure it is—that doesn't mean he doesn't work with a whole slew of more dangerous types." He fidgeted with the valet key dangling off the ring hanging from the ignition before turning his attention back to her again. "And whether you decide you want something more with me again or not, you have to know I'd never want anything to happen to you."

Tenderness for this man—a man who could be so demanding and yet so sweet—made her heart ache for what they'd missed out on nine months ago. What might have been if she'd had the guts to say yes to him? If he'd cared enough to stick around?

Swallowing down her regrets, she covered his hand with her own.

"Nothing will happen to me." Her fingers skimmed the back of his knuckles, up and down over each bump. "But if you're determined to see what's going on with my ex, what are we doing sitting out here when we could find out a lot more by going inside?"

He flipped his hand over, gripping hers hard and putting an end to her tentative explorations.

"No."

"And that's it?" Old frustrations kicked free inside

her, shoving aside the tender feelings. "You say no, therefore, we do it your way?"

"This isn't that simple." The warning note couldn't have been more obvious in his voice if he'd added a siren and a yellow caution light for effect.

Snippets of past arguments—his ability to put a wall up and refuse any kind of compromise—roared to life in her memory. She knew she wasn't the easiest chick in the world to deal with, but he was no freaking picnic himself.

Screw him and his demands. He didn't lay down the law for her, and it would never work out between them if he couldn't appreciate that simple fact.

Reaching for the door handle, she figured she'd better be prepared to sprint. Good thing she was in the best shape of her life since her celibate lifestyle left her with more hours than ever to hit the gym.

"You know what, Emmett?" Wrenching the door open, she ignored his protests. "Too bad."

SHE'D PICKED A hell of a time for theatrics.

But even knowing full well he deserved Jayne's anger didn't make Emmett any less worried about her as she strutted her way across the street in her fluttery dress. Shoving out of the Jeep, he pocketed his phone and keys as he followed her. Watched her. Wished like hell he deserved her.

"Jayne." He called to her as she reached the doors, knowing she wouldn't stop but hoping maybe she'd slow down long enough to glare at him.

She didn't.

The security guards at the entrance were falling all over themselves to open the doors wide for her, and even without seeing her expression, Emmett could envision exactly the flirtatious smile she had on her face at that moment. She couldn't walk past a man without turning his head. It was a frigging scientific impossibility.

He closed the distance between them enough to slide through the entryway while the security guys still gawked slack-jawed in her wake. Reaching out, he caught her elbow in what he hoped looked like a gentle manner since the last thing he needed was to bring down the wrath of local rent-a-cops on his head in some misguided efforts to save Damsel Jayne.

"Wait." Gripping her arm enough to slow her down a pace, he caught up to her and slid a hand around her waist. "You don't know what's going on here."

"Only because you've put me on a need-to-know basis like I'm some kind of cops and robbers neophyte." She allowed him to pull her in between a row of slot machines where a handful of players staked out stools.

"You *are* a neophyte." He sat her on one of the stools at the end of the row, enough to keep her out of sight from the open casino floor.

"Not any more than you, thank you very much." She picked up an empty cup for tokens from a stack on top of one of the machines. Their conversation remained fairly private thanks to the ongoing racket from binging and bleeping slot machines.

"Way more than me." Releasing a gusty sigh, he studied the layout of the room but didn't see Garcia. "Trust me, I know a whole hell of a lot more than I'd like about cops and robbers."

"You can't fool me into thinking you're some kind of ex-special agent, too." She twirled the cup around the top of her finger, agitated and restless. "I knew you back in the day, remember?"

As if he'd forgotten a second of their time together. "No such luck that I'm an ex-lawman, babe." Scanning the baccarat table, his gaze lingered on a familiar-looking redhead.

Thank God.

"What are you trying to say?" Jayne's fingers landed on his jaw with a light grip as she turned his attention back toward her. She stared at him with intent brown eyes in the dim light of the casino. "You don't mean to tell me you've gained the cops and robber experience on the bad-guy end of the equation?"

An old tightness filled his chest, a shame he had never completely shaken squeezing the air right out of his lungs. But he'd done his penance and he didn't share the finer points of his family's past with anyone. And this wasn't the time to freak out Jayne.

Right now, he needed to keep her safe. A task which just got easier since Harrison must be on the scene if Rita Frazer was hanging out at the baccarat tables.

"Not exactly." Tugging Jayne off the stool, he pulled her back toward the front door and hoped he could persuade her back onto the street if she caught the scent of grilled salmon from the restaurant next door. "But I grew up in enough bad neighborhoods to know how to stay safe."

She dug in her heels two steps later.

"I thought you were from New York? Manhattan, right?"

"Among other places." He hoped she'd drop it. Knew she wouldn't.

"You've never spoken much about your family." She stared at him with an intensity unusual for Jayne. But then, he knew she wasn't the fluff-head she sometimes pretended to be when it served her purposes.

He also knew that she wasn't going to let go of this unless he shut down the topic in a hurry. Ignoring the question, he focused on the task at hand.

"Your ex-boyfriend seems to be parting a lot of people from their money lately, and not just at the black-jack table." He spoke quietly into her ear, trying not to notice the way the silky strands wanted to cling to his cheek. "Garcia's been helping some friends set up illegal games outside the casinos and driving a crapload of sucker business toward this alternative action."

He should have probably told her more earlier, before he tried to juggle keeping an eye on Garcia with a day of sightseeing alongside Jayne. Dumb-ass idea on his part. But he hadn't wanted to get drawn into a conversation about why he cared what Garcia was doing or why Emmett should bother helping Harrison nail a ring of slick operators.

His preference to see con artists behind bars was personal and Emmett had no plans to pick open old scabs for her entertainment. But that didn't comfort him much when he saw the flash of hurt in Jayne's eyes at his abrupt turn of conversation. She covered it up with a scowl before she looked beyond him toward the rest of the casino.

He realized he'd completely lost her attention as she watched the movement around the baccarat tables.

"You don't want to talk about your past, fine. That's your business. But I've just spotted Rita so maybe I'll go park myself next to her for a while and spare myself the song and dance routine which I know all too well."

Giving him a haughty sniff, she spun away from him to head across the casino toward her sister.

FROM HIS VANTAGE POINT by a bank of pay phones near the money-changing table inside Golddiggers, Harrison could see disaster about to strike in the form of Jayne Frazer but didn't have a clue how to avert it.

A guy couldn't just throw himself over the lit grenade when the impending explosive device arrived in the form of an extroverted showgirl. At least not in public.

Praying hard Miss Effusive Personality could scavenge up a few shreds of subtlety before she unwittingly alerted Sonia at the blackjack table to Rita's presence behind her at the baccarat station, Harrison held his breath. Rita had proven a surprisingly effective ally inside the casino, scoping out Sonia's whereabouts before he entered and then helping him find a safe place inside to keep an eye on his ex without scaring her off.

And what he'd learned by watching her only confused him more about what had lured her and Trevor to the Caribbean. Were they spending Harrison's 30K to make a killing in blackjack? It just didn't add up. He needed to find a way to confront her before she could run.

Jayne detonated the moment she reached Rita's side, wrapping her arms around Rita and planting an air kiss on her cheek. She twitched and wiggled in all her showgirl glory, but even though she attracted stares from men clear across to the roulette wheel, Sonia didn't even look up from her battle of wits with the fresh-faced young blackjack dealer.

Hot damn.

Rita seemed to be trying to shush her sibling into silence when Emmett appeared at Harrison's side, a pissed-off scowl on his mug that broadcast a fight with his woman more clearly than a shortwave radio.

Knowing better than to go there, Harrison figured he had enough Frazer female trouble of his own without pretending he had any clue how to offer hollow advice, so he kept his mouth shut.

"No sign of your golfer guy?" Emmett paid for a stack of tokens at the money-changing window and then, pocketing all but one, he receded into the nook near the phones where Harrison stood.

"Not the guy." He kept his eyes on his quarry and Rita. "The girl. She's playing blackjack two stools down from where Rita's playing baccarat."

"Your ex-girlfriend left you to gamble away your savings in a podunk casino?"

"She's been playing conservatively, but I don't know what the hell she's doing here in the first place—shit." He shoved back another step into the shadows. "There's our guy."

"The golf pro?" Emmett held his ground, idly flipping the token in the air and catching it, never taking his attention off Jayne.

"That's the one." Harrison couldn't believe his eyes. Trevor strolled in off the street toward the blackjack tables, walking right past Sonia as if he'd never met her and taking a seat at the other end of the table.

Even worse, Rita and Jayne had staked out a new spot alongside Sonia as they joined the game, too. What was Rita thinking?

"Garcia's here, too, you know," Emmett warned, voice tense. "I'm getting fairly uncomfortable having Jayne around."

"No shit. I want Rita out of here, but I'm not leaving until I find out what's going on." Tension coiled through him, reminding him he didn't know nearly enough about what was going on to connect Garcia with Sonia and Trevor. "Besides, I can't go over there without setting off alarms all over the place. And where the hell did you see Garcia?"

That bugged him most of all. Harrison was playing this hand like some small-town rookie if the *Venus*'s dealer had gotten past him.

"There's some doors to the left of the main entrance when you walk in here. I figure that's where the private rooms are." Emmett stepped aside to let a man lugging an emphysema tank while still puffing on a cigarette get to the telephones. "Maybe he's working his angle in a high-roller suite off to one side?"

"Bet the casino loves that." Careful to keep his voice low, Harrison itched with the need to get the Frazer females out. Now. "How can he steal patrons right out from under their noses?"

"I don't know but he put two guys in a limo out front less than an hour ago." Emmett paused his game of toss and catch, snagging the token out of midair. "You know what they're doing?"

"Who?" He followed Emmett's gaze past Jayne. "Sonia?"

"And her golf dude." Pocketing the token, he paced around to Harrison's other side, lowering his voice even further as he walked by. "They're counting cards."

"You're yanking my chain." He squinted at the pair, trying to see something virtually impossible to detect. Or maybe it only seemed impossible to him since he didn't know squat about blackjack. "How the hell could you know that?"

"Strong hunch since your guy just hit on seventeen sixty seconds after he joined the game."

"That's a sign?"

"I'm sure security will be taking a look at the play." He jingled the tokens in his pocket and paced around to Harrison's other side. "You and I have the advantage of knowing the pair of them are probably working as a team, whereas security won't know that. Your ex-girlfriend is some kind of math whiz?"

"She got a degree from Caltech." She'd told him she'd taken the scholarship as a means of getting a great education but she'd never loved the work. Now, as he watched her more closely, he began to understand what Emmett was talking about. Sonia had been sitting there long enough to know what cards had turned up, and a quick math mind would help her calculate the odds of what cards would turn up next.

Information she'd somehow shared with Trevor.

The guy in charge of the casino at the Masters Inn had told Harrison the same thing about Sonia and Trevor—they hadn't come in together. Had they been working casinos all over the Caribbean?

"There you go." Emmett pulled out a paper from his wallet and passed it to him. "Some of the geeks in universities like that hit up the casinos to apply their math knowledge in recreational ways on the weekends. That's the limo's plate number, by the way."

Pocketing the information, Harrison thought through Emmett's idea. That Sonia and Trevor were pulling a scam.

"But she made a fortune in her line of work. So did he, for that matter. Why walk away from a good, legitimate gig to rip off casinos on a—" he clammed up as a waitress walked by "—small-time basis?"

"Doesn't look small-time to me." Emmett withdrew another coin and spun it around the back of his hand in a mighty damn dexterous move. "Did you see how much he cleared with that one bet?"

And sure enough, Trevor was taking his chips and walking away to another table.

"You need to get Rita and Jayne out of here." Harrison trusted Emmett to protect them, but the guy's sharp take on the blackjack game made him wonder where he came by his knowledge of the con-artist scheme.

And the way he'd flipped that token over the back of his hand a minute ago struck Harrison as a move bordering on sleight of hand. Not that he planned to go there now when he needed Emmett's help, but Emmett didn't add up as your average Wall Street magnate even if his background check had shown a successful run in the New York business world.

"What are you going to do about your other friends?" Emmett went still. "Oh shit."

Harrison spotted casino security on the move the same time Emmett did. Two people in dark blue jackets—one man and one woman—moved toward the blackjack tables.

And Rita and Jayne.

Emmett went into action without another word, descending on the redheads while Harrison prepared to resurrect his special agent status long enough to have a heart-to-heart with a couple of treacherous ex-friends.

"WOULD YOU LADIES please come with me?"

Rita stiffened at the polite request from the casino security lady with cool gray eyes and no-nonsense shoes. The Frazer women had been cornered by enough casino personnel in their mother's dark days of gambling to know you didn't mess with these people. They weren't cops and they weren't bound by the same rules as law enforcement.

"We were just leaving." Rita spoke the words in the same breath as Harrison's ex-girlfriend who sat beside them.

"These two are with me." Emmett pulled both her and Jayne aside as the security lady repeated her request for them to come with her.

"Ouch." Jayne seemed to be protesting Emmett's aggressive grip on them as he moved them toward the door, but Rita's eyes were glued to Harrison's ex and the other guy casino security seemed interested in.

A guy she recognized from a photo on Harrison's PDA.

"I'd like to speak with these two myself, ma'am." Harrison stepped between Rita and the security guard, flashing some kind of identification at the woman while gesturing to Sonia and the guy—Trevor, she remembered.

"Come on," Emmett growled in her ear, making her realize her feet had slowed.

"What's he doing?" Worry for Harrison made her hesitant to go. Hadn't she said she wanted to help him? That she'd make a hell of a partner? "I can't leave him. What if they—"

"Out." Emmett proved incredibly strong since he muscled her and her sister through the door despite Rita's protests and Jayne's noisy outrage at being manhandled. "The best way to help him is to stay out of his way."

Emmett steered them all across the street toward a shiny black Jeep.

But Rita couldn't stop thinking about the short guy with no neck who'd followed Sonia into the club when she'd first come into the place. Rita and Harrison had caught up to Sonia quickly enough in the casino, but No Neck had vanished into thin air. What if he lurked in a dark corner somewhere, waiting to get Harrison alone?

Or what if Miss Perfect Sonia turned pleading eyes on Harrison to help her out of trouble? Or take her back. Rita hated it that she thought about something so petty, but damn it, she wasn't ready to say goodbye to the best fling of her whole life just yet. And she didn't trust Miss Perfect as far as she could boot the woman's scrawny butt.

As soon as Emmett relaxed his grip on the other side of the street, Rita backed up a step, closer to her sister in the blazing afternoon sun.

"You've got to dance the show tonight. No mess-ups, okay?" Rita hissed the words in Jayne's ear as she gauged the traffic on the street to go back to the casino. "Stick with Emmett."

"What are you—" Jayne's words were interrupted by an engine revving.

Rita darted into the road, already stepping forward when the sleek little Mercedes they'd seen earlier nosed out into the street and lurched forward with an abrupt punch of the gas.

Right toward her and Jayne.

With split-second thinking, Rita trusted her sister's quick reflexes and Emmett's protection to save Jayne while Rita leaped in the other direction. Toward the casino. Toward Harrison.

Tires squealed as the Mercedes screamed by, missing them both then swerving hard to avoid a bicyclist.

Landing half sprawled on the hood of a white taxicab, Rita disregarded the litany of curses shouted by the driver as she picked herself up off the warm metal fender. Ignoring Emmett's shout on the other side of the street, Rita counted on Jayne to get Emmett into the Jeep so she wouldn't miss her performance tonight. Rita focused on finding Harrison before he got caught by a sneak attack. She might not be a trained agent, but she knew a thing or two about holding her own in a street fight. Protecting Jayne from lecherous old men in their homeless shelter long ago had given her an excellent education in fighting dirty to even the odds.

And she planned to pull out all the stops to give Harrison the backup he'd never ask for. Swiping a small trail of blood dripping at the corner of her mouth where she'd cut it on the taxicab's antenna, she straightened her skirt and slipped down the alley between the seafood restaurant and the casino.

There had to be a back entrance to the building. A way to sneak past the security guards who'd thought she was somehow involved in whatever games Harrison's ex was playing with the casino. High heels clicking down the cobblestones of the narrow alley, she rounded the corner to the back of the building to find No Neck waiting.

Gun leveled at her midsection.

"What do you know?" The little bull of a man smiled as he rose up on his toes in the universal gesture of males with a serious Napoleon complex. "Looks like my lucky day."

CHAPTER FOURTEEN

HARRISON WANTED TO concentrate on the fairy tales his former friend and girlfriend were spinning for him in a locked, humid back room of Golddiggers. But he kept thinking about Rita and wondering if Emmett had managed to return her to the *Venus* safely. If no man could hold onto one Frazer female, how the hell was the guy going to hang onto two?

Harrison should have never allowed Rita to stay at the casino today. A stupid mistake that could have been downright dangerous if what Trevor and Sonia were saying proved true.

"So you're trying to tell me you're counting cards because Yurek is forcing you to cheat as many casinos as possible?" He'd wrangled a private room for the purposes of his interrogation, but he wouldn't be surprised if their conversation was being taped anyway. The security guards hadn't been too keen on turning over the pair who'd cost them a hefty sum.

"Yurek caught me scamming him when I took that cruise a couple of weeks ago," Sonia explained for the second time, the dark circles under her eyes more evident in the bright lighting of the small room containing a conference table and a few mismatched office chairs. She clenched her hands in a tight knot as she cast a wary glance up at Trevor, who stood against one wall. "I only did it to get back at him for luring some friends of mine into off-site poker games where they lost huge amounts of money. I sent a few wealthy customers his way since he's been good about recommending my business."

"What do you mean you sent customers his way?" Harrison couldn't disguise his impatience, an emotion he rarely experienced while doing the work he enjoyed. But he resented that Sonia and Trevor's dangerous games had touched Rita. "What exactly does he do?"

"I *thought* he just set up recreational card games for people who like that sort of thing." Sonia shrugged, her careless gesture striking him as snobbish. "He's been doing business with Shine On for years over the phone even though I've never met him in person. But he'd always been friendly and when I happened to meet a client at the jewelry store who liked expensive travel and the thrill of betting, I'd mention Yurek's games as a favor to them and to Yurek, too."

"Real healthy networking, Sonia." He wasn't sure he wanted to know what sorts of kickbacks Yurek was giving her for the favor.

Trevor stepped away from his spot against the wall, his normally crisp, J.Crew-style clothes slightly rumpled. His dark blond hair was overgrown and his restless movements seemed a far cry from the laid-back golf pro Harrison knew.

"She didn't know what a crook the guy was." Trevor's warning glare shouldn't have tweaked Harrison's conscience since he hadn't been the one to walk off with thirty grand that didn't belong to him, but it did.

"Once a few of her customers started losing big bucks to him she took that cruise to settle the score."

This was the part where Harrison's mind had wandered off thinking about Rita the first time he'd listened to Sonia's tale. He sat forward in his chair now, forcing himself to pay better attention this time. He'd call Emmett in a minute to make sure they got back to the *Venus* without incident.

"And she did this how, exactly?" He looked back and forth between the two of them trying not to let old grudges taint their stories. No matter what they'd done to him, they deserved to tell their side if they'd gotten mixed up in something too big for them to handle.

Sonia cleared her throat and squeezed Trevor's hand. A telling gesture.

Except Trevor didn't squeeze back. Far more telling. Maybe Sonia's card-counting scheme had been more than Trevor was ready for when he stepped into the shoes of Significant Other.

"I thought I'd give him a taste of his own medicine by getting involved in a few of the games he sponsors and taking his dealers deep." She gave him a half smile, a wry glint in her green eyes. "Sometimes a woman just gets fed up with a man who takes advantage of her."

The jab was well placed but Harrison refused to feel guilty about what had happened between them anymore. She'd repaid him in spades for his lack of attention.

Leaning back in his chair, Harrison realized her defection didn't even hurt anymore. Meeting Rita had effectively cured him of thoughts of any other woman.

"You counted cards at his illegal tables and he caught you. And you used my money to do it." Money earmarked for his father's astronomical rehab bills.

His parents' insurance plan had been sketchy at best, a casualty of their focus on getting Masters Inn up and running and not bothering to update an old plan they'd carried over from their days as struggling, self-employed business people.

"I recouped ten times what I borrowed from the store accounts in winnings," she retorted, crossing her legs and swinging her foot in a quick, agitated rhythm. "And I planned to give it back. But when Yurek got wind of it through his security staff, he sent some men to threaten me. Threaten my family."

Trevor put a hand on her shoulder. Comforting her silently while she ducked her head.

"The bastard had a couple of guys pay a visit to her mother in Naples." Trevor scrubbed a hand through his hair. "Didn't hurt her, but they took a few things from the house to show Sonia how easy it would be to…mess with them."

Harrison couldn't deny a twinge of empathy. If anyone went near his folks, he'd go ballistic. Still…

"Why not call the police? Why did she call you and coerce you into lifting more money from the Inn? From my folks?"

"These guys weren't playing around, Harry. Somebody's been watching her since they caught her." Trevor's hand slid away from Sonia, his stance straightening as he faced Harrison. "They forced her to make back the money she cheated them out of by ripping off the casinos the same way she'd played Yurek's dealers.

They let her make one call with a gun to her ribs so she could get together enough cash to stake her bets, only I refused to wire her the money. I flew out that night to figure out what the hell was going on for myself."

"And they're watching you, too?" Harrison remembered the squat guy who'd followed Sonia into Gold-diggers. There was a decent chance they were telling him the truth.

"We've been 'guests' of Yurek's on one of his boats even though neither of us have ever laid eyes on the guy. His people are never far behind her when she goes anywhere. They only let me tag along because it's easier for two people to run a scam than one." Trevor looked toward the room's only high window. "As it is, I don't know how you're going to get us out of here without them seeing. There's no way they'll let you just walk away with us."

Trevor's strained expression seemed to amplify the warning, making Harrison all the more edgy about Rita's safe return to the *Venus*.

"How much backup muscle do you think they had tailing you today?" He could call casino security for help getting Sonia and Trevor out of the building and back to the States where he could sort out the mess with the help of the FBI.

"At least two guys, maybe three."

Sonia leaned between them. "Don't forget they have at least one person working inside the casino to steal business, too." She shoved a strand of hair out of her eyes, her face pink from the heat. "You'd appreciate their industriousness, Harrison. They plant a few gamblers inside the casino to pull aside high rollers for

Yurek's games while I'm inside counting cards to pick the house's pocket."

He ignored the jab at his work ethic, ignored whatever strange relationship dynamics were at work between her and Trevor, and thought about getting the hell out of here.

A rap at the door shattered all hope of focus.

"Who is it?" He gestured Trevor and Sonia away from the entrance, but Trevor took up a spot on the opposite side of the door from Harrison as if to back him up.

Could he trust Trevor? Or was he looking for a way to escape?

Drawing his weapon, Harrison waited.

"Security. Open up."

He didn't recognize the voice.

"We're not finished yet," he called, suspicion gnawing at him. "I'll be up in a few minutes."

The moment of silence that followed was tense and drawn out until he heard a small yelp on the other side of the door.

And then Rita's voice.

"The little man says open the door right now." Her strong, disdainful tone didn't hide a strained note.

Someone was holding her. Threatening her. The vision of someone hurting Rita churned fear and fury through his gut.

"Then the man gets what he wants." Shoving his gun in a hidden holster at his waist, he let Trevor stay behind the door while he opened it slowly. Easily.

As if he wasn't scared as hell of finding so much as a scratch on Rita's perfect pale skin.

There she was, her jacket missing and her red skirt

rumpled where the guy who'd followed Sonia into the casino earlier currently held Rita. His beefy arm squeezed her waist while he cocked a .45 to her head.

"Sorry, Harrison." She gave him a crooked smile even though she had to be scared out of her mind.

The sight of her with a barrel pressed to her temple was enough to make a man's knees buckle. Even a stupid former FBI agent who'd had too much pride to call in for help when he sensed his small investigation of missing money was spiraling into a vast chain of crime. But he couldn't talk to her now, wouldn't say anything to give away the fact that he'd personally take on a firing squad before he let anything happen to her.

Tamping down the self-recrimination he planned to detail later, once Rita was safe and sound and back on her ship, Harrison held his hands up where her captor could see them.

"No trouble here, bud." He watched the guy walk into the room carefully, his face flushed and sweaty with exertion and the sultry Caribbean heat as he kept Rita in front of him at all times.

"Damn straight there's not going to be any trouble." He backed himself into a corner, no doubt so he could keep an eye on everyone in the room at once. "I need your two friends to come with me if you want the lady in red, you understand? They work for my boss and you're done talking to them as of now."

Behind him, Harrison could sense Trevor moving closer to Sonia. Harrison kept his eyes on the pissed-off little fat man, waiting for any opportunity.

"Great. Just great." Rita's words dripped with scorn and

she rolled her eyes even though her assailant would never be able to see her. "You're trading a white-trash seamstress for an upper-crust society babe? Yeah, that'll fly."

"What the hell did I tell you about shutting up?" The fat guy arced his arm back as if to swat her in the temple, but the movement was all the break Harrison needed to strike.

Leaping forward, he wrenched the gunman's arm back until he heard a satisfying snap of tendons. Rita spun out of the man's reach with the dancer grace she'd shown on stage that first night they met. Harrison tackled the goon, landing them both on the floor with a thud. He thrashed the gun-wielding hand until the weapon skidded free, right into Trevor's—no, Rita's—waiting hands.

Damned if she didn't shove his former buddy aside to take it, too. Apparently white-trash seamstresses could hold their own in a fight.

Mood lightening marginally, Harrison slugged the assailant into unconsciousness and pulled himself to his feet in time to see Rita holding the .45 on Sonia and Trevor as she blocked the door with her willowy frame. Her long red hair frizzed into maniacal curls in every direction and the creamy white blouse had lost a button at an eye-popping level.

He couldn't wait to get her alone on the *Venus* and touch every inch of her. Reassure himself she was still whole and strong and as mouthy as he remembered.

"So I'm dying to know," she said finally to break the awkward silence that followed the scuffle. "What excuse did they give you for robbing you blind and making for the Caribbean?"

"WE SHOULD HAVE followed your sister."

Emmett's cranky sentiment reached Jayne's ears even though she was in the shower getting ready for her performance while he stood sentinel in her bedroom just beyond the half-open door.

He hadn't stopped scowling for two hours straight after Jayne convinced him to take her back to the ship. Now, moments before the *Venus* set sail on the last leg of the journey home, Jayne turned off the water and wondered how a man could change so much in nine months that he'd be thinking about her sibling now when she stood twelve feet away and naked on the other side of a shower curtain.

"My sister could fight her way out of a Jell-O pit with one hand tied behind her back." And wouldn't Rita appreciate that little visual? Jayne couldn't squelch an evil grin. "Not that you heard it from me, or anything. But trust me, she can take care of herself."

"Harrison told me to get her out of the casino, not to let her go back in." Emmett rustled around her tiny room, doing God-only-knew what to vent his leftover anger with her.

But she knew it would have been a total waste of time to try talking Rita into leaving. She could have been a kick-ass Army chick with her "never leave anyone behind" mentality. It just wasn't in her makeup. Jayne preferred more of a pirate motto for her life with an "every woman for herself" rule. She certainly had the spoils from her battles at clearance shoe sales to prove how well that was working for her, too.

"I forced you to leave, remember?" She patted herself dry as quickly as possible since her body had become a sensual powder keg in her months of celibacy.

One wrong touch with Emmett around and she'd be halfway to orgasmic like some sort of overenthusiastic porno queen. "I was scared of getting run down by the Mercedes-driving lunatic if you left me by myself to go play hero to her."

Grouchy silence from the other room.

Lord, but how could she be panting over a man who brooded this much?

"Besides," she called into the next room as she reached for Rita's navy-blue silk bathrobe that was a lot more tame than Jayne's butt-skimming white one. "Harrison seemed to have everything in control and he strikes me as the American answer to James Bond, right?"

She peeked out of the bathroom door just to see if that got any reaction from him since she seemed to recall Emmett MacNeil harbored a small degree of hero worship for the superspy.

More silence. And then, finally, he met her eyes across the steam still wafting out of the bathroom.

"I'm sure he can hold his own, but I'd hardly compare him to Bond."

"No?" She stepped out of the bathroom slowly, not wanting to break the mood of tentative reconciliation and feeling suddenly self-conscious. "But he's an FBI agent and doesn't he own a bunch of fancy resorts or something like that? He must have a little of that debonair, rich-boy style going for him."

"No more than me." Emmett rose from his seat at the dressing table. "Damn, Jayne, you must have forgotten what my investment portfolio looks like."

The air in the room turned thick and hot the moment

he stood. Emmett's tall frame seemed to take up all the space, leaving her with no room.

But still he didn't touch her.

"Damn, Emmett, you must have forgotten what my body looks like under this robe for you to still be standing over there." She knew she shouldn't say things like that to him when he'd gone out of his way to be a gentleman, but the words rolled off her tongue before she could stop them.

"This week would have been a lot easier for me if I had forgotten." He clenched his hands into tight fists. "But I'm going to respect your wishes and prove to you I'm not just here to fall into bed with you."

"You're not?" She dragged her gaze away from the taut play of muscles under his shirt to gauge his expression. She couldn't decide if he was giving her good news or bad news.

"Hell no. Although falling into bed with you is a request I'd gladly fulfill should you ever choose to go that route."

"Duly noted." She'd have to voice her preference when the time came. Dictate when they would be together again.

And judging by the steam rolling off their hungry bodies right now, she had to think it was only a matter of time before they touched again.

"But I can't walk away from you again until I can be sure I've given this thing between us a fair shot." His hands landed on her shoulders, his touch strangely comforting in that back-of-the-eyeballs burning way he'd developed since the last time they'd dated. "I let you scare me off too soon last time."

"Me?" Up until six months ago, she'd always been The Sure Thing date, the woman most likely to wind up in a man's bed at the end of the night. "You never looked like you were shaking in your shoes when I was around. Is that why you went running to marry someone else two days after I failed to get back to you on your proposal?"

He slid his hands down her shoulders and away when more than anything she wanted him to wrap her in his arms and tell her he'd only married his wife because she needed a green card. Or because she lacked a good insurance plan.

Ignoring the clock on the wall that would only remind her it was getting close to showtime, Jayne waited for the answer she'd craved ever since she walked into the Last Chance. Emmett seemed to weigh the pros and cons of sharing anything with her, then shook his head.

"You left me hanging more than two days, Jayne. And yeah, I took it personally when you didn't get back to me. I wasn't suggesting a corporate takeover. It was a marriage proposition, for chrissake. I couldn't understand why you couldn't at least give me a yes or a no, so I figured you were just trying to be nice by dragging your feet. And I can take a hint."

"It wasn't a hint." She'd never thought about it like that, although she could see his point.

"Well, it sure looked like a tipoff to me. I took it as a sign I didn't deserve you."

Jayne waited for his words to unscramble in her brain, hoping they'd make sense to her soon, but she still didn't get it.

Or…was he saying he deserved someone better than her? She wasn't sure if she should cry or kick his ass with the pointiest shoes in her closet. She settled for playing it safe until she could be sure what he meant.

"No one deserves a nympho showgirl whose sole life ambition is to have a star on her door, but you had to admit it was fun while it lasted." Her smile stuck to her teeth just a bit, but she forced it out anyhow.

"I meant I didn't deserve a woman with such a soft touch and a big heart." He grazed the backs of his knuckles over her cheek. "I figured I'd be better off with a hard-ass like me, and Claudia was someone who could hold her own. That's why I married her on the rebound—a big mistake for both of us."

Jayne's lips worked silently before she clamped them shut, unsure what to say in the face of such a revelation. He'd seen tenderness in *her?* She was all flash and no substance. A glittering package covering up a wealth of vulnerabilities she knew damn well she never let anyone see. Not even Rita.

How would Emmett have ever spotted something so nice in her when she had spent most of their time together jumping his bones?

When a long moment passed, Emmett's hand fell away from her cheek.

"We'd better go before you miss your performance."

"Wait." She chewed her lip in thought, not ready for the moment to pass her by. She'd been unprepared for his proposal a year ago and apparently the time she'd spent being flustered had convinced Emmett she didn't care. No way would that happen again tonight. "Just so we're on the same page, I want you to know that me being quiet means I'm blown away and don't know what to think, okay? It's a rare—and some would say welcome—occasion for me to be silent, but it doesn't mean anything more than I'm a clueless twit."

She backed away into the bathroom to throw on her clothes out of Emmett's sight.

"You're not a clueless twit, but thanks for letting me know." His voice that close to her while she was na-ked—even if he couldn't see her—turned her on in a big way. "And I remember you have a lot bigger ambitions in life than the star on your door. Have you choreo-graphed any new pieces lately?"

Jayne pitched forward toward the sink as she hopped around the bathroom trying to tug on her skirt. He remem-bered that about her? Maybe they had fit in more conver-sations than she remembered in their weeks together.

"I've got a few routines I'm playing with." In secret. They didn't exactly fit the Roman Cruise Lines mold for what a musical revue should look like.

"You should roll out one of them for the perfor-mance. I bet you'd be great." As soon as she stepped out of the bathroom, he handed her the makeup bag she'd been packing on her bed.

"We'd better hurry if you want to make it on time."

Flustered, Jayne couldn't remember the last time a man had made her so tongue-tied. She was losing her hold on nine months' worth of anger with him, nine months' worth of hurt and resentment. She also happened to be losing her commitment to born-again virginity, and if she weakened tonight, she didn't know how many times a woman could actually be "born again" and still look herself in the eye in the mirror every day.

"Don't be nice to me, Emmett." She yanked her bag out of his hand and jabbed a finger in his rock-solid chest. "I'm not your ex-wife, and I like you better with a temper and a bad attitude."

"Yeah?" He smiled one of those slow, sexy grins that made her knees turn liquid right before he reached around to swat her on the butt. "Then get your rump in gear, babe, or you won't have anyone to show off those high kicks for but me tonight."

"Wise-ass." She felt much happier scowling at him, however, as she pivoted on her heel toward the door.

And with the reassurance of Emmett's strong, solid presence behind her, she could already envision the surprise dance number she'd add to the show tonight as a nod to her long-suppressed choreography skills.

What was the point in having a starring role in a performance if you couldn't occasionally put a little piece of yourself on stage?

CHAPTER FIFTEEN

RITA THANKED GOD for Harrison's cool head when they were detained by ship security that night as they tried to get back onboard the *Venus*. Apparently Harrison's run-in with foreign authorities hadn't gone unnoticed when they disembarked earlier in the day. But she wasn't much in the mood to be quizzed about her activities when *she'd* been the one held at gunpoint by a sadistic SOB who'd left a bruise on her rib cage and a scratch on her cheek from where he'd first clamped a hand over her mouth when he jumped her.

Harrison had been in close contact with his FBI headquarters since he'd made arrangements for Sonia and Trevor to be flown back to the States for questioning and for government protection while the investigation continued into the illegal gambling ring. Local police would keep No Neck in custody until other agents arrived to interrogate him about his business partners. And apparently, Harrison's friends in federal places held a lot of sway with ship security who released Harrison and Rita a half hour after the ship sailed with a terse request to keep his investigation as far away from their passengers as possible.

"That's going to be kind of tough to do considering

they've got crooked dealers on the ship staff," Rita muttered under her breath as they hauled their weary bodies toward the elevators.

The corridors were relatively quiet since most passengers were either in the dining rooms for the late seating or in the amphitheater for Jayne's show.

As they arrived at the elevators, Harrison paused. "Do you need to be backstage for the show tonight?"

"I'm going to let Jayne and Missy cover for me." She couldn't possibly work now. Not when adrenaline still pumped through her, making her legs shaky and her heart jump erratically. Besides, she'd never missed so much as five minutes of her job in the past year. "They ought to know what to do if a button comes loose, right?"

Rita figured she'd more than served her time to the entertainment department considering the dozens of costumes she'd created without so much as a dime in her pocket to show for it. Besides, her technical job description meant plowing through her assigned basket of clothes everyday. Being on site for every performance had been one task among many she'd taken on herself just to be helpful.

"A night off." He seemed to weigh that piece of information as carefully as if she'd just revealed new details in his investigation. His hand fell away from the elevator button. "That's damn welcome news."

"You probably have a lot of calls to make about your investigation." She expected that, but she braced herself anyway. They only had two days left at sea before the ship docked in Fort Lauderdale. No sense getting too attached to a man who would only be saying goodbye soon.

"I've done all I can for the night." He drew her away from the elevators as a family with three little girls dressed in matching blue dresses piled out of the lift. "I need to check in first thing tomorrow for a conference call with my former superiors, but I've got tonight free."

A wealth of implication underlied the words. Rita heard it. Felt it. Her skin practically vibrated with the need to touch him.

"Did you have anything in mind?" She didn't know how much good it did to play cool now when she'd risked her neck to check up on him this afternoon. Surely he already suspected she felt something for him beyond raw lust.

"Hell yeah, I have something in mind." The rough edged growl in his throat rumbled right through her as he took a step closer, backing her up against one wall. "I've had a crap day and I want you all to myself for as long as you're willing."

The proximity of his body clarified his purpose quite well. Rita found herself licking her lips.

"O-kay. Can it involve a night swim?" She wanted him, too, but she couldn't wait to wash the fear off of her, to dip herself in cleansing waters that would take away the gut-clenching scariness of having a cold metal barrel dig into your temple.

"Every pool onboard is bound to have at least a small audience." Frowning, he seemed to think that over. "But I'm game if you are."

"Really?" Apparently her practical temporary lover had uncharted wild depths. "An enticing thought for another time, perhaps. But the entertainers have access to the spa and gym after it closes and since I'm an honorary member, and everyone else in the show is still putting on a performance…"

A flash of heat sparked in his eyes as he pulled her back toward the elevator.

"Mercury floor, right?" He was already pushing the button.

They shared the ride up with an older couple who couldn't keep their hands off each other and Rita wondered if they weren't the only ones making plans to enjoy the ship's quietest corners. Parting ways with the other couple once they reached the locked door for the gym, Rita and Harrison pushed the door to the darkened spa shut behind them.

Harrison grabbed her before she could turn on a light. His hands found her waist in the dim interior illuminated only with a few emergency floor lights and he spun her to face him. She had a brief glimpse of his sleek, muscular silhouette outlined against a backdrop of Nautilus equipment before he lowered his head to kiss her.

The scent of sweat and Harrison and the chlorine from the hot tub in the next room filled her nostrils as he swept his tongue over the seam of her lips, urging her to give him more. His touch roamed fast and urgent under her jacket, as if he'd been waiting for this. For her.

Fears from earlier in the day melted away as she warmed to his roving hands. Her knees went liquid beneath her and she would have fallen if not for his arms steadying her. Her fingers flexed against the collar of his shirt, urging him closer as he kissed her. His lips moved with an overtly sexual, seductive rhythm. If kisses were dances, this one would be a tango. Her hips moved in blatant invitation.

"Damn." He scooped her off the floor in a Rhett Butler move that would have made the most cynical woman's heart flutter faster. "Where's the pool?"

"It's a hot tub." She wondered if he even noticed her weight as he navigated his way around rowing machines and free weight stations toward the back of the room. He carried her as easily as if he went around bench-pressing women on a regular basis. "Through the door on the left."

He kicked open the door and backed through the entryway to the spa area. Steam enveloped them, the whole room misty with damp heat wafting off the sunken tub surrounded by Mexican tiles. The bubbles had been turned off, but a light below the surface illuminated the room in a watery blue glow.

"Nice." Harrison lowered her to the ground, his hands never leaving her even after her feet touched the tiles. "Are you going to play mermaid for me?"

"I'm going to wash away the feel of No Neck's hands first and foremost." She peeled off her jacket, eager to douse herself. "But after that, I'm open to suggestion."

A shadowed expression crossed his face and she half regretted bringing it up. But then his fingers reached for the buttons on her blouse as he helped her undress.

"You're not going to remember any hands but mine after tonight, I promise." His fingers tunneled under the cotton to explore the skin beneath.

A rush of heat spread through her at the simple caress, his confidence tingling nerve endings and seriously revving her motor. His touch made her realize how badly she wanted to be naked with him, to feel the press of hard muscles and hot skin against her.

Shrugging out of her blouse, she fumbled for the skirt fastening at her hip, but he chased her hands away, claiming her whole body as his territory. A scrumptious idea that had her clenching her thighs against a jolt of longing.

Lowering her zipper one tantalizing inch at a time, he slowly unveiled the rest of her custom-made pink lingerie, a silk and lace panty that matched the bra she'd sewn in a moment of optimism that she might one day take a lover again. The imported silk was completely decadent, the merest brush of it enough to give a woman a shiver of pleasure.

"It's so soft." He ran his hands over the fabric covering her rump. "I can't tell where the silk ends and you begin."

The small part of her that had been a smidge jealous of his ex-girlfriend today now sighed contentedly at the compliment. Basking in the warmth of his absolute attention, she refused to let any old insecurities take away from the feel of steam heat and even hotter Harrison seducing her mind, body and soul.

She tugged his belt free, enjoying the play of his abs against her knuckles as she reached inside his shorts for an experimental feel. And ooh, was this man built for sex. She wriggled her hips against him, ready for more.

Whether it was her touch or her hip roll that spurred him into action she couldn't say, but Harrison started pulling clothes off with gratifying speed. His shirt landed across the room on a bench while his shorts and boxers fell to the floor and then skidded over the tiles at his kick.

She might have changed her mind about the need for

a dip in the tub to straddle him then and there but he stepped away to turn on the jets, sending the still water into a bubbling frenzy. The scent of chlorine grew stronger, reminding her she ought to ditch her best lingerie before it lost its delicate color.

"Ready?" She hooked her hand in the clasp at the front of her bra, only too happy to play the stripper for a man who seemed to enjoy watching her perform. She'd never forget the way he saved her butt on stage with his hot, steady gaze.

"Damn straight I'm ready." He sank into the tub to watch her, his arm reclining on the tiles as he leaned against one wall. "Come on in here with me and I'll show you exactly how ready."

Flicking the clasp of her bra free, she rolled her shoulders enough to make the straps curl down her arms. The cups slid away from her breasts, exposing taut nipples that ached for Harrison's touch. He watched her with blue eyes turned smoky, his gaze fastened to her body.

Encouraged, Rita spun around on the tiles, her bare feet moving easily over the floor in a solo tango. She added a little shimmy to her step, and she peered back over her shoulder just to make sure he was still watching.

"Like that?" She hooked her thumbs in the lace waistband of her panties, tugging the material upward enough to give herself a cheap thrill, the silk damp against her sex.

She gyrated around, toying with the lace band, stalking closer all the while to where Harrison sat in the hot tub. Circling around behind him, she watched him spin with her, his gaze never wavering. A completely captive audience.

Not knowing where she found her nerve, she simply danced her way toward the spa, driven by some reckless and naughty impulse she always ignored. Almost always. Now, she ground her hips in circles, lowering herself closer and closer to where he sat until she performed a private table dance for his viewing pleasure. Splaying her thighs wide, she exposed herself to him for what she thought would be just a teasing moment, but his arms snaked out of the tub to catch her. Hold her.

Warm wetness streaked off his arm to drip down her thigh where he gripped her as he rose up on his knees on the built-in bench seat. Putting his cheek right at thigh level.

A moan escaped her as he pulled her closer to plant a kiss on her inside thigh. Her heart slugged with fast, heavy beats, her skin on fire where his rough jaw grazed her soft flesh. She reached to anchor herself on his shoulder, to steady her shaky arms on his. He seemed so solid, so capable of grounding her when everything else slid out from under her feet. Her hands skimmed over the damp heat of his skin as she leaned into him, suddenly very ready for more.

Another time, Harrison would have gladly feasted his eyes on Rita's body for hours on end, relishing every lush sway of her hips until they were both crazy for each other. But this afternoon at the casino had scared the hell out of him, demolishing his store of patience where she was concerned. The need to hold her, touch her, get inside her was fierce.

He straightened enough to pull her into the water with him, careful not to let her skin brush against the tiles above the edge of the sunken tub. Her curves molded to his, their bodies slippery from the steam and water. She wound her arms around his neck in a way that made his heart clench, the gesture so sweetly at odds with the rest of this brazen woman.

He ran his hands over the sides of her breasts and down her ribs. She winced slightly, not enough to make him think he'd hurt her—only enough to make him think she'd been hurt.

"What?" Dazed with lust, he blinked fast to focus on her face. "Are you okay?"

He peered down at her body in the pale blue light reflected in the water and spied a hint of shadow on her skin a few inches below her right breast.

"It's nothing." She cupped her fingers under his chin but his attention couldn't be distracted.

"That son of a bitch hurt you." He'd left Yurek's goon in the custody of local police until the FBI could spare a couple of agents to launch a bigger investigation into Yurek's dealings in the Caribbean, but now Harrison toyed with the idea of going back to St. Maarten so he could personally take the man apart.

"Not hardly." She shook her head, wet red curls slapping lightly against her shoulder. "It would have hurt if something happened to you because I came back to the casino. I'm sorry I put us all at risk, but I worried that maybe you forgot about No Neck."

He continued to touch her under the surface of the water, his hand savoring the lean muscle of her thigh.

"If you and Emmett hadn't been there today I wouldn't have known about the card-counting scheme." His finger traced the lace waistband of her panties. "I owe you for convincing me to follow Sonia today."

For that matter, he might still be sitting in an interrogation room with the St. Maarten police if she hadn't
helped him out that morning with an alibi.

"Yeah?" She covered his hand with her own under the
water and drew his fingers lower along her hip. "Then
how about you start paying me back for all my help?"

All thoughts of gentleness and gratitude incinerated
as she guided his hand between her legs. He watched
her eyelids slowly fall shut, her spiky dark lashes
fanning out along her cheeks as she tipped her head
back. The sight of her—the feel of her—fed his senses
until fire sparked through him like a gunpowder trail and
every inch of him strained from the heat.

The bubbles churned white all around them, water
swirling in powerful streams from the jets that ringed
the tub at varying heights. The hum of the motor filled
his ears, almost as loud as the rapid-fire swish of blood
through his veins just looking at Rita, the tops of her
breasts visible above the water. Every now and then he
spotted a hint of the tight crests that made him want to
pull her into his mouth for a taste.

It was all he could do not to shove aside the little
scrap of underwear she wore and take her now. The
silky material clung to her like a second skin, but he
didn't want to take them off until he'd had the chance
to do one more thing. Wrapping an arm around her
waist—careful of the bruise on her ribs—he pulled her
into his lap and spun her around at the same time until
he cradled her rump against his erection. He'd already
scoped out the jet situation in the tub since he'd had to
move away from one threatening to put him over the
edge while Rita danced around the spa.

Now, he nudged her thighs wider as he steered her closer to the nozzle perched at just the right height to pulse over her sex. She huffed a breathy little moan as the stream of water hit her, the sound acting like a turbo boost to a libido already in overdrive.

He pushed aside her hair to nip the soft column of her throat, savoring the feel of her skin against his tongue as she whispered throaty sounds of satisfaction. He reached between her legs to spread her thighs wider, opening her to the relentless stream of water and she bucked against him with a shriek of pleasure.

The intimate press of her round little ass while she came made his eyes damn near roll back to the other side of his head. He held onto her tightly and held onto his self-control even tighter, praying for restraint until he could get inside her. Reaching for some towels off a nearby cart, he spread two on the tiles at the edge of the tub so he could lift her out of the water since prophylactics were iffy at best when exposed to chlorine. Kissing his way up her neck, he spun her around in his arms as she sagged against him.

"Come here." He wrapped her arms around his neck and lifted her with him as he rose up to sit on the towel. While she sat warm and panting on his lap he leaned over her to tug her underwear down her endless legs.

"We can go back to your room," she offered, her gaze sweeping over his makeshift haven of white terrycloth.

"You give me credit for a lot more patience than I have." He shifted her thigh so she straddled him. "I need you now, babe, but the good news is, you get to be on top."

No siren's smile could have been as wicked as her grin. She pushed him to his back so that he reclined on the bed of towels.

"You're putting me in charge?" She twirled a wet red curl around her finger and pretended to be deep in thought. "Whatever will I do to pay back the man who forced me to have sex with a hot tub jet?"

His Johnson bobbed in response, obviously full of ideas.

But Rita was already lowering her lips to trace her tongue down the length of his shaft and back up again, spiraling around the head before taking him deep in her mouth.

Payback could be a damn good thing.

Her breasts brushed his thighs as she moved, her heart-shaped rump high in the air as she leaned over him. The visual alone nearly jacked him off into the stratosphere.

And then he couldn't take the payback. He hauled her up to stretch out over top of him, lining up their bodies before he reached for the condom that had been riding around in his pocket all day like a good-luck sex talisman.

"Let me." Rita took the foil packet from his hands, her thighs swaying against his as if she heard music he didn't. With quick efficiency she rolled it over him before guiding him to her slick heat.

He gripped her hips in his hands, fingers sinking into her softness as he steadied her. Moved her over him in the rhythm his body demanded. He couldn't remember ever being so driven to take a woman, so consumed with need. She made him crazy. Hungry. Hot.

With her head thrown back and her high, full breasts swaying in time to her movements, she followed his rhythm, jutting her hips forward as he drove deep. He slid his palms up her sides to her breasts, tweaking the tight pink nipples between his fingers.

Her breath grew shallow again, her throaty mewling sounds a precursor to her last orgasm. His restraint shredded, he allowed himself to simply enjoy the tight feel of her around him, her feminine muscles starting to squeeze…

He came so hard he had to hold on to her for fear she'd fall back into the tub. Gripping her waist he kept her captive on his shaft as the surge of heat pumped through him, curling his freaking toes and crossing his damn eyeballs. His legs twitched in the aftermath as if he'd just been shot.

And hell, maybe he had been. For all he knew, Cupid had been taking target practice on his sorry ass ever since Rita Hayworth Frazer sashayed her way into his life.

"Damn."

His piss-poor excuse for words hung in their steamy haven for long minutes afterward, failing to convey the magnitude of how he felt after the best sex of his life. Hell, the best sex of his last ten lives, if he were reincarnation-oriented.

Rita just smiled that gorgeous smile of hers, the one that made him feel like a hero even when he was saying stupid things. He really ought to know better than to try talking after the earth moved.

Still, that didn't stop him from blurting the very next thing that jumped into his mind.

"Marry me, Rita."

CHAPTER SIXTEEN

EMMETT COULDN'T HAVE been more blown away by Jayne's dance number in the show that night. He'd spent enough years living in New York that he'd seen a few Broadway musicals. After he'd made something more of himself than the slick con artist his parents had raised him to be, he'd had standing seventh-row seats to whatever he wanted to see. Yet he'd never seen such a fast-paced, edgy routine that combined so many types of dance styles and yet remained quintessentially Jayne.

And she did it all while draped in feathers and rhinestones, the in-your-face sexy outfit only enhancing the cool confidence she exuded as she stalked around the stage with crisp jazz moves and slow, sensuous ballet kicks.

"Brava!" He rose to his feet when she finished, the overall performance only halfway done even though she'd completed her part for the night.

The cruise ship crowd was a little slower to acknowledge her dance, but at his enthusiastic whistles and shouts, they seemed to shake off their surprise enough to give her a rousing cheer before she hurried offstage to make way for Sammy the Somersaulter's performance before the nearly nude revue.

Would Jayne's boss be upset that she'd changed the

routine at the last minute? Emmett remembered she had long-standing creative differences with the woman in charge of the show. He planned to make sure Jayne heard nothing but encouragement tonight after she'd finally taken the plunge and tried something different. She'd grown bolder and more confident since he'd known her before, and damn but he admired that.

Returning to his seat at the end of the bar, he pilfered an orange slice from the tray of drink garnishes and waited for Jayne to shower and change while the next troupe of acrobats took the stage. Since Jayne had a tenuous relationship with the production manager, she asked him not to venture behind the scenes in deference to a rule she used to ignore when he'd first met her. But he didn't mind. She was a quick-change artist after a lifetime onstage and besides, he needed the extra time to get his head on straight for what he wanted to talk to her about tonight.

The carnival-style music filled his ears, but he didn't bother looking back toward the show now that Jayne wasn't there. He watched the bartenders flip glasses and fill drinks, missing his days at the Last Chance even though he knew he'd settled things with Claudia to the best of his ability. He'd given her the bar in the divorce, hoping she'd forgive him for his half-baked proposal and she'd seemed content with that when they'd said their goodbyes. She'd even admitted that she'd rushed into the marriage, too—for reasons she had never really spelled out.

Maybe Emmett would buy another bar someday. Right now, he needed to figure out what to say to the woman he was still crazy about.

Jayne had told him her long silence on the subject of marriage hadn't been her way of saying no. For that matter, she'd made a point of explaining her silence meant she was thinking and—sometimes—confused. He could have pounded his head against a wall to hear her say as much because ever since then he couldn't help wondering if maybe she would have eventually said yes.

Too bad he'd been so busy being defensive he hadn't really bothered to understand her. No, he'd run out and married a woman he thought he *did* understand.

Reaching for another orange slice, he didn't expect a feminine hand on his shoulder to stop him. But all of a sudden Jayne was there, behind his seat at the bar, her face scrubbed clean, her expression strained.

"Jesus, Emmett. You'll never believe it." Her rapid appearance in the back of the theater surprised him since the final act was only just leaving the stage. The shaky tone in her voice surprised him even more. "You'll never believe what the Demon Witch Danielle had to say about my dance."

Tensing, he braced himself against the inevitable desire to roar his fury at anyone who upset Jayne.

"If she said anything besides how amazing you are, she's dead wrong." Standing, he gave her his seat at the bar and waved over the bartender to order Jayne a drink.

But before he could ask what she wanted, Jayne made a mewling little sound in her throat that came dangerously close to a cry.

"Can't be she thought it was too amazing because she just fired me."

He pulled her into his arms, not sure what to say to fix something he had no control over. Waving the bartender away, Emmett kissed the top of her head and told himself he'd be the lowest life form on the food chain if he allowed himself to get turned on while holding a woman who'd just lost her livelihood.

"Can she do that?" He pulled her back to look her in the eye, figuring they'd both be safer if her hips weren't so close to his own. "This woman sounds like a temperamental nutcase since she fired somebody else this week and then gave her back her job a few days later. Maybe she'll cool down and realize what a mistake she's making."

The show ended on the stage behind them, the audience applauding the performance but not with as much enthusiasm as they'd clapped for Jayne.

"I doubt it." Sniffling, she grabbed a handful of cocktail napkins off the bar while people began to spill out of the theater toward the exits. "She's been mad at me before, but she's never threatened my job because she knows I'm the best they've got."

"Damn straight you are." He stroked a palm over her silky red hair and gave a nod to the bartender who brought Jayne a drink without being asked—looked like a seltzer water with a lime perched on the rim. "What makes her think she can still have a show without you?"

"She said my unauthorized dance tonight was the final straw." Reaching for the drink, she took a long sip then held up the glass in a silent toast to the bearded bartender who'd brought it. "She hates any choreography that isn't classic showgirl stuff or borderline stripper porn. Not that I mind the titillating routines. I've been dancing them for years because it's popular with audiences and physically challenging at the same time. But why can't I try anything else? Why let the show go stale because she can't see beyond the end of her own freaking high kick?"

"What did she mean about it being the final straw?" Emmett couldn't think about Jayne and erotic dancing in the same breath or the gentleman act would be out the porthole. "What other reason did she give you?"

He set her glass back on the bar for her when he noticed her hand quivered. Tension? Anger? He didn't know enough about her finances to understand how much the loss of the job might hurt her.

"Apparently Danielle has been asking questions about what went wrong with the show that night I wasn't onstage and she figured out Rita danced my number. That's part of the reason I'm getting booted."

Emmett tried not to remember Jayne's reason for skipping out on her show that night. The thought of her with anybody else torched his insides. Then again, if that loser blackjack dealer of hers had showed up to elope with her back on St. Kitts, Emmett would have never had this chance to fix the things he'd messed up with her before.

"You don't need her or her job, Jayne." He couldn't stand to see her swipe at her eyes with the cocktail napkin, her shoulders drooping with the weight of bad news. "You could dance anywhere with your talent."

"You know how many dancers would kill for this job?" Sniffling, she gestured toward the stage. "It may not look glamorous to you since you've probably seen shows like this in New York and Vegas, but it's good, steady work with a lot of nice perks. And Rita told me to make sure I didn't lose this gig until we had something else lined up and I haven't done anything to check out other opportunities. God, I need to make some phone calls so—"

"Stop." Emmett gripped her arms, determined not to let her run around the boat distraught and frazzled. "This isn't about your sister. This is about you."

"You don't understand." She tossed the wadded-up napkins in a bin behind the bar. "I need this paycheck. The mortgage payments on our condo require this paycheck. That is, if my mother hasn't somehow gambled it away in my absence."

"You and your mom can move in with me." He figured he had to be head-over-heels for this woman if he'd just offered to take in her mother, too. But if it meant he could have another chance with Jayne—hell, he'd give just about anything.

Jayne blinked slowly, her whole body going unusually still.

"Have you been drinking?" She leaned closer to sniff him, as if he might be rip-roaring drunk. "Do you have any idea what you're saying?"

"Of course I know what I'm saying." He knew he wanted another shot at life with a woman whose background was nearly as humble as his own, a woman who'd managed to make peace with it and come away holding her head high. Onstage and off, Jayne Frazer dazzled him. "I'm fresh out of a home, if you'll recall. And I've got a bank account stuffed with savings to buy a new one, but until right this second I didn't care about trying to find anything because my main goal has been to fix the mess I made with you the first time."

"And you think playing sugar daddy to me and my gambling mama will win me back?"

Somehow it sounded more sordid than he'd intended.

"I've been trying all week to win you back by treating you with the patience and respect I failed to show you when we first met." And he didn't give a rat's ass if the bartender, or the guy two stools down heard every word he said. He wasn't letting this opportunity slip out of his grip without pleading his case. "Why do you think I've been so determined to stay out of your bed even when your willpower faltered? It's because I want you to know that I'm not just crazy about the sexpot showgirl. I want the sweet-hearted Southern girl with the wicked sense of humor who hides underneath the feathers even more."

He knew he was making progress when she was quiet for a long moment. That meant she was thinking, right? Not necessarily plotting ways to turn him down.

Finally, without saying a word, she pulled him away from the bar at the back of the theater toward the exit. When they reached a window seat overlooking the dark sea below, she tugged his shirtsleeve, pulling him down to sit beside her in the quiet corner.

"I am not a woman to be trifled with, Emmett MacNeil. I'm in the middle of a life crisis here, so now is not the time to try and rope me into playing house with you until you get tired of me and boot me out along with the rest of the Frazer clan."

He wondered exactly how many people she considered clan for about a second before concentrating on the rest of what she'd said. A gaping hole in his heart yawned open as he realized how much he continued to miss the mark with Jayne.

"I would never mess with you like that." He'd proven

it to himself this week even if he hadn't convinced her. He'd walked away from the transparent dress. He'd ignored the urge to pull her into his lap when they were in the Jeep and he'd threatened to put his hand up her skirt. She'd even showered five feet away from him through a half-open bathroom door and he'd left her alone. The fact that he had to sit on his hands to accomplish the task hardly mattered. "And there will be no playing house since I'd never expect you to sleep with me unless you wanted to. Being apart from you these past nine months has only made me realize how much I just want to be with you. Only you."

Emmett's words echoed around in Jayne's head as she searched for hidden meanings or loopholes or anything to indicate he wasn't sincere. Yet her every instinct screamed for him, cheered for his cause, told her to hold onto him with both hands this time.

"You'd really let me sleep alone in a house we shared?" She knew Rita would never believe that a man could possibly mean such a promise, but Jayne had kept a flame of optimism alive even through the worst of times for the Frazer females. No matter that her big sister considered optimism the equivalent of fairy-tale thinking, Jayne liked to believe the best of people.

"You make the call on sleeping arrangements. Not me."

Jayne knew he'd been trying to tell her all week that she could call the shots regarding intimacy. But trust came slowly where Emmett was concerned since she didn't much care to be pushed for what he wanted. Her sister was pushy. And although Margie had mellowed as her life got more and more screwed up, she'd pushed Jayne harder than anyone in an effort to raise the most attractive, talented daughter in the state of Florida. Margie still had shelves full of trophies and sashes to show for her efforts, but all Jayne had was a flare for accessorizing with rhinestones and—up until twenty minutes ago—a dancing gig.

But now Emmett seemed to really be trying to tell her that he wanted her in his life. In his home. Whether or not sex was involved. And even—God forbid—if she towed Margie over to his place with her.

No man made those kinds of offers lightly. She threw her arms around him, wondering if she could trust this man after all. The way she'd wanted to so desperately a year ago.

"That's the nicest thing any man's ever said to me." She buried her head in his shoulder, inhaling his warmth. His strength.

And oh my, how the feel of him in her arms could supercharge her sex drive.

"Nice?" His strangled words soothed her ego, so she didn't hold back the urge to feather light kisses along his cheek. His jaw.

She'd be damned if she'd hold onto her born-again virgin status any longer with Emmett making heart-meltingly sweet offers.

"Yeah, nice." She blew on the spot she'd kissed, sending a cool stream of air across his jaw. "Sweet. Sexy without making me feel cornered."

"Uh, Jayne?" He gripped her arms even as her hands were beginning a journey down his chest.

"Mmm?"

"If you want to stick to the nice-guy route, we'd

better lay off the kissing." His jaw was stiff as he edged out the words.

"Not a chance, MacNeil." She scooted closer to him in their private window seat until her knee grazed his. She wanted to make him as crazy for her as she was for him. To force him to his feet so he could find the fastest way back to his room. Her room. For that matter, she'd gladly settle for a stairwell. "You're such a nice guy, I've decided I need you to take me to bed right now so I can show you how much I appreciate all you have to offer."

She glanced down toward his lap and licked her lips with calculated effect.

"Hot damn." He hauled her to her feet so fast her head was still spinning as Emmett's long strides carried them closer to his room through the endless ship corridors. She could feel the tension in his grip, see the tension in his shoulders.

The knowledge that he wanted her so badly fueled her steps to keep up with him. She couldn't believe she was finally going to break her born-again commitment with Emmett after he'd been the one to drive her to such desperate measures. No man seemed worth it to her after having him, although she'd tried to convince herself she'd feel differently once she was married. A stupid rationalization that would have blown up in her face the same way Emmett's brief marriage had exploded in his.

Now, reaching his cabin on the highest deck available for passenger suites, Jayne didn't care about getting fired. Didn't care about the cruel words Danielle had used to try to erode her self-esteem about a dance Jayne knew had been good. Right now, she only wanted to feel

Emmett hot and hard against her in real life instead of his recurring role in her dreams.

He pulled her inside the suite and she barely had time to take in the spacious living area dominated by a king-size bed. The drapes off the balcony were pulled closed, the lights low except for that lone recessed reading lamp the cabin stewards liked to turn on over the mattress. But that's as far as she got in her perusal of Emmett's highbrow quarters before he slanted his mouth over hers and kissed her.

Hell's bells, did he know how to kiss.

His lips moved over hers with excruciating tenderness totally at odds with his rock-hard strength pressing her back against the closed door. Her breasts ached at the contact, her hips restless, but still he took his time to kiss her as if they had all the time in the world to savor that lone intimate act. Sighing her pleasure, Jayne let her head thud back on the door, giving in to his slow, carnal kisses and subtle physical dominance that she'd missed so much.

He bent over her, shoulders curved down toward her because he was taller. His strength, his desire, surrounded her, seeming to come at her from all sides until she was completely swept away by the spicy scent, the citrusy taste, the substantial feel of Emmett. The gentle sweep of his tongue heightened the scratch of his chin and the prickly patch of trimmed hair beneath his lower lip.

She wriggled and squirmed against him, her whole body responding instantly to the rough-soft feel of the kiss. He cupped her jaw in one hand, his hard, capable hand adjusting her, fitting her to the angle he craved. His thumb slid between them to skim her bottom lip, to roll it down so that he might kiss her more deeply. Wetly.

The union of mouths became unbearably hot, igniting bursts of flame all over her skin as she imagined what it would feel like to have that expert mouth transplanted elsewhere. Her neck. Her breasts. Her belly…

A shiver coursed through her hard, awakening nerve endings and coiling through the very core of her being. She reached up to twine her arms around his neck, to anchor herself against the rising tide of dark, hot sensation churning inside. But Emmett caught her arms and pinned them to her sides. Helpless. Captive.

Ooh.

He knew things about her, sexual things, that she had never shared with any other man. For that matter, she never even knew the power of her own wicked appetites until Emmett had made her realize them. Before Emmett she had been unaware how much she would enjoy peeling off all her clothes on a nude beach and savoring the warm sun on her skin as a prelude to sex. And before Emmett she'd never allowed a man to bind her wrists or—even better—tie her legs. But she dearly enjoyed that, too.

She'd trusted him enough to try so many things with him. Why had she never realized that kind of trust revealed a depth of feeling, intimacy she'd fought so hard to hide? No wonder he'd been surprised when she turned down his proposal with silence. She'd said yes to him on so many other levels.

Now he pinned her wrists to her sides, one in each of his hands, as he kissed her at his infernal leisure. Her insubstantial green dress, the one she loved because of its erotic brush against her skin and delicate swish, became an instrument of her own torment as she twitched and writhed to get a more fulfilling feel of him. Her full breasts strained against the sheer fabric, her back arching toward him for more. The hemline fluttered gently around her knees, tickling her thighs with its flounced ruffle, making her crave the strength of Emmett's hand there instead.

Just when she thought she would scream for more, he lifted his head to stare down at her in the half light, his lean muscles silhouetted to mouthwatering effect.

"I never stopped dreaming about you." His nostrils flared, his eyes dilated. "I tried. But I couldn't. I'd think I was holding you and then you'd slip away while I was waking up."

The naked truth in his eyes inspired an answering pang in her heart. She knew their relationship still wasn't quite right, knew she needed to understand him better if she wanted it to work between them, but for right now it was enough for her just to hold him.

"I'm not going anywhere." The cool assurance in her voice made her feel smart and strong like her sister. She could do this, damn it. Her days of serial dating ended tonight.

Flexing up on her toes, she stretched to kiss him again, to lose herself in the taste of him.

With a groan he released her hands to pull off his shirt and then tunnel his way up her skirt the way he'd threatened to in the Jeep earlier. There was no finesse in the disrobing. He dragged the silky underslip and sheer overskirt up her body until he could shove the whole mass over her head and off. Her hair danced with static to follow the dress, hovering around her cheek with as much electrical charge as the rest of her.

She dove for him in her moment of freedom, her hands splaying across his chest to soak up his strength. At the same time, her enthusiastic exploration pushed him back a step, catching him off guard as she molded her hands to the angular planes of taut sinew and hot muscle. She walked him backward, his gaze hypnotized—or so she liked to think—by the sight of her garbed only in a flesh-colored body stocking she wore under her feathered outfit for dancing.

The lightweight spandex covered her curves like a swimsuit, the clear straps invisible unless the light hit her just right. He stopped the backward trek as his calves hit a wingback chair, his hands coming to life again to hook the straps of her undergarment and slide it off her shoulders as he stepped out of his shoes. Another time she might have shimmied her way out of the outfit to tempt him, but she didn't think either of them was capable of teasing at this point. Instead, she helped peel away the garment, letting it fall down her legs before she kicked it aside.

But she left her rhinestone shoes strapped to her feet, unwilling to part with the extra height that put her closer to his mouth. He stared at her a long moment, his breath rasping in and out of his lungs as loudly as her heart hammered in her ears.

"I've never had a virgin before." He unfastened his belt and trousers, unveiling something she hadn't seen in too many long, lonely months.

A thick, fully erect male member straining in her direction.

"No?" Jayne's voice wobbled on a gulp of anticipation as she reached to touch him, stroke him. "Well, don't believe everything you hear about innocent girls. I won't cry if you're not gentle."

Stepping out of his pants, he retrieved a condom out of his wallet before kicking them aside. Then he surprised her by lifting her up, skimming her body over his as he held her off the floor until he anchored her hips level with his. Reaching under her thighs, he held her as he lowered himself into the wingback and seated her on top of him, her legs thrown over his to rest on the arms of the chair.

"Oh!" The position surprised her, suddenly putting his heavy length within inches of where she wanted him most. He slid against her easily, her slick heat betraying exactly how much she wanted him.

"Are you sure you're okay with this?" Emmett caught her hair in a long rope at her neck and twisted the end around his wrist. "Because I may have left gentle back at the door. Maybe in the theater."

Her tongue swelled in her mouth, making talking impossible. Nodding, she circled the head of his shaft with one finger as he passed her the condom. Fingers shaking with nervous excitement, she fumbled the foil and rolled on the protection.

He aligned their bodies, lifting her by a fraction, placing her hands over the back of the chair so that she bent forward over him. As he pressed himself inside her, he pulled one nipple into his mouth, rolling it between his teeth until she cried out.

He edged in carefully despite his assertion he couldn't be gentle. He felt impossibly thick inside her, her whole body already quivering with the beginning tremors that would turn into toe-curling convulsions before long. He filled the places she ached the most, reminding her no other man could make her feel the things he could. No other man could touch her in the ways he did. Gathering up what little sexual fortitude she had this first time out, she levered herself up high before lowering herself back down, finding a rhythm that pleased her. Up and down she rocked against him, on him, her hands sinking off the back of the chair to grip his shoulders.

Heat built and built inside her, threatening to level her and she felt a scream build in her throat as Emmett palmed a breast in each hand, circling the crests with lazy shifts of his thumb until pleasure blinded her for one white-hot second. An orgasm jolted through her like a lightning bolt thrown from above, squeezing her insides until sweetness blossomed low in her belly with a breathless sigh.

At the same time, Emmett's whole body went rigid, as if he'd been caught by the same electric current. She wrapped her arms around him, savoring every shared heartbeat until their breathing evened out into easy sync with one another.

Head still swimming with raw feelings and uncertainty, Jayne wasn't prepared for the tender way Emmett tipped her chin up to look at him several long minutes later. The brooding look of the last few days had vanished, replaced by an expression of quiet determination.

"No pressure, Jayne, but I'm open to a visit to the ship's captain if ever the mood should strike you."

Puzzled, she couldn't imagine why Emmett would suddenly want to meet the man in charge of the *Venus*.

"I hear it's tough to get an appointment with him, but I suppose I can give it a shot."

"It's your call." Emmett raised his hands in the universal language of the Caribbean that said, "no problem." "But do you really think he'd pass up an opportunity to preside over a wedding for one of his ship's star entertainers?"

CHAPTER SEVENTEEN

MARRIAGE?

Rita broke out in a cold sweat, the condensation on her body from the hot tub flash-freezing at the new set of fears Harrison's completely unexpected proposal inspired. She envisioned herself as he must see her now—mouth hanging wide open in disbelief, her head already shaking "no" even though she honestly hadn't given any thought to his off-the-cuff suggestion.

Hiding her confusion behind a smile, she could only assume he must be joking.

"I do believe that's the best endorsement I've had of my sexual prowess in a long time." Grabbing another towel off the cart, Rita wrapped herself in terrycloth and dangled her feet in the churning, sunken tub.

She knew she wasn't the kind of woman who men lost their hearts to in a matter of days. And she'd never believed in love at first sight no matter how many times Jayne came home swearing she'd found The One. If anything, her sister's propensity to fall in love and the inevitable emotional explosions that followed only confirmed Rita's opinions about the fleeting nature of rose-colored glasses inspired by lust.

"It's actually not such a bad idea." Harrison levered

up to sit beside her on the edge of the sunken spa, dragging a towel with him to wrap negligently about his waist. "I'm crazy about you, Rita, and I've never been the kind of guy to get tied up in knots over women."

Her heart fluttered in her chest, hopeful and optimistic, even while she told herself he was probably just thinking out loud—never considering that she might take him at his word on a super-casual, post-coital proposal.

She knew better. Right?

Yet, she couldn't help but savor the moment just a little since no man had ever been crazy about her.

"I'm liking you pretty well, too, Harrison Masters." She owed him that bit of truth after what they'd just shared. Still, her growing feelings for him were too new, too fragile to trot out for discussion yet. "But I don't think you'd be making those kinds of offhanded proposals if you spent more time with the Frazer women." She remembered how many men Margie had scared off for her and Jayne. "It's easier for me to be myself when I'm not with them, but they're family, you know?"

The sound of the hot tub motor humming rumbled through the silence between them. Rita twirled her foot round and round the water, stirring circles of bubbles against the current of a nearby jet. And wasn't that the story of her life? Always swimming upstream. Fighting the current.

"I'm serious, Rita." His hand slid over her thigh— warm, gentle, and reminding her how much she already wanted him again. "When I saw you today with that bastard's gun pointed toward you—" he turned dark blue eyes on her "—I knew right then and there I wanted nothing more than to have you by my side the rest of my life. Everything else fell away in that moment—the money, the way my best friend betrayed me, the gambling ring. None of it mattered as much as holding you."

She blinked hard. Fast. His words crawled right under her skin to warm her insides and turn her cynical resolve to mush.

"I never thanked you for saving me." She'd been so scared. And if she allowed herself to think about those moments, she might throw herself into Harrison's arms forever and never look back.

But would that be fair to him when he was probably still riding an adrenaline high from wrestling a psychotic gunman to the ground to protect her? Would he one day regret his impulsiveness in proposing to her after they'd known each other for such a brief time?

"You don't need to thank me." He curled his arm around her back to toy with the wet strands of her hair. "Hell, you saved yourself by pissing off that guy and giving me a chance to grab the gun. But what I really want to know is if you're willing to give us a chance once we get back to Fort Lauderdale."

"This is all kind of…sudden for me. We haven't even known each other that long—"

"That's the strange part about all this." He turned her to face him, his hands gripping her shoulders. "I've always been a practical guy. Straightforward. Realistic. I think we're a lot alike in that way. Normally, I would never proposition a showgirl or let a first date almost turn into sex. As a rule, I'd never mix business with pleasure by dragging a girlfriend all over town to look for a missing person. And hell, I would have never dreamed that I'd propose to a woman I met less than a week ago, but I'm also smart enough to recognize someone I'd never want to lose."

Oh God. Oh God. Oh God.

Panic skittered through her belly even as she listened to the nicest things anyone had ever said to her in her whole life. He really was serious about this. He hadn't been joking. This incredible man wanted her in his life forever? She didn't even mind that he'd never suggested he loved her since—like he said—she was practical and realistic and didn't need a bunch of flowery words. But she did need rock-solid assurances. Absolute trust that he wouldn't run and trample her heart in the process the first time her mother picked his pocket or used his credit-card number to place a bet.

She was quiet for so long Harrison seemed to move on to his next round of ammunition.

"And I know you like your work on the *Venus,* but if you ever decided you'd be content to sew in Florida, I've got a vacant storefront at the Masters Inn in Naples. You'd be close to your family if you wanted to set up shop and—"

"Stop." Her heart pounded with a mixture of hope and dread at the mental picture he'd created for her. As much as she might be enticed by those visions, she never thought she was destined for that kind of happily ever after with her mother on the verge of breaking her no-gambling commitment and her sister picking up new men while trying to elope with a criminal.

"Just thought I'd put it out there." He shrugged like it was no big deal. "There are FBI offices all over the country, so if you wanted to go somewhere else, that could work, too."

"I don't know." Her body still humming with all those happy sex endorphins, Rita didn't know if she could trust the voice inside her that urged her to take a chance for once. Harrison seemed so steady—the only kind of man she'd ever pictured herself with. "We haven't even talked about how we could be together after the cruise. You're on the west coast of Florida, and I'm on the east when I'm on the mainland at all, which is rarely."

"Then we start talking. We're smart people. We could figure out something." He brushed his fingers idly over her arm, arousing a deeper hunger no amount of sex would ever fulfill. "I understand if you need more time. We can have a long engagement. But when you meet somebody so right—damn, Rita, I just want to be with you."

The thought of a long engagement made her pause. That part of the idea was practical, at least.

"I guess it wouldn't hurt to explore options for how to see each other." She was crazy for not just telling him no since she'd never have a normal life with normal expectations for love. But sitting here next to him, wrapped in the strength of his arms, she wanted to believe that anything was possible. That maybe, just maybe, a Frazer female could find true love and happiness.

She saw him smile before the sound of muffled giggles drifted to her ears.

With no other warning, Jayne burst into the spa area, her high heels sliding on the wet tiles before she caught herself on Emmett, who stepped through the door behind her.

"Ah! There you are!" Jayne squealed, face flushed with happiness. "Guess who just got engaged?"

She thrust out her hand to show off what looked to be a cherry stem tied around her left ring finger. Waggling her fingers as imperiously as if she wore a three-carat diamond, Jayne ignored the fact that Rita and Harrison were both wrapped in towels to descend on them.

"Wish me luck, big sister. I'm going to be a bride after all."

Like a bucket of ice-cold water on her dreams, Jayne's announcement brought Rita firmly back to reality. How many times had she seen her sister crash and burn for committing the kinds of rash acts Rita had just been considering? She hugged and kissed her sister and Emmett in a daze, her heart not really in the moment since seeing Jayne rush impulsively through life reminded Rita of all the reasons why it didn't pay to act on a whim.

What had she been thinking to entertain the idea of marrying a man she'd only known for a few days? She could not—would not—turn into an eccentric old lady who inspired people to cluck sympathetically when she walked by.

But as Jayne and Emmett left the spa and a long silence fell over the hot tub area, Rita realized she had no idea how to tell Harrison the way she felt. So she draped a second towel around herself as she gathered up her clothes and figured she'd better just spit out her concerns instead of letting them fester and grow bigger.

"I don't know about us seeing each other after the cruise." She didn't realize she was shaking inside until she tried standing still long enough to speak to him. Damn Jayne and her timing.

"Come on, Rita." Harrison moved closer, dark brow

furrowing. "Just because your sister can set up multiple engagements during a cruise doesn't have any bearing on you and me."

"I know Jayne and I are very different people." Major understatement. She hugged her bundle of clothes in her arms as she backed toward the women's locker rooms behind the spa area. "But maybe part of the reason we're so unalike is because I'm smart enough to learn from her mistakes."

Or so she hoped.

"But if you never take any chances of your own, how can you really call that learning?" Harrison plucked his shirt off a bench and fought his way inside it, muscles tense. "Has it ever occurred to you that by being so careful not to make mistakes you could be missing the big payoffs that can come with big risks?"

Her retreating step faltered as it occurred to her she was literally backing away from him and the tempting risk he'd offered. Since when was she scared, damn him?

"I didn't retreat today when I thought you might get cornered by one of Yurek's guys." Anger bubbling in her veins, she stood her ground to make sure he knew she took risks all the time. "And I didn't flee the scene when Jayne didn't show up to dance her routine the other night. My fear of dancing didn't slow me down then, did it?"

Harrison's big, broad body halted a step in front of her, the heat of him reminding her how recently they'd been tangled up together.

"When it comes to saving someone else's butt, you're fearless." He brushed a thumb down her cheek before his hand fell away, fisting at his side. "I think you'd risk anything to save your sister, and I'm humbled by what a gamble you were willing to take for me. But when it comes to taking a chance for *you*—a chance at love, or a shot at a career *you* want instead of a career that will allow you to watch over Jayne—I don't see you rushing to lay anything on the line. Why isn't that even an option?"

Rocking back on her heels with the force of his accusation that she was a play-it-safe coward when it came to men or fashion design, Rita couldn't begin to sift through her feelings. How could she explain her confusion and uncertainty when she normally knew exactly what direction to take with her personal life? For the first time, she wasn't sure.

But one thing was certain. Rita damn well knew she wouldn't follow in her sister's footsteps.

"I'm sorry. I just can't accept your proposal, Harrison." And pivoting on her heel, she walked away from the most tempting offer of her life.

HARRISON OBSERVED HORATIO Garcia was noticeably absent from Jayne and Emmett's quickie ceremony aboard the *Venus* the next afternoon. The outdoor nuptials on the Jupiter deck seemed to be attended by everyone else who worked on the ship, however, including the stage manager who had apparently fired Jayne the night before. The temperature had cooled down a few degrees as they sailed north toward Fort Lauderdale, giving the newlyweds mild sunny weather while the ship's electrician—a good-humored Texan who was also a chaplain—pronounced them man and wife. The marriage might not be totally legal until the paperwork was filed back on shore, but still…a wedding.

Of all the ways to sprinkle salt into a shredded

wound, seeing Emmett and Jayne get hitched today had to be the worst. Just when Harrison thought he was making headway with Rita last night, she'd shut down the second her younger sister burst into the spa to announce her good news.

His chest yawned with emptiness while cheers went up all around as the bride—wearing a pink halter dress with a headpiece of rhinestones and feathers—kissed her groom with unabashed enthusiasm. Rita withdrew a disposable camera from her purse to snap a picture, her face more strained with worry now than when she'd been held at gunpoint the day before. Harrison wondered if she'd shared any of yesterday's experience with her starry-eyed sister or if she simply kept all her problems to herself.

No, scrap that. He didn't wonder. He knew damn well Rita wouldn't have said squat about his proposal or the handful of minutes when she seemed to actually consider the offer.

"We need to talk." He moved out of his position next to Emmett as the groom's impromptu best man. Crew members flocked around the couple to offer their best wishes before returning to their posts. The captain hadn't been able to attend, but he'd given the okay for any off-duty crew members to help their former star entertainer celebrate her big day.

Harrison suspected he was trying to make nice with Emmett's bride since MacNeil had personally spent a small fortune onboard the ship during the few days he'd been part of the cruise, purchasing all his clothes, an expensive ticket and a catered wedding package.

Now, Rita looked up at him with a wary gaze, her

smile halfhearted at best as she tucked her camera partially in her purse. Had she listened to the ceremony and thought about what might have been if it had been him and Rita tying the knot today? Hell, he would have settled for Rita to even consider the option down the road.

"I've been meaning to talk to you, too." She didn't protest when he motioned her toward the rail, away from the receiving line full of waiters, cabin stewards, chefs and dancers. "Ever since Jayne sprang the big news on us, I've been running in circles trying to help her get ready."

"Did you make the headpiece?" He didn't know much about Rita's work as a seamstress since—for the days they'd been together—she apparently did most of her sewing at night when everyone else was sleeping.

"I thought she ought to have something custom made for her big day. Only Jayne would request a little showgirl sizzle in her bridal attire." Rita ran a finger along the rail around the deck, a hint of affection in her voice even as she grumbled. "I asked her to wait until we got back home so Margie could have been part of the wedding, but Jayne wanted to be able to marry him on the *Venus* as a last hurrah with her friends before she left for good."

Harrison would have preferred she ask Jayne to give her more breathing room for a personal life, but what did he know? Frustration ate away at him that Rita had backed off completely after seeing her sister's decision to forge ahead with a wedding.

But since he knew she wouldn't appreciate hearing his opinions on that matter, he changed the subject.

"You haven't heard back from your mother yet?" He

withdrew her camera from where it poked out of her purse, hoping that snapping a few wedding pictures would clear his head. He'd thought watching Jayne and Emmett get married was tough until he stood side by side with Rita again and wondered what he could have done differently yesterday.

"She left a voice mail message for us last night to say she was fine, but she neatly avoided mentioning anything about what's going on with the video poker machines and if she's in the middle of a gambling crisis." Rita mustered a smile for her sister who waved their way between hugs and kisses doled out to everyone on deck.

A band of waiters rolled in an appetizer cart full of hors d'oeuvres and champagne glasses around an ice sculpture of Cupid. Someone had frozen a few feathers in Cupid's head, making the ice statue look more like an Indian princess than a mischievous Roman cherub. Missy squealed at the sight and promptly crowned the sculpture with her rhinestone bracelet. Harrison recorded a photo of showgirl Cupid with Emmett and Jayne in the background before he turned back to Rita.

"I talked to headquarters this morning and they have reason to believe the guy behind our illegal gambling ring is headed toward southern Florida." He'd climbed the walls last night after Rita's lukewarm response to his premature talk about the future, so he was running on a few hours' sleep for his conversation with his superiors who expected him to be back to work in three days.

"You think he's following you?" Rita's expression morphed from strained to downright panicked. "Could he know who you are? Do you think your ex-girlfriend sold you out to this creep?"

"No." Gripping her shoulders, he hadn't expected the show of concern after her hasty retreat last night, and her worry for him now soothed something raw inside him. "Hell no. And I can take care of myself even if this guy does know who I am."

Some of the tension seeped out of her shoulders, her posture relaxing as the sound of champagne bottles popping signaled preparations for the wedding toast.

"Then what?" Rita peered over her shoulder for a moment before returning her gaze to him, the afternoon breeze playing havoc with her unbound hair.

"Jayne's ex-boyfriend was in the casino yesterday and by now he's got to know your connection to me." Just the idea of someone using Rita to get to him turned his blood to ice. "I'm more worried they could be targeting *you*."

JUST WHEN YOU THOUGHT a day couldn't get any worse, the sexy stud you'd turned down because you couldn't get your head together went and informed you a psycho crime lord might be stalking you.

Rita tried not to fidget during Harrison's wedding toast even though her brain churned at high speed with too many fears, worries and questions. Jayne had tied the knot after years of threatening to run off with the next man she saw. Did Emmett have the guts to stick it out with a woman who could try the patience of a saint and changed her mind about what she wanted out of life on a weekly basis?

Rita had quizzed her impulsive sibling about where she and Emmett would live, what she was going to do for work and what Emmett planned to do for a job now that he'd apparently given his bar to his ex-wife. Jayne couldn't answer a single one of Rita's questions, pissing both of them off until Rita decided the hell with logic and simply sewed her sister's headpiece.

Now, she raised her glass to the newlyweds and admitted to herself that part of the problem might be just a smidge of envy that Jayne had the guts—possibly foolishness—to try what Rita feared most. Harrison's totally unexpected proposal had caught her off guard since nobody—well, nobody but Jayne's boyfriends— proposed after a handful of days together. Granted, their days had been action-packed, their bond growing strong in a hurry thanks to the life-and-death circumstances they'd faced in St. Maarten. But she'd never expected someone as practical as Harrison—someone who freely admitted to ignoring his last girlfriend to concentrate on his work—to make such a wildly romantic suggestion.

And oh God, the memory of it still made her heart clench with the sickening fear that she might never have another chance at a lasting relationship. Another chance at love. Harrison probably had a valid point about her being a coward, but had he really given her enough reason to take such a monumental risk? Sure, the sex was phenomenal, but didn't she have the right to more assurances than that?

Polishing off her slice of wedding cake, Rita reminded herself that no mention of love had been made in Harrison's proposal. A pretty big oversight, in her estimation, and yet, she could almost appreciate his practical approach. They would be good partners, wouldn't they? She'd searched for him at the casino yesterday to prove as much.

And yet…

Fanciful Frazer blood ran through her veins no matter how much she told herself she was a sensible woman. There would always be that piece of her that actually liked a few well-placed feathers and rhinestones, damn it. And that part of her craved the assertion of undying devotion that Jayne had nabbed with Emmett.

Blinking hard, she stacked her plate on a busboy's cart and went to give her sister a hug. Rita wouldn't let anybody rain on Jayne's wedding day. Not even a cranky old-maid big sister. She didn't know if Jayne and Emmett would last two weeks, two months or two years in this marriage, but Rita thought they deserved a fighting chance and the support of friends and family. Besides, Emmett was a far cry from Horatio the ass-grabber. Maybe he could find happiness with Jayne and vice versa.

Or maybe Rita was only softening on her stance toward Emmett in some lame attempt to give herself permission to be as wild and crazy as the newlyweds.

The crowd began thinning on the Jupiter deck since the captain had only offered up a small window of time for his crew to celebrate when they had a ship full of passengers to entertain. Jayne glowed with happiness as Rita approached her at a table next to the Cupid ice sculpture.

"Congratulations, Mrs. MacNeil." She planted a kiss on her sister's cheek. "The ceremony was beautiful."

"Wasn't it the best?" Jayne glanced at Emmett who—for once—didn't retreat to the sidelines. He winked back at her as if she'd just made him the happiest man in the world. "The sky was gorgeous. The vows were perfect." She leaned close to whisper in Rita's ear. "And even Danielle showed up to see my day of triumph, the hateful old hag."

"I'm sure she'd give you your job back if you want it." Rita couldn't even imagine sailing on the *Venus* without Jayne. Their lives had been wound together in cheerful dysfunction and a united cause to protect Margie from herself for as long as Rita could remember. "Danielle just can't stand for anyone to take her by surprise or make her think she doesn't have utter authority. I'm sure she showed up today to let you know the door is open if you want to work things out."

"And wouldn't she love to see me grovel?" Jayne shook her head, a few strands of her upswept red hair tumbling loose to brush her cheek. "Not this time. I've put in enough time on the *Venus*. I'm going to see where else I can take my dancing now that I don't have to worry about money every day of the year. Emmett said Margie can always move in with us if she—you know— got into any trouble with gambling this time around."

Rita's guilty conscience cringed at the mention of money and Margie since Danielle still hadn't reimbursed Rita for the new costumes she'd made. Rita's income alone would never be enough to cover the mortgage and the expenses associated with the condo.

"You can't let a crazy mother into your house while you're a newlywed." Rita didn't know how she'd get by with Margie on her own, but she wasn't about to sabotage Jayne's new marriage by letting her take in their mom. "I know Emmett's wildly in love with you, but Margie could scare off the most devoted of men in ten days flat."

She'd only been trying to make a point, but she immediately regretted it when she spied the moment of panic in Jayne's expertly made-up eyes.

"I'm sure we'll be fine—"

"I'm kidding," she hurried to reassure her sister. "There's no way in hell Margie could have figured out how to use the video poker machines with no credit cards to her name. It's all good."

Except for the psycho crime lord following Rita to Fort Lauderdale. The lie stuck in her throat, reminding her she needed to get the hell out of this conversation before she said something stupid to mess things up for Jayne.

Emmett would protect Jayne since Harrison would no doubt fill him in. Emmett could take Jayne anywhere in the world with the money Jayne swore he'd made in the stock market before she'd met him a year ago. Maybe they'd go to New York so Jayne could finally take on Broadway—if not as a dancer, maybe as a choreographer.

"I'd better get back to work before I get fired, too." Squeezing her sister's shoulders, Rita hoped she'd been supportive enough today since her own heart seemed to be quietly breaking despite her most stern talks with herself. "I'm proud of you, Jayne. I hope you know that."

Clearly, she'd caught her sibling off guard since Jayne was uncharacteristically silent—a trait she exhibited only rarely. But Rita knew her well enough to know she was touched.

And why did that make her want to cry all the more?

Turning on her heel, Rita left the newlyweds to their celebration while she went to settle a score with Danielle and to pretend her world wasn't crashing around her ears.

CHAPTER EIGHTEEN

OF ALL THE TIMES to have her brain cells malfunction.

Jayne replayed her conversation with Rita in her mind after her wedding, wishing she could have shaken loose her tongue long enough to say something nice to the sibling who'd been there for her more times than she could count. But the moment had evaporated before she could slough off her surprise at Rita saying she was proud of her.

Jayne stood at her dressing table in the cool and cavernous backstage late that evening, slowly packing up her things from the showgirl gig she'd loved. Emmett had promised her a real honeymoon soon, understanding that tonight she had a lot of people she needed to say goodbye to, a lot of things to do before she walked away from the *Venus* forever.

Fingers tracing the outline of the aluminum-covered cardboard star Rita had given to her their first week on the ship, Jayne smiled at the wealth of glitter and sequins her sister had glued on the ornament to spell out Jayne in sparkly cursive letters that could be spotted from clear across the dressing area. The decoration had dangled from Jayne's mirror every day that she'd danced in the ship's show, a silent, showy talisman that never failed to lift her spirits. It hadn't been quite the same as having a real star on her dressing room door since Jayne shared the spot with twenty other dancers, but the homemade star reminded her how far she'd come from those dark days when Margie's gambling had been at its worst, when the only thing standing between Jayne and sexual assault at a smelly homeless shelter had been a sister who wasn't afraid to risk her own neck to deliver well-deserved ass-kickings.

Blinking away the fear of that old memory, Jayne tugged down the star and concentrated on remembering Rita's vocal eruption that had brought half the shelter into the women's bathroom to see what was going on. A bunch of hard-luck females had been equally incensed to see a dirty old man trying to take advantage of teenage Jayne in a crappy stall and the women had delivered swift vengeance before someone brought in the police.

After the near rape, Jayne held on to her sanity by clutching her femininity with both hands, refusing to hide curves and exuberance for life out of fear. Every time she reached for silk and organza, feathers and rhinestones, she gave herself a little dose of "I am Woman. Hear me roar."

She'd never stopped thumbing her nose at the guy who'd imprisoned her with his filthy hands for those few terrifying seconds before Rita arrived.

Sweeping off the rest of her dressing table, Jayne packed up her combs and brushes, makeup and hair-pieces she'd used for an assortment of shows over the year. Regret nipped as she thought about never performing again. Surely, she would own a stage again, but it would never be onboard the *Venus*. Never with her sister at her side, calling out orders, warning her to behave, smoothing over the inevitable bumps in the journey.

Smiling, she could almost hear her sister shouting now. Assuring her she'd be sorry…

Wait.

Setting down the bag stuffed full of her belongings, Jayne realized the shouting was indeed Rita yelling, not in Jayne's mind but in Danielle's office a few feet away. Jayne hurried toward the office, debating whether to wait or interrupt and try to help Rita. So she did what any sister would do. She eavesdropped.

"…I'm in no position to reimburse you for those outfits until I know whether or not corporate approves of the show." Danielle still sounded as pissed-off and on the edge as she had when she fired Jayne. "We're being visited by the Roman Cruise Lines' Entertainment Director next week and we'll let him make the call about the outfits."

"But I made those clothes on good faith," Rita argued, her voice rising even more. "Our deal didn't have a damn thing to do with the success of the show. You've been dragging your feet on this for weeks after you told me you already had approval for the payout."

Jayne struggled to process the new information as she huddled behind a dressing table near the wall to Danielle's office. Danielle hadn't paid Rita for the costumes? And Rita let her get away with that?

Damn it. Why didn't her big sister possess half as much avenging-angel attitude on her own behalf when people screwed her over as she had whenever Jayne got into trouble? If Jayne had been stiffed like that, Rita would have gone ballistic. Now that it was *her* in the hot seat, she seemed content to wait things out.

"Take it or leave it." Danielle the Dreadful's voice floated through the thin walls more softly, and Jayne could almost picture the production manager's bitchy smile.

Debating marching into the office then and there, Jayne started toward the door when she heard footsteps approaching from the other side.

"Good enough. But I'm going to need that leave I requested for the next month, whether or not you approve and I damn well will be expecting the check you owe me before I come back to the *Venus*."

If Danielle argued, Jayne didn't notice since the office door flew open as her sister suddenly stomped out, her red hair swirling around her shoulders as if it had a temper of its own.

"Hi!" Jayne flashed her brightest smile and hoped Rita wouldn't wring her neck. She deserved a free pass for eavesdropping on her wedding day, didn't she? "I was just packing up my table when I thought I heard you. Everything okay?"

Rita studied her hard. Assessing. Then she surprised Jayne completely by ignoring the eavesdropping possibility and ushering her closer to her dressing table where her packed bag waited.

"Things are fine." Rita hefted Jayne's bag over her shoulder before heading toward the supply closet where she kept her sewing supplies and fabric samples. "I just told Danielle I needed to take that leave time I've been storing up. The cruise line has been dragging their feet on renewing my contract anyway."

"Sounds great," Jayne lied, thoroughly confused why Rita wanted time off between contracts when she normally worked nonstop. Besides, if the corporate suits would be onboard next week to decide whether or not they wanted to buy the costumes Rita had apparently loaned them on a consignment basis, wouldn't she want to be present to make sure the scales tipped in her favor?

"I'm going to reevaluate our arrangements for Margie now that you're not going to be chipping in on the condo."

"But I will," she protested, certain she'd already explained to Rita that Margie could move in with her and Emmett. Hadn't she? The cruise had been a bit of a blur from being left at the altar to tying the knot with a man she hadn't seen in months. But everything would be fine.

She hoped.

"That's fine if you'd like to help down the road, but as of right now, you don't have a job, remember?" Rita tossed fabric bolts, scraps of lace, ribbon and other trimmings into a box as she spoke.

"But Emmett has tons of money. Not that I plan to mooch off him, but if we got in a pinch I'm sure he'd help us out. And either way, Margie can still move in with me, and you won't have to worry about her at all." Jayne's gaze roved over the satin theater masks on the supply closet walls, so many faces staring down at her. Judging her.

"Sure, hon, but for right now, you and Emmett don't even have a place picked out, let alone the preparations ready for moving Margie." She chunked an old-fashioned Rolodex in the box on top of everything else.

"Oh." She hadn't really given much thought to where she and Emmett would go once they docked. "Right. Um, Sis?"

"Yeah?" Rita swiped her eyes before looking Jayne's way.

Making Jayne feel like total crap for losing her job.

For getting married without any thought to how things would be tougher for Rita now. For not having one thing in her life organized—not even something really basic like a house. Hell, she didn't even know where she wanted to pursue her dancing career as a married woman.

"Are you sure you want to stay with the ship's staff now that I'll be leaving?" Rita had only taken this job to ward off the Horatio-types that Jayne seemed to attract. Funny her sister never tried to dissuade her from marrying Emmett even though he'd already screwed up one marriage with lightning speed. "You could come with me on my next gig once I get settled and it'll be just like old times."

"So I can be a seamstress?" Rita peeled her design sketches off a bulletin board in the back of the tiny room. "Now that you're well on your way to achieving your dreams, I figure it's high time I followed mine—once I figure out what they are."

"What will you do?" The thought of life without her big sister scared her. Together, they'd always been able to tackle any odds. Separate…

Jayne swallowed a bubble of panic.

"Sewing isn't so bad when you're not mending a torn-out toe or a hole in a coat. I kind of liked making all those costumes for the show. If I can scrape together some start-up cash, maybe I can—I don't know." She shrugged like it was no big deal when Jayne had the sense that this actually meant a lot to Rita. "Maybe I'll try my hand at a few other designs."

"But you're not quitting now, are you?" This seemed like an awfully rash act for Rita, while Jayne hadn't thought twice about taking big risks to get *herself* fired. She'd skipped out on a performance. Changed her whole routine without telling anyone.

Seeing her big sister packing up her box full of saved-up dreams sure made Jayne feel two inches tall and selfish to boot.

"Ha!" Rita's laugh held no humor as she taped up the cardboard container. "I definitely can't afford to do that. But maybe if I have my things with me on leave I'll be inspired to try something creative. Explore some new directions since the old ones have left me face-to-face with a dead end."

"What about Harrison?" Jayne couldn't have read that situation wrong. They were crazy about each other. "You guys looked pretty friendly when Emmett and I found you in the spa to tell you about the wedding. Are you going to be seeing him while you're back home?"

Shoving past her to push the heavy box out the door, Rita shook her head.

"Not with us living on two different coasts and me not even sure where I'm going career-wise. You and Emmett have known each other for a long time, but Harrison and I…" She flicked off the light, walking away from the supply closet where no one had made a star for her door—not even a homemade job like Rita had fashioned for her. "It just wouldn't be very practical."

And that was a concern…why?

God, Jayne wished someone could convince her sister to take a few chances. Unwilling to venture deeper into a topic her sister obviously didn't want to discuss, Jayne debated how she could help Rita and Harrison find as much happiness as she hoped to find with Emmett. For now, however, she simply settled for helping Rita push her box down the hallway as they left behind the glitter and glitz of their floating home away from home.

"YOU WANT TO go where?"

Harrison hailed a cab outside the debarkation area for the *Venus* the next morning while Rita stared at him like he'd just busted her for possession.

"I'm taking you to your mother's house," he repeated, waving over a yellow taxi and motioning for the guy to pop the trunk. "No arguments allowed, because if I don't ride to your house with you, I'll only be waiting on your doorstep when you get there."

He hefted her bags and the box into the cab along with his suitcase, then held the door for her. Waiting.

She stared back at him, unmoving on the sidewalk crowded with ship passengers meeting their rides and making calls on their cell phones now that their ten days at sea were over. Vaguely Harrison wondered if any of them had a trip even half as memorable as his had been.

Rita looked so damn good it hurt. Too bad her gaze slid from him to the car and back again as if she wasn't sure to trust him. The look tore him up inside since he knew it was based solely on his premature need to talk about a future between them.

Scavenging for a little more sensitivity, he remembered she'd left him a message late the night before when he'd been going over new evidence on an illegal gambling ring at work in the Caribbean.

"This will give us a chance to talk anyway." Reaching for her hand, he pulled her toward the taxi and the driver who was starting to get antsy. "Didn't your message say you wanted to talk to me last night?"

Giving the cabbie the address, Harrison settled in the seat beside her, his knee hovering within touching distance of hers. He'd give anything to go back in time and put a muzzle on himself before uttering the stupid words that had put a wall up between them faster than a champion mason. What the hell had happened to society to make women bolt at the mere mention of marriage?

"Actually, I wanted to talk to you about what happened with us the other night." Rita rolled down her window, allowing the mild southern Florida breeze to whip through the back seat as their driver headed toward the highway.

"I'm all ears." He told himself not to get too hopeful, but he couldn't help but wonder if she'd changed her mind.

"I'm sorry if I didn't say that I was—am—extremely flattered because I was just so taken off guard." She smoothed a muted green skirt over her knees, her fingers slowing each time they came to one of the miniature daisies embroidered around the hem. "I didn't really consider the possibility of…forever because it seemed so out of left field when we've known each other such a short time."

"I know." Harrison had been thinking over his proposal almost nonstop since he'd put it out there in a moment of sex-inspired optimism. But damn it, he knew that patience paid off with a woman like Rita—had learned that lesson their very first night together when he'd been forced to wait. "And maybe I was too hasty to make you all mine, but I hope you can credit that to a boatload of appeal on your part."

She cast him a skeptical glance before he forged ahead, pressing any advantage he could.

"Look, I know I may have gotten ahead of myself the other night, but why does that mean we have to put an end to the whole thing? What's to stop us from getting to know each other more slowly?"

He cracked his window, too, needing the fresh air and a fresh perspective. And hell, if there was any inspiration floating around outside, he'd be damn grateful for it.

"I don't know." She peered out the window for a moment where palm trees and strip malls whipped by in a blur as they sped north on the interstate. She anchored a handful of hair at the back of her head to keep the red strands from blowing into her face. "What did you have in mind?"

"I'm going to be spending some time around Fort Lauderdale anyhow until we nab Yurek and anyone else working with him." He hadn't mentioned the full-scale surveillance he'd planned for her once she got home, but then he'd only just realized this morning that she was taking leave from the *Venus* so he hadn't had much time to set things up. "Why can't we get to know each other better over the next few weeks?"

She was quiet for so long Harrison wondered if she hoped to be saved from comment by arriving at her house since the cab pulled off the highway. But finally, she turned to look at him, her yellow blouse sliding to the edge of her shoulder and giving him a mouthwatering view of her skin.

"I am not a coward." Her level gaze told him his accusation two nights ago had gnawed hard at her pride.

"I didn't mean to suggest you were." Okay, maybe he had, a little. But her cutting and running had slugged him hard. "Does that mean you'll give us a chance? On a slow basis only?"

"If you're going to be in town anyway," she shrugged, exposing all the more shoulder, "what's the harm?"

Yes.

She might not be cutting him much slack on the dating suggestion, but at least she seemed willing to give it another try. And Harrison didn't have any intention of squandering a second chance.

"And this time I'll let you set the pace because I obviously don't know jack about timing with women." He'd sit back and let Rita call the shots this time. A new approach for him, but what did he have to lose? "Sonia wanted to box my ears for taking too damn long to see her as wife material. You practically ran screaming out of the spa when I suggested we think about long-term. So I'm going to let you decide where to take things now."

At her clipped nod he realized they seemed to be closing in on her house. Not the best area of town, he noted, peering out the window at the overgrown lawns and squat housing that could benefit from updating. A small residential building lumbered at the end of a block situated behind a grocery store near the highway. The noise had to be constant here, the proximity to a dilapidated strip plaza raising the possibility of crime. He hadn't expected such a hard-luck address for the Frazer women since both Rita and Jayne must earn decent livings, even though the cruise industry wasn't noted for high wages. And they shared this place, right? That doubled their financial muscle.

"It's right here, sir," Rita called to the cabbie through the Plexiglas screen as she fished for her wallet in her purse.

"I've got it." Harrison beat her to it, having already

agreed on a flat fee with the cabdriver while they'd been waiting for Rita to get in the car. "I figure you deserve a free ride since I gave you company you didn't want."

"Thank you, but it's not that I didn't want company." Rita put her wallet away, glancing around her street as though the place put her on edge, too. "It's just that I knew we were heading to my house and my mother... Well, put it this way. Brace yourself."

With no further warning, she bolted from the cab the second the driver slid the vehicle into park. Leaving Harrison more than a little uneasy.

Brace youself?

Hell, he'd needed to brace himself to meet Jayne and Rita hadn't warned him her sister was hell-on-wheels with her man-eater smile and refusal to see how her behavior put an unfair burden on her sister. What would the mother be like who even made Rita jumpy?

Floating the cabby a few extra bucks to lug the bags, Harrison followed Rita's quick footsteps across a broken sidewalk over the brown lawn toward the building that looked to be a fourplex. There were no cars in the parking area, not really a surprise since most people worked during the day, although a teenager pushed one toddler over the burnt grass in a faded plastic car while she hefted another one on her hip.

Rita waved at the teenager who wasn't a sitter but— holy crap—a mother, judging by Rita's promise to drop by later with treats for the woman's daughters.

"Does your mother know you're taking leave this week?" Harrison forced himself into special agent mode, knowing he needed to get his head out of the ways he'd messed up with Rita so he could figure out how to protect her until he finished sewing up his case. He just hoped she wouldn't change her mind about taking it slow once she found out he wasn't letting her out of his sight until he had her house thoroughly protected from Seva Yurek and his goons just in case Rita was a target.

"No." Rita tugged a key out of her bag and inserted it in a patio entrance on the ground level. "She also doesn't know about Jayne's marriage so mum's the word on that one, okay? Jayne said she and Emmett would meet me here."

Frazer women liked their surprises, apparently. Harrison filed away the knowledge as he scoped out the condo while Rita called out her mother's name.

Not that anyone would be able to hear it over the orchestra music blaring from the stereo. A sultry-voiced soprano belted out a tune over top of a rising violin crescendo, the music vibrating the thin wooden shelves where the stereo had been nestled along with a record collection that spilled onto three shelves and the floor.

"Mom?" Rita set her purse down on a small kitchen table practically hugging the patio door before stalking deeper into the dim town house with shades pulled over all the windows except for the glass entryway.

A hint of incense wafted through the place along with a light scent of cigarette smoke even though he'd never seen Rita or Jayne take a puff. Fashion magazines lay open on a couch, an empty wineglass perched on a coffee table nearby, as if the magazine reader had been overcome with the urge to go to bed or do something else and had simply left everything wherever it fell.

The furnishings were simple but sturdy with hints of

Rita and Jayne's personalities in an occasional leopard-print hassock or a red sequined pillow. Black-and-white photographs covered the walls, all starring one redhead or another in ballerina costumes, tap shoes or sequins. Usually one auburn-haired beauty would be smiling and preening for the camera while the other scowled back, vaguely menacing despite her slender size and be-ribboned ponytail.

"Is that you, baby?" A slightly raspy southern drawl drifted down the stairway at the back of the two-floor home.

Harrison observed the tight set to Rita's jaw as she paced closer to the stairs, her shoulders tense.

"Yes, and I have a gentleman caller, so could you make sure to wear real clothes please?"

A girlish squeal at odds with the raspy throat floated down the stairs.

"A gentleman for my Rita?"

Harrison could hear the floorboards squeak overhead as the woman hurried to the stairs.

"Actually a law-enforcement gentleman, Mom. He has a few questions he needs to ask you and then he'll be on his way." Rita shook her head as her mother descended the stairs. "A smoking jacket and pajama pants do not qualify as real clothes. And for crying out loud will you quit with the smoking already before you have no voice left at all? I've been in here five minutes and the smoke has already penetrated through my whole head of hair, and that's saying something."

Harrison got his first look at Margie Frazer as she turned the corner at the landing and swept into the room. A slighter version of Jayne and Rita, their mother wore impeccable stage makeup that sat a bit heavily around her crow's feet, but otherwise showed a deft touch on a woman who couldn't have been much past fifty. Her hair was brighter than either of her daughters, possibly the result of hair color, and where Rita and Jayne both had shoulder-length curls, Margie had a straight, chin-length bob with bangs brushed straight down to her eyebrows.

But the most interesting facet of her appearance had to be the belted crimson smoking jacket over black satin pants. She wore black satin high heels trimmed in fur that looked like something a Playmate centerfold might have worn fifty years ago.

"Law enforcement?" Margie peered from Harrison to her daughter and back again, not bothering to squander any maternal affection on Rita as she passed by her even though Rita had told him they hadn't seen one another for months. "How clever of you to finally win one over to our side, darling. Introduce us, will you?"

She was already positioned face-to-face with him, but apparently this was a woman who preferred to stand on ceremony. Rita huffed a noisy sigh from across the room as she went around the house systematically opening windows.

"Mom, this is Harrison Masters. Harrison, the crazy lady in the smoking jacket is my mother, Margie Anita Frazer, headliner at the Broken Palm Lounge twice a week."

"The bar used to have a branch in Palm Beach, you know." Margie extended her hand as if waiting for it to be kissed.

Harrison squeezed.

"Pleasure to meet you, ma'am, and I'm sorry to stop

by unannounced but I had a few concerns about Rita's safety and I wanted to check out the security in her building."

"Rita?" Margie waved away his concern before tucking her manicured hand into her quilted pocket. "That one knows how to take care of herself, trust me. And don't you worry about dropping in, young man, my girls do it all the time."

"It's our home, Mom," Rita reminded her, silhouetted enticingly in front of a window she'd opened wide, skirt plastered to her thighs as a mild breeze wafted inside. "And don't think I didn't notice that you completely cleared out the cash drawer. That was for emergencies, remember?"

Harrison pulled his eyes away from the view with an effort, eager to impress upon her mother the importance of keeping the condo safe. If he could win her over, he'd obviously be a lot closer to his goal of sticking by Rita until his case was closed.

While Margie made noncommittal humming sounds to Rita's various concerns, Margie kept her eyes on him.

"You haven't seen anyone new or unusual around the place this week, have you, Ms. Frazer?" Harrison spotted ten different ways the building could be breached without even looking closely. If one of Yurek's lackeys came looking for Rita, it wouldn't be hard to get to her here.

"Other than you?" Margie batted his arm before shouting over her shoulder to Rita for a glass of lemonade for him. Turning back to Harrison, the older woman smiled broadly. "Actually, there has been another man who's been asking for Rita this week. First time that's ever happened to you instead of Jayne, isn't it, baby girl?"

A bad feeling crept into his veins, a premonition that left a sick feeling in his gut.

"Who was it?" Rita called from behind the kitchen counter, her body going still for the first time since she'd set foot in the place. "Did you recognize him?"

Margie seemed to savor the secret, letting the moment spin out until Harrison wanted to shake her. And then finally, she smiled.

"I've never seen him before, but he seemed eager to see you again, my angel." She hugged her arms, her red nails gliding over the scarlet satin. "But I don't think he was from around here since he had the most charming accent. Russian, maybe?"

Oh shit.

Harrison wished he were closer to Rita to lend her an arm. Some support. The assurance he wouldn't let this scumbag Yurek near her.

"Margie, this is important." He took his time to make eye contact even though he had the sense this woman rarely troubled herself with reality. He'd known her for two minutes and had learned a lifetime's worth of information about her daughter in the process. No wonder Rita was so damned self-sufficient. "What exactly did he say?"

Rita slipped away from the kitchen counter to listen and Harrison resisted the urge to touch her since he wanted to let her make the call on their relationship.

But man, did it suck holding back.

"I guess he stopped by around seven-thirty last night asking for Rita, so I invited him in for some lemonade."

Rita's low gasp echoed his thoughts. What the hell was Margie thinking to let total strangers inside? Screw good intentions. He reached for Rita's hand to give it a squeeze for his own sake as much as hers.

"He came inside?" Rita's hand trembled lightly within his.

"No, he said he had a lot of things to do and he wouldn't want to impose. Very nice manners, you know."

When no one seemed overly impressed with the social graces of a guy who could easily be a hit man, Margie forged ahead.

"But before he left I mentioned my act at the Broken Palm which led to a little chat about our favorite casinos and all the things Rita doesn't like me to talk about." She reached out to lay a finger atop Rita's nose as if Rita was five years old. "Anyway, he told me he knows a gentleman who runs a very upscale card game he thought I might enjoy, but of course I told him I never venture down that path anymore."

She held her head high, a suffering martyr for the loss of her favored pastime. Damn, but she was a piece of work. And not once had she bothered to ask why Harrison wanted to check out security around the place or if he thought her visitor might pose a threat.

Determined to protect Rita with or without any help from her family, Harrison excused himself to call his office and set up a plan to guard Rita 24/7. Yurek was obviously on the move in Fort Lauderdale, putting both Margie and Rita in his crosshairs.

CHAPTER NINETEEN

TWO DAYS LATER, Rita told herself she wasn't a coward for retreating to her bedroom while Harrison worked with a private security company and local police to protect the Frazer residence. Truly, she escaped upstairs to go over the piles of mail and bills from the last two months that her mother never thought to forward. Rita's need for privacy had everything to do with getting her personal finances in order and could *not* be attributed to Harrison's continued presence in her home.

He'd slept on the couch, proving a resolute gentleman and true to his word about letting her set the pace. But he was leaving tomorrow once the condo met his specs for security. He had a case in progress and a job to report to with the FBI after his yearlong absence. He seemed utterly at home with his work already, so much so that Rita couldn't believe she'd ever envisioned him as a business owner.

But she wasn't being a coward to dance around the issue of "seeing each other" that she'd agreed to in the cab ride to her house. She hadn't been prepared for having Harrison move in with her for a couple of days. Frankly, sleeping in the same house with a man made it difficult to go back to dating and his intensive involvement with the gambling ring case didn't leave much free time for dating. Therefore, she remained in a holding pattern where he was concerned and she concentrated on getting her life together instead, seeking out her own dreams instead of supporting Jayne in hers.

And the more she thought about it, the more she liked the idea of designing. She could have some measure of independence and still fulfill the creative itch that scratched her in a different way than the rest of the family. But instead of making exotic show costumes, she could create clothes women really wanted to wear— everyday clothes to incorporate a little bit of glitz and glamour with something practical, too.

While she sketched out drawings for possible garments, Harrison seemed to be fitting in just fine around the Frazer household. She'd been disconcerted by how politely he'd worked his way around her mother with a minimum of fuss, allowing Margie to maintain her illusions of torch-singer grandeur while quickly extracting any information he'd needed. All without getting frustrated. She could take a page from his book to help her deal with her mother.

Ensconced in an old leather chair, Rita opened another envelope from a company who claimed her credit-card account was overdue, even though she didn't own a credit card. Apparently she did now, however, and judging by the bill, she'd been dropping a lot of cash at Neiman Marcus and…crap…Vernon's Electronics. Rita would bet solid odds—no, take that back since she wasn't a gambler—that Vernon's Electronics would be the company behind video poker. Picking up the telephone, she figured she could wait five minutes to cancel the credit card until she found out if her suspicions about video poker were correct.

"Hello?" A strange man barked into the phone before she even dialed the number for Vernon's. "Can you hang up, please? We're doing some work on the line to keep you safe."

Settling the receiver back in the cradle, Rita reminded herself to be grateful for police protection, even if it robbed her privacy and invaded her whole life. For that matter, maybe she shouldn't be making phone calls to gambling establishments that skirted the law since she could unwittingly point the investigation in the wrong direction.

Making a mental note to discuss Margie's recent bout with video poker with Harrison, Rita returned to her review of the bills as the telephone rang. And rang.

On the chance it might not be a test of whatever equipment they were installing on her phone, she answered.

"Hello?"

"Ri—Rita?" Jayne's voice on the other end of the phone was broken by a hiccup.

"Yeah, it's me." She hadn't been thrilled when Jayne had skipped out on her promise to meet her at their mother's house so Jayne could break the news of her marriage to Margie, but Harrison said he'd spoken to Emmett and they decided maybe it wasn't such a bad idea to keep Jayne away from the house in case Yurek's people were watching. And since Jayne wanted to tell Margie about her marriage in person, Rita was stuck having to pretend she didn't know anything. "Everything okay?"

"No." Another hiccup. "I'm afraid I've made a colossal mistake by marrying Emmett."

Oh dear God, not already.

"What do you mean?" She figured Jayne was simply experiencing the inevitable adjustments that come with big life changes, but Rita's protective streak remained alert, just in case. "Didn't you tell Emmett going into this that you don't do compromise?"

"I can compromise, damn it. But how can I stay married to a man who won't tell me squat about his past? He could have been a bank robber or a grave robber or a…"

In the background, Rita could here Emmett shout, "Don't forget cradle robber! I could have been pirating away underage women to my wild and wicked lair before I met you."

Rita smothered a laugh, clamping her hand firmly over her mouth so Jayne wouldn't hear any snickering. But having held Jayne's hand through a lifetime of anxiety attacks followed by seemingly fearless, kick-ass performances, Rita appreciated that Jayne could be a tad high-strung.

"You probably were!" Jayne shouted back as she made a poor attempt to cover the mouthpiece so Rita wouldn't hear. But smothering the phone didn't disguise the sound of a door slamming on the other end. Emmett leaving? Then, sighing, Jayne spoke directly into the phone again. "Sorry about that. He walked out again because he's annoyed with me, but I don't understand why he can't tell me anything about his past without getting all bent out of shape. If you love someone, don't you want to share who you are and where you've been in life?"

Hearing the wistful note in Jayne's voice forced Rita to take the question seriously since it apparently meant a lot to her. Pushing the stack of bills away, she spun around in the worn leather office chair to stare up at her mother's wall of fame with framed photos of Margie and a whole host of minor movie stars.

"Maybe his childhood sucked." Rita's gaze paused on a photo of Margie with Elvis in his Vegas days. Margie liked to tell the story of how her winning streak had compelled casino management to give her great tickets to an Elvis show. "You and I never talk about parts of our teenage years. Did you tell him about nearly getting—"

"Of course not." Jayne cut her off quickly, as she always did on that particular topic. "No guy wants to hear the gory details of me getting manhandled by some toothless lunatic."

"You're wrong." Rita had always known Jayne should have gone for counseling about their days in the homeless shelter, but she'd freaked any time Rita brought it up and basically scared Rita into shutting up about it. "Emmett would be indignant on your behalf. You can't expect him to spill his guts for you if you're not honest with him. For that matter, if you're planning on keeping your own secrets, don't you think you need to be more understanding about him staying silent with his past?"

Rita knew she made it sound simple when it wasn't, but she couldn't bear to have Jayne walk away from her wedding vows after less than a week. Somehow Jayne's marriage had become a benchmark for Rita, a gauge for how Frazer women might succeed in love and relationships. Her gaze traveled down the wall to the photo of her mother and father on their wedding day. A brief, happy marriage before their father—a college basketball player turned plumber—had a massive stroke while fixing a neighbor's sink. Margie had never shown any interest in marrying again.

Now Rita wondered why. Would her parents have stayed together if her father had lived? Would Margie have still fallen victim to her addiction? As she thought about it, Rita wondered if Margie's gambling had become a way to compensate for the loss in her life since she'd professed to love her dead husband for years after the fact.

On the other end of the phone, Jayne launched in another direction, abruptly halting Rita's thoughts about her mother.

"And what about my career? Emmett says I could dance anywhere I want, but what if he's just saying that to be nice? I don't want to fall flat on my face in some big production. Yet I can't let Emmett pay all the bills or I'll feel like a total sponge."

"Do any of these questions ring a bell to you?" Rita tapped a pen against the stack of mail, thinking maybe she needed to confront her mother about dating again. "These are all the same concerns I had *before* the wedding and you had no interest in figuring out any of the answers."

"What do you want me to say, Ree?" Jayne snapped, unusual for her since she normally sugarcoated any irritable words with a more subtle barb. "You were right and I was wrong. I have no clue what I'm doing or why I thought I was ready to get married, but since I'm drowning in worries in a set of unfamiliar circumstances, do you think you could step out of holier-than-thou mode long enough to help me think this through?"

Rita might have been more annoyed, but the breath-less panic threaded through Jayne's voice inspired every protective, big-sister instinct that had been drilled into her head.

"Sorry." She trotted out the word she rarely used, but she didn't blame Jayne for being scared. Rita hadn't even been able to work up the courage to say "I do," so she ought to be able to empathize with the onslaught of problems brought on by a marriage that hadn't been super thought out. "I'm cranky today because Margie applied for a credit card in my name and charged some Neiman's stuff and several hands of poker, but I don't mean to take it out on you."

"Do you need me to come over?" The breathless quality faded from Jayne's voice as she focused on Rita's problems instead of her own. "Or do you want me to confront Margie on the phone? I know what a headache she can be when she tries to deny the obvious."

Gratitude for the offer made Rita feel like twice the bitch for giving Jayne a hard time.

"Thanks, but I'll talk to her. I'll feel better knowing you're safe where Harrison and Emmett put you." They'd agreed on a hotel outside town until Yurek was captured or Emmett and Jayne went on their honeymoon.

"How are things going with Harrison?" Jayne zeroed in on Rita's biggest source of worry with the utter accuracy bred by spending most of their lives within ten feet of one another. "I know you said he was a dead end, but I thought maybe since he'd set up house with you and Mom—"

"Actually, this phone is wired now, Jayne, so I'd rather not—"

"They bugged it? Cool." She sighed on the other end

of the phone, and somehow the lonesome utterance made her sound a thousand miles away. "So I guess that gives you a convenient excuse not to talk about him, even though you let me rattle away about Emmett in front of God-knows-how-many people who could be listening."

"Call me back on my cell phone tonight and we'll figure out some things, okay?" Rita wasn't sure what to suggest to help her sister's fledgling marriage stay on its feet, but she'd help however she could. Too bad she couldn't make a living taking care of people. She'd be rich by now. "Emmett's a good guy and if you ask me, he's crazy about you. Anything else, we can fix."

The words rung hollowly in her ears long after she said goodbye. If they were true—that a marriage could be saved if you were with a wonderful man who adored you—then Rita had screwed up big-time by turning down Harrison. Still, a little corner of her heart protested that those practical ingredients could only propel a relationship forward so far without the most important element of all.

Love.

EMMETT STRUGGLED FOR patience a week later as he stomped through the living area of their hotel suite and listened to Jayne dial the phone in their bedroom for the fifth time in as many days. Calling her sister, no doubt.

His feet slowed before he could leave the suite as usual when they argued. Out of deference to Jayne, he refused to get involved in any more shouting matches, so he'd quickly developed a habit of splitting when they butted heads about everything from where they wanted to live to what Jayne wanted to do for a job.

She'd been really dogging him to talk, so fine. He'd told her fifty times they could go wherever she liked, chase whatever dreams she chose, but that didn't help. She'd always trot out some small idea—what if she went here, what if she tried working as a production manager—and then ask what he thought. All sorts of strange questions about what decision would make him "feel" better and where did he "dream" of spending his life.

Good God, she was speaking another language. Confusing as hell Chick-Speak.

Proceeding with caution, he tried to say as little as possible so he wouldn't screw up until she pressed. And then he'd offer up an objective list of possible pros and cons. Unfortunately, she took the list personally and went on to argue every single damn pro and con he'd mentioned.

And this time he'd learned that saying "I don't care" was definitely not a good Band-Aid fix for the problem. Those words—intended to give her freedom to do whatever the hell she wished—elicited tears the likes of which he'd never seen.

But before he could reach the door to their suite at a historic hotel in downtown Miami, Emmett heard Jayne hang up the phone again before crying even harder.

What kind of an ass would he be if he fled the scene of a sobbing woman—who happened to be his wife—when she didn't even have the solace of a trusted loved one to pour out her heart to?

Pivoting on his heel, he grit his teeth and prepared to go back into the war zone to see if he could straighten out some of the mess that had tangled them up ever since they'd said their vows. He loved Jayne. Adored her with a depth of feeling he'd never experienced in his whole life. He just didn't know how to give her emotional support she seemed to crave, and apparently the combination of getting married and other radical changes— loss of a job, separation from a family she was close to, totally different surroundings—had her stressed out in more ways than he could appreciate.

But that didn't give him the right to walk away. Telling himself he'd never again raise his voice to a woman who cloaked a fragile core under thick layers of feminine wiles, Emmett forced himself to put one foot in front of the other as he headed back to their bedroom.

"Jayne?" He rapped on the closed door, realizing he needed to start connecting with her if he didn't want to lose her.

"Go away." She sniffled before he heard a resounding thump against the door right by his ear, as if she'd thrown something at him.

He tipped his head against the door, wishing he'd taken the time to pound some sense into his head before things had gotten so out of hand between them. She should be talking to him about how to resolve their problems, not calling her sister every day. A notion which gave him an idea. "Let me in and I'll remind you why you made the best decision of your life by marrying me."

"If you think you have any chance of seducing me when I'm this angry, Emmett MacNeil, you are not nearly as smart as I gave you credit for."

"That's not what I meant." Although he appreciated the mental image of getting her naked, he hadn't been thinking along those lines. "I want to talk to you."

"I'm mad and I'm crying." Her voice sounded closer, as if she'd moved near the door for a face-off. "You have no wish to be around me when I'm mad and crying, remember? You bolt for the door like you're going for a land speed record."

"That's because I hate to see you cry and I figure that since I'm the source of your frustration, you'll feel better if I'm out of your face." Claudia had always seemed grateful to shove him aside when she was angry with him. A tendency for which he'd been grateful since he'd never been keen on confrontation. But he ought to know by now that Jayne had nothing in common with his ex-wife. "Since that method obviously sucks, I have an idea how to fix it this time."

A long silence followed before the bedroom door opened a couple of inches. Jayne peered through the crack, her eyes puffy and red-rimmed as she confronted him wearing a white silk bathrobe that showed an incredible amount of thigh. Not that he would ever ogle a crying woman. But he'd have to be blind not to notice the long expanse of killer legs exposed by the thin robe belted around her curves.

"You want to fix things?" She lifted an eyebrow in curious surprise, as if she couldn't believe he cared enough to solve their problems.

That moment of unguarded vulnerability tugged at his heart even more than the killer legs called to his libido. Seeing that look of wary hope in her eyes made him want to leap tall buildings in a single bound for her. Straightening out their marriage might be as tough as any superhero feats, but if it made her happy, Emmett would apply himself to the task. James Bond wouldn't walk out on a weeping woman.

"I not only *want* to, I will." Seized with renewed determination to make her happy, Emmett stepped through the doorway into the bedroom to relay his plan. "It occurred to me today as I was walking out of here that the first thing you do when we fight is call your sister."

Sliding his arm around her waist, he led her toward the bed where they'd spent countless hours relearning each other's every hidden desire and sensual need. Tugging the bedspread over the bare sheets still tangled from morning lovemaking, Emmett pulled her onto the edge of the mattress to sit beside him.

"I only do that because you leave." Jayne reached for the box of tissues on the nightstand and blew her nose. "I wouldn't have to call Rita if you'd help me figure out anything."

"Then I'm not going anywhere today or tomorrow until we figure out whatever you'd like—where we're going to live, what jobs you'd like to pursue, you name it." Maybe if he wrote the pros and cons on paper that would help Jayne decide what she wanted without arguing every point with him. Then again, maybe she could tell him what kind of advice she expected from him instead of getting upset whenever he failed to provide it. "How does Rita help you figure out things when you talk to her? Does she offer ideas or does she just listen?"

Jayne snorted. "We're talking about my big sister here. Rita Frazer *always* has an opinion."

"Out of curiosity, do you argue with her every time she makes a suggestion?"

"Of course not. Okay, maybe sometimes." She folded her arms and stared at him crossly. "But whether I argue or not, she never sprints for the door whenever I try to solicit advice."

"So I'm sitting here for the duration until we have a plan." He reached for the notepad in the nightstand drawer and prepared to write down the results of their planning session. He'd do his best not to hurry her through her decision process since he knew she didn't appreciate being pushed. "Anything else you want to add to our list while we're developing our marriage mission statement and five-year goals?"

"Emmett." She pulled his pen out of his hand. "Can we just talk without taking notes? If you really want to know how Rita helps me, I can tell you that there is no long-range planning, no mission statement development and no pros or cons in our conversations, okay? We talk. We share what's important to us."

He gripped his notepad tighter, but what was the point in maintaining his paper if she wouldn't give him back the damn pen? Sighing, he set aside the notes.

"Fine." He scavenged around in his brain for some depth of sensitivity to handle a discussion that clearly meant a lot to her, but all he came up with was a pressing urge to sling an arm around her shoulders and draw her closer. Which he did. "What do we tackle first?"

"How about—" She stopped abruptly, her gaze gravitating to his as she twisted a tissue mercilessly between restless fingers. "How about I tell you something about myself first so you can understand me better? Don't you ever feel like you married a total stranger?"

"Hell no." He lifted a hand to her chin to cradle her face. "I love you just the way you are and you don't owe me any explanations."

Part of him hoped if he released her from any compunction she felt to tell him about her past that maybe she'd do the same for him. Besides, wasn't their conversation supposed to be about planning for the future instead of looking backward? He'd thought he signed on for deciding where to set up house.

"Really?" She flashed him a crooked smile as she released the tissue she'd crumpled into oblivion. "Well, I love you even more, and I don't think of it as giving each other explanations, but rather as sharing what makes us tick."

He froze as he realized there would be no reprieve on opening old wounds today. Jayne apparently saw it as a bonding ritual, a far more painful version of a blood oath to share life crises. Oh joy.

When he didn't answer right away, she sucked in a deep breath.

"Aren't you even mildly curious to know why I tend to call Rita like my own personal 911 line every time life goes awry for me? Or why my extremely talented sibling signed on to work as a seamstress onboard the *Venus* even though she's got enough talent in her left pinkie to make an incredible career at anything she chooses?"

He should deny any and all interest since his preferred plan was to write off history in order to make a clean start. But damn it, now she had him curious.

"I just figured she'd made it her life mission to be your personal guardian since it sounds like your mom clocked out on the parenthood deal at an early age." He knew compulsive gamblers didn't have time for much in their lives outside their addiction.

"That's part of it." Jayne reached for a pillow and clutched the crisp white cotton-encased feathers in her arms. "But Rita's overprotective streak has more to do with a nervous breakdown I had at sixteen after I'd been assaulted in a homeless shelter."

For a moment, Emmett thought she had to have been speaking in tongues since none of the words made sense. Jayne in a homeless shelter? Where she'd been attacked? Fury singed his veins as fear for her threatened to level him.

"Somebody hurt you?" She'd been a kid, for Chrissake. His arm around her tightened. "What happened?"

"I didn't get hurt—not physically at least. Rita found me before a guy molested me in a deserted women's bathroom, but I'd never been so scared in my life." She shivered at the memory, blinking away whatever demons she still carried.

"Thank God she got you out of there." Brushing a kiss across her forehead, he couldn't even imagine two teenage girls facing down a rapist. Emmett wanted to ask about ten questions all at once, but he limited himself to only one as he smoothed a palm down her back. "Did they catch the guy?"

"Actually, a bunch of women in the shelter wreaked their own brand of vengeance before the cops picked him up. But I don't know all the details because I tried to put it behind me since Rita and I were up to our eyeballs in trouble with Margie losing our house in a poker tournament." She took a deep breath, moving past that rotten time in her life even now. "Things seemed okay for a while, but then I ended up having a nervous breakdown a few months later when I got the lead in a high school play. The chorus teacher came up behind me to ask me if I was nervous on opening night, and I lost my mind when he touched my elbow. I screamed for five minutes straight until Rita carted me home."

"Didn't you ever get any counseling?" His chest ached at the thought of her dealing with so much crap at that young of an age. Anger at their mother for checking out on them spiked his pulse as he clenched his fists. But then he remembered he was supposed to be helping Jayne and not indulging his own frustrations. Forcing himself to relax, he tipped her chin up. "That's supposed to really help put stuff behind you."

Not that he'd ever tried it, but a school guidance counselor had mentioned it to Emmett once before he graduated and Emmett had promptly told the guy where he could shove his psychobabble bullshit. Which only proved he was a punk in high school, but he'd scraped through the best he could until he got to college on the other side of the map where no one knew his delinquent past or his grifter parents and he had as much of a chance as anyone to succeed.

"No." Jayne shook her head, loose red waves sliding over her white robe. "Rita pushed me to go, but I was trying so hard to forget it, I couldn't see the benefit of hashing it out with a shrink every week, you know?"

"How long were you in the shelter?" He couldn't picture Jayne living in those dank conditions. She had a natural sparkle, a vivacious personality that would be a downright sin to dim.

"Five months." She peered down at her nails and rubbed the brightly polished tips across the rumpled sheets. "My mother got some counseling help after that, but her having her head on marginally straighter didn't do much good in reclaiming our old house. We were in cheap rentals after that until Rita and I saved up enough for a condo. But even back when we rented, Rita footed most of the bills with odd jobs until I graduated from high school. Then we tended to stick together to pay the mortgage and keep an eye on Margie, who has opted to live in fantasyland as often as possible since our homeless shelter days, although she has a knack for adding a touch of irreverence to life when times get tough."

"I'm so sorry you had to go through that. All of it." He hauled her closer, grateful she'd been wise enough to suggest they share something about themselves since her story sure as hell explained her tight bond with her sister and possibly a little of her urgent need to figure out where they were going to live next.

"I didn't tell you to make you sorry for me." Her words were muffled against his shoulder as he held her. "And I didn't even *want* to tell you, but Rita said I should and I could see her point."

He scrubbed his hand across her back, knowing she probably had another motive for telling him. She wanted him to repay her openness with some of his own, and by now he could hardly deny her. He'd tried his best to protect her from his past, but after spending the last tumultuous week with her, he'd realized how much he needed her in his life. All of her. And if that meant forking over all of himself in the process, then so be it because he'd do anything to keep this woman.

Figuring he'd offer up something before he lost his nerve, he decided to relay the one significant fact of his past that he'd omitted. Bending to plant a kiss in her hair, he was grateful not to meet her eyes.

"My parents aren't all that different from Margie." He hadn't talked to them in years, couldn't understand their justifications for a lifestyle that had always rankled his moral sensibilities. "They thrive on taking chances, gambling with their freedom instead of money."

She inched back, but he held her tighter. He brushed his jaw over the top of Jayne's hair, his unshaven cheek snagging on the strands. Before she could ask any questions, he forged onward, hoping she wouldn't be sorry she'd married him.

"For years I thought my dad had the best job in the world because he was home all the time. It wasn't until I was seven that I realized his job actually sucked because he was a crook. A charming con man who fell in love with my mother when they were competing for the same mark." So Emmett hadn't even been able to take solace in his mother's sense of honor since she was as much of an operator as his father.

Jayne wiggled in his arms with more insistence, freeing herself enough to look up at him, confusion in her gaze.

"*Your* parents?" She cocked her head to one side as if seeing him anew. "I thought you were a blue-blooded New Yorker with the Ivy League education, the Wall Street career and all that goes with it."

"That's what I led people to think." There'd been a tremendous sense of freedom when he left home in Seattle to start college on the east coast since he knew he'd never look back. "I legally changed my name to disassociate myself from my parents—a couple of small-time grifters who had pressed me into pickpocketing by the time I was ten."

She may as well know all of it because Emmett sincerely wished to avoid the topic for the remainder of their marriage. This was a one-shot deal in an attempt to assure Jayne he could be open and honest and not always the first to bolt at any sign of trouble.

"Were you any good at it?" Jayne arched a curious eyebrow, dark eyes alight with mischief.

"Jesus, Jayne, what kind of question is that? You should be revolted you married someone with a criminal background." He'd worried for two decades that someone would discover he'd once stolen a neighbor's wallet even though he'd incurred his father's wrath by returning it three days later under the pretense that he'd found it. The nice old guy had tried to give him a dollar for his trouble, but Emmett had fled the scene and the dangling dollar bill, figuring if he took the money that the gates of Hell would open wide for him.

"How could I be upset when I know better than most people you don't choose your family? You love them—or do your best to love them—flaws and all. But that doesn't mean you're to blame for their choices." She toyed with the tie of her robe, twirling one loose end around her finger. "And just like it's not my fault that Margie's a compulsive gambler whose habit forever destroyed my credit record, it's not *your* fault your folks tried to drag you into a life of crime. The test of character is what you do on your own."

She batted his knee with the robe tie, her mood more calm, her tears long dried. Which was fortunate, since he figured he'd be reaching for the damn box of tissues himself any minute.

"You're too good for me, you know that?" Eyes burning, he pulled her into his arms and squeezed. Hard.

"I think we're doing pretty well for ourselves, all things considered."

"My seven-month marriage notwithstanding." He breathed in the floral scent of her hair, the permanent hint of Chanel No. 5 that clung to her. "I'm sorry I didn't wait around last year after I asked you to marry me."

"I'm sorry I couldn't get my head on straight back then. But you know what?" She arched back to see him. "You're getting a much better wife in the bargain."

"Is that right?" He tugged her long, bare legs up and over his lap, wondering if they could afford to spend all day in bed.

"I grew up a lot after you walked away." She unfastened the top button on his shirt. "I think I'm stronger now that I know I won't have another nervous breakdown if someone I love walks away from me." She paused in her unbuttoning efforts to flash a warning glare his way. "Not that you'd better ever try it again."

"Never." He slanted his mouth over hers, their lips meeting in a slow mating dance. On their wedding day, he had thought he couldn't possibly love Jayne any more than he did, but already he'd proven himself wrong. Her easy acceptance of who he was and where he came from had cracked open his heart all the more, assuring his wife had an unshakable claim on his love.

While he didn't delude himself that they wouldn't ever disagree again, at least they'd made it over a major hurdle. They were both talking…and listening. And that counted for something.

His pulse thudded so loud his ears rang with it. When the ringing grew incessant he pulled away and realized the hotel phone chimed beside the bed.

"Damn." Knocking the receiver off the hook, he pulled it to his ear with every intention of running off the caller as fast as possible. "Hello?"

"Emmett, it's Rita. Is Jayne there?" Brusque and efficient, the elder Frazer didn't waste time with niceties.

"Yeah, but we're a little bit busy—"

"I'm sorry and I wouldn't bother you if it wasn't urgent." She barreled on before Emmett could get a word in edgewise, let alone pass the phone to Jayne. "I booked a ticket for Margie on the *Venus* tomorrow because I can't leave her alone. She's gambling again—big-time. I wondered if you and Jayne would consider taking your honeymoon on the ship because we need to have a *serious* family powwow before Margie digs herself a hole so deep we'll never be able to pull her back out."

CHAPTER TWENTY

MAKING POLITE CONVERSATION with the woman who
dumped you sucked.

Harrison helped Rita and her mother with their bags
the next morning as they boarded the ship along with
the next round of passengers for another ten-day cruise.
The *Venus* took on guests for a new excursion the same
day another trip ended. The international crew lived
aboard the ocean liner for months on end, only disem-
barking for occasional shore trips.

As Harrison paid for his ticket and walked around the
metal detector thanks to his renewed FBI status, he
watched the other passengers in Hawaiian shirts and
straw hats gearing up for their vacation. He could see
Jayne enjoying that kind of lifestyle, but he wondered
how much Rita liked her seamstress gig in the nonstop
party atmosphere.

He'd checked in with her most days that she'd been
on leave, but she hadn't done anything but work for the
past two and a half weeks that she'd been in Fort Lauderdale. Not that he could blame her, since he hadn't
been able to find time for much else besides his case in
progress either, especially since nabbing Yurek meant
protecting Rita and her family.

After so much time apart, it was tough to recapture the tenuous connection they'd agreed to that day in the cab. So it was no surprise that a bad mood rode him hard today when he'd barely slept the past two weeks and he didn't know what to say to the woman he wanted more than anything. Seva Yurek hadn't put in any more appearances after Margie Frazer mentioned the man with a "Russian" accent, but his boat, the *Over-Under* had been spotted in a nearby marina on two different occasions. Unfortunately, local police hadn't contacted federal agents in time for them to haul Yurek in for questioning.

Since then, the boat and the man seemed to have vanished into thin air.

"I don't feel right about sleeping on this deck when I have room for Margie in my cabin downstairs." Rita hesitated in the hallway as Harrison opened the doors to connecting rooms on a deck reserved for passengers. "Isn't this considered gratuitous government spending to buy me a spacious suite on a cruise ship when I already have a place on the employee deck?"

Her mother seemed less concerned about government spending, skirting past her daughter to claim one of the rooms.

"How charming!" Margie picked up one of the tiny bottles of champagne from the display on top of the minibar. "They give you champagne, too?"

"For a fee, Mom." Rita didn't set foot over the threshold although Harrison suspected she battled a strong urge to wrench the overpriced bubbly from her mother's hand.

No doubt about it, Margie Frazer was a handful. Harrison figured her practical older daughter had been more mature than her by the time Rita was eight years old.

Heart softening at the thought of all the responsibilities Rita juggled for her family—regardless of whether or not she *should*—Harrison didn't bother resisting the urge to palm her back and give her a nudge toward the small suite.

"Don't worry about the room." He lowered his voice for her ears alone while Margie investigated the freebie basket perched on the television. Leaning close to her ear, he inhaled the clean scent of her hair as he spoke. "Roman Cruise Lines wants to put an end to Yurek's ring as badly as we do since he's cost their passengers a lot of money. They comped your suite and assured me they're willing to cooperate in any way necessary to finger everyone involved with illegal gambling."

He found it nearly impossible to pull his hand away from the knit tank top she wore with a knee-skimming skirt. He'd avoided touching her at all costs while they were in Fort Lauderdale, knowing he needed to let her make the next move if he was ever going to convince her they could take their time and get to know each other better. But now that he had touched her—mostly in an effort to reassure her—he found himself swamped with memories of other times they'd touched.

She didn't move away. Not even when another couple walked past them juggling margaritas and carry-on luggage as they hunted for their room. Rita just stood with him in the entryway, the heated look in her eyes assuring him he wasn't the only one plagued with memories.

"Seems like old times being back onboard the *Venus*, doesn't it?" She cast a glance over her shoulder to where Margie flipped through television stations while she read the ship's welcome letter out loud. "Do you have a minute that we could talk?"

"Sure." He pulled the door shut to Margie's room and tugged Rita into his, hands never fully leaving her waist.

"I've got a question that won't take long." Fanning herself, she stepped out of the circle of his arms. "Just how did you expect we were going to get to know one another better if we never speak to each other?"

Her question blindsided him, relegating the sound of kids running down the hall to the back of his mind. "What do you mean?"

"I mean why did you tell me you were willing to slow things down between us and then pull a total disappearing act?" She perched a hand on one hip, the heat he thought he'd seen in her eyes obviously more frustration than passion. "I know you've been busy, but I've been working myself silly trying to plot a new course for my life and the man who suggested he wanted to marry me totally checked out."

The silence that followed her outpouring seemed all the more quiet for the contrast. Harrison thought he might hear her heart beating. God knows he could hear his own.

"I tried to call most nights." Hadn't they talked then? "Besides, I thought you wanted more space." Had she said that? Or had he simply opted to read her rejection that way because her answer to his proposal had about ripped out his heart?

And what was this about charting a new course? Vaguely, he remembered her walking around the Frazer house with a sketchpad for the two days he'd been in residence. Had she been thinking about her own dreams for a change?

"I hate to be the bearer of bad news, but you were only half present for most of those phone calls. I got the impression you wanted to know I was safe and then you were racing to hang up the phone. It would have been nice to—you know—talk."

Damn. He hadn't seen the opportunities right in front of his eyes. "I'm sorry, Rita. I started coordinating the operation to smoke out Yurek, but I probably threw myself into the work with twice as much effort because I've been worried he'd come after you or your family."

"I appreciate that and while I want you to know I understand the need to take care of business, I'm going to hold you to your offer for a date once your schedule frees up." Rita smiled slowly, but their conversation was overrun by commotion next door. Talking, laughter and the distinctive sound of a champagne cork popping.

Rita was pushing through the connecting door in no time, perhaps recognizing Jayne's and Emmett's voices. Her automatic reaction to rush toward her family reminded Harrison how much he needed to be on his toes this week to keep her safe. While he didn't expect Yurek would be dumb enough to book himself passage on the *Venus* just to get to Harrison through Rita or her family, he knew the gambling network probably had more than one connection onboard.

"Rita Hayworth Frazer." Margie gave her daughter a mock glare as she came into the room, her eyes bright. "Don't you dare tell me you knew our Jayne went and eloped!"

Margie had her arm looped around Jayne's waist, her whole demeanor changing around her youngest, almost as if she tried harder to behave. Harrison suspected that while Jayne was the undisputed favorite, Margie knew perfectly well that Rita was the daughter who kept her bread buttered, so even though she nitpicked her older daughter, she remained careful not to alienate her goodwill.

Crafty old broad.

"I knew." Rita removed the champagne bottle from Margie's free hand and poured minuscule amounts into plastic cups Emmett passed to her. "But I was sworn to secrecy because Jayne wanted to surprise you."

"She knows how I love surprises. And now I want to propose a toast to the bride and groom." Lifting her glass, she fluffed her carefully coifed auburn hair around the collar of her dark linen jacket. "May you live the love you've always dreamed of, and may your romance be an inspiration to everyone who sees you."

Margie tipped her glass to her lips and downed her portion first.

Rita seemed as surprised as Harrison at her mother's toast. He clinked his glass to Rita's in an effort to second Margie's sentiment, then polished off his drink while Rita did the same.

"Let's take this party on deck," Margie urged, pinching Emmett's cheek as if he were five years old. "I feel guilty keeping these handsome men to myself."

"They're not yours, Mom," Jayne reminded her mother, swatting Margie's wrist with her boarding card. "And I'm sure Emmett would rather not be bruised the first day he meets you, okay?"

While Emmett made polite protests about Margie's gentle ways, Jayne attempted to nudge her mother out the door along with the men, but Harrison didn't have any intention of leaving Rita's side.

"Can I have a few minutes to talk to Rita?" Jayne's batting eyelashes might be tough for some men to resist, but Harrison couldn't help think how he preferred Rita's directness.

"I don't want to leave Rita alone until we capture everyone involved in this gambling ring." He'd spoken to Emmett about the need to be careful, but then Emmett hadn't shown any desire to take his eyes off his new wife so it wouldn't be tough to look out for her.

"She won't be *alone* since she'll be with me," Jayne wheedled, her gaze following Margie's progress into the hallway with Emmett. "What if we lock the door and Rita promises not to leave unless she calls you to come down and get her? I need to talk to her about our mutual problem."

The pleading look in Jayne's eyes finally won him over. He could definitely empathize with the way Margie's gambling habits had put both her daughters over a financial barrel. "Okay." He switched his attention to Rita, trusting her to follow through on a promise more than her sister. "You'll call me when you finish up?"

Nodding, she wrapped her arms around herself. "Count on it. We hadn't really finished our discussion from before."

Despite the warning note in her voice, he actually looked forward to that talk. If there was any chance he could still sway her into considering a future with him…hell, he couldn't sign on fast enough.

THREE DAYS LATER, Rita had all but given up on ever speaking to Harrison alone again. The *Venus* docked in St. Kitts on the fourth day of the cruise, and despite the fact that Rita had an upgraded suite free of her sister's perpetual clothes tornado, she still figured this had to be the worst trip of her life. Trying to corner Margie for a family meeting had proven more difficult than wrestling a tomcat into doll clothes, a feat Rita and Jayne had accomplished more than once. Rita could almost think someone had tipped off their mother that her daughters meant business this time. The credit-card scam had put Rita over the edge.

Peering out her stateroom window overlooking the harbor on St. Kitts, Rita remembered the last time the boat had docked here and Jayne had hightailed it to shore to elope with her boyfriend the crook. Now, within less than a month, Jayne had already married someone else and was planning a new career as a choreographer while Rita still sewed costumes for Danielle the Dreadful, who at least had finally coughed up the dough for the outfits Rita had sewn.

Which meant Rita didn't have an excuse in the world not to start following her own dreams. Blinking against the relentless sun glinting off the turquoise water all around the dock, Rita knew nothing held her to the *Venus* since Danielle fired Jayne. And with the recovery of their savings plus the small profit she'd made on the costumes, Rita could pay off the credit-card debt Margie had run up with video poker. The amount loomed high enough to pinch her purse hard, but it hadn't come close to the devastating amounts her mother had lost in the past.

Nothing was stopping Rita from handing in her resignation today and taking a chance on the design talent she'd only flexed as a hobby in the past. Nothing but bone-gnawing fear of failure.

And the knowledge that she'd be going it alone.

Someone rattling her door handle from the outside made her jump, startling away her dark thoughts.

"Land ho, ladies. Let me in so I can roust you from your beds to go ashore." Jayne's voice chirped singsong style on the other side of the door and Rita smiled in spite of herself. How many times had her sister awoken her with her Mary Sunshine B.S. when they'd lived together?

Pausing before opening the door, Rita called through the barrier, "You know, I always dreamed of locking you out in the hallway whenever you used to wake me up too early and at last I've got my wish."

"Yeah, sure. You've got Margie sleeping like a dead woman in there. That ought to make for a real fun day for you."

Relenting, Rita clicked open the lock.

"Does it give you much sense of victory to know you won out over a woman who sleeps like the dead?" Rita turned to stare at their mother's slender form wound up tight in her sheets after tossing and turning half the night.

"You never give me credit for any maturity, you know that?" Jayne stood by her side to stare at their mother, who didn't look like a holy terror while sleeping.

"Well, you should have been here a minute ago, because it happens I was just mentally singing your praises." Rita cracked open a bottle of water that she'd smuggled onboard in her suitcase just to spite the out-rageous minibar charges.

"Oh, do sing them out loud instead." Jayne seated

herself on the love seat in the sitting area of the suite. "You know how I adore praise, especially when it comes from that most rare of all sources, my cynical big sister."

Tossing Jayne a second bottle of water from her private stash, Rita sank into a wingback nearby and considered how just a few weeks ago, Jayne's observation would have rankled. Not much. A minor irritation in an ongoing sibling battle to point out one another's flaws.

But after spending two and a half weeks away from Jayne, Rita found she missed her.

"I was just thinking how scared I am to go into business for myself."

"That doesn't sound at all like praise for me." Jayne sipped her water thoughtfully. "And since when are you scared of anything?"

"Since all the time." Rita capped her bottle and sat straighter in her chair, still surprised by her new revelation. "Since I was old enough to realize somebody should be looking out for you when Margie ditched us for a week to gamble. Since realizing how fast a person can lose everything. I'm always scared I'll mess up something big, or that the IRS will take away all our money after finding out Margie didn't claim some gambling winnings she blew ten minutes after she won it."

"Well, take heart that you put on a good show, lady. You'd never know you were scared of anything to look at you." Jayne flipped through Margie's collection of colorful paper umbrellas from exotic drinks she'd ordered during the cruise. "Remember when you launched on top of Toothless Joe to pull him off me? I figured he was a dead man the moment you arrived. Not for a minute did I doubt your ability to mete out justice, but now that I think about it, I guess you were only—"

"Seventeen years old." Rita had never been so petrified in all her life as the moment she'd seen some creepy pervert on top of her sixteen-year-old sister. "But that's what I was trying to tell you before about singing your praises. It only just occurred to me today that you're really good at making me forget I'm scared."

"Me?" Jayne didn't give her usual humble turn-of-the-shoulder the way she did when men gave her obvious compliments. Her eyes practically bugged out as she leaned forward. "You think *I* do that?"

"I know you do." Rita smiled inside to think she gave her sister a gift she hadn't been able to before—acceptance for simply being Jayne. "I guess it's obvious that the desire to play superhero outweighed my fear the day I lifted Toothless Joe off of you. But there have been other times— like on all those damn auditions Mom made us go to before I was old enough to tell her where to get off—that I would have hid in a corner if it wasn't for you breezing around every strange dance studio like you owned the place."

"I'm so brave I lost my job for dancing a never-before-seen routine on Danielle's stage, right?" Jayne jammed one of the paper umbrellas into a grommet of her purse for decoration. "I probably need a healthier dose of fear, but I appreciate you making me see the plus side of a reckless streak."

"No problem." Just putting the acknowledgment out there filled Rita with a new sense of satisfaction. "So how's married life treating you?"

She'd been dying to know. There hadn't been much time to talk to Jayne one-on-one amid Harrison's preparations for their island excursions where the chances of running into Seva Yurek's goons ran higher. Even

Margie had gotten in on the investigation, timidly offering up that she'd heard about a big game open to high rollers in St. Kitts today. Harrison hoped to track down the lead while Rita and Jayne finally cornered Margie alone for a talk about her broken promises and return to her old ways. Their attempts earlier in the week while on the boat had always resulted in Margie running off to join some activity or another, so this time, Rita figured they'd take her to a beach where she didn't have anywhere to go but the ocean.

Assuming Margie ever woke up so they could go ashore.

"Married life is divine." Jayne hugged her arms around her waist at the thought. "Emmett had to go ashore for some kind of errand before he meets up with us today, but he is so good to me. I'm going to try my best to make him happy."

"What about all the fights before?" Rita hopped up to nudge their sleeping mother, wondering if they could simply corner her right here as soon as she showered and seemed alert. Rita wanted the whole emotional mess of this talk about counseling over and done with so she could look ahead.

At her empty life without Harrison.

Heart aching at the thought, Rita waited for Jayne to answer while Margie shuffled toward the shower and a knock sounded on the connecting door of their cabin.

"Rita?" Harrison's voice still shot a thrill through her for a split second before she remembered she'd turned him down. "You ready to go ashore?"

Opening the door to admit him, her chest ached at the sight of him in khakis and a crisp blue shirt rolled up at the sleeves as if he'd already been hard at work this morning. His broad shoulders ate up the better portion of the door frame, the kind of shoulders any woman would long to brush kisses over or hold on tight while making love….

"Rita?" He shoved his phone in one pocket and a PDA in the other. His service weapon made a slight bulge just above his hip in a place a jacket would cover.

"Jayne and I are ready but my mother just rolled out of bed so it will be a few minutes." She was tired of making apologies for a woman who would never care all that much about other people's schedules. Or finances. "Do you think Margie was right about an illegal game in the works today?"

"There haven't been any sightings of the *Over-Under* in this part of the Caribbean, but it's possible Yurek found another home for his poker haven. A second boat. A hotel room." He raked a hand through his hair.

Margie peeked out of the bathroom in a purple bathrobe, blow dryer pointed at her head. "Did someone say poker?"

Rita's patience threatened to wear right through until Harrison's hand materialized on her back. The simple touch soothed her and gave her the first inkling of what it might be like to not be alone.

"No poker for you, Margie," Harrison answered for Rita over the hum of the dryer, his hand sliding south a few toe-tingling inches before disappearing again. "And to make sure we keep you all safe, I figure we'll stick to the quieter side of the island. Jayne, maybe you know where I'm talking about. I guess Emmett used to own a bar over there."

"I'm not setting foot anywhere near my husband's ex-wife," Jayne announced, rising off the love seat with the dancer grace that had long made Rita look like an also-ran.

"I'm not going anywhere if there are no cards," Margie chimed in from the bathroom over the hiss of an aerosol can while she sprayed her hair in place.

"Everyone's going if I have to hog-tie you together and drag you by your high heels, so I suggest you get the lead out." Rita didn't know what would come of their day ashore, Harrison's quest for justice or her mission to talk to him privately, but she damn well knew her family wouldn't be leading her around by the nose anymore.

Sighing, Jayne relented.

"Okay, fine. But if we're going anywhere in the vicinity of Emmett's ex, I'm asking Missy to help me with my hair so I don't look like a train wreck." She picked up her purse and moved toward the door. "No offense, Ree, but you don't have the same finesse with a brush as Missy. Why don't you come with me while Margie finishes her five-hour wrinkle maintenance routine? The ship's practically empty since today's the first island stop and I've been wanting to show you something special backstage at the theater anyhow."

"You'll stick together?" Harrison scowled. "This big game is supposed to be off the ship anyhow, but I can't wait much longer for your mother to finish. If Yurek has something going down as scheduled today, I need to put local police in place around the marinas."

"We'll only be a minute." Rita figured it was just as well to go with Jayne so her sister didn't try to escape the sticky confrontation with Margie for the sake of avoiding Emmett's former wife. "If we're not back when she's done, you can stop by the theater since it's on the boarding level anyhow. Jayne told Emmett to meet us by the customs checkpoint."

As Jayne half pulled her from the room, Rita conceded the fact that she'd never be alone with Harrison again in her life. Every time she got close to having two minutes of private conversation, something happened to spoil it.

"I can't imagine what you have to show me," Rita groused, striding down the corridor toward the theater where Missy had been practicing every day since Jayne had started working with her a few weeks ago.

Jayne slowed down to link arms with her.

"I've been doing a lot of thinking about what's really important since Danielle fired me." Jayne's bracelets jingled in time with her steps as they entered the deserted theater and made their way toward the backstage area. "Close your eyes."

Knowing Jayne loved surprises as much as their mother, Rita closed on command. She let Jayne guide her around the dressing tables, their footsteps echoing off high ceilings and bare floors.

"Okay." Jayne halted their progress. "You can open."

Blinking, Rita noticed they were standing in front of her supply closet door. Except the door wasn't a bare expanse of unpolished wood anymore. Someone had installed a tiny silver hook on the front and from that hook dangled a skinny golden ribbon sewn on a silvery silk star stuffed with some sort of fluff to give it a little pouf. Rita's name had been embroidered with red thread in elegant cursive letters on the fabric.

"I noticed all this time you've never had a star on your door." Jayne stared at the creation she had obviously made herself. "And I felt like a total schmuck to realize how much you've cheered me on my whole life while I—I guess I just wanted you to know I'm rooting for you, too."

"You sewed it yourself?" Rita reached to touch the shimmering silk and the neat stitches.

"Yeah well, my sewing is kind of like your dancing. We can fake it well enough when the need arises, right?"

Touched more than she could say, Rita squeezed her sister tight.

"It's gorgeous. Thank you."

"And I want you to know that I've already talked to Emmett about taking over with Mom from now on." Leaning back, she swiped a tear off Rita's cheek, ever mindful of makeup smudges. "I saw her flirting with an old guy at the singles dance by the pool last night and it occurred to me she'd probably be the life of the party if I can find her a great retirement community where she can give singing lessons and chase old men to her heart's content."

"You'd move Mom?" Rita wondered how Margie would feel about a change. She certainly loved the social aspect of the cruise, so maybe a retirement community would be just the thing to keep her busy and give her some new hobbies that didn't involve poker.

"I'll put her close to wherever Emmett and I decide to settle. We're going to research that soon." Jayne fished in her purse and pulled out a lipstick. "But I want you to know you're done. You've gotten us this far and given me every chance to find happiness. Now it's your turn."

Rita smiled, standing still while Jayne fixed her lipstick for her. She would find her happiness, too, damn it. She'd just needed time to get her head on straight.

As she realized maybe she'd already accomplished that the past few weeks, the door to the supply closet swung wide open from the inside, revealing Horatio Garcia standing beside an acrobat in Danielle's stage show—Samuel the somersaulting guy.

Inside Rita's supply closet. And—holy crap—Sammy the Somersaulter clutched a gun in one hand.

"That does it." Sammy reached out to grab Rita while Horatio snatched Jayne half off her feet. "Any more heart-to-heart sister chat and I'll hurl for sure."

CHAPTER TWENTY-ONE

"TIME'S UP, MARGIE." Harrison summoned what little patience he had left to keep his tone light. Non-threatening.

But Margie had been applying makeup for fifteen minutes straight until Harrison thought he'd lose his mind if she swept one more layer of eye shadow across her lids. He had a bad feeling about today, an itchy sense something was about to happen.

"Hurry, hurry, hurry," Margie muttered, clicking closed her makeup case that looked suspiciously like a converted fishing tackle box. "That's the problem with your generation. You're all going to hurry yourself into premature heart failure because you've forgotten how to take your time and enjoy life."

"Any other day, I'd agree with you, ma'am." Flattery went a long way with Margie, he'd learned in the course of his brief time as her houseguest. "But I'm concerned for your daughters' safety and we need to catch up with them."

He'd feel better once he had Rita back in view, but until Yurek and his operation had been caught, he'd worry any time she left his sight. Even within the relatively safe confines of the ship with a crew lending all possible support to his investigation.

"My girls?" Margie's eyes narrowed, her sun-weathered wrinkles hiding most of her carefully applied makeup. "Why didn't you say so?"

She jammed a wide-brimmed straw hat on her head and moved toward the door.

Harrison's phone rang as they shut the door behind them.

"Masters."

"It's Emmett. Do you have Jayne and Rita with you?" The connection crackled, the sound quality suggesting Jayne's new husband wasn't right around the corner.

"No." His bad feeling about the day increased. "They're at the theater and we're heading there now. Why?"

"I disembarked to look around the pier for anyone who might be headed to the game Margie mentioned." A buzz of interference hissed through the connection. "...talked to a couple of high rollers who were meeting someone from the ship, but when I mentioned Garcia, they looked blank and clammed up."

"You don't know who their contact was?" Harrison jogged past the boarding area of the ship and Margie wasn't doing a bad job of keeping up.

"I think they were worried I was a cop and they wouldn't say any more, but it's safe to say there's someone else working the inside of the ship besides Garcia."

"Harrison!" Margie's yell interrupted his forward momentum and he had half a mind to just sprint toward the theater and leave her to her own devices.

"I'll call you back," Harrison muttered into the phone before shouting to Margie. "Come on!"

"But this is the Russian!" She pointed toward an easel in the center atrium of the ship where the business offices and welcome center were housed. The ship changed the displays according to what floor show was being staged each night.

Wait to look and get to Rita two seconds faster? Or maybe get a leg up on the enemy by identifying him ahead of time?

He sprinted back a handful of steps, ignoring startled looks from a few late-rising passengers lined up to exit the ship for a day ashore.

"It's Samuel the Somersaulting Albanian," Margie called over a photographer's head who seemed to be asking her if she'd like her picture taken. "He's the man who came to the house asking for Rita shortly before you arrived."

Harrison waved away the photographer, took one look at Somersaulting Sammy's face and knew in his gut he'd discovered yet another alias of Seva Yurek the Ukrainian mastermind behind the gambling ring that had roped in countless vacationers looking to get rich quick.

Tossing Margie his phone as he took off toward the theater, Harrison called over his shoulder. "Hit redial for Emmett. Tell him to get here now and bring security to the theater."

He turned face forward just in time to avoid slamming into a couple of preteens coming out of their room in the narrow ship corridor. At nine hundred feet long, the huge cruise liner seemed endless to a man trying to get from forward to aft in a hurry. Finally reaching the theater, he drew his weapon as he burst through the door to the backstage area, trading speed for stealth. If Samuel-Seva had gotten hold of Rita and her sister, he was bound to be desperate.

"Rita." He shouted her name, spinning around the sea of dressing tables to peer into the dark corners of the echoing back room.

A scuffling sound alerted him to movement on the other side of a wall of speakers.

"Harrison!" Margie's voice projected from the doors of the theater with the lungpower of a former singing diva. "Do you see her?"

Wishing like hell he'd never let Rita out of his sight today, Harrison edged close along the wall of speakers, praying Margie could keep out of the way. Rita would never marry him if he let anything happen to her mother. And if anything happened to Rita...

Gut tight, Harrison edged out from behind an amplifier, leading with his .45. Peering around the wall of electronics, he saw them—Jayne and Rita bound together against the velvet curtains tied to one side of the stage, mouths gagged. Their feet rested about a few inches off the ground since they stood on some sort of wheeled conveyance used in the show to deliver dancers onto the stage.

Horatio Garcia pointed a 9 mm at Rita and Jayne while Samuel—Seva—turned an archaic derringer that looked like a stage prop on Harrison. But since he had no proof the thing couldn't fire, Harrison planned to treat the weapon with the utmost respect.

"Close enough, Masters," Yurek warned, a receding hairline the only clue to the fact that the lean acrobat neared retirement age. His reflexes looked quick enough, his arms wiry with strength. "For that matter, you've come far too close already."

Harrison chose to simply remain still, gaze steady on Yurek since he knew damn well who was calling the shots and it wasn't Horatio the ass-grabbing flunky. Although they were slightly offstage, out of view of the theater seating, they were shrouded in shadows since no one worked in the backstage area at this time of day.

"I can stay put right here, Yurek, but you're going to need to release the ladies if you want to make your life a whole lot easier before a slew of Feds descend on you." He didn't dare look at Rita bound back-to-back with her sister for fear of going ballistic on the guy and losing focus when concentration and timing were all that mattered right now.

At least Margie seemed to have decided to stay safely on the other side of the wall of speakers since the rest of the theater loomed quiet.

"Not a chance." Yurek laid a hand on Rita's shoulder, a gentle, almost fatherly gesture that made Harrison want to upchuck. "Surely a man in your profession understands you don't risk the big mission for the sake of a few stumbling blocks. Perhaps we can reach a compromise with the incentive of the Frazer women to inspire you?"

"No deals." Harrison didn't trust the guy not to pull a fast one, especially when he didn't know how far away Emmett might be with backup. His best bet now was to stall and hope help arrived before bullets started flying.

Before anything happened to Rita.

"Don't be hasty." Yurek's gaze was steady, confident. "I have many ways for slipping on and off the ship, and I can easily kill you here and take the ladies with me through the loading area. They would fit neatly in the oversize crates used to cart bananas onboard, don't you think? No one will find my hostages in a banana crate. For that matter, no one would find your body, Masters, if I wish to package you up and ship you back to Fort Lauderdale."

The concrete image of Rita and Jayne suffocating in a packing crate had Harrison's heart plummeting in stone-cold fear. Harrison didn't doubt for a moment that the guy knew the inner workings of the ship like the back of his hand. And hell, no one else knew to connect Seva Yurek with the acrobat except for Margie who must still be eavesdropping on the other side of the wall of amplifiers and speakers.

"Okay, I'm listening." Harrison didn't lower his weapon and, since Yurek hadn't asked him to, he wondered if the guy was getting nervous. Three people were a hell of a lot of witnesses to whatever he had planned. "From what I've seen of your operation so far, I know you don't need to use brute force to work effectively. Where do you propose we go from here so no one gets hurt?"

No one. He couldn't risk anything happening to Rita. Memories of the first time he'd seen her—the zing of instant connection that had been more powerful than anything he'd ever experienced. He'd known on some level even then that they were meant for each other. He should have made sure she knew that rather than giving her all the damn space he thought she wanted.

Determined to have that second chance with her, he waited for Yurek to lay out his demands.

"I don't know, Masters." Yurek gestured toward Garcia. "Now that I think about it, maybe I don't need to deal with you at all to get what I want and get everyone safely off the ship without calling any more attention to beloved Sammy the Somersaulter."

At Yurek's cue, Garcia began to push the conveyance Rita and Jayne stood on, wheeling them backward.

Harrison only had a split second to decide how to protect them since he didn't hear any help on the way.

"Maybe I will simply eliminate all my problems here and now." Yurek lifted the derringer higher and Harrison couldn't wait any longer to act. If something happened to him, who would protect Rita and Jayne?

He lunged toward Yurek, knowing Garcia would have the opportunity to take a shot at him, but willing to take the risk.

What he hadn't counted on was Margie leaping into the fray from behind him.

"I'm here," Margie cried, perhaps confused about whose life had been threatened. "No one eliminates my girls!"

A shot blasted from somewhere as Harrison ripped Yurek's arm backward to knock away the derringer. He had a vague impression of Margie's straw hat falling as he turned toward the second gun—Garcia's 9 mm. He drop-kicked the weapon from Garcia's hand, just enough to make sure it wasn't turned on Rita. Another gunshot rang out, pinging into the rafters and sending a stage light crashing to the floor inches from Rita and scattering glass everywhere.

In the moment he turned from Garcia, Yurek slugged him in the kidney while Garcia jumped him from behind. Harrison landed a blow to Yurek's head, smashing him squarely on the temple. Garcia's fingers clamped around his throat momentarily, but then his whole weight lifted away thanks to the arrival of Emmett. No doubt, Emmett MacNeil had plenty of reasons to enjoy taking a shot at the blackjack dealer.

Harrison clocked Yurek in the gut this time, sending him buckling to his knees while behind him he heard Emmett shouting an impressive litany of obscenities as he threw successive blows at Garcia's head.

He glanced toward Rita whose wide-eyed gaze rested on a fallen pink form.

Shit.

Security guards poured into the backstage area along with a couple of cops Emmett must have rounded up on his way back to the ship. A security guard kneeled by Margie, who was sitting up and talking even though her arm was bleeding.

"You okay, Margie?" Harrison shouted through the mass chaos backstage as he vaulted over Yurek's fallen form to help untie Rita and Jayne. Two ship stewards already struggled with the knots while security closed off the theater and the police cuffed Garcia and Yurek.

"It takes more than Somersaulting Sammy has got to stop this old broad," Margie called back, smiling at her daughters, her eyes shiny with tears. "Frazer women are tougher than they look."

The second she was free, Harrison pulled Rita into his arms and held her tight for a too-scant moment before following her over to Margie's side.

"You're damn right about that." He suspected these three strong, stubborn women had been through enough together to keep them battling happily with one another, and supporting each other, for the rest of their lives.

Which gave Harrison an idea for fixing things with Rita when that moment finally arrived, because he didn't have any intention of letting *his* Frazer female walk away.

"You could have been killed," Rita admonished, falling to her knees to hug her mother's good side in a billow of red hair and silky skirt. "God, Mom, what were you thinking?"

"I nearly had a coronary," Jayne agreed, peering over the old security guard's shoulder where the man pressed a clean cloth to Margie's arm. "Is she going to be okay?"

The *Venus* medic had already pushed his way through the crowd to where they all gathered.

"I'm going to be fine," Margie answered for herself, her skin pale but her focus still alert. "And if you must know what I was thinking, I can tell you that no matter how much I've screwed up things for you girls in the past, all I've ever wanted was to provide beautiful things for my beautiful daughters. I can't fix the way I've hurt you, but I'd do anything in the world to protect you."

BY THE TIME another hour passed, Rita had never battled so many tears in her life as she sat on a vacant dressing table, waiting for the police to finish exchanging information with Harrison and ship security. Jayne passed her a hankie—a charmingly stitched linen she wouldn't dream of actually using to blow her nose—and offered her a silent hug before she retreated into some dark corner with Emmett after he'd given a statement to local police.

Rita and Jayne had gotten to give their version of events to the police together, for which Rita was endlessly grateful because she'd been scared out of her mind that she'd never see Jayne again after today. Before Harrison arrived, their captors had promised she and Jayne were going to get tossed into the ocean off the back of Seva Yurek's newer—smaller—boat that he'd purchased after Harrison made the connection between the *Over-Under* and the gambling ring.

"God, I've missed you, Rita. You okay?" Standing near the velvet curtains bracketing the stage, Harrison turned from his conversation with an FBI special agent who'd flown over from St. Maarten to follow up on Margie's lead about a big game in town. Sure enough, a game had been planned, and Yurek and Horatio had been sabotaging Rita's supply closet before they departed for the day, hoping to scare off Harrison for good.

When Rita and Jayne had arrived at the theater, the two of them had been in the middle of loosening bolts in her heavy metal shelves to stage an "accident." But once Rita and Jayne had shown up, Yurek—who was apparently half Ukrainian and half Albanian and skilled with either accent—had figured it would be more efficient to simply nab both women and feed them to the fish.

"Fine," Rita lied, praying Harrison would finish soon so she could lock her arms around him and never let him go.

Apparently her acting job was unconvincing since Harrison walked away from the other agent, warding off questions from security guards who still swarmed the area as police gathered evidence.

"Did the police tell you it was okay to go back to your room?" Harrison's blue gaze remained unwavering as he locked in on her.

"I'm free to leave." They'd needed contact information in case they had more questions, but Rita suspected with all of Harrison's investigative legwork, they'd have more than enough evidence to convict the biggest illegal gambling operator the Caribbean had ever seen. "I can't believe all that time the big criminal mastermind was an acrobat working right on the ship."

"Entertainers have the most leeway with their contracts to get on and off the ship, right?" He waited for her nod, then continued, "It sounds like he was able to attract a continual supply of new gamblers through his contacts on the ship, and the security guys figured out Yurek had been smuggling contraband in and out of the ship along with the food supply company who restocks the *Venus* each week. He could get weapons onboard and transfer money off the ship in crates of vegetables or boxes of canned goods."

"I thought I'd die when he said he'd put us in a banana crate." She shuddered at the thought.

"I would have torn the *Venus* apart if you hadn't been in the theater today." Harrison pulled her past her supply closet door where police were investigating the sabotaged shelving. At the very back of the dressing area, he tugged her behind a rolling rack full of costumes where they were hidden. "Just because you weren't ready to marry me doesn't mean I've stopped loving you."

"You do?" Her heart skipped a beat. "I mean, you haven't?"

His sudden proximity after so long apart had her blood racing through her veins.

"No." He smoothed his thumb over her cheek where the scratchy, cheap bandanna had been bound around her mouth. "And I learned something about you today that I didn't realize when I first proposed."

"Really?" Her hand reached for his shoulder, seeking his strength. His solidness. "Nothing bad, I hope."

"Hell no." He shuffled nearer, his big body closing in on her in ways that sent heat screaming through her whole body. "After watching your family in action the past few weeks, I discovered I needed to put a lot more emotion into my argument the way all the Frazers do to get their points across. I probably seemed pretty laid back to you when you're used to everyone around you speaking with so much...vehemence."

Her heart turned over at his gentle touch, his intense expression. She thought she might just dive right into those blue eyes of his and warm herself in his love.

"We Frazers are pretty good at arguing," Rita countered, pleased to think Harrison hadn't simply written off her crazy clan as a bunch of disagreeable creative types. "What makes you think you could have ever won an argument with me?"

"Ah, you still don't see the most important point. Because we *both* win if you simply concede that we belong together." He lowered his mouth to hers, covering her lips for a kiss she'd never forget since it promised new beginnings, burning away old hurts as it tantalized her with new possibilities.

"You don't have to argue with me, Harrison." Rita loved her family dearly, but she wouldn't trade this man's rock-solid steadiness for anything. "Because I love you like crazy and you won't ever talk me out of that."

"You mean—you'll take the idea of a future together under advisement?" He went still against her, the heavy beating of his heart the only sign of life for a long moment.

"I don't know how long I can think about it since I still have enough Frazer impatience in my veins to know I won't be able to resist the lure of marriage to a Masters man for long."

His kiss was hard and swift, his arms steadying her against an onslaught of hundred-percent pure, undiluted Harrison. And oh God, how she loved that. He lifted her right up off her feet, holding her a few inches above him for an endless second before sliding her back down the length of all that hard, male muscle she'd been missing these last few weeks.

"You're not going to regret this." He squeezed her hand as he stepped away, a new light in his eyes that she hadn't realized until this moment had been subtly brooding ever since the first time she'd spotted him peeling the label off his bottle of beer.

"Neither will you." She'd make sure this career-driven special agent remembered to make time for his family while he made sure she didn't let her family take over her life. They'd be perfect together. "Oh, except maybe at your company picnics when my mom tries to flirt with all your friends. But other than that, you're going to think marriage is all wine and roses."

"Fortunately the Bureau isn't all that big on company picnics." He kissed her, smiling, while from somewhere down the hall the security guys were shouting for Harrison. "But I'll bet your mom will like visiting the Masters Inn. I've been thinking I need to convince the new management team that it would be great for business to arrange a talent night like they have here on the *Venus*."

"Oh God." Rita squelched a giggle, not ready to let

the rest of the world intrude on their moment just yet. "My mother won't rest until she's the lifetime defending champ of open-mike night. But are you going to have any pull at the Inn now that you're going back to the Bureau full-time?"

She had a design career to launch. Jayne wanted to test her choreographer skills. And Margie finally seemed interested in finding love and romance for herself again after twenty years without her first husband.

"I thought I'd invite Emmett and Jayne up to see if I can get Emmett interested in the property. He seems to have a better head for business than I ever did, and besides, I caught him helping out behind the bar on the Neptune deck the other night, so I have the feeling he's missing the Last Chance."

"How did I ever find a man even more practical than me?" The rightness of the plan settled over her like a perfectly sized new dress. Rita blinked back a fresh batch of tears as she arched up to kiss the man of her dreams—her vacation fling turned the Real Deal.

"You picked me as a focus point, remember?" He kissed her back with slow thoroughness, ignoring the voices still shouting for him in the echoing backstage area. "It was a pleasure to help you stay on your feet that first night on stage and it's going to be a constant pleasure to get you horizontal for the rest of your life."

"A practical man with a wicked streak." Her body revved at the heat in his voice, the warmth of love in his eyes. "The perfect combination."

EPILOGUE

One Year Later

IF YOU THOUGHT THIS story ends with Rita and Harrison smooching, you've obviously forgotten who's the star of the Frazer family. *Me*. Jayne Mansfield Frazer MacNeil. I can tell you exactly how things turned out because I've had a bird's-eye view of the whole thing. Actually, I've had a view from the raised platform of my stage, which is almost as good since it perches up high above the rest of life.

And tonight, as I corral a really cute new crop of dancers into their dressing rooms at the dinner theater inside the Masters Inn—*real* dressing rooms, mind you, not just an explosion of tables in the middle of an over-crowded backstage area—I can safely say that Rita and Harrison are getting along adorably and that my big sister is completely gaga over her FBI stud who should be showing up to join her at the premiere of my new show any minute.

"You need any help?" Rita calls from the edge of the stage, her pregnant belly just beginning to show now that she's hit five months.

For a woman who wanted to slow things down in her

personal relationships, she sure got into the spirit of married life in a hurry between her baby on the way (a girl, if ultrasounds can be trusted), and her prominent position in the lives of Harrison's parents at the Masters Inn.

"Don't be silly." I try very hard not to take Rita's offers of help although she's still the most capable woman I know. "But you can call your husband and remind him that attendance at my new show tonight is *not* optional."

I look at my watch meaningfully as I brush off her offer because even *I* know pregnant women are supposed to put their feet up instead of running helter-skelter to help other people. And let's face it, now that I have a fabulous new production in the works, everyone finally has to admit I don't need all the help they thought I did.

Even my new shrink says so, and she's got more degrees than I have men in my past. That's saying something.

"He'll be here." Rita has total faith in that man.

She peers around the elegant Naples dinner theater that holds a thousand people and routinely attracts vacationing bigwigs from all over the country who try to buy Frazer family talent to market on a big-city basis. Designers from New York slobber over Rita's fashions in the eclectic boutique she created out of the vacated Shine-On storefront. Theater managers of all stripes try to woo my choreography talent away from the Masters Inn. Even Margie got an offer from a Granny Follies show in Palm Beach after her performance on open-mike night since she's the sexiest soon-to-be grandma in Collier County.

But by now, all the Frazer women agree we're confirmed west coast Florida girls. This is where we belong.

"Jayne MacNeil." Margie breezes through the dinner crowd to approach the stage, her expression happy even if her hand flutters at her chest like she's anticipating heart failure. Her new man trails two steps behind, his suit neatly pressed with a hot-pink hankie in the pocket that could have only come from his girlfriend. "You didn't tell me your name was on the marquee out front!"

"That was Emmett's doing." He'd bought fifty-one percent of the Masters Inn from Harrison's folks and had thrown himself into the lifestyle of a resort owner with an enthusiasm I hadn't expected. And while I don't need star billing these days since Emmett always makes me feel like the undisputed queen of his whole world, the surprise of seeing my name on a marquee was a nice touch. The man has made it a mission to ensure our marriage thrives, and a girl could hardly complain about that. "He thinks I need a lot of ego stroking for some strange reason."

Rita disguises a laugh behind a cough, but I don't care. A few ego strokes never hurt anyone, after all. These days, I try to make it a point to give out as many as I rake in, and that philosophy seems to promote excellent karma in life judging by all the happiness surrounding me.

"Hi, Gil," Rita greets Margie's boyfriend, the only guy to have lasted more than two weeks in Margie's renewed burst of enthusiastic dating since we convinced her to get into some addiction therapy and see a shrink. And since her psychologist is the same genius woman that I visit on occasion, there's every reason to believe Margie will beat her compulsion and rejoin reality. She certainly has applied herself to the task of enjoying life—and men—again. "Let me show you and Mom to your seats. I put you at a table right near Harrison's parents."

As Rita bustles off to seat Margie and the lovesick man with the pink hankie, I spot Emmett serving cocktails to Harrison's folks who have adored him as one of their own since the moment we first set foot in the place eleven months ago. They never asked Emmett about his lack of a family, but seemed content to play adoptive parents as if they'd somehow intuited he needed them.

See what big words come from visits to the shrink? I try to "intuit" wherever possible, but apparently I'm not emotionally evolved enough to be supersensitive to others. But I understand my family better. Plus I'm sweet to my dancers and treat them like talented people instead of like worker minions to scare into submission, which had been Danielle's school of thought. Still, she's promised to come see the new show once it opened, so she wasn't all bad.

Maybe she's forgiven me for hiring Missy away from the *Venus*.

Oh—back to Emmett. He gets along great with Harrison's folks, but maybe they appreciate having him around as much as he likes them. Harrison had managed the Inn just fine, but he'd never been all that hip-hop about mixing killer margaritas or whipping up passion fruit surprise smoothies for overworked dancers. Whereas Emmett seems to have perfected the low-key lifestyle now that he's come to terms with his past and made peace with himself.

And lest you worry about the ex-wife he married on the rebound, let me assure you Claudia is thriving on St.

Kitts now that she's embraced her natural sexual pref-
erences and lives with an adorable girlfriend she'd been
seeing before she married Emmett. Apparently she got
hitched to him on the rebound as well, and was trying
to kick the alternative lifestyle in deference to a disap-
proving family. Who'd have thought she'd marry a man
to kick an all-girl hankering? It just goes to show you
that we Frazer females aren't the only confused chicks
walking the planet.

Now, before I run and give my dancers a last-minute
pep talk, let me assure you that Rita and Harrison
Masters are going to be together until they're old and
gray and watching me in my own Granny Follies productions. The two of them never argue that I've ever
seen, and while I think that's slightly against the natural
order of things, I can't help but be happy for my kick-
ass big sister who always wanted a life with less stress.
She never even worries about Harrison's FBI job since
she's seen him in action and knows how he handles
himself. He's as practical as she is, which gives her
heaps of confidence he'll always come home safe at the
end of the day.

Besides their absurd commitment to never arguing
and their mutual understanding of one another, I personally think the two of them must share some hot and
heavy sexual encounters behind closed doors since
Harrison likes to occasionally lock the hot tub room for
the two of them late at night. They walk around with
matching smiles on the days following their spa nights,
so that's my theory about what else holds that marriage
together like superglue.

Sure love and understanding are important. And in

my case, a shrink helped, too. But bottom line, hot sex is *always* a plus.

Although a few feathers and rhinestones thrown into the mix can be fun, too....

Everything you love about romance...
and more!

Please turn the page for Signature Select™
Bonus Features.

The Pleasure Trip

BONUS FEATURES INSIDE

Deleted Scene from
The Pleasure Trip

Writing The Pleasure Trip *was a labor of love. Revising the book into the polished version you now hold in your hands—not so much. They say great books aren't written, they're rewritten. But my stories always feel freshest when they're actively taking place in my brain, unveiling themselves as my characters chatter away and share their adventures with me in their own words. So to hack away parts of their dialogue with me always feels a little disrespectful to the characters who've been gracious enough to fill my pages.*

But after having written numerous books, I can see the wisdom of occasionally forcing my characters to be more succinct. Especially the characters who have so much personality—and so much to say—that they'll probably be with me my whole life. Jayne Frazer was that kind of character, and a section of the story that was in her point of view

4

*was one of the scenes that needed to be trimmed
from* The Pleasure Trip.

*The following scene originally appeared after her
first phone call to Rita in Fort Lauderdale and
before Emmett figured out what he needed to do to
make his marriage work. I like the scene because
of Jayne's realization that a good romance isn't
always fairy tales and roses. Solid relationships
require hard work. But while I enjoyed this
moment with Jayne, my editor and I ultimately
decided this section didn't really move the story
forward the way every scene in a good book should.*

JAYNE'S FINGER SHOOK as she dialed her sister's
phone number a week later from the luxuriously
appointed suite she still couldn't get used to.
Her wardrobe looked pitifully underdeveloped
in the yawning closet space, her rhinestones
clashing with the polished brass fixtures and
Italian marble in the bathroom.

Slamming the receiver back into place, she
tried waiting for that damn finger to stop
shaking. She stared at it in vain, and finally
picked up the phone again to call her sister
and vent from the king-size bed swimming in
high-thread-count Egyptian cotton.

"Jayne Frazer," Rita's voice answered
without prelude since she'd probably gotten

used to Jayne's calls after her fights with Emmett had become a daily event. "I hope you're calling to say you've cleared the air with Emmett."

At least Rita's voice grounded Jayne, soothing away some of the shakiness that threatened to level her every time Emmett walked away from her during a disagreement.

"We're getting nowhere." She sighed into the phone, slumping down into the sumptuous bed at the luxury hotel where she and Emmett had spent long, delicious nights followed by days of total noncommunication. "And no, I haven't told him yet."

"How can you keep calling me when you refuse to take my advice?" Rita sounded more short-tempered every day she spent cooped up with their crazy mother, especially now that Harrison was knee-deep in catching a criminal. "You can't be mad at Emmett for not pouring out his heart to you if you don't share anything of yourself with him beyond sex. You're being unfair."

"You know, you usually sugarcoat this talk a little better for me." Jayne swiped away a tear, knowing damn well Rita didn't appreciate people who felt sorry for themselves. "How about I agree to come clean with Emmett tonight if you promise me you'll quit tiptoeing around Harrison and tell him to come on over so you can jump his bones the moment Margie goes to bed?"

Usually Jayne and Rita did things together—from tap dance lessons to waitressing, they'd tackled so much of life together that Jayne hated to be out on the marriage limb all by herself. And if that made her sound like a self-absorbed crybaby, so what? Committing your heart and soul to a man was scary business. A girl needed allies to strategize her relationship.

"Oh yeah, that's a really fair compromise. You're already married to your man, Jayne. News flash—that means you've already promised to come clean with him in the form of marriage vows."

Jayne stared down at her wedding ring glittering brightly against the white cotton sheets of their unmade bed. They'd barely ventured out of the hotel room all week, but after their fight two nights ago, Emmett had returned with an incredible chunk of diamond set in gorgeous platinum with a whole host of smaller diamonds around it. Showy and splashy but built to last. Jayne adored it.

Maybe Rita had a point about being committed to telling Emmett the truth about her past. Who'd have thought marriage would require this much work when two people totally loved each other? She'd always been so focused on the big event of falling in love, she'd never thought about what happened afterward. Now she was stuck improvising, and while she might have been great at winging it on stage, this loomed way more important than any dance routine. Jayne desperately wanted her marriage to work.

"So I'll work up to it in a few days." She just needed to scavenge some more courage because marriage was nothing like dancing. She didn't have the endless supply of courage when it came to love. "I promise."

"In the meantime, you've got to give up on surprising Margie with the news of your marriage because I'm getting tired of trying to keep it a secret. She still thinks you're onboard the *Venus*, Jayne. I couldn't tell her you got fired or she would be hysterical without the other half of the story—that you're settling down with a man who's crazy about you." The wistful note in Rita's voice surprised her.

"Soon." Was it so selfish to want to tell Margie in person? "I've waited forever to introduce her to a hot man who was all mine. Can't you just not talk about me for a few more days?"

"Assuming they catch this Seva guy in a few more days," Rita grumbled. "Hiding out really sucks, especially since the longer I stay away from Harrison the more awkward it feels to talk to him on the phone."

"Awkward? Since when does Rita Frazer let a man rattle her cage?"

At Rita's snort, Jayne hung up the phone without feeling at all reassured she'd solved her sister's problem, but she thought maybe she'd finally fixed one of her own. She'd be damned if she'd let Emmett call all the shots in this marriage that he'd professed to really want. Making things work between them would no doubt be a lot of work, but Frazer women were damn hard workers.

He'd have to put himself on the line. But because she loved him more than she ever imagined loving any man, she would take Rita's advice and put herself—and her past—on the line first.

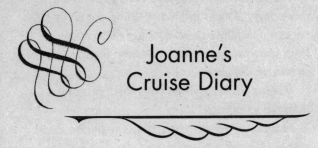

Joanne's Cruise Diary

I was so thrilled to persuade the editors at Signature to let me try my hand at writing *The Pleasure Trip*. The only catch was I'd never been on a Caribbean cruise in my life. Didn't I owe it to my readers to create an authentic experience?

Convinced my cause was just, I embarked on the task of selling the concept to my husband. For one thing, we'd never had a real honeymoon, I explained. Plus, we'd just passed the ten-year mark of our wedding anniversary. After three kids and moving eight times across six states together, didn't we deserve a romantic cruise vacation to celebrate the milestone? By the time I got to my big guns— it'd be a great tax write-off—my husband was already logging on to Expedia to seek out the best deal. And while our experiences onboard Carnival's *Inspiration* ship weren't quite as action packed (or dangerous!) as Rita and Jayne's, we had a blast.

Day One: We arrive in our Florida port in time to marvel over the vast floating hotel that will be our home for five days. While 2,600 passengers prepare to board, I quickly do the math of the lifeboat seating capacity after seeing *Titanic* one too many times. Assured there's plenty of room for all of us, I have to laugh that my husband is busy buying extra bottles of champagne for the trip from the local wine shop, while I'm obsessing over safety issues. It's not always easy when you're a mildly neurotic Virgo married to a fun-loving Aries, but on vacation, it's a very good thing.

With the booze safely stashed in our suitcases, I take careful notes on the embarkation procedure and keep an eye out for friendly security folks who can help me iron out some of the boarding logistics for my characters. Armed with my books and bookmarks, I'm careful to announce myself as a writer so the security folks don't think I'm trying to figure out how to smuggle in illegal aliens.

After much exploration of the huge ship that's already giving my legs a workout, my husband and I find a spot against the rail to enjoy mimosas and the scenery as we sail out of port and into the open seas. Feeling the effects of the champagne, I'm reminded of Johnny Depp as Captain Jack Sparrow— "Welcome to the Caribbean, love." Whether this trip is a belated honeymoon, a ten-year anniversary celebration or a Machiavellian tax write-off, the cruise was a fabulous idea.

At night we hang out at the outdoor disco and make plans to see the floor show the next evening. I can't wait to see the stage area since so many of my scenes will take place there on the *Venus*.

Day Two: Breakfast in bed. The first thing one realizes while cruising is that food is abundant and available twenty-four hours a day. I begin to doubt the authenticity of my characters who make their living aboard a cruise ship and still manage to maintain showgirl-style figures. I make a mental note to seek out the showgirls onboard for an interview and discreet inventory of their physiques. Thinking Rita could still high-kick with a few more curves, I indulge in another raspberry Danish and review my *Carnival Capers,* the ship's daily newsletter.

Itinerary decided, Dean and I raid the shops onboard and revel in a few hours of duty-free fun. Great makeup and fragrances abound, but so do a million and one inexpensive tchotchkes that Jayne would love. I scoop up a handful of sunglasses, sequined bags and shell necklaces that my fashion muse could make look like a million bucks. The T-shirts are nice, too, but I can't help but think designer Rita could do better. Already the cruise is working since my characters are now firmly perched on my shoulder, giving me their opinions as I walk through their world.

Due to the miracle of vacation time, lunch awaits us in the dining room as soon as we're done shopping. In an effort to gain less than ten pounds on the trip, I go for the spa-recommended vegetable fajitas, but end up sneaking half my husband's crabmeat sandwich served on a warm baguette. If I didn't order it, it doesn't count, right? Besides, I'll be getting a workout tomorrow when we spend eighteen glorious hours in Cozumel, Mexico.

Later that night, Dean and I dress for the formal dinner and wonder if boat shoes can successfully be worn with a sport coat since we made it a priority to pack lightly. I throw on jeweled flip-flops with my taffeta skirt and declare us ready. I think Jayne may be dressing me, but it looks just right for our brand of cruise ship formal. Over dinner we chat it up with our waitress, Katarina, whose sexy accent comes from Polish heritage. While I wonder if it's too late to take up a second language, Dean quizzes her about her time on the ship and what life onboard is like for crew members. Smart man. Thank goodness one of us remembers we are not only onboard to shop and wolf down seafood. We're here for research!

After dinner we take in the floor show and hit the bars for entertainment. We dance to a rock-and-roll band's kicking covers of a few Van Halen tunes and cheer for our shipmates in the karaoke lounge.

Day Three: The history buff in me wants to check out the Mayan ruins on the mainland when we stop in Mexico, but the stories of potential choppy waters to travel there dissuade me since I refuse to spend a moment of my shore excursion being seasick. My intrepid husband decides we must rent mopeds for the day and explore Cozumel on our own instead, even though the cruise lines do not endorse this kind of trip due to the high rate of accidents. Undeterred, we scout out a man with some mopeds, rent snorkel equipment, and take off for parts unknown. *Wheeee!* We're zipping by crystal-blue water in eighty-degree weather in January, when I know the temperature is ten degrees below zero in my hometown. We see tropical birds and iguanas in the foliage as we whiz past acres of undeveloped acreage in the middle of paradise.

The road around the island takes us right along the coastline, so the beaches and turquoise water are in sight at almost all times. There are gorgeous flowers and low jungle terrain. Every breath we take on the southeastern portion is floral scented.

Stopping at a Mexican bar perched on the water, Dean and I quiz our waiter about life in Cozumel, and Dean tries to talk me into regular trips to the Caribbean. (Like I'd argue.) We set up our beach towels right beside our little table where we eat awesome guacamole and down huge margaritas. We allow ourselves to get a bit schnockered since our shore time is a glorious eighteen hours, leaving time for us to eat, swim, laugh hysterically over nothing and sunbathe until we recover ourselves. I get sunburn stripes on the insides of my arms—the only place I'd forgotten to slather sunscreen.

Later that day we stop at Chankanaab where the coral reefs are easily accessible so we can snorkel. I've never snorkeled anywhere that you didn't have to ride out into the water by boat to access the reefs, but here, there are fish of every color all around the moment you step into the water right off the beach.

At night, we shop and check out the local bands, finally returning to the ship loaded down with presents for the kids we left behind.

Day Four: I begin to see the appeal of the ten-day cruise since I'm ready for more islands, and yet we've got to head back to Tampa. When we booked the cruise, we weren't sure if we'd like cruising. Ha! Who wouldn't get used to this lifestyle? We make it our mission to eat like fiends since we were very athletic yesterday with all the swimming and dancing. Surely we can indulge in more fabulous food?

In the late morning we park ourselves on lounge chairs around the pool and listen to the calypso band and people watch. After a quick dip in the pool, we head to the hot tub and enjoy the antics of a few semi-badly behaved children since it's a nice reminder that we have another kid-free day all to ourselves. (Are we so smug?) This cruise marks the first vacation we've ever taken without our boys, and while I miss them, I'm also really glad we took some time to celebrate our tenth anniversary. Squeezing my hubby's hand, I'm glad this trip hasn't been all about research.

Day Five: Sniff! How can it be over already? In a last-ditch effort to thank all the right people and scribble a few more notes, I chat with the cruise director, our cabin steward and a few other ship employees to cement this great experience in my head and remember that I need to think about life from the employee point of view. I carefully observe debarkation process and the security procedures, not unlike the methods used in airport terminals.

As we try to leave Tampa there is a hard crash back to reality: our flight to Cleveland is two and a half hours delayed because of a snowstorm and then our connection decided to fly out without us. We are stuck in snowy Cleveland for an extra day when all we want to do is go home! By the time we finally return to the Burlington, Vermont airport the next day, the temperature is an oh-so-chilly negative seven degrees, and our van is iced over so badly we can't drive for another half an hour until we chop it out of its icy coating. Ick.

I quickly decide that if I'm ever a huge and smashing success in the writing world, my first big purchase will be a house on an island somewhere where we can ride mopeds every day and drink many more margaritas. All in all, the trip couldn't have been more fabulous since it inspired three romances—one in real life and two in my head. As I head back home ready to write, I'm already debating possibilities for a sequel....

Author Interview:
A Conversation with
Joanne Rock

What's your idea of a pleasure trip?
I love vacations that are leisurely and allow plenty
of room for spontaneity. I'd rather spend time in
the local venues than exploring tourist traps, and
I'm happiest when I'm savoring regional foods
and soaking up the culture. If that means a night
of clams and beer on Nantucket or testing out
the conch fritters in Key West, I'm equally happy
because I'm more interested in the "how" I
spend a pleasure trip than the "where." Although,
now that I think about it, Nantucket and Key West
are both right up there on my list of great
vacation destinations.

Did you need to do research for this book?
The Pleasure Trip required more research than
any contemporary story I've ever written. And
although I surely could have found a great deal of
information for the story via online sources, I

have to say I enjoyed researching this one firsthand. This book provided the perfect opportunity to talk my husband into a cruise and we loved every minute. Research becomes an absolute pleasure when you can walk the path your characters walk and see the world they live in with your own eyes. My Caribbean cruise provided a level of authenticity for this story that I don't think I could have achieved without taking my own trip. Aside from that, I also researched a variety of cruise lines and Caribbean islands with travel guides, and I conducted some firsthand research about the cruise industry from local merchants who see thousands of tourists every week.

Why did you become a writer?
After years of studying literature in college, there came a point where the only way I could crawl deeper inside a book was to write my own and experience the process from the inside out. I had always enjoyed writing, but crafting a good book takes more than skill with a pen. It also requires a keen eye for storytelling, and it was this facet that I struggled with as a new writer. The learning journey opened up a whole new world for me and it has been an endlessly rewarding adventure from the moment I typed my very first opening line.

What matters most in life?

Family, friends and the legacy of love we leave behind. I think it is important for all of us to understand our calling in life and to use our gifts and talents in ways that touch other people. For the man who loves math and science, maybe that means making sure that the houses on his block always have electricity through his gig at the local power company. For the stay-at-home mother, maybe that means throwing the best backyard barbecues on the block and conveying a sense of home and family extending beyond her front door. And for the romance writer, I like to think that providing happy endings to readers is a gift of mental escape or emotional satisfaction. Whatever your strengths, I think it's important to use them in ways that make the world a better place.

What gives you pleasure?

Lots of things! I think it's important to build your life in a way that you can receive pleasure (and, hopefully, provide it) every day. For me, I am pleased with a fulfilling day of work where the words came together just the way I wanted, or a day of rest and relaxation with my family where we take a drive around and stop to explore something new and unexpected—an old church, a nature path beside a rushing stream or a horse farm we hadn't seen before. I also love to visit with friends old and new, and to pass whole days talking up a storm with people I haven't seen in a while. Oh, and great dinners on the deck with good wine, fresh local veggies and something savory to grill.

When you're not writing, what do you enjoy doing?
Reading, talking and teaching. I guess I really love the whole communication chain! But I also enjoy seeing new things and people watching. For years, my family has relocated frequently for my husband's job and we always make it a point to explore the terrain and get a feel for each new place. In Kentucky, we did Derby Day and croquet

tournaments. We learned to two-step and we spent a lot of time in Cincinnati watching the Reds play baseball. In southern Utah, we went hiking in all the gorgeous red-rock canyons and saw the sights in Las Vegas. Our vacations meant drives along the California coast that once culminated in pilgrimages to Candlestick Park in San Francisco and Oakland-Alameda Coliseum for a rare day/night baseball doubleheader involving the Bay teams. In northern Louisiana, we discovered a love of crawfish and made the Mudbug Festival and local Mardi Gras celebration an annual event. For our baseball jaunt, we checked out the Ballpark in Arlington, Texas. Three states later, we're in upstate New York and rediscovering our love of northern summers and the thrill of cutting our own Christmas tree from a snowy mountainside.

Do you believe in love at first sight?
Absolutely. And I think books like Malcolm Gladwell's *Blink,* where he discusses the power of quick thinking and rapid cognition, only gives more credence to the concept that romantics have understood all along. We can make intelligent, emotionally accurate judgments very quickly. That fast intellectual processing applies to trusting our instincts when making business decisions as much as it applies to finding love at first sight. Often when we meet The One, we know almost instantly. Even if we don't always trust the instinct, it's very much there.

Is there one book that changed your life somehow?
I can credit three books with having a profound effect on my life. *Black Beauty* was the first book to absorb me completely and sweep me away into a fictional world that felt real and important. This story made me a dedicated, lifelong reader, which in turn, helped me to excel in every facet of my school education. I think a love of reading is a gift that gives back to you your whole life. Second, *Wuthering Heights* forged my worldview (at all of fourteen years old) and helped me understand that I would always see life through the lens of an

optimist and a romantic. Third, Alice Walker's brilliant book *The Temple of My Familiar* made my spirit soar in the way only great fiction can. I dreamed about the book for weeks afterward, and found the characters resonating through me even though my life experience was a far cry from anyone's in the book. Walker's ability to create such vibrant characters is a testament to her power of storytelling and was my first inkling at the incredible effect of a well-told tale.

What are your top three favorite books?
I have a very difficult time choosing favorites, but I would have to cite Zora Neale Hurston's *Their Eyes Were Watching God* because the author has such a beautiful way of phrasing profound thoughts using the simplest of words. For romance, I'd fill out my list with Susan Elizabeth Phillips's *Breathing Room* and Teresa Medeiros's *Charming the Prince*. For classic Gothic-style stories, I'd add Wilkie Collins's *The Woman in White* and Henry James's *The Turn of the Screw*. For classics, I'd have to add *Gone with the Wind* and... Oh wait, did I mention I have some trouble with favorites?

What are you working on right now?
Right now I am delving deep into medieval history to re-create one of the most exciting moments in history from a romantic and

feminine perspective. As I write *Lady Ivy*, slated for release in 2006 from the Harlequin Historical line, I am using Eleanor of Aquitaine's court of love as a setting for several scenes. The book is set in 1174 during Eleanor's rebel years where she parted ways with King Henry and set up a court full of poets and thinkers on her own lands in the wealthy Duchy of Aquitaine. My heroine is a troubadour in the court, a member of the group who set the code of courtly love that was handed down through the ages. From a feminist angle, the chivalric code marked an important turning point in the way women were viewed. Instead of bargaining tools in men's power struggles, women became lofty ideals for gentle behavior and noble undertakings. Historically, it's an exciting time period. And for a romance writer, I have to say my characters' discussion of courtly love is leading to some very interesting scenes....

 Signature Select™

COMING NEXT MONTH

Signature Select Collection
BOOTCAMP by Leslie Kelly, Heather MacAllister, Cindi Myers
Strong-willed females Cassandra, Rebecca and Barbara enroll in the
two-week Warfield crash course to figure out how to get what they
want in life and romance!

Signature Select Saga
QUIET AS THE GRAVE by Kathleen O'Brien
Mike Frome's ex-wife is found suspiciously dead—making him the
prime murder suspect. Believing in his innocence, Mike's ex-flame
Suzie Strickland offers her support. But sudden murder evidence
against Mike is discovered, testing their newfound trust and love....

Signature Select Miniseries
COFFEE IN THE MORNING by Roz Denny Fox
A heartwarming volume of two classic stories with the miniseries
characters you love! A wagon-train journey along the Santa Fe Trail
is a catalyst for romance as Emily Benton and Sherry Campbell
each find love.

Signature Select Spotlight
VOWS OF SILENCE by Debra Webb
A secret pact made long ago between best friends—Lacy, Melinda,
Cassidy and Kira—resurfaces when a ten-year-old murder is
uncovered. Chief Rick Summers knows they're hiding something,
but isn't sure he can be objective...especially if his old flame Lacy is
guilty of murder.

Signature Select Showcase
LADY'S CHOICE by Jayne Ann Krentz
Juliana Grant knows she's found "the one" in high-octane real-
estate developer Travis Sawyer—even if *he* doesn't realize it yet.
But Travis has arrived back in Jewel Harbour for retribution, not
for romance. And it doesn't help that the target of his revenge is
her family!

SIGCNM0206